FAGIN UK

Crime pays until the end…

To John

Mike Pattison

Mike

not just
another book

First Published in 2017 by not just another book

Copyright © Mike Pattison

(for not just another book: email)

hampton.joyce14@yahoo.com

Cover Design and copyright © Mike Pattison

Main Text Set in Times New Roman 11.0

Published by: not just another book

ISBN: 978-0-9935665-1-6

Printed and bound in Great Britain by Clays Ltd, St Ives plc

Disclaimer

This is a work of fiction. Names, characters, businesses, places, events and incidents are either the products of the author's imagination or used in a fictitious manner. Any resemblance to actual persons, living or dead, or actual events is purely coincidental.

Contents

1

The Meeting

Sammy Finklestein and Harry Margolis were both born and reared in Stamford Hill, north London - a very pleasant, mixed area of Jews and Christians with a liberal sprinkling of Pakistani and Caribbean peoples all living together in harmony. Both boys had a reasonable education, first at a junior school in Stoke Newington, and then at the comprehensive school in Hackney, an adjoining borough. Both had a semi-religious background, which, when translated within the culture of their two families, meant they 'took it as it came'.

Sammy's dad – Ivor - worked with Harry's dad – Morry - in the furniture trade at a factory in Bethnal Green, just down the road. They were both cabinetmakers by profession and shared a lively business in Hackney Road making 'occasional' pieces of furniture, gate-leg tables and china cabinets. Ivor was thick-set and strong-looking, possibly as a result of all his years of hard graft, and his physique had passed down to his only son, Sammy - the sole difference being that his son was lighter-skinned, but still with a mop of very dark, slightly curly hair inherited from his Jewish ancestry. Standing at five feet eight inches, Sammy was already noticeably taller than Harry, who, his father had always said, was a 'late developer', who would acquire his pulling power in his twenties rather than his teens. Harry kept his thoughts about this particular comment to himself and his deep-brown eyes often chose to keep the world at bay rather than embrace it energetically as many a youngster might have done.

It might also have been about how he viewed his life prospects: having not found any subject at school much to his liking, he already felt adrift and without much to look forward to as an adult. Like Sammy, he helped out at the shop during school holidays and sometimes at weekends simply to earn a bit of pocket money. They were both expected to learn the workings of the whole trade so that one day they would take over the business from their fathers. As younger boys, this had for a while just seemed natural, but with the onset of adolescence they began to resent their fathers' expectations and tried - in vain it seemed - to plan ahead for something a lot better.

Still mulling this seemingly dismal prospect over in their last years at school, they talked to each other - and no one else - about how they felt they were surely destined for bigger and better things than lifting heavy gate-leg tables, which had been the cause of poor old Morry's injury - a rupture that hurt so bad it showed through his trousers. Even now, they knew that Morry worked with it, gritting his teeth sometimes through the pain, simply because he was too scared to have it treated.

Finally, the day came when the boys left school for the last time, to start work at the shop and learn the ropes of working in a full-time commercial business, known as 'Making'. It started off as best as could be expected, both the boys agreeing in private that it was at least a source of wages every week; on the other hand, they knew they were not going to get rich very fast - and more than likely not at all. Nights were usually spent at the local youth club and in pubs to unwind from the day's hard graft. But, on one such night while they were having a laugh with a couple of ex-school friends, something would happen which would change their whole future, a complete U-turn in fact.

This was the time when they met Yiddel Davis - the 'Master', as they would later refer to him - the man who was to shape their lives forever. The boys had been standing in the pub watching two darts players trying to get the better of each other in a game being played for the grand prize of twenty pounds. The extraordinary, disproportionate tension felt by all those watching was palpable. All the gallery of watchers was silent...each man carefully working out the next throw of the darts and how it was to be executed. Nobody spoke a word, just in case the action of the players was upset. Finally, the winning throw was made, a raw cheer of emotion went up and the money handed over. The noise level in the bar resumed its normal pitch.

Ideal territory for a man like Yiddel Davis. He was the ultimate 'ducker and diver'. Now in his early forties, with a strangely confident and affluent bearing, he got his living - an increasingly lucrative one - from anything he could sell or steal. His eyes missed nothing. He casually turned to the boys and made a seemingly offhand remark about 'earning that sort of money ten times over in as many minutes'.

"What business are you in, then?" asked Harry, more out of politeness than anything else.

"I, me old mate, am what is known as a dealer." He said no more than that.

Both boys now took a good look at the man. He was wearing a tonic mohair suit, a quality tailored shirt and tie with a gold watch and gold cufflinks. Everything about his appearance seemed to exude a unique self-assurance, an indescribable ability to read people instantly, probing the far reaches of a person's mind in spite of whatever they might do to try to prevent this. And although he was dressed in some style and affluence, the boys, although still only in their teens, knew instantly that he was drawn from a very working-class background. Yiddel could indeed take care of himself in any situation, and not necessarily just through a display of physical strength – although he was taller than they were and of a stocky, naturally muscular build – but more significantly through those all-important life-skills that a person either does or doesn't develop, yet which everyone has to call upon during their lives.

If anyone had ever said to Yiddel that he had good survival instincts in the urban jungle, then his only remark might well have been "You've either got it or you haven't". His view was that life for most was unrewarding drudgery where most were locked into thankless jobs and sub-standard, overcrowded housing. No light at the end of the tunnel. No thanks to all of that. To get out of this had been his goal from before adulthood when he had been 'apprenticed' by his dad in the ways of the grandfather, the original 'Mr Davis'. If only he had met him – but that privilege had been denied of Yiddel and he had never forgiven Fate for it.

Life in east London demanded that you kept your wits about you and Yiddel Davis had plenty of these. His dark hair, swept back courtesy of an expensive barber, was only just starting to grey at the temples, part of a very real self-made man, not just an image as was the case with many out there. So, the impression the boys immediately felt was already enough to remove them – in their imagination for now - from the lives they were expected to lead by their fathers.

They were impressed enough to ask, "What does a dealer do?"

"I make money from anything that makes money, lads!" he said, adding, "what do you do then?"

Trying to sound very important, Harry said, "We work for our fathers in the furniture game. We are directors".

Simultaneously, he shot a quick glance sideways at Sammy that clearly advised 'shut up and say nothing, this guy could be offering us something', and, suddenly awake to a chance of escaping what they had both since long ago agreed was a dead-end life, he ventured, "but we are always looking for anything that might come up in the world, ain't we Sam?"

Sammy nodded and thought he would sit it out and say nothing for a while. Unusual for Harry to be so enthusiastic about anything but maybe let him do the talking for now – it probably is just some modern-day spiv anyway, although maybe not? Something about him...a certain "edge", a cut above the rest. Harry and Sammy could never have guessed where this conversation would lead them. Money – yes, but the stakes would be high, and with that would come much risk.

First, though, some things about Yiddel. His grandfather had been quite a man. He had been brought up in the East End of London by a family of fellow Jews after he had narrowly escaped the last pogrom in the Ukraine. The Cossacks had nearly hacked his head off simply for being a Jew and he knew that his father and mother had not been so lucky. At only twelve years of age, he had somehow made it out of the Ukraine to the Baltic port of Danzig (Gdansk when part of a future Poland), and with the only bit of money he possessed, had paid his fare on the boat to London where he had been told his family had friends in a place called Brick Lane in the east part of that city.

Arriving in the days just before the Great War, he lived with a friend of the family in the old Brick Lane, close to Spitalfields and Bethnal Green that had become part of the new ghetto for Jews in the East End. For the first few years of his new life in a new country, he worked hard and had numerous jobs to help with his keep, clothes and occasionally a little money to enjoy some sort of life in London.

When he was seventeen, he got a job making table lamps for a frummer (religious man) in nearby Stepney, where he met Yeidel, his wife to be. She was working as a machinist, making fabric lamp shades at the same factory. After a few months of seeing each other after work, they decided to get married and rented a room just off Brick Lane and a year later, Yiddel's father was born. The grandfather had already adopted the name of Davis when he arrived at Tilbury docks. He saw the name on the side of a building as the boat was berthing and thought it was much better than the unpronounceable Russian name he had. 'A new country, a new name,' he thought. The beginnings of a new Davis family had arrived in England.

Yiddel's grandparents did a splendid job of bringing up their only child on the extremely poor wage that the grandfather earned from the lamp maker company, and for a few years it was a real struggle to survive. He eventually left the lampshade business in a fit of temper one day over the poor wages and terrible working conditions of the sweatshop. And he told the old frummer exactly where to put his badly paid job. Now out of work with a wife and a young baby to support, he was desperate. They were living close to the booming busy docks of 1930s' London and he decided to see if he could get a job of any sort there. Despite all he did, no one would give him work, advising him that the only one way to get a job in the docks was to have a member of the family already working there or to get someone to buy a 'ticket' to work (a ticket being a trade union card demanded at that time for getting into the dock).

One morning, feeling down and wondering how he was ever again going to put food on the family table, he overheard some of the local spivs who were talking in a greasy spoon café; they were saying how easy it was to steal what you liked from the sheds in the docks, mainly because the security was so bad.

When they left the café, he decided to follow them to the West India Dock to see what they were up to. At the huge front gate, they all split up and went their separate ways on what was a carefully pre-arranged plan. On the dock gate was one lone police officer directing traffic in and out and checking people leaving the docks by foot. When the spivs came out of the bonded warehouse, one of them was carrying a bag while the other three headed off to the opposite side of the gate and started to make out in front of the policeman that they were having a fight, making enough noise to attract the attention of the lone copper. He saw what was going on and rushed over to break up the 'fight'. And the bagman meanwhile slipped through the unguarded gate and away! The police officer, having sorted out the affray, had told them to 'fuck off and stop making trouble'.

The act continued whilst they thanked him for being so lenient in his action and walked through the gate and away to catch up with the other member of the gang. The spoils were bottles of rum and vodka, which they then sold to a local off-licence at half-sale price; the proceeds were then split between the four. Watching covertly from the corner of a nearby building, Davis was more than duly impressed by the whole operation and saw a very easy way to make money, and at the same time, his idea of teamwork now included his young son. He could see that a diversion to distract the gate man

7

was essential. This lone individual, after all, had to carry out all the checks on vehicles and pedestrians as they left to make sure they only went with what was on the collection dockets. He also had to check people's bags to prevent anyone leaving the bonded dock with the odd bottle.

Around the docks of London at that time were numerous dock gates with all manner of things coming into the country from all over the world. Davis would soon learn where all these gates were. Back at home, he began to teach his eight-year-old son a new game. He had noticed on one of his recce trips that the port officers did not bother with young children as they walked in or out of the port. "Perfect," he thought, "that's the way I'm going to get rich." He got his wife, Yeidel, to make an overcoat for the boy with large pockets on the inside, enough room to take four bottles. Two each side for balance, which was tested in the flat to see if the boy could carry the extra weight. It worked and Yiddel's father, now eager to help earn a living for the family, was launched into the world of 'ducking and diving'.

The next day with the larder empty, the duo made their way into the bonded warehouse of West India Dock. They walked past the duty officer into the dark and cold of the vast store of alcoholic spirit; past stacks of barrels of wines and spirits, on to towering boxes of bottled spirits, still completely unchallenged. Davis did look the part, he was suitably dressed as a dock worker, with cap and canvas waist overall. He swiftly slipped four bottles of spirits into the prepared pockets of the boy's overcoat and told him to walk straight and to not on any account wobble as they walked to the gate exit.

Just before they got to the gate he went left of the officer and said, "See yer tomorrow, mate," as though he was just finishing his shift as a porter. In doing so, he drew attention away from the little boy who just walked through the gateway completely unnoticed and away into the busy street, to be joined by his father a short distance away. He then helped him to carry the ill-gotten gains to the local dealer in exchange for cash - enough to be able to take home some bread and fish for the dinner table that night. The young apprentice had just done his first job of many.

Father and son carried out every fiddle in the docks that any two people could over their years of working together. They were never caught because they always played the act of dock worker and visiting young boy to the letter. It wasn't long before the youngster started to think up clever ruses of his own and as he busily set up his own ideas – and making himself a lot of money on the side – he realised that this was far better than anything he would otherwise have done in 'normal' jobs. In the end, he had a scam for anything; he would say to those nearest to him, "If it's not bolted down, I'll have it."

As the years passed, leading to another global war, Yiddel's grandfather refused to allow his only son to be evacuated and instead kept him close as they exploited wartime conditions to further their 'business' dealings. Venturing into the ruins of nearby buildings to obtain anything that could be of value and dodging the attempts of the local police and air raid wardens who tried – often in vain – to control the massive black market that was feeding off the chaos and trauma of those years. The family remained defiant and closer together than ever, and as Britain emerged into an uncertain post-war era, it seemed as if everything was indeed rosy in the Davis garden. The boy was now an adult and had found himself a beautiful wife, who bore him a healthy son, and he had acquired enough money to buy a home they could all be proud of.

9

He knew his father admired him, seeing the fruits of all the knowledge, guts and determination that had passed from grandfather to father. And who knows, possibly again from father to son?

They would still go out together, but this time to pubs, not on jobs anymore, or maybe as a family to the coast, with Yiddel's father driving the new, fast car that was easily affordable for him, but not for any of his contemporaries. And it was on the way back from the coast one Sunday, with this successful young man driving them all back home along the main road from Southend to east London that it all came to an abrupt end. Poor mum. No seat belts then. And dad's legs all mangled, half-buried under that lorry's wheels because the driver had been drunk at the wheel. Although just a young boy in the back seat who had smashed into the rear of the fronts, he could all too vividly recollect that day. It had been so confusing being in hospital overhearing the news of his parent's deaths and it was all too unjust to simply accept. The tragedy broke the old grandfather completely – the man who had survived the sabre-wielding Cossacks of pre-revolutionary Ukraine and the carnage of two world wars succumbed to a massive heart attack on hearing the news of the accident, leaving young Yiddel alone and seemingly defenceless in the world.

The story he told himself was that now, after years of working with his dad and then working alone, he was moving on to new ventures: 'keep busy,' that was the thing, 'stay occupied and alert, stand on your own two feet. Take the world on if needs be, but one step at a time. Moreover, do unto others before they do unto you.'

This latest idea was about looking for a couple of clean, crime-free boys to further his plans, and to make his fortune. Yiddel had an idea of a scam and he needed two young eager men to pull the job off. It would be an ongoing thing and all going well it could go on for years.

Offering to buy the boys a drink, he took them to one side away from the darts players to a corner of the lounge. He asked them first if they were interested in making some real money without them having to work their balls off to get it. Both the boys eagerly noticed the 'without having to work your balls off' bit and were now more than a bit curious to find out what their new friend had to say.

Being what he was, Yiddel had over the years been very careful not to say too much too soon, but to see first if others were in or out. He was also checking if they were as keen as he had been to start a life of crime all those years ago in the docks. He felt that he wanted to keep his business in the family of Jews. So, what he had learnt about the boys within the last couple of weeks simply by blending in with the rest at this run-of-the-mill pub had proved invaluable to him. No gold cuff links on those occasions, but now it was different. He went on to tell the duo that they were to tell no one what they did at all, never to let their guard down and only let people know what they want them to know, nothing more.

"Why did you choose us?" asked Sammy, naively.

"If you had been looking, I have been in this bar for the last three weeks and I have been close enough on many occasions to be able to listen to you both bleating off about the shit job that you both do as 'directors' of the old man's firm. In addition, it's about time you found something else. So, in a way you came to me, sunshine! Now - do you want to listen or not?"

The two boys, still only sixteen, were about to make the decision of their young lives, to break the mould of the family tradition, and to at last say: 'Fuck to the furniture trade'.

"Yes!" they said together.

"Right," said Yiddel, more pleased than he chose to show. "Tomorrow morning, go to your fathers and tell them that you are leaving the firm to become 'technicians' in an old established business in, let's say, Birmingham, starting from next Monday. That will give you time to move out and move into a flat I own in Hackney. Tell your parents that all will be well, and that you'll be back to see them when you are next in London, but don't tell them where you are living, in fact tell no one where you are living. I want you to disappear - no records, no phones, nothing. All that you want, I will get you…clear?"

Without hesitation, despite the momentous decision that this was – a real leap into the unknown - they both nodded, and the team headed by Yiddel Davis was about to be forged together.

2

The Team: The Early Days of Apprenticeship

The working fathers, Ivor and Morry, were not happy about losing the two boys. Now they would have to do all the lifting that the boys did for them and that was going to add pressure to a certain rupture. Tears from the mums and farewells from the neighbours and families as the two boys left the security of the family home - to all intents and purposes off to central London for the train to Birmingham, but in reality, this was going to be just three miles down the road to a spacious, well-decorated flat in Hackney.

Yiddel Davis proved to be a master to the boys: how to size up a situation and make it work, how to read people quickly to your advantage; indeed, all the knowledge he had learnt from his father he was now going to pass on to Sammy and Harry. They started the basic preparations of the business with Yiddel conducting lessons on how to tackle everyday events. One crucial element was how to see and observe, yet not be seen or observed - how to become part of the street or surroundings.

Their first job in the street was an art form of crime at the time, known as the 'Jump up'. Very simple, very quick, but not always successful in the final outcome. Yiddel took them to west London and from the shadows of a large lorry parked up at just the right spot showed them what was expected: a Carter Paterson delivery van stops outside a shop, the driver gets out, goes to the rear of the van, opens the roller shutter and checking his delivery notes takes a parcel and delivers it to the shop.

Still observing this for the first time, the boys listened keenly to Yiddel's instructions: "Because of the size of the parcel or perhaps because there is another parcel to go, he never closes the roller shutter. As soon as the driver enters the shop, Harry – you jump up into the back of the van, take a quick look at the parcels, decide which is the good one and pass it down to Sammy, then jump out of the van and away. Don't even look back. Head straight for the nearest place of safety as I've told you, where you can open the parcel and find out if you have picked a box of diamonds or a box of baby's napkins. Leave all the wrappings at the spot and only walk away with the good gear in a covered bag, which you will have with you. Walk away separately, not together. Leave the scene entirely, don't even look round and head where we can meet in private. Here endeth the first lesson."

The next day, the trio headed for Brixton in south London. This was unknown territory for the boys, the pair had never been south of the river before and kept giving backward glances - a common reaction of north and south Londoners - as Yiddel's car crossed over London Bridge. Arriving near the market, Yiddel took great care to park his car in a place where it fitted the surroundings, and not too far from where he hoped the action would take place. All three moved off around the back of the market near the Brixton Road shops. Just as they arrived, Yiddel signalled to Sammy that a Carter Paterson van was slowing down to stop.

Sammy checked where Harry was and waited. The van pulled up and the driver went around to the back, rolled up the shutter and pulled a large box towards him; he checked the paperwork on his clipboard and sure enough staggered off with the box to make the delivery. Straight away Harry was up into the rear of the van; checking the parcels he grabbed one, tested its weight and pushed it over to Sammy, who lifted it as Harry jumped down, and the pair, now both sharing the weight, carried the box away from the scene of the crime.

As advised by Yiddel: not a look back, not a falter in step - exactly how Yiddel had told them to.

They got around the back of the shops and quickly cut the package open to reveal a box of bedside alarm clocks.

"Not bad for the first hit," remarked Yiddel, "they should fetch three quid each, easy. Quite a good start for the first Jump- up, boys."

The boys perfected their Jump-up to a fine art many, many times until the Carter Paterson company got a grip on the situation and advised the drivers to always close the back roller before leaving the van to make the delivery... but not locking it.

Harry and Sammy were now working alone and doing very well, leaving Yiddel to 'fence' the stolen loot. Moving on with the new law placed on the drivers, the two boys were getting quicker on the Jump-up: getting to the van quicker, quicker with the roller shutter, quicker into the van, quicker grabbing a box and finally quicker closing the shutter and away. Always careful, but enjoying every moment of it. Until, that is, one day, when they were going through their well-rehearsed routine, and Harry - moving like the wind - jumped up into the van straight into the jaws of an angry, snarling, menacing dog coming straight at him. He fell backwards, luckily into the arms of Sammy. The pair left the dog itching to tear them to pieces and terminated the Jump-up forever. Carter Paterson had moved up a gear with their new protection and it was time for the duo to stop while they were still Ok and not torn apart by large, angry dogs.

Yiddel was not disappointed when the boys told him of the near calamity and rightly so as it was clear that the time had come to move on. After all, they'd had a very profitable two-years of doing the Jump-up operation across greater areas of central London – though mainly in the west where the pickings were good – sometimes doing three vans a day and netting the trio ever greater amounts of money. But, as Yiddel said, "It's time anyway to move on to bigger things," and he wasn't joking. The boys were well and truly convinced that under the directorship of Yiddel they were on the road to 'earning a few bob'. And over the next two years they learned and listened to Yiddel much more intently. They could afford good clothes, could eat well, enjoy London night-life more, and begin to feel proud of themselves and even prouder of their Master. On trips back home, both families would look at them and smile that their boys were doing so well in Birmingham, so much so that the fathers were told by their wives that they should dump the old furniture business and become 'technicians' and not toil away at the wood trade to scrape a living.

"Look at our son," Harry's mum, Anna, said, beaming from ear to ear. "Look how well he is doing." She could, after all, detect significantly more confidence in her son who had lost a lot of his former quietness and insecurity even though, like Sammy, he had to keep up this pretence of working as some kind of 'technician' in an established business that no one had ever heard of, somewhere in or near Birmingham. The soulful, slightly withdrawn, shy expressiveness of his teens had without doubt given way to a maturing sureness of purpose, and the young man who stood tall in front of her did so with deep, untroubled, brown eyes that masked an adventurous new world of crime, villainy and considerable risk.

The low profile that the two boys kept was all about obeying Yiddel to the letter: don't flash money around, only own a modest car, keep the mouth closed, tell no one about the business. Money from the jobs was put into separate accounts and the trio lived very well. Yiddel, of course, was the master to the success of the operation so far; he had an assortment of different fences that he sold the stolen merchandise to. He knew the right man for each box of goods that was stolen, be it gold watches or baby clothes; he always knew a man, and always got a good price. He played the game fairly, always cutting the money three ways and the boys trusted him and so did the fences. They knew Yiddel would never take them on.

Yiddel now introduced the boys to his new idea. He had been setting it up during their last Jump-up which he had always known would not last forever – not at the rate it was being stolen from the vans. He had heard that someone had been caught at the Jump-up and had been accused of all the jobs, even the ones that the trio had done. It was good while it lasted, but it was time to move up a gear to better things, so that's exactly what Yiddel did.

The boys were now eighteen and getting very streetwise, taking in all the advice from the Master and, more than that, they were picking up on their own ideas. One of these was that they had noticed the routine on Saturday mornings for all the milk and bread delivery rounds men to collect the weekly cash for provisions that had been delivered to the homes throughout the week. At the time, all rounds men carried money satchels for all the silver and copper coins they were paid by the housewives. After a while, the weight of the satchel was so heavy that the bag was left hanging from the float. Sammy had seen this, and the idea was hatched. He knew it would not last long, so his plan was to hit this little swindle as quickly as possible.

The two boys set to work with the aid of a small motorbike. They would drive around the streets, see a rounds man's van or cart, and pull up alongside. Harry would nip off the back of the bike, grab the heavy satchel off the hook and away they sped, netting on average about fifty pounds in small change. They then drove to where they had parked their car, emptied the satchel into a box in the boot and threw it into the nearest rubbish container and away again to find the next unlucky milk or bread delivery man, making sure not to go back anywhere near the last heist. This little caper went on for a few months of Saturdays - they did very well out of this nice little earner, but as with all these little earners the makers of the vehicles came up with an idea: in this case, to fit a locked metal box welded to the floor like an onboard safe. That was the end of that one!

In the meantime, the caper that Yiddel had been keeping his eye on was a haulage yard in Stepney to which loaded lorries were brought back to be locked up for the night so that the drivers could arrive early the next morning to deliver the load. Bringing back the load to the yard was so that the drivers only worked their allowed driving hours and then could run out the next day and not break the ministry rules regarding excessive time in the driving seat. Yiddel had heard about this and was observing from his usual discreet distance, at the same time keeping his ears open when he 'ate' inconspicuously in the café the staff from the haulage company used for breakfast. It did not take long for him to hear that the yard only had an old pensioner on duty at night, and according to what he heard the old boy got his head down at about 9pm and 'nothing woke him up'.

'Well,' thought Yiddel, 'that *is* a nice old man, a sleeping minder and no yard dog. What could be better?'

Yiddel briefed the boys on how he wanted the job to go. He had already established the place for the 'slaughter' out in Essex, so all the boys had to do was to make sure the goods got there safely. They ran over the plan repeatedly over the next week. He had heard, on one of his discreet breakfast eavesdropping visits, that the haulage company had just won a contract to pick up and deliver bottled whisky all over the south of England.

"That will do very handsomely," said Yiddel to the boys, adding, "we've got the slaughter all ready for it." He knew exactly how lucrative it was going to be after a couple of phone calls to the right men – those who would like a load of whisky at a good price, no questions asked.

Sammy questioned Yiddel about the slaughter in Essex. "Is it necessary to have a place so far out?" he ventured.

Yiddel told the boys that the essence of the job was as it had been in the days of the Jump-up. Get in, get well away from the scene of the crime and do not be observed. In the case of the stolen lorry, for as long as they had the load on it the more chance they had of being caught, but once they unloaded it, they could lose it for good, and all being well be home and dry for the deliveries via another clean lorry. They chose Monday night to do the job because Yiddel had heard that the first load was being picked up and brought back to the yard for early delivery on Tuesday morning.

The trio arrived at the front entrance to the yard at 9.30pm in a dark blue van, specially stolen for the job. Preparing to go to work on the gate with a set of bolt cutters, they noticed that the outside lock was already off. Thinking that perhaps the silly old sod of a night watchman had forgotten to put it on they nevertheless approached the huge gates with a fair bit of caution. Looking around the gate into the yard, they could see to their absolute amazement the lorry standing loaded and sheeted - up all ready to go. There was no sign of the night watchman; the yard seemed to be empty except for the loaded lorry. Yiddel could not believe his good fortune, even the door of the lorry was unlocked and ready to drive out. He had a quick look under the tarpaulin to make sure that the load was indeed the right one of whisky. It was…Harry leapt up into the driver's seat.

With Sammy quietly opening the gates, he drove the vehicle out of the yard, Sammy jumping up into the passenger side as he picked up speed, Yiddel following behind in the van.

'What a result!' thought Yiddel to himself as both vehicles drove along the road heading for the A13 and the slaughter in Essex. "And hopefully not too good to be true…"

The former pig farm was as safe as houses. Yiddel had made sure of that before he had rented it from a letting agent, using one of his many names and paying cash for a two-week let. Within an hour of leaving the yard they were there and Yiddel directed Harry to drive the lorry into a very large old barn. They quickly got to work unloading it, stacking the boxes neatly along one side of the barn; in half an hour of the three working flat out, all was stacked very discreetly.

Back on the road, they headed for a large transport café near Epping Forest, forty minutes' drive away. Harry parked the now empty lorry at the back of the parking area alongside the others. Yiddel parked a short distance away from them, watching all the time to see if they were being observed. They walked across to Yiddel, got into the van and were soon heading back to Hackney along the main road through the old forest.

The term 'slaughter' had come about in cockney slang - it was a word meaning the cutting up of stolen goods into smaller parcels, which were then dispensed through all the regular channels of fencing.

'This job has gone well,' reflected Yiddel, as he tried to find any flaws in the plan. 'Quick, easy pick-up, no one around at the yard…that was the bit that was odd – where had the night watchman been? Sod worrying, it's done now. No one saw us at the car park as far as could be known from watching it.' The lorry was completely clean of any fingerprints – that was another of his rules. Always wearing gloves and never taking them off until clear of the scene equals leaving no evidence. This self-imposed rule went back to the downfall of the Great Train Robbery gang, where all was discovered by one palm print found at the farm - when one nobhead failed to do his commissioned job of burning down the farm, which would have got rid of any fingerprints and evidence. This had led to the capture of the whole gang. This had always stayed in Yiddel's mind and constantly made him ensure they wore gloves and overalls on any job.

Over the next week, the whisky was disposed of little by little from the farm to dealers known to Yiddel until it was all gone, and the farm was again empty. Yiddel shared it out fairly, which netted them all a tidy sum.

About a week later, Yiddel was in a club in east London having a drink and talking to a villain he knew who worked for the Smiths, a particularly notorious gang operating on the south side of the Thames. After a few shorts, the villain started talking about the bad luck that the gang had suffered over the last few weeks. He told Yiddel about cars that failed to start, people they were relying on

21

who did not turn up and also a load of whisky that they'd had ready and loaded to drive away when their look-out spotted a dark blue police van pull up outside the yard. So rather than wait to get their collars felt they all escaped out through the back exit and left the area fast.

Yiddel felt the hair on his neck stand up and he hoped that any reaction that his body was showing did not give him away. He sat there struggling, hearing himself utter empty phrases like: "What a bastard, mate, never mind, maybe your luck's going to change; better luck next time."

After he left the club, still in a hot sweat, he was thinking at a rapid rate of knots. 'They must have been setting the job up at the same time. I didn't see anyone I knew in the café or on the street. Christ, they must have had an insider in the haulage firm.'

He called the two boys to a meeting as soon as he got back to Hackney. When they arrived, he told them the story he had just been told and by whom, and said, "If it ever gets out that we have stolen a load from the Smiths we might as well say goodbye now. We will be fitted up for a concrete jacket and finish up in some roadworks somewhere, inside a motorway support pillar."

All Yiddel said about it later was that he reckoned the Smiths ought to get a better look-out in future.

Despite this close shave, financially the boys were having the time of their lives. They were very well dressed, very well fed and the apartment they shared was really something else in style. They bought their clothes from designer shops apart from the working clothes, which came from charity shops, replacing them after every caper to prevent identification through a certain piece of clothing. They drove around in an old car so that nothing was given away of the wealth that they now had. Their money was put away under

22

Yiddel's guidance in separate bank accounts in fictitious names, well hidden away in safe banks.

The only money they ever kept either in the apartment or on them was just enough cash to live on for a week so that, God forbid, as Yiddel said, "If you ever get a pull, you are potless."

The account books were also put away in a safe place and when they did have a good earner, they only had a certain amount put in the accounts at a time so that staff at the banks did not get suspicious and become tempted to inform on two young men putting loads of money away in one go.

"Do not take any chances," was the advice from Yiddel, and they obeyed it to the letter.

Such were the early days, but what was to come would blow all these things to kingdom come.

3

The Oxford Street Caper

Things had been relatively quiet for a short while, but they both knew that Yiddel was grooming them gradually for, one day, the 'big 'un'.

Moreover, they had the feeling that when it came it was going to be a real sizzler - much riskier, maybe some violence -so they had to be quicker and craftier. In the meantime, the Master was indeed working on this next caper, this time in the West End of London. With the exception of some very lucrative Jump-ups, this was going to be unknown territory to Yiddel and the boys, but if what he had heard was right it was well worth the bus fare to go and get it.

A well-known high street store was apparently taking great care to save money by burning its old, dirty bank notes on the premises. This way they did not have to pay a security company to collect it, take it away and burn it...Burn it! Not all the money was burnt, only what was classed as old and dirty, the good stuff being collected as usual by a security company. Yiddel had heard that what the bank had in the store was a staff member responsible for deciding at store level what was good and what was bad. He gave the store a receipt for the burnt money that was then paid into its bank account with the good cash and the cheques. It saved having to send the money all the way to Debden in Essex to do what he was doing in Oxford Street and was cheaper in the end for this multi-national.

Yiddel had heard of this going on through one of the cleaners who worked at the store and who happened to know his girlfriend.

It was reckoned that it could be close to half a million pounds a day being taken on a Friday or Saturday. He had met the cleaner 'incidentally' when his girlfriend had invited her round for a chat and who should be there, paying a visit at the same time, but he, Yiddel Davis. And so, the two were introduced and the next night the pair were out on the town clubbing and dining. At the end of the night, Yiddel had this new acquaintance, Sheila - whom he found out he knew from her family - eating out of his hand and well and truly stitched up for a nice piece of the money if the job came off. Sheila was very keen to be of any assistance when she heard how much money was possibly coming her way.

Sheila started her cleaning shift immediately after the store had closed for the day as was the case at all the major West End stores. She detailed every move that the night staff had to perform to get in and how they were watched, to stop any pilfering from the stock, either on show or in the stock rooms. As Yiddel listened to Sheila, the plan started to form in his mind. He knew that the burner of the money only arrived at the end of the day and usually worked through the night until 6am. The incinerator was in the basement and only two men were in that room at the same time: the bank man and his assistant. The entrance to the room was only through a small service lift, which the bank man had control of by way of a key - the only key. This was the bit that Yiddel was getting into his head: how to get into the vault and how to get the money out?

He guessed that the best day to do the job was going to be the Saturday night because there was no collection on Friday according to Sheila, and what two better days to have? The shop would have been at its busiest then, taking more money in two days than the whole of the rest of the week. The huge store at night when it was closed was a hive of activity and industry. Security, cleaners, shelf

25

and stock fillers as well as painters and decorators doing alterations and in-store modifications were all there. The security staff in one way or other were hard pushed to watch everybody and everything that moved – surely?

Yiddel spent a few hours on the first observation day walking around the store, just as a normal shopper would. Looking and touching garments and products, pondering if value for money. At the same time, he was checking where the inner doors were and the staircase to the little lift to the vault and who, if anyone, was checking him. He kept his eyes on the garments only lifting his gaze enough to see if the mobile cameras were tracking him. 'All that went well,' he thought, and he left the store to head back to Hackney very much wiser as to the layout of the store, and the risks the job presented.

The next day he took the boys with him, both fully briefed as to what they were looking for and getting the plan of the store firmly in their heads. The three worked completely independently of each other, not even going near one another, looking and checking so as not to bring one ounce of suspicion from the ever-observing security camera operators who might bring their cameras to bear on them for the slightest of reasons. Yiddel knew these people were experts, trained to spot crooks like him. He and the boys even entered and left the store by different doorways. After they left they met at a café at the rear of Oxford Street, safely out of reach of those trying to foil capers like the one he had now hatched.

"This job 'as got to be done and dusted as soon as possible," he said, once they were seated. "The longer we take to check it out, the more chance there'll be that we'll be getting some unwelcome attention - these guys that operate the cameras are not mugs - if they start seeing the same faces the alarm bells will start to ring very quickly. Either that, or another team of crooks get smell of it and beat us to it," he said, smiling. "You know what I mean!"

Later that night they had a conference and went over the job, checking all the information they had in hand. Yiddel knew what he needed and laid it out like a military operation.

"In the morning, I want you to get some workmen's overalls, gloves, full face masks, some good large holdalls and a couple of large plastic sacks. I will be returning to the target on my own after dark to see what it looks like at night, then I'll confirm the job's on for the next Saturday night. All the equipment needs to got – that's down to you two. I will put the final plan together as to what roles each of us is playing."

Saturday night came. A van was stolen and parked nearby ready for use. The three arrived at the store with the night staff and booked themselves in with security as building workers whose company was already on site, using the company name and fake ID. Yiddel had checked this out on one of his 'listening' visits. Once in, they headed for the storeroom where the builders kept all the tools for each task. Taking a tin of paint each they headed for the basement looking as best they could like painters about to start work. The lift which the bankman used was locked after he and his assistant had let themselves in to the incinerator and counting room. Sheila had advised him that there was also a door in case of emergencies if they needed to get out other than the lift.

The moment had come. Hearts pounding, minds focused, time seemed suspended for a moment. Then, putting on their facemasks, the two boys shoulder charged the door and burst into the room. For a second the bankman and his aide froze with shock at the noise of their workplace door – which they'd previously assumed to be impregnable - being smashed in by three masked men. Quickly, Sammy and Harry grabbed hold of the two men, who were now madly protesting about the intrusion with lots of "Who the fuck do you think you are?" Harry and Sammy swiftly overpowered any resistance and gagged and bound them securely without saying a word.

Only Yiddel spoke: "Don't even think about being brave, gentlemen. We will be out of here as soon as possible, so don't try to be heroes." Just a few words, but the tone of his voice made the two of them realise that from now on until this was over, bravery was not on the agenda and whatever these three villains wanted they were going to get. The trio looked at the mountain of paper money stacked up on the counting table and were gobsmacked. Yiddel had never seen so much cash; the two boys immediately started to load the bundles of money - all neatly stacked up, just waiting to be burnt - into the bags. Yiddel had by now secured the smashed door, and was now jamming it from the inside. As soon as he had fixed this in place, he joined the boys in the loading of the bags. No more words were spoken throughout and no masks were removed. Silence was never more golden, and the task was soon done. Before filling the big black bags with the cash, the boys had tipped the contents of one of them onto the floor to see what Yiddel had loaded in it...large lumps of asbestos.

The filled bags were now partly zipped up and the asbestos was laid on top of the money. Yiddel searched the bankman's pocket and found the key to the lift into which they loaded the bags. As a parting gesture, he turned and waved goodbye to the two trussed-up men and they swiftly left.

The three made their way to the staff exit, telling everyone as they passed not to breathe because they 'had to get rid of life-threatening asbestos right now and right out of harm's way'. In fact, having heard the gist of this simple statement, all the security guard at the door could do was to mumble behind his handkerchief: "Yeh, get it out of here!" The three villains all thought the same thing at the same time with a united "We sure will!" and exited the building. They had taken no more than thirty minutes to pull off the entire caper.

Outside, they dumped the pieces of asbestos in a doorway. At the van, Sammy threw the back doors open and chucked the big bags into the back as Yiddel started it up, and, still not daring to believe they had got this far this quickly, they drove away – keeping it careful and steady on the speed. Yiddel knew that the men in the basement would not be found for a good few hours, and by that time they would be well away from the store. He knew that no one could get to the men quickly because the door was jammed from the inside and the lift could only be used by the one key, which was now down a drain hole at the back of Oxford Street.

They stopped the van at a car park in the West End and changed vehicles - two loading, one watching, alert as always. Everything went into the boot: the overalls, masks and gloves in a large waste bag would be burnt at the first chance. They drove home elated that the caper – their first bank job - had gone so well and too excited for words to discover what they had earned out of it.

Back at the boys' flat, before any counting began, the first thing Yiddel could say was: "Put the kettle on, Sam, my throat's like the bottom of a budgie's cage!" Harry cleared the table for the mammoth task that was about to begin.

After four hours, they still hadn't made much of an impression and already they were into the one and a half million pounds area. Yiddel looked at the pile of counted cash and then at the stacks still in the bags and a slight panic caught him. Was this too much? Were they out of their depth on this one? If they weren't really careful, this might be their downfall. And then, looking at the boys eagerly digging into the bags and getting more and more out to count, joking and laughing as they went, he thought: 'What the fuck, it's done now!'

He got stuck in with the boys, counting and piling and starting to enjoy the feeling of 'this is what I have always dreamed of, the pot of gold, the last job, the Shangri-La'. He stopped counting every now and then for a swig of his tea and a cigarette and looking at the piles of counted notes that were getting bigger and bigger.

Finally, it was the last bundle. Sitting back exhaustedly, they looked at each other, said "Fucking hell!" and burst out laughing. "Lads," said Yiddel. "I think we have cracked it this time. I have never seen so much fucking money in all my life."

The two boys were seated behind what had now become such a huge mountain of bank notes that they could only just see Yiddel on the other side of the table.

"What do you make it?" he wanted to know.

Sammy, looking at the tally sheet, and after taking a deep breath, announced it was "two million five hundred thousand pounds," and then, glancing at Yiddel, cheekily added, "give or take a pound or two."

They sat still and stared as if hypnotised at the cash, each with his own thoughts of what he would do with his share, and said nothing more for a long time. Eventually, with the adrenalin of the caper at last slowing down, it was Yiddel who broke the silence: "I don't 'alf fancy a sandwich!"

He knew that by 6am the shit must have hit the fan in the store back at Oxford Street and the hunt would now be on for them. He turned on the TV and clicked on the Teletext news sheet pages. Big bold headlines declared that a daring raid from one of England's biggest multi-national stores had been carried out, 'aided by unknown security staff'.

The story went on to discuss a team of villains who had managed to get into and away from the store without arousing any suspicion. There was a piece in the copy that said how well the gang leader had treated the bankman and his aide and how these 'Robin Hoods' had escaped into the night before anyone knew that a crime had been committed. Reading the news bulletin, Yiddel felt pumped up that they - three snot noses from the East End - were being put on the same par as Robin Hood.

Putting the bags of money out of sight in the bathroom, the three managed to get a couple of hours sleep and at 10am Sammy slipped out to get some beigels and doughnuts. The first edition of the *Evening Standard* was on the streets, so he bought two for them to read back at the flat. The headline splash on the front of the *Standard* was: 'WHO ARE THESE MEN?' with a large reward offered by the store. As the day went on, the TV networks were having a field day with all the possibilities of who the gang were. The figure of the amount stolen grew all day, estimated by the media as anything from four million to twenty million pounds. The store held a press conference at its headquarters, which the trio watched as various people described the gang and what they did to get access to the fortified store.

"Fortified store!" Yiddel exclaimed. "It was like walking in and out of the local park."

The security guard had at least been honest and told the true story of how cheeky they had been when leaving the store, claiming to have bags of asbestos to carry out to be dumped.

"Yeh," Harry said, "in someone else's doorway."

The trio stayed in the flat, only Sammy slipping out to get some fish and chips. They were quite happy sitting back, eating their humble fish and chip lunch, watching this amazing saga unfolding on TV. Now was the time to reflect on all the care that Yiddel had taken in not involving anyone outside of the three and planning the whole job as clandestinely as he had done. The only possible weak link was the cleaner, Sheila, but deep down Yiddel knew that she could be trusted. He knew her family and how much old-time loyalty was in place to 'yer own', as they said in the East End. He had heard of her father, an ex-docker who would fight anyone for a pound and always won. Of her two brothers - small-time villains, sure - but loyal to the back teeth.

He felt that Sheila was 'as safe as houses' and that he could trust her to the hilt. He knew that she would not talk about the caper – even to her family - in case by some fluke it was overheard by some nosey listener. The next morning, Sammy went out for the morning papers and some fresh food. He usually only bought *The Sun*, but today it was all the papers on the news-stand.

The headlines were mind-blowing. The three sat around the kitchen table grasping a piping hot cup of tea on what was a chilly November morning, reading about what they had done – or apparently done - at the store. Headline banners like 'WHOW!' on the front of *The Sun*. 'DARING RAID' said *The Mirror*; *The Mail* followed the *Standard* with 'WHO ARE THESE MEN?' and so it went on, each paper doing its own splash. In every paper, the story was different in many ways; all the tabloids were having a field day with eye-catching, very expert, sensationalist journalistic terminology. The crime writers had gone mad writing prose not used since the days of The Great Train Robbery, of course making the stories sound even better than the first time they were told.

The heavies played it a lot calmer and as near factual as they could get it without the dramatic prose of the tabloids, all stating what a great deal of trouble must have gone into the planning by this gang in pulling off such a crime in the middle of London, but also mentioning that no one had been hurt - only the dignity of the store and the bankman had been dented. A large reward was splashed over most papers, offered by the store and the bank. As this second day wore on, the more far-fetched the whole operation was getting; things that never happened were being written into the column inches, making the crime story expand in every paragraph. With considerable self-control, the trio kept out of sight, staying in the flat all day, listening to the radio and watching the TV news bulletins updated on every hourly and half-hourly news reports. Again, the stolen amount grew constantly.

If Sheila was preparing herself for anything, it was because she knew that the police would soon be knocking at her door and checking her out; it was mainly because of her brothers that she would be a suspect. But, she also knew that, all being well, and if she got through it, she would be set up for life - as promised by Yiddel. Just got to be very clever and extremely careful, now, though.

Less down to earth, the two boys were virtually floating over the amount of money they had (now stacked in their bathroom). Better than all the Jump-ups and all the satchels! They also considered the fact that, come what may, even if they never did another job, they were from here on in, set up for life. Yiddel was buzzing inside his chest and being very careful not to show any sign of being other than his normal self when he was out and about, especially around the market, where tongues had a particular tendency to waggle uncontrollably. Yet, everyone he met was talking about it; they all had their own thoughts and ideas of who could have pulled it off. Always in hushed voices, and from behind a hand, all seemed to have a theory of who did it, ranging from certain figures of the British underworld to an imported foreign team from Italy. Yiddel always went along with their thoughts; he just listened and agreed, never arguing. His own thoughts were concentrated on the cash not one mile from where all these unknowing people were talking about it.

The trio met as often as was safe at the flat, discussing what could top this one and how, if at all, it was going to unfold. Yiddel, as always, had the ideas, but was looking much more into the future rather than the present time. He told the boys that if they were caught on this one, because of the size of it and because of the amount of publicity the caper had generated, they would go away for a very long time. The boys knew that the Master was right. After a week, the press had moved on and the story dropped off the front pages.

Sure enough, Sheila had been spoken to by the police who very quickly had visited the family home in Hackney. They had searched every place in the house for the slightest piece of evidence and had gone through her personal phone book and the rest of the family's,

34

looking for names of known criminals. They found nothing to link her or the family to anything, and left thanking them all for being so helpful in their investigations. All the old man said afterwards was, "I told you we would get a visit, as you worked there."

Yiddel's next move was, on the face of things, a surprising one. He got work on a fruit and vegetable stall in Ridley Road market, telling the boys that it was better that he joined the working classes for a while as it gave him a chance to listen to what was going on. He had worked for 'Dodger' on his stall before and was good at weighing the produce up and serving the locals. He was well liked because of his style and cheek; he would say rude things to the old people and make them shriek with laughter. "A man you would have to go a long way to beat," some said. Once, a woman called him a 'likeable rogue' and she was right.

Working one day, he looked up and met eyes with Sheila.

"Hullo, love, how are you? How's yer dad?" he enquired.

She acted as though she was an old schoolfriend, making sure no one was looking at them too closely.

"Everything's fine," she said, calmly.

And that was it, they had made contact, reassuring each other that they were safe and there were no concerns. Yiddel was pleased he had encountered her and told the boys later that he had met the person who had helped set up the job. He asked them if they were Ok he slipped her a few quid the next time he saw her. They agreed instantly.

"Leave it to you, Yiddel," said Sammy.

Two days later in the market, Yiddel saw Sheila walking down through the stalls heading in his direction. She came over to look at the fruit and affected interest in the apples.

"Are they all right?" she asked.

"Are they all right! I've just picked 'em from some woman's garden, love," he responded, cheekily.

"Well, Ok, I'll have two pounds, please," she said, by now unable not to smile at his fine acting skills.

Yiddel weighed up the apples and slipped two fifty-pound notes into the brown paper bag, saying as he passed it over: "You'll like them, miss, they are really tasty."

She smiled and walked off; if anyone had been watching them all they would have seen was her buying apples from a stall and simply passing the time of day with the seller.

The boys met Yiddel for a drink in the local pub near the market for a chat and to find out if he had discovered anything.

"Not a dickie bird," he said, using one of his many cockneyisms. "Not a word!" They told Yiddel that, as it was nearly a month since the caper, they were thinking of going away for a week to have a break from lying low and doing nothing.

"Well, that's a very good idea. I might as well come an' all. Go over the travel shop and get a brochure and I'll meet you round home tonight and we'll sort something out."

The boys were glad he had said he would like to go as well - they had realised that out of the three of them he needed a break the most. They knew that although he was all calm and serene on the outside, the inside of Yiddel was going at two hundred miles per hour all the time.

Later that night after looking at the offers in the brochure, they picked on a hotel in the middle of Benidorm surrounded by thousands of English and foreign holiday makers, all hell-bent on enjoying their annual holiday in the sun. The next day Sammy booked up the three to jet off in two weeks' time. Harry was sent

36

to the West End to get 'a few pesetas', enough for a week in and around the hotel getting drunk every night.

The two weeks passed, with all still Ok. The story dropped out of the news, with only an occasional voice grumbling about the police doing nothing to find the perpetrators.

Sheila occasionally passed by the stall stopping for some produce and a fifty-pound note in the bag along with the fruit. "I'm going away for a week, tomorrow, love - to Benidorm. See you when I get back," he said as he was serving her.

"Why not? Have a nice time." She smiled, but inside was sad not to be going with this handsome benefactor.

'At least she knows where I am,' thought Yiddel, 'in case she thinks I've done a runner.'

4

The Gold of Heathrow

The morning of the departure for Heathrow came. They had a mini-cab booked to get them to the airport, but the little Asian cab driver could hardly speak English let alone know in which direction to go for the world's busiest airport so Yiddel guided him onto the right road and, that done, sat back in the car to start enjoying his holiday – or so he believed. The boys thought this hilarious, all three of them in the old Vauxhall Cavalier heading for the airport with a driver that had just left Bombay. Driving up the motorway, they saw the first signs for the terminal building and left it to Ali, as they now knew him, to get them there – a bad move as it turned out as they soon found themselves not at the flight departure area but in the cargo area on the west side - though with at least with ample time to spare, still.

Surrounded by large lorries and cargo vans all dropping off freight for flights to foreign parts, the taxi slowed up, Ali now being not just lost but quite disorientated. As they were giving him the verbal about his knowledge of England and how simple it really was to get to the departure area, Yiddel saw three *Securicor* lorries pulling into one of the huge cargo sheds. He knew that these types of vehicles only carry heavy cargo…like bullion. In addition, the amount of police in attendance endorsed his theory.

'Well now,' he thought, his mind starting to race with various possibilities. 'What a nice way to start your holiday.'

The break did all three of them the world of good and after a week of sun, sand, sangria and lovely women they were on their way back to London. All the time Yiddel was on the Costa Brava, his thoughts kept returning to the cargo sheds at Heathrow. Now they were back in London he was preparing himself for a trip out to the airport to have a proper look around. He had a chat with the boys about there being a possibility of something coming up – something to put a cherry on the cake - and naturally they were both up for it. Now that he had whetted their appetites, the desire for another, immediate caper came flooding back into their otherwise dull routine.

"What makes this one better," said Harry to Sammy when they were alone, "is that now we are rich, it makes it much more enjoyable. It's like we can now afford it."

Yiddel had borrowed a moped scooter from a mate who had used it doing the London taxi knowledge run outs; he had finally passed it, but did not bother to sell it; he just kept it in his back yard. It was still rigged out with the clipboard and waterproofs for those odd rainy days when his near-penniless friend had trundled around the streets of the capital doing the 'knowledge'.

With a full tank of two-stroke, and under an azure-blue sky, he headed for the airport. He enjoyed the long ride in the sun; arriving at the cargo side of Heathrow, he rode around with no one taking any notice of him at all - looking like a new learner, riding the right machine, just learning about this place as well as the streets of London. Around the cargo areas he stopped every now and then to make notes on his clipboard as discreetly as he could, yet never too far away from the huge shed where he could observe the bullion lorries going in to.

Nearby, he noticed a small café that catered for the drivers and staff. He parked the moped and went in for a cup of tea. Doing his usual thing of sitting with his tea, and a newspaper in front of him as though engrossed with the page three picture, he listened attentively to all that was said by the cargo workers who were in and out all the time, snatching quick tea breaks and then back to work.

Yiddel surreptitiously did this for four days by when he knew the first names of all of the day and night staff including the managers - what they were like, all their hates and all the rest of it. Childlike, these men unwittingly passed over all their secrets to Yiddel's expert ears. And one name that kept coming up was a certain Richard. It seemed that Dick, as they called him, was into a much more sordid life than most men. Dick was gay, and he liked the seedy side of being gay, enjoying taking part in sexual acts at a club in Knightsbridge, which was noted by Yiddel. The men from the cargo shed all thought this was extremely funny and would laugh and make jokes at what Dick apparently liked.

Yiddel, however, calculated that this priceless information might be his way into the bullion shed. It meant that there was one essential thing to do on this fourth day and that was to check what Dick looked like and to follow him home. He did this easily by parking within safe distance of the shed exit from where he could hear one of the men say that Dick was off early tonight and that he was going to the club, and others laughing about not turning his back when Dick was about. An hour later, the day duty men were all leaving. All the men that had been in the cafe were all saying goodnight to Dick and advising him to 'be careful'.

'Perfect,' thought Yiddel. 'This is easy. Everyone has just played into my hands and pointed out to me who Dick is. Now I just need to find out where he lives.' Keeping a sensible distance behind, it proved to be just a ten-minute drive, to nearby Hounslow. He watched him go into his house, watched the light go on and saw him close the curtains. He noted the number and name of the road and set off for the East End, well pleased with his four days' surveillance work.

"Now the real fun will start," he murmured to himself.

Yiddel had learnt so much in watching the cargo workers and listening to their banter both in the café and out around the airport buildings that he had compiled a dossier of this knowledge. He knew most of the workers by sight, he knew a bit about the manager Richard aka Dick, what type of bullion was handled and to where it was shipped, how many times a week; day and night arrivals, by whom and to what. He knew about unfair workloads, the men's grievances, who was a shit and who was a nice guy and most of all - how the cargo system worked - all by drinking cups of tea in a café, and a little legwork.

The trio met to see what was going to happen once the Oxford Street caper had died down. Yiddel had not been idle; he had met with a local man whom he referred to as Mark Joseph. Joseph had set up three separate accounts. Yiddel had assured the boys that the accounts were as safe as anything else was and all they had to do was to remember seven numbers. The boys were happy about this. Yiddel promised to introduce them to Joseph when they felt it was safe enough to move the money.

"Right, the next thing on the agenda: what shall we give Sheila?" asked Yiddel.

All three had roughly the same figure in their heads and agreed when Yiddel announced "two hundred and fifty K'!"

"A nice round amount for her, which should help her and the family out for the rest of their lives," said Harry, bringing the bags out of the bathroom. He pulled a wad of banknotes out onto the table and they counted out the quarter of a million pounds.

Yiddel bagged it up in some Tesco plastic bags ready for the pass over to Sheila. The rest of the money was split up into three different piles amounting to seven hundred and thirty thousand pounds each. The final part of the meeting of the 'Board of Directors' as Sammy called them was for Yiddel to put to the Board the new caper to see if they were ready to do it.

Yiddel had his own thoughts on this and was keen to see if they were still as interested on going on a new caper now that they were rich. He told them just enough about it and no more. Except that it was a totally different type of job. He said to them not to rush and give it a bit of thought, but to make up their minds as soon as possible. But, even he was surprised when the two boys, without waiting, said together, "When do we start, Yiddel?"

Yiddel phoned Sheila and carefully put it to her that he had 'found her purse by the stall', and, if she wanted to come to the market he would hand it over. Sheila thanked Yiddel, understanding the coded message enough to emphasise to him how grateful she was and that she would be at the stall in fifteen minutes, before ending the telephone conversation. He waited for her on the corner of the market and quickly ushered her into his car and drove off.

"I'm glad you got the message, darling!" he said.

"I thought for a minute, what the bloody hell are you talking about and then the penny dropped, and I knew you wanted to see me. You're right, they could still be listening on incoming calls."

42

"Is everything all right with you?" he asked, with some concern.

"Yeh. No probs at all. The money's been very handy every week, thank you." Sheila's smile said it all.

"Well, it's even better this week. In the bag on the back seat is your share of the money for your part in setting it up for us."

"Thanks for that, it will help get some extra shopping this week. Its dad's birthday and I want to get him a cake." Naively, Sheila had not even considered how much it could be.

"I don't want to scare you, darling, but it could be a bigger cake than you could possibly imagine..." He let the inference sink in for a moment before continuing, "You've got two hundred and fifty thousand pounds in the bag!"

"HOW MUCH?" she exclaimed in loud disbelief – and genuine shock.

"Shush, the whole street will hear you," said Yiddel, stopping the car. Sheila was so shaken she just sat there, looking at Yiddel with a glazed expression on her face.

"I won't say it again, but you are a very wealthy lady, and I am more than pleased to give this to you," he said, with heartfelt honesty.

Trying hard to compose herself, she leaned over to Yiddel and kissed him on the lips. "I can't thank you enough. I didn't expect that much, Yiddel."

"Well, as we have both got a few bob, why don't we have a night out together and maybe you let me spend a little of mine on you, then?"

"I'd love to, Yiddel. Let's do that!"

He dropped her off a short distance from the house and both promised that on the first available opportunity they would have their much longed-for date.

Later, Yiddel gave the boys a bit more of an outline of the next caper. He told them about Dick and what was going to be needed to pull the job off. He detailed some ideas of what was going through his mind. They agreed that Dick could be the key to the caper, but the question was: how to use him?

"My brain's been trying to come up with an answer and I think I have just come up with it," Yiddel proudly announced. "Now, I have known a gay guy for years, and don't take it wrong, you two!"

Sammy instantly jumped up and posed all girly, giving them a laugh at his actions.

"I know he is also into the other side, like Dick is, and I also know that he, unknown to most that know him, is a guy that can be trusted, because his family are all villains and thieves. His two brothers are members of the Smith gang and if anyone found out about him, they would fit that person up with a pair of concrete boots and drop him into the Regent's Park Canal. So, if it's Ok with you, I will pay him a visit and see if he is interested in joining up with us on this caper. I know he would like to get away from Hackney but has never had the chance to break from the family and if I put it to him right it could be his way out – and our way in!"

Yiddel phoned the man in question, named Roger, and they met in the Prince of Wales public house in Kingsland Road. After carefully broaching the plan to him and what he wanted him to do, it wasn't long before Yiddel had Roger's agreement - with a good deal of enthusiasm.

"All I want you to do is get to know this bloke, strike up some sort of friendship, getting as much information out of him as to how we can get into the Heathrow shed, without giving him any idea what we are intending to do. I know the name of the club in Knightsbridge, Rog. Meet him there, and I'll leave the rest to you," he explained, glad that Roger seemed keen to do the job. "We'll go over there next Saturday to do a recce."

However, it was to turn out better than Yiddel had thought. Yiddel met Roger in the same pub on the next Saturday night and took him over to Knightsbridge. Roger was extremely well dressed and looked very smart, thought Yiddel, not for one moment thinking anything else. He went over the plan again, making it clear on the way there as to exactly what he wanted. Yiddel wanted Roger to spend the night with Dick at the club and get as friendly as he could.

"Go over the top, if you must, Roger, but get us in that shed."

Roger understood exactly what was meant, and as he got out of the car, he said "leave it to me". Yiddel leant across and gave him five hundred pounds.

"That's for your expenses, and I don't want any change!" Roger was well pleased, a night out doing what he liked doing and being paid for it too.

Yiddel paid the entrance fee for them both and they made their way to the bar. Yiddel ordered the drinks and were standing there being asked by several of the regulars as they passed, "Hello, first time here?" to which Yiddel nodded and Roger smiled.

This was not what Yiddel was used to in any shape or form and he was going to be very pleased to see Dick, hopefully, arrive and then be able to direct Roger to the target - and make a swift departure from this underworld of an altogether different kind.

After about an hour of this torture, he at last noticed Dick sweep in through the front doors, making a 'grand' entrance and enjoying attracting the attention of several of those already there. Dressed all in black leather with chains hanging from his jacket, he was looking very different to when Yiddel had seen him at the cargo sheds. He seemed to know everyone there, they all waved and smiled or 'hallo'd' him.

Yiddel discreetly pointed him out to Roger, wished him "best of luck mate" and hurriedly left.

'Right, it's all up to you now, Roger, me old mate,' he thought, 'and rather you than me', thankful that he could at last leave the premises. Driving away, he reflected on some of the various places he had been to in his life so far and began to realise that, if he thought he had seen everything, tonight made him realise he definitely hadn't. What would his father and grandfather have made of the last hour of his life? Just a little bit different to the docks of Empire when he'd had to help his dad steal all those bottles of booze and been forced to navigate the world of hardened, small-time villains and the law - both dangerous territory - as a young boy.

'Danger of an alternative nature in that club tonight', he thought, smiling now as the compulsion to begin the next caper in earnest overtook him and the adrenalin flowed through his veins.

Yiddel thought it best for the boys to take a trip out to Heathrow to see for themselves what he had been looking at, checking out the terrain and the layout of the cargo area. He told them they would need to be able to carry this one out swiftly under cover of darkness so "get familiar with the layout and don't hang around in one place

46

too long. Act as though you are looking for one of the businesses around here."

On Sunday afternoon, Yiddel called for a meeting. They all met at Roger's flat and 'dear Roger', as Yiddel light-heartedly called him, had indeed passed over all the information that Yiddel wanted from him. Roger explained that Dick was infatuated with him and thought he was 'the best thing since sliced bread' and wanted to do it again. Yiddel was very impressed, but didn't want to go any further into the 'do it again' bit. Roger said that Dick told him he could not meet him next week because they had a lot of work coming in and he was expected, as he was the night manager, to stay at the shed with one other man and pass the shift over to the airline loaders in the middle of Sunday morning. He told Roger much more - all about the dull work routine he was so bored with, about his life in general and how he wished he could get out of the 'rat race' and have a much better time.

He had asked Roger if he wanted to come for a visit during his shift and explained he would only open the door if Roger rang his office number first when the other man was out taking his hourly break and then they could be together in comfort for a short while in his office. "At least I will see you, Roger!" said Dick, excitedly.

Roger told him he would look forward to a little cuddle on the next Saturday night and left Dick absolutely bubbling over with anticipation at the prospect of having his new lover visit him in the office.

"Roger, you're a diamond, I couldn't have done that better myself! I think you are a real star. I don't think you should make contact again, though. Just make that call to him next Saturday, I'll give you a call immediately before we go in to confirm we are outside." Yiddel had made his mind up on the final plan.

He made it clear to Roger that he could tell no one at all what he had done or where he had been. Roger replied that Dick had asked him where he could contact him, and he'd said that he was in the police force and it could therefore be a bit difficult, but he would see what he could arrange when they met on Saturday night. Dick had appeared to accept his answer on the grounds of security and they had parted company the best of friends, with Dick declaring, "See you next Saturday then, Roger!"

Yiddel sent the boys shopping for the usual overalls and gloves as well as a dark blue uniform with shiny buttons and a cap, 'like a policeman's', he had specified. They were also instructed to acquire a good sturdy truck and another car. "Make sure that the truck is a good 'un," was his instruction.

Late on Saturday evening, the trio left Hackney for Heathrow. Taking the underground from Bethnal Green, they changed onto the Piccadilly line for the airport, each of them travelling in separate compartments all the way, each carrying a large holdall complete with travel labels hanging on the handles, but inside they had all the clothes ready to change into. For now, though, it was a case of all three giving the impression that they were heading for the airport simply to jet away to sunnier climes.

The truck was driven to a car park just outside Heathrow near the tube station at Hatton Cross and the stolen car taken to a pub car park near the truck and left.

At five past ten, Yiddel phoned Roger to make the call. Yiddel watched the other night watchman depart for his break, leaving Dick on his own. Roger made the prearranged number of rings to Dick's office. Simultaneously, Sammy arrived with the truck to a parking bay opposite the shed. Yiddel was now dressed in his bogus police uniform and he knocked gently on the steel personnel door. Dick opened the door with a big smile on his face to look straight at a man dressed in uniform whom he had never seen before.

"It seemed a shame to have to knock him out," said Yiddel later, musing over Dick's naivety and shock.

Once inside the door, Yiddel and Harry checked to see if it was all that Dick had said and that it was just him there. Harry hit the electric button to lift the shutters and Yiddel signalled to Sammy to start reversing the truck up to the shutters as they were opening. Once the truck was inside, they closed the shutters and removed Dick's unconscious body to one side making sure he was safely out of the way of the truck and the doors.

In the middle of the warehouse were the steel pallets loaded with bars of gold. Sammy opened the back doors of the truck and jumped in as the other two began passing the gold in to him. For the first time, all three were experiencing the true weight of one bar of gold. Yiddel and Harry passing them into the truck as fast as they could to Sammy stacking it, hearts thumping with the tension of the moment and the physical exertion of the weight of it all. After a short time, all three were panting like old men instead of the strong and healthy types they actually were. A whole pallet of gold bars was loaded in twenty minutes. Yiddel looked around to see if they had left any behind and he saw another pallet, full of what he thought was silver.

"Quick, grab some of them as well," he ordered. They pulled the pallet nearer to the van using a hoist, throwing the empty one to one side. Harry jumped in this time and Sammy helped Yiddel pass them in. Feverishly, and sweating so much it got in their eyes and stung, they loaded the contents of the whole pallet into the truck.

"Ok, enough is enough." Yiddel knew when to stop and not push lady luck too far. "Let's go!"

Sammy jumped into the driving seat and Harry hit the electric button for the shutters to rise; Sammy edged the truck forward and out of the shed as Harry hit the button again to lower the doors. He took a quick glance at Dick's still motionless body and left, closing the personnel door behind him. Walking into the cool night air, and glad of it, he jumped into the front of the truck and on to where the car was parked.

As they were leaving the cargo area, it became apparent that there was a very real problem. The sturdily built truck was struggling to get along the flat road towards the car park. It was only now they realised how much weight they had in the back, and no way were they going to be able to transfer all this bullion into one car.

"Get the car, H, and follow us as close as you can," said Yiddel.

Never in a million years had he given any thought as to what a large consignment of bullion weighed. What they had in the truck was too much even for this workhorse of a vehicle let alone putting it into a car.

"The truck's got to stay with us, Sam," Yiddel decided, now feeling nervous. He feared the journey that was in front of them - travelling from west to east London at night in a vehicle that was making so much noise - the bodywork was rubbing agonisingly on the wheels – and this could all too easily get some very unwanted attention as it chugged along. He knew that to make the slaughter in Essex was out of the question.

'So, where oh bloody where are we going to go with this lot?' he was anxiously thinking.

"Where are we going, Yiddel?" Sammy wanted to know the same thing – and quick.

"I'm thinking just that, mate. I had thought we could go to the slaughter, but we will never make it there. We're chancing our arm on this bit of road, let alone Essex. Let me think a minute!" he told them.

Harry held his fears back as long as he could, but now felt compelled to break the silence. "By the sounds of it, this truck must be right down on its springs…we can't go too far like this. We've only got to go past the old bill and they're bound to stop us…"

Suddenly, maybe due to the exertion on his brain from the night's fatigue, it came to him. "I've got it," he shouted, above the ear-splitting revs of the protesting engine. "Head for south London – Southwark. I know who will look after us."

Sammy drove the truck more gingerly than he had ever driven before. Around the streets of the capital, he was extra careful turning corners trying hard not to make it squeak too much and trying even harder not to rev the engine too hard to avoid inadvertently making it sound any worse than it already was. 'It could give out any moment,' he thought. He drove on the edge of his seat for what seemed a never-ending nightmare, praying every light would be green, and no cop car waiting, hidden down some side street, ready to pounce on them. How could Yiddel explain this one?

Eventually, Yiddel directed him to a yard under a railway arch. "Stop here. My aunt owns this place and since my uncle died, never uses it. She lives here on her own. There's a great big empty yard at the side of the house." He jumped out of the truck and rang the doorbell, to be greeted by his old aunt.

She was overjoyed to see him: "Yiddel, my baby, how are you?" giving him a kiss and a hug. She was small in stature but her voice instantly commanded respect and attention. "I don't see you so much these days now that you've got a few bob," she added, slightly reproachfully, looking him straight in the eye as if to demand some sort of a reason.

Yiddel was always going to bypass this inevitable point, shrugging his shoulders and gently implying that it was because he "led a very busy life" and so on. He went on to ask if it was all right to put some gear in the yard.

"Of course, Boobolla," and she gave him the key to the gates. They opened into a cavernous yard that could easily take the truck and a few more – incredible, all this space so close to central London. Sammy drove in. Harry parked the car a short distance away and came back to the yard, where they closed and locked the gates from the inside and were in Auntie's front room having tea and toast within ten minutes of arriving.

"She's one of the best!" exclaimed Yiddel to the boys in front of her. He knew that was what the old timer liked to hear, especially from her nephew. "My dad's sister, she is. My dad had to leave her in Germany and she followed on later. My old man helped her get here and she has never forgotten that. She is one of the old-school Jews; she would give you her last piece of bread. Trouble is, I don't see her too often, but she still loves me, don't you, auntie?"

The old girl was grinning from ear to ear hearing her nephew talking about her in this way, her blue eyes sparkling with delight. They stayed with her for an hour; Yiddel knew the truck was safe in the yard and that she of all people would not allow anyone in the yard until he came back.

"See you tomorrow, darling," she said in her Cockney-Ukrainian accent.

Yiddel, under his breath, said loud enough just for the boys to hear, "you can bet on that."

Harry fetched the car up to the house and the trio drove off through the dark streets, wet now from a recent shower, waving goodbye to auntie standing at her door to see them off. They kept to the south side of the Thames, keeping away from the City and driving through Bermondsey, heading north through the Rotherhithe Tunnel, then cutting through Roman Road to Hackney. They dropped Yiddel off first then took the car to Shoreditch, where they left it in a car park in the grounds of a block of apartments they knew of, and 'innocently' caught the bus back to their flat.

The next day Yiddel expected the media to have a field day about the job. He thought the papers and TV would be on overdrive...Not a thing! He made a few phone calls, had a shower, dressed and went out to meet a very old friend whom he had phoned earlier. The man handled diamonds and precious metals - that's all he did - as long as they were stolen. On the way there he expected, by then, to see something on the news stand placards about the caper. But still nothing! This was puzzling, but on the other hand, maybe a good thing, he thought, 'it's giving us breathing room and we are not being pressurised by the exposure of the crime'. Arriving at his friend's business address (a front to the real business, this false concern being a company set up to import carpets from India and Europe), he rang the bell and was met by Sidney Harris, one of his Dad's old friends from their younger days. Harris, older than Yiddel at fifty-two, now suffered with a painful 'condition of the

53

spine', which he would tell no one anything about, but it was plain to see by the lines on his face that 'painful' was something of an understatement. He stooped slightly as he took Yiddel into his office and before Yiddel had sat down he had placed a large scotch in front of him. They then gave a toast to the old man and all the Jews they had ever known.

"What can I do for you? If it's money, forget it," Harris said, laughing.

Yiddel knew that if he was short of money Sidney Harris would be the first to give it to him. "I've got a little bit of business for you, Sid, if you're interested?" he enquired, looking over his shoulder to make sure the door to Sidney's office was closed so that the attractive little girl sitting outside polishing her nails and acting like a secretary could not hear what he was about to ask Sidney. "I've got some gold and silver to sell, Sid. A lot of gold and silver. In fact...so much that we could hardly get it away."

"Has it come on top yet, Yiddel? 'Cos I've heard nothing."

"Not a word, I've had the radio on, the TV, watching the papers and still nothing!"

"Yer know what I think don't you, son? I think that what you have done is so fucking big the old bill has put a blanket on any press knowing, and I'd bet any money that they have now sealed up the place and completely closed shop on the company you've nicked it from. That way they have time to start putting out the feelers and see if they can drag somebody in before the papers get hold of it."

Yiddel agreed. "That must be the reason why there's no word about it."

"How much yer got?" Sid was getting seriously interested.

"A pallet of gold bars and a pallet of silver. Look, I've got to go down the yard where it is - come with me and see for yourself."

Sidney looked a bit worried. "Is it safe?" He needed to know; if he ever got found out for even a fraction of the criminal dealings he had been involved with, they would send him down for the rest of his years, and that he did not want one little bit. Yiddel looked deeply at his friend's expression, knowing that Sid was only acting as carefully as he would do in the same situation.

"Course it is, I've got it in Auntie's yard!"

"Oh, that makes it Ok then…Auntie's yard!" exclaimed Sidney, looking towards the heavens.

So, now things were rolling. They caught a taxi to the nearest pub to Auntie's, had a quick drink to allow the cab driver to drive off and then the pair walked the short distance to the yard. Yiddel rang the bell and the old girl let them in, recognising Sidney immediately.

"Sidney, my boy! How's yer Mum, darling?" she asked.

Uncomfortably, Sidney gave Yiddel a glance before replying: "she's dead…last year, luv!"

Auntie shook her head and went back to her chair muttering, "they are all dying. All my friends…"

Yiddel steered Sidney through the rambling house, cluttered with the stuff of ages past, and out into the yard. There was the truck, still securely locked up. Yiddel opened the back door and Sidney saw what had to be the biggest pile of bullion he had ever seen in his life – and all of it in the back of an old Ford truck in an old yard in Bermondsey.

"Fucking hell!" was the first thing that came out of his mouth as he picked up a bar. "This is not silver, Yiddel, it's platinum, far better than silver." He now had a bar of gold in one hand and a bar of platinum in the other and he knew that just this would last him a long time in cash, but to have a mountain of the stuff was too much to grasp even for this old villain.

Sidney Harris was unable to move from the spot at the back of the truck and just stood there looking at it all, and clearly now lost in his own thoughts. Eventually he came back down to earth, put both bars back on the stack and dusted his hands as though that precious metal was still somehow on them.

"What do you want me to do? And how are we going to work the deal?"

Yiddel said nothing until he had locked up the truck. "Let's go inside, my friend. Now you've seen what is here, you can come on board as an 'adviser for wages', Sid."

They went back into the house and told Auntie they were leaving and would be back later. Yiddel and Harris kissed Auntie goodbye, she in turn waving them off, hoping that she would now see more of her nephew and his friends. In the next passing taxi to the East End, neither said anything, just some small talk for the people-wise taxi driver, until they were back in Sidney Harris' office. Sidney was for the first time in his life dumbstruck. Seeing them arrive, the girl remarked, "you was quick, I thought you'd be out all day."

"No, love, we only popped out for a beer - if you like, you can get away now and go shopping up west."

Her coat was on in seconds and she was on her way. "See you in the morning, bye," was all she said as she hurried out of her office.

Clearing his desk of all the rubbish that had accumulated on it, Sidney made them both a coffee and a glass of Scotch whisky as a chaser.

"How do you want me to do it, Yiddel?" he wanted to know.

"I haven't got a clue; I'm entirely in your hands. I came to you because I know I can trust you, you're like family and I know you won't turn me over."

There was a pause as Sid thought about how this might work. "Right, then," he began, taking a deep breath. "I did a rough tally up, and I reckon there's about eighty million pounds' worth of precious metal that you've nicked."

"How much?" Yiddel almost dropped his coffee cup. "You must be joking, Sid!"

Sidney Harris was not joking; his penetrating stare over the top of his glasses indicated in no small manner that he meant every word. Sitting back in his chair and starting to enjoy Yiddel's astonishment, he added, "In fact, Yiddel, to be really truthful, it may be a great deal more!"

The two men sat in silence as the extraordinary scale of just what this caper had turned into sank in. Eventually, Sidney sat upright, leaned forward and solemnly stated, "I will get the best price I can for it."

With the Ok from Yiddel, Sidney became the middleman for placing the bullion. He knew that this was going to be the biggest job he had ever been asked to look after and he was not going to make a mess of it. He was very uneasy about the stolen truck sitting in the yard and told Yiddel to organise a visit to Auntie's to start unloading the bullion and to get rid of the truck. He was all for keeping the bullion there but definitely not the truck.

Yiddel and the boys headed for Auntie's yard. She was once again pleased to see her nephew and the two boys: "I haven't seen you for years, then I see you every day - but I like it," she told Yiddel.

Once in the yard, Yiddel had a look around to see where they could stack the bullion once it was unloaded. The old uncle had intended to straighten up the yard before he died, and have it cemented over to even up the surface. He had had a large amount of sand delivered in preparation for doing just this. The sand was still in a huge pile where the delivery driver had tipped it, in a corner at the far end of the yard.

"We'll use that as a cover," said Yiddel. "Reverse the truck over to the rear of the yard as near to the sand as you can, Sam."

Sammy opened the back doors and reversed the truck back. Even for just those few yards, it groaned in protest.

"Hold it there!" shouted Harry, as Sammy neared the edge.

They began by putting scaffold boards down on the floor, and stacked the unloaded platinum along the wall on the boards. Putting down the rest of the boards in front of the platinum, they piled up the gold bars, which they then covered with sand until finally all that was visible was just a pile of sand totally covering everything.

"That looks exactly like it should - a pile of sand ready to cement the yard. Well done, boys," Yiddel congratulated them.

Sammy started the truck up, while Yiddel said goodbye to Auntie. Sammy drove the truck out of its temporary two-day place of concealment. Yiddel locked up the gates and the three drove off, Sammy and Harry in the truck with Yiddel following on. After fifteen minutes, they parked the truck on some waste land at the back of an old factory estate.

Once that was done all three drove on to Sidney's yard to see what he had done. Now, as they were heading back to East London, Yiddel saw what he had been waiting for: *Evening Standard* placard splashed in large black letters: 'GOLD BULLION STOLEN FROM HEATHROW'.

"That's it, it's out in the open now," he said. "No going back."

Sammy stopped the car and Harry ran over to the stand and bought a copy of the paper. "It says: 'A heavily armed gang used a policeman to gain access to a bullion shed, injuring the manager by hitting him with a gun'," said Harry.

"What a load of bollocks!" Sammy was indignant.

Harry went on reading: "They are saying it is the biggest haul of bullion ever stolen in the world, and the police are looking for a ruthless and very dangerous gang."

"Would you say that we are ruthless and dangerous, Yiddel?" asked Harry with a cross between a smile and a sneer on his face.

"I don't think I have ever lost my temper," replied Yiddel. "Well…maybe once when two lads that I know didn't listen."

"Well, that makes you the ruthless one then!" reckoned Harry with a laugh, causing Yiddel to stop the car and make out he was going to hit both of them, but then suddenly changing his mind and turning it into a huge hug for both of them.

Yiddel was relieved that at last it was out, at least they could follow the news and see what was being done. The story in the *Standard* got even better as Harry read on. "I won't tell you anymore, wait 'til we get home and you can read what a lot of shit is in this paper. It's a lot of made-up puke. Fuck knows where the reporter got his information, but it certainly wasn't at Heathrow."

Arriving to meet Sidney, who had also seen the news bulletins, Yiddel told him what they had done at the yard - losing the truck and hiding the gold and platinum. That pleased Sidney, he had felt that the truck sitting in the yard was a reason for a nosey copper to

59

check it out and find everything. But now he felt that Auntie's was the safest place in the whole of England. Yiddel was delighted that he had got Sidney on board; he had realised the size of the caper was way above his head and welcomed Sidney alongside them. He knew that he was now well on the case and would soon be in a position to start placing the bullion. He told the boys to leave Sidney to do the selling. They left him to it and went back to Hackney.

Once they were back at the flat, Sammy turned on the TV news – predictably, the news channels were talking about 'What is being done to catch these crooks?' As to what had been seen that night, the amount of gang members grew from four to twelve including a fleet of trucks that were used to haul it all away, guns everywhere. One eye witness said that he had to duck for cover when one of the gang opened fire. Another stood in front of the camera and told how he was threatened by two members of the gang waving guns in his face; he then sobbed, shaking with fear. 'Eyewitnesses' were certainly coming out of the woodwork now.

The next morning, Harry got up early and went for the papers as Yiddel arrived at the flat. He came back with all the morning editions and some fresh beigels. The stories lurched from bad to worse, the dear old 'hacks' from Fleet Street were also contributing to the confusion by writing a load of fiction and nothing at all factual in any of their precious papers. Yiddel hated this press, he wished that he could ring up the news desks and tell them what had really happened on that night.

Back at Heathrow, the heat was being turned up to find the perpetrators of the crime. A huge public and political demand had been generated by the sheer scale of the media splash to find these criminals. They were also throwing in the Oxford Street job as another that the police had not got a clue about. Scotland Yard was in more ways than one being put under serious pressure to find the gangs responsible. The senior officer in charge of the Heathrow robbery had instructed all his officers to 'pull out all the stops' to get some sort of a lead. He believed firmly that it was an inside job because the crime was performed so well. Nothing was left out. He knew now that the night manager only caught a glimpse of the 'copper' and that not one single person on the outside had seen a thing. A few had claimed to see something, but once they were checked out, he deduced they were only after the reward money…and had not actually seen anything. Great!

He said that the people who had done the job were like ghosts: they came, and they went, taking with them eighty million pounds' worth of bullion in the process. He did not even have a vehicle that he could say was used in the robbery; true, there were tons of stolen motor reports, but not one checked out as having been used on this job. One truck discovered in south London was found to be stolen, but had already been set alight by vandals before his men could check it out. He said he believed that it must be a very shrewd, professional gang that had pulled this one off, but who were they?

In desperation, the officer in charge instructed all the officers working on the robbery to put some heavier pressure on all the workers at the airport warehouse and see if any of them buckled under a bit of sustained questioning. So, they had a go at every single employee, from the menial tea boy to the senior management. But they all told the same story - they had seen no one acting suspiciously or hanging around the place in the days leading up to the crime.

Yiddel had played his part so well; he was the ghost they were now looking for. He knew that even the night when Roger met Dick was completely unrelated, according to Dick, to the robbery at Heathrow. He knew that Dick would not put at risk his beautiful liaison with Roger by openly stating that had had anything at all to do with the crime. It was totally removed from work, in Dick's eyes. After all, Dick had enjoyed a 'magical' night with Roger at the club and then at his home - no one knew this so why should he repeat to the police what he did in his own time? Yiddel had dealt that hand so well and he knew it. As far as Yiddel was concerned, that part was as safe as houses. Dick, meanwhile, had assumed that the reason his lover did not turn up that night was because he must have seen somebody there when he arrived and had decided to leave. Dick was now hoping that Roger would contact him again or meet him at the club.

A short while later, Yiddel got a phone call from Sidney to meet him at his office as soon as possible. When he arrived, Sidney was behind his desk with the girl outside still doing her nails. 'She can't have any nails left, she don't stop,' thought Yiddel as she told him he could go in.

"Close the door, Yiddel, and come and sit down," Sidney said, grinning all over his face. His whole manner indicated he was now fully engaged in doing what he did best in life: "I think I have placed about half of the gold and a large piece of the platinum. And I believe, under the circumstances, they will take the rest once we have got the first load safely delivered and they have got it. I have negotiated a very good price for them - under half the face value plus 'expenses' for a safe delivery". Sidney sat back in his chair contentedly and smiled. "We have to get the first load to Holland, and I can see no problem with that at all, Yiddel, me old mate.

62

Why? - because I have a load of carpets that I am redirecting to Amsterdam and our little lot can travel with it. I already have the transport ready to take it away. All going well on the next phone call it'll be off on Monday. Tell your two boys I want to see them later today!"

Yiddel made the phone call immediately and told his two very reliable fellow crooks - after all, they were no longer apprentices - to get ready for work and to report to Sidney by 4pm. Once they arrived, Sidney took them to his transport yard where in one of the sheds was a brand-new, heavy-duty Scania lorry being worked on by Sidney's 'fitters' - busy putting in a false wooden under-floor. Sidney explained what was being done and made it clear that he wanted all the gold and platinum at the yard by the next day ready for loading.

"We will be doing the actual transferring once the fitters have left the yard, so keep it in the truck when you arrive and wait for them to go home," he said.

The two boys made their way over to south London to arrange the pick-up of the valuable cargo and getting it back to Sidney's yard. They decided not to take the risk of stealing a truck for this journey, so they finished up borrowing one from a friend of Harry's for the price of a drink or two.

They arrived at Auntie's to be warmly greeted as usual with tea and cake that she said she had just made. Then came the physical task of loading it all. Once they had loaded up, they bid Auntie farewell and left, locking the remaining bullion in the yard, hidden below the sand.

All the way back to Sidney's yard, the truck – now carrying way above its allowable weight limit – was groaning and rattling on every turn in the road. The engine revs were way above what it could sustain for very long, and for Sammy this was almost as bad as it had been on the night of the bullion raid itself, except that this time he knew in advance what to do. Sidney had detailed exactly how many of each he wanted. Sammy pulled into Sidney's yard and parked close by the Scania, the fitters just washing their hands, almost ready to leave.

"Timed that right, mate!" Harry said to Sammy, a little mockingly.

Sidney came out of the shed, asking how everything was at Auntie's, plus a load of old small talk, waiting until his fitters had all left. Once the last had gone, Sidney closed and bolted the yard doors to prevent any unwelcome visitors from gaining entry.

"Ok, Sam, reverse it into the shed alongside the Scania," he advised. The floorboards of the truck had been peeled back and left on one side. Jumping up on the back of the larger lorry, Sammy and Harry started placing the bullion into the recesses between the joists of the deck. The gold and platinum bars fitted nicely into these recesses, and Sammy for a moment envied the driver of the Scania his much easier driving experience to the port. Sidney, meanwhile, was carefully wrapping every piece in a plastic bag and laid them like floor tiles to stop the bullion from shifting about inside the floor area once the journey began. Once all the bars had been placed tightly together, they brought back the top wooden floor and began nailing it into place, totally covering the bullion, now sealed in between two lots of wooden flooring.

"That's great," said Sidney. "Now, tomorrow morning, the driver has got to take the lorry over to north London and have the carpets loaded ready to go to Amsterdam. Don't worry, I'm going with him."

64

Sidney had told the driver before he left to collect him on the following morning because he wanted to supervise the loading of the carpets, currently stored at the depot in Edmonton. All twenty tons of them were being returned to Holland because the purchaser had found they all had a fault in the pattern and Sidney had the job of returning the consignment to the Dutch manufacturers, who were not very pleased that such a large load was coming back to them, but as Sidney had told them: "Put it right and I will pay you, but not until."

Sidney had told them that he was coming back with the load to show them the problem, so he had a very valid reason to be there – of more concern to him, now, was making sure the first load of bullion also arrived safely. All the documentation had arrived from Holland and the custom papers made out for the return load.

"It's all Kosher and under board," said Sidney to the boys, grinning. His elation had eased his pain, Yiddel noted, and he was glad of this for his old friend.

A day later and Yiddel got a phone call from Sidney in Holland to say that all was well, and that he would be back in a day. That's all the trio wanted to hear, those words: 'All is well'.

Yiddel took a ride down to Auntie's to check that things were still Ok in the yard, and to thank her he took her a bunch of flowers. She was always pleased to see Yiddel, flowers or not, and more pleased these days that she was seeing him so often, though she had no idea of the real motive.

The newspapers were still printing all their ideas about 'Who has it?' and where it was now and so on. Once again, the stories got more glamorous the longer no real facts came out, and *none were coming*, certainly not from the police. They were still chasing cold leads and tips from people who claimed that they were there and had witnessed 'something' - and still hoping to cash in on the reward money. None of the tip offs stood up, of course, but the police were nevertheless duty-bound to investigate every little bit of information, pulling in for questioning any known villain who might or could have been involved in the crime. Dick had now been interviewed several times as he was the prime witness at the scene of the crime. The police had checked him out thoroughly; they knew he was a single gay man who had no money problems and who owned his house. He had no past criminal form and led a quiet life. He told them exactly what had happened on the fateful night, leaving out the bit about the expected, unofficial rendezvous with his new lover, who, as far he was aware, happened to be a police officer. His face was not badly marked from the right hook that Yiddel had delivered. His fellow workers were all feeling so sorry for him that he was beginning to enjoy his 'hero' status.

Truly, the only thing that he was worried about was that Roger had not come back to him so that even now he still couldn't tell his new lover what a terrible thing had happened to him on that night that he did not turn up. As it was, Roger had no intention of ever seeing Dick again or of going to that seedy club in west London.

Sidney got back from Holland and called Yiddel the minute he was in his office.

"How'd it go?" asked Yiddel, excitedly.

"Like fucking clockwork." Sidney sounded pleased with how things really had gone. "We sailed through the customs at Dover. We went through the customs on the Belgian checkpoint and had a fast run right into Amsterdam. The carpet man was not very pleased though, he had the right arsehole over the carpets, trying to say the fault was done here. In the end, after I told him he was just behaving like a fucking prick, he settled down and said he would call me when they were remade, fucking idiot."

He threw Yiddel a pack of two hundred *Rothmans* and a small box of cigars as a present from the trip and poured them both a glass of duty-free Scotch whisky.

"After the carpets were unloaded we drove into town and left the vehicle in a lorry park. I told my man to have the rest of the afternoon off and go down to the red-light area of Amsterdam while I made some calls to see if we could get a return load. Once he was gone, my Dutchman turned up with his little team of men. We drove a little way out of town into his yard. He lifted the boards and unloaded the lot, checked it all out and paid me off, every penny.

"I put all the money back into the hollow floor so that if we were stopped we would seem as clean as a whistle," Sidney continued, stopping for a long swallow of whisky. "Yeh, the money is still in the truck and locked up in the yard, just in case Customs and Excise had any reason to follow us back. I gave 'em no reason to, but it's always best to be safe, don't you think, Yiddel?"

"I think you have done very well, Sid," replied Yiddel, with more than a little honesty and admiration.

He had good reason to. "Yiddel," came Sid's voice down the phone, "we are ten million pounds better off than this time last week!"

Sidney had expected to hear from his man in Holland about the rest of the bullion and when it was to be shipped during the course of the next few days, but having heard nothing at all, he phoned the Dutch dealer, anxious to know if everything was all right. He found out that his client was more than happy about the deal, but they would not be taking the rest due to the large amount they already had in their possession.

"No hard feelings, Sid, but keep in touch," was how the Dutchman ended the conversation.

Slamming the phone down Sidney was livid. "The bastards, they promised me, the Dutch fuckers!"

He ranted and raved for five more minutes and was still going off - by now that everyone in the world was a shit - when the office door opened and Yiddel walked in. Having heard the rage from outside Sidney's office, Yiddel was starting to think about the police having possibly got a lead on them. But, after calming Sidney down enough to get the gist of the real reason for his outburst, Yiddel in his typically laid-back style said, "Sid, me old mate, look at it on the bright side, we have shifted quite a lot of it. We have ten million in cash and we still have a pile to sell. Why have a heart-attack over it? We are doing all right. Surely?"

Sidney dropped his arched shoulders and realised Yiddel was right; 'ease up, the pain is coming back,' he thought to himself. He opened his desk drawer and took a few pills out, gulping them down with yet another whisky. What the pills were, Yiddel could not see. Sidney lurched back into his chair, breathing heavily and for a moment looking drained, his lips turning a slight bluish-purple. He focused on Yiddel. One of the reasons he loved the big Yiddisher boy was that ever since he had known him he had never seen him lose it, he was always cool and calm, and he wished he could be the same. Everyone he knew liked Yiddel. His attitude to life was what pleased all that met him; he had that sort of easy-come-easy-go way about him.

The two boys were of the same opinion - from the first day they had met him, and possibly to the last, whenever that might be.

Surely, nothing bad could ever happen to their Master? He gave off a deceptively carefree attitude, seemingly no real rush to do things but in the end, it always got done – properly - whatever the obstacles in the way.

Sidney trusted Yiddel with his life and vice versa.

"Sidney, don't worry, my boy, one door closes and another one opens," mused Yiddel, raising his shoulders in his interpretation of an old Jew doing a bit of business. They both laughed at his antics and Sidney poured them both some more duty-free scotch.

Later in the afternoon, Yiddel took a ride up to Stamford Hill for his favourite snack, a salt-beef sandwich, and eating it as the tradition has it - standing outside the shop while watching the world of that part of London walk past. He had always done exactly what he was doing, even when he was a young boy. And it *was* a tradition, he would say. Munching away at the huge sandwich and deeply, happily engrossed in its flavour, he suddenly saw a huge figure of a man coming towards him. Swallowing his mouthful sharpish, he bellowed at the top of his voice: "ELVIS!!"

The big man nearly jumped out of his skin at the volume of this voice. Now it was that he recognised his old friend.

"Yiddel, my boy, you frightened the life out of me, shouting like that! I can see already what you're doing on my manor - eating as usual."

Elvis was a rabbi. The pair had grown up together in the same street, they had been close friends from childhood, and the only difference now was that one was a rabbi and the other a thief.

Elvis got his famous title when he and Yiddel were young boys and he used to do a very good impersonation of 'The King'. Elvis was a giant of a man, all dressed in black with his big brimmed hat covered in plastic to protect such an expensive item from the drizzle.

"These hats are not cheap," he would say to Yiddel when remarks were made about it.

"So, what are you up to, Yiddel?" he asked.

"You know me," came the reply, "a little bit of this and little bit of that - ducking and diving as ever."

The Reverend Rabbi Schlomo knew exactly what he meant all right. Rabbi Schlomo, to give him his right title, helped to run a small charity at Stamford Hill supported by those in the local Jewish community who could afford things to help destitute Jewish people in the north London area who had fallen on bad times. He was exactly like Yiddel in temperament. He was of a soft and gentle nature that did not at first glance fit with the size of the man.

"So, how's yer luck?"

Yiddel told the rabbi a little, but not too much; then he told him some more but only enough, just enough to fill him in as to what he was 'ducking and diving' at the moment.

In the past, when he had had a good week, Yiddel would send a couple of hundred pounds up to Elvis at the charity. "Not as a penance," he would always say to Elvis when they met.

"You will never get into heaven," Elvis would always reply.

Yiddel knew that because of where they had both been brought up as kids, Elvis possibly knew even more fiddles than he did. Now, Elvis listened to Yiddel's having been let down by the Dutch and said, "Have you tried the Russians?" assuming that Yiddel had something to sell on the quick.

Yiddel finished his salt-beef sandwich as they were talking, getting all manner of looks and sometimes nods from the frummers walking past. They walked along together for a short while and

Elvis was telling Yiddel that his charity was taking many unfortunate kids to Israel for a week to show them the country, and that he would see him, all going well, when he got back. They shook hands and gave each other a hug and the big man was gone, rushing along Stamford Hill with his long black coat blowing out behind him, hurrying to get back to the charity house.

Thinking about what Elvis had said and about Sidney's failed load to Amsterdam, Yiddel made his way up to Kensington via the underground from Manor House station. He knew where he was going. He knew a man who ran the *Ukraine Club* in Kensington who might have a connection with what Elvis had said. Arriving at the club, he found his man sitting at the bar.

"Hallo, Yiddel, to what do I owe this pleasure?"

The man was portly-figured, in his forties and was the owner of this club for ex-pats from the 'old country', as he put it, but in reality, all this was a cover for a gambling club for all those with a few pounds or more to lose. Yiddel himself had over the years lost and won a lot of money here.

"Igor, you old rogue. I'm looking for one of your rich clients with plenty - and I mean plenty - of cash, who would like to do a deal in gold and platinum. Put me onto someone, my friend, and you are up for a few quid."

Igor poured him a beer, and they talked generally about life.

"Leave it with me, Yiddel, and the minute I hear anything I will phone you," he said in his heavy Ukrainian accent.

Yiddel stayed for a couple of drinks and they talked about former times; then he headed back to Hackney, pleased that he had gone to Igor's and possibly put another iron in the fire. He was hoping that something might come out of the trip to Kensington.

5

Amsterdam and Beyond

Sidney had invited the trio to his office for a conference - a 'team meeting' he called it.

"I just want to have a jaw about what was doing and who are the players at the moment."

Yiddel opened with his piece about the Russians. Sidney followed with news that he had again phoned the Dutchman to see if he was still in the deal, but it did not sound hopeful. The two boys said they had been to Auntie's, as all now affectionately called her, which had also become a code word when they were talking about the rest of the bullion, and all was well there.

"Right then, there's nothing more we can really do for now. As you say, Yiddel, we are in front, so let's take it easy, keep it careful and see what develops."

Yiddel took a long look at his old friend and thought, 'At last, Sidney, you *have* realised what I've been saying'.

"The last thing on our little agenda today, gentlemen, is the money. I suggest we go to your yard, take it all out of the Scania and split it up. We've got to pay out a little, but we can't leave it any longer just in case we get turned over and then we could lose it all. We've also got to settle up with Roger. Is there anything else, Sid?"

"What about Auntie?" was Sid's only question.

"I'll give her something, let me do it my way."

"And Roger?"

"I was thinking about a figure...what do you all say?"

They all looked at each other and Sammy said, "He did it for us, and very well too. He did it with no connection to us at all. I say let us go for five hundred thousand pounds! Or is that not enough?"

They all agreed that was the right figure.

"Ok, let's get the money and then we can start divvying it up," said Yiddel.

Sidney phoned the yard to see who was still there and who was out. Two of the fitters were out on a recovery job and the one who answered the phone said he was just leaving for the dentist and was locking up and not going to be back today.

All four jumped into Yiddel's car and were at the yard in ten minutes. It did not take long for them to lift the floorboards and put the money into bags. The two boys quickly got to work putting the floor back, and the whole job was done in minutes. They then drove over to the more secure flat of the two boys.

Once there, they tipped the bags of money in a heap in the middle of the room.

'This is easier,' thought Sammy, with all the money now on the floor in ten-thousand-pound bundles. Last time they did this had been with the Oxford Street money, and most of that had been loose.

They put Roger's money to one side in a Tesco bag and then split the rest into four equal piles of…a hell of a lot of money.

"Is everyone satisfied with that?" asked Yiddel. All of them gave the thumbs up and picked up their own pile. Rogers's bag was to be delivered by Yiddel. After Sidney had left, Yiddel asked the boys if they wanted to do what they had done with the last lot of money to which both readily agreed. Mark Joseph would be in possession of the money the following day.

The next morning arrived and Yiddel was also paying a visit to Mark's office for the same purpose. Mark noted that the boys had not arrived yet; Yiddel reckoned they would be on their way: "When they can actually get out of bed, that is, Mark!"

Yiddel had phoned Roger the night before to say they should meet. They met in a small park near Roger's house. Roger was expecting to get a couple of thousand pounds for his night's work. As they sat on a park bench, in the middle of an open expanse of grass well away from the path, Yiddel began to tell him how much money had been agreed for his share. Roger nearly fell off the bench. He was understandably taken aback by the vastness of the sum and had a lot of difficulty calming down. When he had finally gathered enough composure to be able to speak, it was just "Oh my God, I can't believe it!" and he sat there shaking with pleasure. Yiddel worried for one awkward moment Roger was going to kiss him 'which just isn't on,' he thought to himself. He pulled back slightly to make sure, and then he laid it on the line to the shocked, overjoyed man.

"You did exactly what I wanted you to do on the night - it was spot-on. You got the man's trust and gave me a way in. That is all I wanted, you know that, Roger. Now, I want you to be very careful; don't be seen splashing money about, specially round here. Take it easy, you are part of my team now, look after the old man and just enjoy the fact that you have not got to go to work for the rest of your entire life."

Yiddel did then allow the man to give him a big hug. Yiddel, the big softie, and in reality, understanding the scale of the news he had just given Roger, returned it likewise.

"Thanks, Rog, remember what I advised, please," was all he said as they left the park.

About a week later, Yiddel got a phone call from Igor, simply saying: "Could you pop over today?"

Yiddel caught the next train from Bethnal Green and arrived at the *Ukraine Club* within the hour.

"Yiddel, I have asked around my clients and one of the men I was telling you about, a big spender in here, said that he would like to meet you this afternoon in a bar in Sloane Street. *The Blue Anchor* at 3pm…is that all right?"

"You're a little diamond, Igor," Yiddel said, pinching his cheek affectionately, and left for the rendezvous.

He got a taxi to the bar and found when he walked in that there were only two men in the bar. One was sitting by the door and the other was at a table in the far corner. This was the man who looked up as Yiddel arrived.

"Are you a friend of Igor?" came the strongly-accented voice.

"I am," Yiddel replied calmly, walking towards the man.

"Come and sit down, my friend, what would you like to drink?"

Yiddel ordered a beer. The Russian looked at the man by the door and lifted his head as much as to say, 'Get it'. The man duly got up and went to the bar, bringing the beer and what looked like a glass of vodka for the Russian and then returned to his position at the door.

'Ah, minder,' thought Yiddel to himself.

"What is it you have got?" the Russian asked.

Yiddel was still weighing up the man on the door and shot a meaningful glance over his shoulder in that direction.

"Oh, he's Ok. He works for me. He is what you Brits call a 'minder', yes?"

"I thought so. How long have you known Igor?" Yiddel was still checking the man.

"I have known Igor for about twenty years. We served together in the Soviet Army. And after the Cold War I came here and we both went into businesses of our own. He came to England first and I followed with his help. I trust him completely. See? Here *we* are, two strangers, talking."

Yiddel by now was fairly satisfied with the story and demeanour of the smartly dressed man in front of him, but needed to know for sure what exactly the man was interested in otherwise this would just be a waste of time.

"I have a large amount of gold and platinum," Yiddel declared, studying the man's expression closely. The Russian's eyebrows immediately raised, and then Yiddel knew he was interested. "In fact…it is a very large amount of bullion, consisting of a ton of gold and about a half ton of platinum. The retail value of the lot is about fifty million pounds. I want twenty million for the lot; you can turn over fifty million overnight."

The Russian sat thoughtfully looking at his glass of vodka, not saying anything for two whole minutes.

"Is your merchandise the same as the Heathrow haul?" he finally asked.

"Yes, it is."

"So, I can be sure it is one hundred percent pure?"

"Yes, one hundred per cent. We have already traded part of the load." It was now Yiddel who was feeling very interested and was sure now that the man was definitely no time-waster.

The Russian got up and went over to the bar to use the phone. He spoke to someone for about a minute and returned to Yiddel at the table. Downing his vodka, he said proudly: "So, we are in business! When can we exchange?"

Yiddel was taken aback by the suddenness of the man's unequivocal agreement to do the transaction. No haggling over the price demanded – that was very unusual. If this encounter hadn't been set up by Igor, Yiddel would have backed off here and now, minder at the door or not. But, now was the moment to clinch it properly.

"As soon as you want, I can have it moved to wherever you want it within a few hours. You do understand we want paying in cash?"

"But, of course, like we want ours in gold and platinum," replied the Russian with a wry smile, as if it was the best joke of the week. "We have to now get your money together, which should take only a day or two, so that will give us time to set up where it is going to. We will exchange at the same time."

He paused and this time Yiddel could feel it was he who was being scrutinised. He said nothing, letting his new business associate continue.

"For safety, we will have our assessor there and you will check the money there also, yes?"

"Sounds fair enough to me," agreed Yiddel. "I will have my men there with me."

"Good, it is done," said the Russian with clear satisfaction. "Igor will call you and tell you where."

Standing up, he shook hands with Yiddel. The minder simultaneously got up and stood by the door as his master swept past him into a waiting car and was gone.

Yiddel felt as though he had been put through a spin dryer, it had all happened at such an alarming speed. He was sure, thinking about it afterwards, that he had held his breath throughout the whole encounter.

Now he really needed a drink. The 'usual' barman had been allowed to return from his temporary dismissal, and Yiddel ordered a large whisky before phoning Sidney to relay the news. With barely concealed excitement, he said, "Sid – Yiddel...Do you want the good news or the bad?"

"Anything, just talk," was the impatient response.

"We have just had a good day, my friend. It's all done and dusted... they want it – and at our price!"

Yiddel could hear Sidney gulp first and then say quietly as though in acute shock, "Fuck me," as he put the phone down.

Not having known Sidney to ever react like this before, Yiddel phoned back with some concern to see if he had heard correctly. Sammy answered the phone: "Yeh, he looks Ok, he's sitting on the floor looking at his hand. What did you say to him? He looks like he's in a trance."

Yiddel repeated the same thing he told Sidney. Sammy turned to Harry and told him, who, becoming so excited, began whooping like a Red Indian on the warpath. Yiddel had to grin and hung up. In a moment, though, he was really starting to feel the immensity of what they were now involved in. After another double scotch and sitting alone in the club for some time, he eventually got up and made his way home in the back of a taxi.

The next morning Igor phoned him to say that the Russians had been in touch and they were all go for the next day and that the delivery place was in Kent. He said they had a house there; he then gave Yiddel the address. The boys were sent to a friend of Sidney's, who had a heavy-duty truck that they could legally use to deliver the bullion to Kent.

As Sidney said, "The last thing we want is to get stopped in a bent motor. It's too long a drive to risk it."

They were told that, once they got the truck, to meet at Auntie's. Yiddel and Sidney headed straight there from Hackney. As soon as the truck arrived it was driven into that old, almost derelict, yard in Bermondsey, and all the sand brushed away from all that precious metal, which was carefully dusted off and loaded into the truck. The boys were told by Yiddel to stay with the truck all night and then first thing in the morning, they would all go to the Russians' place in Kent.

By mid-morning, the whole gang was on the move, driving down the Old Kent Road in the direction of the 'Garden of England'. Sammy was driving under strict instructions from Sidney not to go anywhere near, let alone exceed, the speed limit.

"Take it nice and easy," he had advised with noticeable seriousness. This was the worst part of the plan for him, and Yiddel could see the tension on his friend's lined face. Thinking to lighten the mood, in true Yiddel style and always looking for a laugh, he pointed to a café on the A20 road. "Ok, Sam, let's pull in for tea and toast, I'm a bit peckish."

"No fucking way, not with that lot in the back!" shouted an enraged Sidney.

"I'm only kidding, Sid," Yiddel calmly replied. And then, as an afterthought: "On second thoughts, I'll just have the tea!" He glanced back at Sid, who was now smiling at and cursing him simultaneously.

The main road became a narrower one as they neared the village, and after travelling up a few lanes they eventually found the drive that led up to the manor house.

"It's like fucking Colditz!" was Sidney's immediate verdict.

And in some ways, it was. There were two no-nonsense men on the closed-gated entrance who, once they said they were 'expected', opened the huge iron gates to let them in. Sammy reckoned later he could see shooters from inside their jackets. Now, they were driving slowly up the long, gravelled drive to a substantial Gothic-architecture building, forbidding and imposing, and which had an air of criminality about it that made even Yiddel and Sidney hold their breath. If this was reflective of the reception they were going to get, they would need to be on their guard – and if those inside had shooters? Yiddel tried not to think about that. His only consoling thought was that Igor had set this up, and Igor would not have let him down, not allowed someone to do that to him, surely?

Looking about the place, he could now clearly see that there were a host of attendant outbuildings, built originally to serve the masters of the main house, but now quite possibly utilised in a very different way. Another two men were directing Sammy, pointing to the rear of the house – to an entrance for goods and supplies in former days.

Sammy stopped the truck. The back of the house garden was shrouded with trees, and standing by the back door was the Russian whom Yiddel had met in the bar.

"Reverse the truck to the door, please," instructed the Russian, "and then follow me into the house."

Sammy was a bit reluctant about leaving the truck on its own, so he locked the doors and followed the others inside. As they walked through the storage room and into the main house, they were all astounded at its splendour. Yiddel said later that he thought it might have been a royal retreat at some time - long ago. In a

80

cavernous room with a massively high ceiling and life-scale portraits of gentry or perhaps royalty of past centuries, a long central room table was the sole item of furniture, and on this was the money, all stacked in neat piles. Yiddel sent Sammy back to the truck to fetch a bar of each as a sign that they had honoured what they had agreed. One of the Russian's foot soldiers escorted Sammy, whether he liked it or not. They brought back the bars and gave them to the Russian.

The Russian had his man there, who now scraped a small piece off each bar, and dipped the scrapings into a jar of fluid; then, he announced – with no visible emotion whatsoever - that they were 'as good as gold'.

Which caused the Russian another wry smile. "Ok, gentlemen, please check your money!" he said.

All four counted the piles and after conferring came up with the same total. "All correct," said Yiddel, shaking the Russian's hand.

"Please stay for some lunch before you go," said the Russian.

After they had eaten, all the 'payment' was put into beautiful luggage cases and packed into the truck. Shaking hands with all the Russians the four left, promising them that if anything else came up they would be the first to know. This registered, and as they drove away, Yiddel could see in the wing mirror the Russian watching them very closely.

Out of the country lanes and back on the road to the big city, Sidney started to sing, "Hi Hi Hi Hi Mozzeltoff, Hi Hi Hi Hi Mozzeltoff. Now we can stop for a cuppa. Eh, Yiddel, or have you lost your thirst, my friend?"

"No way," came the response. "No way, that is, to stopping. Do you know how much money we've got in the back? Don't stop,

Sam, until we are back in your flat." But he knew Sidney had simply got his own back.

Arriving at the flat, they took all the bags inside while Sammy ran the truck back to the owner.

"Now we can have a cuppa, Sid," said Yiddel, doing a little arms-raised Yiddisher-style dance around the coffee table.

The mood of the team was sky-high - they had no reason for it to be otherwise. All four were now millionaires and it had taken just a few weeks to do it.

"We have money coming out of our ears," reflected Sidney.

Sammy returned, saying that all went well, and he had told the truck man that Yiddel would see him in the week to settle up for the loan of the truck.

Yiddel nodded in agreement and said, "Ok, Sam, thanks for that. Now, once again, gentlemen, we have to share out and get light of it. Let's get it sorted and split up and then we can relax for a while."

Checking and putting the money into four bundles took a long time. When they had finished, each one had a huge pile of banknotes.

"If Harry goes," suggested Yiddel, "I'll buy us all a ruby murray and a bottle of wine."

All the others instinctively responded with, "Are you sure you can you afford it?" and "Leave it, Yiddel, you're a bit short this week."

Harry duly left to get the order from the Indian restaurant and some red and white wine. By now, all the divided cash was piled into bundles of five million pounds which took up the whole of the lounge floor. They all sat on the floor eating a takeaway curry on the top of the money, using it as a table. They could have passed for four paupers eating as though they hadn't had a meal for days on end – except that all around them were not old belongings of no value, but almost enough money to make moving around impossible.

At the end of the meal, Yiddel declared he would like to say a few words. "The only big expenses we have are for Igor. I think we should give him ten thousand for his efforts, without him we would still have it at Auntie's and it could have become a greater risk to have kept it there for much longer. And even more seriously...I'll pay for the loan of the truck as well as the supper!"

The boys loved his sense of humour. "Do you think you can manage that, Yiddel? Let's have a whip round to help the poor old sod out!"

"And all I can say is, we have enjoyed it, and I hope you two..." pointing at the boys, "have learnt something from this caper?" He still did not mention Oxford Street by name, not even in front of Sidney. "And we have a newcomer to the gang, and with help from Sidney, will make a few more quid in the future. Thank you, Sid, long may you be lucky!"

They all nodded and raised their glasses to each other. 'MOZZELTOFF' was the toast.

The next day Yiddel went again to see Mark Joseph about depositing the money in their foreign accounts. Joseph, an accountant of ill repute but always for the client, was as crooked as the day is long; he had pulled more strokes than the Oxford and Cambridge boat race crews combined, so it was said, regarding 'investments' and taxes and funds.

Yiddel had paid him well for his recent services and he knew he would now be well paid again. Yiddel noticed, as he entered his office, a very impressive, brand-new top of the range BMW in his parking bay, and it was odds on that it was from a satisfied client - as well as his actual 'fee' for doing whatever he was instructed to do.

"Hullo, Mr Joseph, I see you're supporting the German motor trade this week!" said Yiddel with a grin.

"Do you like it, Yiddel? Of course, it was just a little pressy."

Exactly as Yiddel had guessed. "Listen, I've got another job for you, Mark. Something I want placed exactly like the last lot." He told him how much it was and that it was to go into the same three accounts.

Joseph was always agreeable to huge sums of money. "Give me a bell when you want it done." After shaking hands like a good businessman, Yiddel strode off down Ridley Road market. He stopped at Dodger's stall for a chat with the old trader there, and then into the Jamaican café for a coffee and a beigel.

"Hullo, Ansel, how's the business doing?" he asked.

The owner of the café was a big London-born black man. "Wotcha, Yiddel, me old flower!" he replied in his broad cockney accent. "Still ducking and diving…or are you going to go straight and get a job? It's not our lot in de dole queues any more – it's all you Jews and de Pakis."

Yiddel grabbed hold of the big man and pretended to throttle him to the great delight of the nearby stallholders, who had been listening to the banter from the café. One of them shouted out: "Go on, Yiddel, strangle the bastard, that's the only way we'll ever keep him quiet."

Everyone in the market enjoyed Yiddel when he turned up; they knew they were in for a laugh.

84

"You know, Ansel, that's not a bad idea. I think I might get a stall down here to get a bit of beer money. It's been a bit rough lately and I can do with earning a quid or two." Yiddel was thinking on his feet as usual. And the thought was, 'What could be better, to have a little job? Pull a stall out three or four times a week and be seen by all to be working for a living. In addition, use it as a cover for other activities. Perfect!'

"I hope it's not near my cafe, Yiddel. I won't get any customers if you're around," retorted Ansel, with that unforgettably broad Jamaican grin.

Still laughing with them all, Yiddel ambled up the market, seriously wondering about his idea of getting a stall, something particularly good if he could fit the two boys in as well.

Later at the boys' flat that night, Yiddel put it to them. They both readily agreed with Yiddel that now they had so much money put away it would be a good way to look kosher working on a stall. Yiddel knew that the boys got their buzz from doing the jobs; they enjoyed the excitement and the thrill that it gave them.

"You're right, boys, ask any thief why he has to keep going and he will tell you that they get such a kick out of planning and then carrying them out, they can't stop. You two have got that feeling and can't let go, not yet, anyway, but there will come a day when, as you say, you've got money put aside and you will never need to worry about paying the gas bill or the car tax and that for me is a lovely feeling too." He could sense he was becoming a bit too sarcastic at this point. "Ok, what shall we do? Shall we have a look around or shall we open a stall in Ridley?"

"What the fuck are we going to sell in Ridley Road market, Yiddel?" exclaimed Harry. "Gold bars?"

"No, you silly sod, I thought it would give us a chance to slow down, we can have a look at other things and at the same time we are legit... for a while anyway."

Both the boys did not like the sound of the market, it meant getting up early to do a dreary old job that paid nothing - and that to them was a real frightener.

"What would we sell, then?" Sammy wanted to know.

"I thought toys," said Yiddel. "A definite 'no' to fruit and veg. Besides, the stock goes off."

6

The Three Marketeers

Sure enough, a market pitch for one stall was obtained through his market trader friends, and the trio opened a stall selling cuddly toys, bears and dolls. Yiddel had a contact in the wholesale toy trade who would deliver the merchandise to them. They did not really care if they sold any or not; they were going to be seen to be trading and that was the whole point of the exercise... They took it in turns over the four market days in the week to work the stall and it turned into a very nice, lucrative, little business. Yiddel called it 'TOYS AINT US' and it thrived.

Mark Joseph had called: all the money had been shipped down to his office ready for transacting. He phoned later to report that it had passed to the bank in Jersey and the offshore deals were in place.

"So that's taken care of that," said a very happy Yiddel to the boys. "Mark's been paid, too."

Ironically, the three were now enjoying the market life, and indeed the whole razzamatazz of Ridley Road.

Yiddel was always sitting, standing or walking around with one expert ear always trained on the spoken word of others. Even if he was reading a paper, he was listening. And it was on such an occasion when, sitting in a local pub one lunchtime, he overheard two men talking about the house they were working on in Hampstead. They were both electricians and it seemed that they were rewiring an old property. They were saying: "the bloke who owns it must be loaded." Yiddel's ears immediately picked up on the word 'loaded'.

"Did yer know," one was saying, "he is richer than anyone else in the world?"

And the other said, "What, richer than Bill Gates?"

"Richer...he's so rich he's listed as number one in the world."

"Never! What does he do then?"

"I heard from the painter that he is into arms dealing in the Middle East and since the collapse of the old USSR he buys all their guns from them. My mate said he can't sell 'em fast enough. He said all the Arabs and extreme militant countries are crying out for weapons, so this bloke buys 'em and passes 'em on plus his commish."

'Nice work if you can get it,' was the verdict of these two men, completely unaware that their remarks had not only been heard, but would be acted upon in a way they could never have imagined as they went back to looking, so abstractedly, through their newspapers.

Just a few yards away, the ever-imaginative Yiddel was immersed deep in thought. 'An arms dealer...now that's an idea.'

What was in his mind was that as he had just done a very good deal with one of the emerging Russian mafia this same man could be the key to finding the right people to talk to. First, though, he had to do his homework on who had the guns and who wanted guns.

The market stall was working well and between the three of them they were to all intents and purposes 'making a go of it'. Harry would now go to the warehouse to choose a lot of soft toys, and in fact anything he bought would sell. The other two had left it to his choice of what to buy and so far, it had paid off well enough; it was turning out exactly how Yiddel had planned - a very good cover for other things. He reflected the irony of their situation in now being a registered company and all of them paying National Insurance stamps each week.

"We are so kosher," declared Yiddel, "it's frightening."

Early one morning it was Yiddel's turn to be at the stall. He was busy putting all the assortment of toys up on boxes and hanging dolls from strings, when a voice behind him gave him a start.

"Morning, Yiddel."

"Cor, stone the crows, Elvis, what are you doing down here - especially at this time of day?"

"I've come to talk to you about a bit of business," answered the rabbi. "Is it all right to talk here?"

"Yeh, just keep your voice down, my friend, and then all the earholes in Ridley won't be tuned in to us." Yiddel 'casually' glanced around him to see if anyone was near.

Elvis went on. "I have a problem, and I hope you might know someone who can help me or advise me what to do."

He checked around, just like Yiddel, to see if it was Ok to carry on talking. Seeing it was, he said, "Yiddel, I know that I can trust you. I don't think you are aware of this...but I am a member of what some would consider to be an extreme militant group. We're based here in London, but have support for our cause all over the world. You know what I'm going to say...We believe in Israel. We believe that the Arabs should not be in any position to dictate to us the way that they do. My particular organisation takes care of certain people in the party without the Israeli government 'officially' getting involved."

Yiddel was truly taken aback. After a moment to reflect on what his old friend the rabbi had just advised him of, he asked, checking around him "What do you mean 'take care of'?"

"If we find out through our undercover network that we have a particular assassin or bomb maker on the Arab side, we take care of him or her as quietly as possible."

Yiddel had to halt the conversation to serve a customer, but came back to his old friend, eager now to find out what Elvis was after from him.

"Now, we need to find a way to get some new arms and munitions out to Israel from the UK," he said.

"It's funny you should ask me this, Elvis, because I have just heard of a certain man not five miles from here, who by the sounds of things could be very useful – more than useful, in fact. As far as I can make out, he is operating as an international dealer in ex-Cold War army weapons." Yiddel paused, knowing he was getting into very deep water, unsure if he could swim, but also aware that the challenge of it all was too much to resist. He looked hard at Elvis. "My friend, trust me. Leave it with me for now and I will try to find out a bit more."

After Elvis had left, Yiddel felt more than a bit stunned that the man whom he always thought was such a passive, peace-loving sort of a bloke was now running a global militant cell in Stamford Hill. He knew he had been lucky being in the *Ridley Arms* when the two electricians were in there, but where else could he expect to find them again? Hopefully they would be in there next Saturday morning as before. All Yiddel wanted from them was the address at Hampstead where they were working from.

Friday passed, with the stall still doing a fabulous trade. On Saturday morning, Yiddel left Sammy in charge of the stall and walked up the market road to the *Ridley Arms* arriving at about the same time as last week, newspaper tucked under his arm, and casually strolled in as if just for a pint. And there, sure enough, sitting in the saloon bar reading his paper was one of the electricians, a slight man of about forty years, clearly at home in his local, enjoying a bit of downtime away from work and those indoors.

Getting himself a beer, Yiddel went over to the man's table. "Hullo, mate, is this your local?" he asked.

"Yeh...I live just over the road. Usually meet me mate in here," replied the man, barely looking up.

"I hope you don't mind me joining you, but I would like to ask you a question. I was sitting at the next table to you and your friend last week, and I hope you don't mind, but I heard you say the bloke you were working for is in the arms dealing trade and, well, I have a mate who I know would be interested in speaking with him. Y'know, maybe put a bit of business his way for a few quid, that sort of thing."

The electrician, suddenly looking worried, said, defensively, "Now, look, the only thing I can say about what you heard us saying is...see, we hear a lot of things while we're out and about working, mate - I can't know for sure if there's any truth in it. I was just going about my business, quite legit, y'know?" He was now looking at Yiddel suspiciously, and clearly thinking of making a hasty departure.

Yiddel realised what the man naturally thought and was prepared. "Look, I'm not the old bill or MI5, mate. It's Ok, I work in the market, that's all, but I get to know a lot of people – all sorts of trades - and I only need the number of the house and the street to do my mate a favour." And then, reassuringly, to lighten the tension, and with that Yiddel air of congenial openness, added: "Gotta be worth a pint, surely!"

That helped. The electrician looked relieved and Yiddel went on: "Really…all I need is the address, and then my mate can just go round and see him, check if he can do any business; if not, no problem. Nothing ventured, nothing gained. There's no harm in that, is there? And I promise - you won't even get mentioned".

"Well, I s'pose not," conceded the sparks. "Ok. It's in Bishop's Avenue, Hampstead. Do you know it?"

"Yeh, he'll find it," answered Yiddel, quietly breathing a sigh of relief.

The electrician put the name of the house on a piece of his newspaper and passed it to Yiddel. "By the way, there ain't no houses over there – only mansions and bloody castles."

"Much obliged. It all helps the world go 'round, I always say. So, what yer drinking, mate?" Yiddel asked him, and then, fetching the man a pint of his favourite tipple, he thanked him again for his help, just in time as his friend was now arriving.

Yiddel phoned Elvis on Saturday and gave him the details of the house in Hampstead. "What are you going to do to make contact, Elvis, go 'round there?"

"I don't think I can go round there dressed as I dress, just in case he's anti," said the rabbi. "Maybe we could go together or perhaps you can test the water first."

"Somehow I knew you were going to say that! When will you be clear to go then?" Yiddel mocked his old friend slightly.

"What about in the morning? It being a Sunday, he'll probably be in. I can't do anything today, it's the Sabbath for me."

"So, what are you doing answering the phone?"

"Well...I guessed it would be you ringing! For some things, I make an exception."

The next morning Yiddel picked Elvis up and they drove over to Hampstead to Bishop's Avenue.

"Oy!" the rabbi was exclaiming. "There's a few bob over this side of London, and that's for sure."

Yiddel pulled up outside the name the electrician had given him. It was indeed a residence of an altogether different dimension – the size, almost of the manor house in Kent, but of a much more modern vintage. He left Elvis sitting in the car and knocked on the door. A well-dressed, middle-aged man answered it. To Elvis sitting in the car looking on, intently watching them, they seemed to be speaking for ages. Then Yiddel came back to the car and said, "He's invited us in!"

The man was not an Arab, that much was certain; he apparently was a third-generation London Jew. The family was from Poland originally and he was quite at home talking to them both. Whatever Yiddel had said to him had evidently smoothed the way for doing a deal – the man confidently took them through to an expensively furnished living room overlooking extensive, well-manicured gardens at the back of the property. Indicating leather armchairs for their discussion, he asked some questions about Yiddel and, in particular, Elvis. 'Good questions,' Yiddel thought, as he helped the business talk to flow forward in style, giving the man the necessary reassurance he knew he, Yiddel, would want under the same circumstances. The man's name, apparently, was Jeremy Store - a very English name, thought Yiddel, scrutinising him carefully through the cloak of his outwardly relaxed demeanour. Mr Store's complexion betrayed something of a Middle Eastern ancestry, but he was otherwise a very affluent Englishman living a very comfortable 'early retirement' earnt through hard work and, as was becoming clear, a very astute business mind that could size people and situations up with great intelligence.

Yiddel's mind was turning this over when Mr Store asked them whom they had spoken to about him. Yiddel quickly said it was a contact he had made a long time ago and of which he could not remember the name, but he had kept the address, lying through his teeth in his well-practised manner; out of the corner of his eye, he could see a big smile from the rabbi for doing it so well.

"So...what can I do for you, then?" Store asked them eventually, the poker game entering a new stage.

Elvis took over at this point and explained what he was after and whom he represented, telling Store that the money was available in cash and they had means of shipping it.

"It is very obvious, Mr Schlomo, whom you represent, but I cannot believe your organisation would have any trouble at all in the Middle East getting guns," said Store.

"It's not guns we are after, Mr Store. It's the more *technical* equipment now." The rabbi was speaking slowly and deliberately, in almost hushed tones despite the privacy that the house afforded. "We are after the latest laser-guided missiles. Same as the ones used in the Gulf War. We have special targets that we need to destroy and the only way we can get at them is by using this type of equipment."

Yiddel sat back in his chair and thought 'Fucking Hell! The rabbi wants nukes!' Jeremy Store, on the other hand, had not batted an eyelid to the request that was being put to him. He had also guessed Elvis' vocation, or cover, in life. "I see no problem with your order, rabbi. You say that the money is available?"

94

"Yes, Mr Store, the money, whatever your price, is available."

"Do you know from your colleagues how many are required?"

"No. Now that I have made contact with you, and am understanding that you can help me, I will make contact with them again and find out."

The men exchanged phone numbers. Their host saw them to the door telling the rabbi he would wait for a call from him 'clarifying' what the demand was. Shaking hands, they left. Back in the car, Elvis - according to Yiddel - was "like a dog with two dicks." He was so pleased that his old friend had so easily found someone who could look after the 'supplies'. Yiddel was still reeling from the fact that his mate Elvis from Stamford Hill, a frummer, had just put an order in for nuclear weapons from a total stranger living in Hampstead, who, despite appearances to the contrary, was highly delighted about it. Yiddel had to marvel at Store's ability to conceal it so well. And, amazingly, all this had arisen from a chance eavesdrop in a pub in Hackney - two average sparks talking carelessly to each other – was all that was needed to get them an introduction to an international arms dealer.

In the meantime, the two boys were doing so well with the stall that both had now fitted into the street market in its running, getting on famously with all the other traders. The stall was making money; in fact, it had not failed since the day it was opened... Yiddel's comment on this was: "It just goes to show, if some poor bastard opened a stall like us to earn himself a living, put bread on the table, you can bet on it that it would fail. Us lot, just because we needed a cover, have got a thriving stall business selling bloody stuffed toys of all things."

The morning ritual at the stall was always the same: get the stall set up with all the stock displayed, order two or three cups of tea and a cream cheese beigel each. Then the day can commence. Fridays and Saturdays were their best-selling days, and were also the best chat-up days for the women. Every unescorted attractive female never failed to have a remark aimed at her, like, "Blimey, I thought Marilyn Monroe had come down Ridley to do her shopping," which always got them a grin in return. Yiddel had a thing to say to every pretty girl. From the little blonde girls to the larger black girls he made each feel that she was the only woman in the street and, of course, they all loved it. They in turn would respond, telling him what they thought of him too! His charm was well known in the street market and everybody liked him. He was called a rascal by many, a scoundrel by some and a 'saucy bastard' by most, but he loved it, and so did they. The two boys had even finally got around to telling their parents that they were now living in Hackney and no longer in Birmingham. The two mums were glad that they had their boys now not too far away from them. The boys, however, kept up in every way the pretence of their colourful, criminal lives with the one and only Yiddel, the sole exception being that they shared a flat together now that they had decided not to be 'technicians' anymore; the flat, they said to their mums, was handy as a base now that they ran the very successful toy stall in Ridley Road market.

The British press finally went quiet on the Oxford Street caper. Occasionally a police spokesperson would have to stand up to declare, if a question was raised, that enquiries were 'still ongoing' but that was about all.

The Heathrow caper was a different matter. That was still making significant splashes on front pages. Maybe only in small column inches, but still there. Questions were asked in Parliament regarding the robbery and what was being done about it. At police conferences, the moment the press sensed they had a chance they made the senior officer squirm by not asking about the relevant issue, but about the outstanding one and "What are you doing about it?" To which they always got the same answer: "We are making new enquiries." But they did not have a clue.

7

The Southampton Caper

A few months had now passed and Yiddel was getting itchy feet, as he said, to get on to another caper. The deposited money, for all three, was making more money, which Yiddel checked with Mark Joseph every week. To his exact reckoning, they had acquired some thirty million pounds, which of course was growing with investments at a good rate of return thanks to the ruthless, well-honed financial instincts of Mark Joseph.

While sitting on the edge of the stall one morning, reading his favourite paper, *The Sun*, Yiddel's attention was suddenly drawn to page two where he read that an American company was putting on an exhibition of priceless antiques due to arrive in the UK soon after a global tour before going back to the USA. The exhibition consisted of precious gems found at tribal archaeological sites in America. The piece went on to say that the exhibition's worth was in excess of one hundred million US dollars and it would be on show for four weeks at various venues around the UK.

"This is tempting," he said under his breath.

Later that morning he phoned *The Sun* news desk to enquire if they had any more information about where the exhibition would initially be. They said that a full-page advertisement was being put in all papers by the American promotion department the next day and he would be able to see where it was planned to be at. Gathering the boys together at the stall, Yiddel showed them the article in the paper and sat back to see what reaction it got from them. Both of them read it at the same time.

"What do you think, lads?" asked Yiddel after giving them both a moment to reflect.

"Are we up to this?" was Sammy's cautious response.

"I don't know yet… once we see the paper and find out where it will be held, and if it's not too difficult. We will see, boys! If it's within a game plan, let's a have a look at it first - agreed?"

Both boys nodded and left it at that.

The next morning Yiddel was up early and rushed out to get the morning paper. Sure enough, there was a full-page advert detailing all the locations during the four weeks that it would be on before going back to America. The exhibition was to be held at four major venues. The first was in the city centre in Manchester, the second at City Hall, Birmingham, the third in *The Ballroom* at Grosvenor House and the final one at the *Grand Hotel* in Southampton. Lots of information was added to the advert plus a detailed itinerary of the content of the show, which would have on display one of the biggest diamonds ever found in America. At each venue, the article said, it would be there for four days only, giving the dates and times and where to send for tickets to avoid buying at the door. The whole show was due to start in two weeks. Yiddel's appetite was whetted in no small measure at the 'one of the biggest diamonds' description, and he came to the decision that it would be worth looking into. Asking the boys to join him at his place later that night, they sat down to a fish and chip supper. "So," said Yiddel as they sat down to eat, "How do you feel about it, you have both read the score?"

The boys felt that old 'buzz' starting within their bodies and the words of Yiddel were ringing in their brains. They were already hooked and raring to go for the next 'Big One'. No mistake.

"I'm ready," said Harry.

"So am I," echoed Sammy.

"That's what I thought you would say. Right, let me get all the information about it, if it stands up, we'll do it, right?" Yiddel was also getting the adrenalin buzz.

"Right!" both boys said together. The decision was made.

But the next thing that happened was a phone call from Rabbi Schlomo asking for Yiddel to come up to the charity house at Stamford Hill for a meeting at 2pm the next day. Yiddel arrived and was greeted by one of the elders of the charity, a man he remembered well from his days as a young boy when this same man had given him Hebrew lessons at his school. Shaking his hand warmly, the old man was truly pleased to see one of his old pupils again and then showed Yiddel into Schlomo's office. A dreary, drab, old-fashioned room, its style in keeping with the 1940s rather than the present day, Yiddel also recognised that distinct smell that always was present in these old premises. It certainly was a good cover for international arms dealing.

"Hullo, Yiddel, thanks for coming up," said Elvis, greeting his friend as warmly as ever. "I have had a chat with Mr Store and he said that what I ordered was no problem, and where it will be coming from, it would be no trouble in delivering it - with a little help from my colleagues in Israel. I asked him why he had not run a security check on us to see if we were kosher. He said he had, but it was the first time he had ever had a rabbi come to him and place an order, and that was enough for him, he knew we were Ok."

"I suppose he's right," said Yiddel. "Who else would dress up as a rabbi and go and order nukes?"

"Yiddel, they are not nukes, they are missiles," Elvis reproached him, looking very cross; he felt that he should correct

100

him once and for all. "They are purely…missiles!" he underlined his last word very strongly.

"Ok, I stand corrected, Elv. So, is the order going through or not?"

"Yeh, all's well, it's being taken care of as we speak. Oh, here's a little something from my associates for you."

"What's that for?" asked Yiddel, genuinely taken aback. He opened the box and found himself looking at a brand- new Rolex Oyster watch. "I only introduced you to the man!"

"They said it's for you and to you it's been given, so shut up and be lucky, Mozzeltoff," said the rabbi, beaming all over his face at seeing his old friend actually blush.

Thanking his friend, and the elder, who was hovering outside the door also smiling broadly, Yiddel headed back down the 'Hill' to Hackney, muttering contentedly, "Another satisfied customer."

On the bus, he happened to glance over the shoulder of a man who was reading that day's *Daily Telegraph* and saw that all the information of the American exhibition was printed in much more detail than in *The Sun*. As he got off the bus, he went into the nearest newsagent and bought a copy of the paper. The first venue was confirmed as being in Manchester, City Hall, starting at 10am in two weeks' time. Yiddel told the boys about the date and said they would be going to Manchester on that day to have a look at it and see how it shaped up. He told them not to book anything on that day. It was also to be a trip of secrecy, so "tell no one where you are going," he said.

"It's a good day," announced Sammy, checking his diary. "It's a non-market day!"

"Yeh," said Yiddel. "I already checked that."

Both the boys looked at each other and Harry said, "What did you expect for him, old clever clogs, not to have checked already?"

Two uneventful weeks went past and now it was the morning to go to Manchester. Yiddel held a full briefing before they left London.

"Travel separately on the train. When we arrive at City Hall, just do your own thing and have a good look at the exhibits. Get as much literature about it as possible. Do not draw attention to yourselves and do not hang around too long at any one showcase. Watch for cameras."

All three browsed around the exhibition for an hour, taking in as much detail about it as they could. The two boys saw Yiddel start to head for the door and that was the signal for them too to leave. They followed Yiddel for about two hundred yards whereupon he went into a pub.

Discreetly, he asked their opinion. "Well, lads, what d'yer reckon?"

"The security looks good," said Harry. "The protection around the gem cabinets looks very flimsy, but the actual gems look fabulous."

Yeh, exactly what I thought as well," said Sammy.

Yiddel listened to their comments, then threw in a couple of his own observations.

"First one, did you notice the big guy standing by the door? He was rigged with walkie-talkie, the other smaller guy by the window was looking at everyone who passed him. He took a double look at you two, but that was all."

As Yiddel was going in to the exhibition, he had helped a young mother open up her pram as she put the baby inside. Yiddel decided to stay close to her as she walked around the room with himself nearby looking like he could be the father. He spoke to her as they passed the security guard and the man did not even glance at him.

"I should think that the cabinets the stuff is in will travel all around the venues, that is why they look so flimsy, so that they travel well and are easy assembled at each show. Did you notice any cameras inside the hall?" he asked.

"No, not one," said Sammy.

"That's right, nor did I. That means that we have not been filmed looking at the stuff. Ok, let's get out of Manchester and get back home."

While they were travelling back to Euston, Yiddel was putting a plan together. He would pay another visit to the exhibition when it was in Birmingham, on his own. Leave the London venue alone and make the hit in Southampton. Later that day he phoned Roger and asked him if he would like to work for him on a job again. He also phoned Sheila, apologising that he had not been in contact, but would she like to do some work for him? They both said 'Yes', providing they were both clear. Yiddel agreed to phone and make a meet for as soon as possible for both of them. He had been thinking for a while about bringing new members into the team. He knew that with these two he had trusted people who would fit into his 'Game Plan' - to carry out the job successfully.

He met Roger, who now was leading a very stylish, pleasant life of man-about-town, doing all the shows and films, shopping and having a carefree life, but he was more than pleased to hear that Yiddel wanted him for the next job, which would top up his bank balance and investments nicely. Yiddel instructed Roger to go to Birmingham with him, have a look at the exhibition, doing the same as Yiddel and the boys had done in Manchester.

103

Sheila met Yiddel in the usual little park and the pair discussed the part Yiddel wanted her to play in the next caper. She said she was still working at Oxford Street because she felt to leave too soon might make the police take a closer look at her and she did not need that. She said she had two weeks' holiday due and that she could take it when she liked and when Yiddel wanted her. Yiddel gave her the date for Southampton. He wanted her to get herself down to the south coast a week before the date and to get a job at the *Grand Hotel* as a maid or cleaner.

"I know it might be difficult, but see if you can change your appearance somehow. Change the colour of your hair and anything else so that you cannot be identified afterwards. Tell the hirer at the hotel that you are a student from Ireland or somewhere and that you are on summer leave from the university. That way they don't expect any National Insurance cards - they just take you in for a short term, pay you bad wages and you leave at the end of the term."

Sheila was quite happy to be involved with Yiddel; she was getting to like the man more than a little.

'That's that,' thought Yiddel. He now left it to Roger alone to get as much data at the Birmingham venue; he was sure Roger would be more than able to see as much as he would if he was there. Sheila, he knew, would do what he had asked her to do and both of them could be left alone until he gave them both their final briefs for the day of the caper.

At last, the exhibition started in Birmingham; it got as much press as the Manchester venue. All the papers and TV channels were saying what a magnificent exhibition it was and 'well worth seeing'. At Birmingham, Roger had a good, careful look at it and reported to Yiddel that it was exactly as he had detailed it: same guards, same cabinets and still no inner hall security cameras. Yiddel then sent Roger for a trip to Southampton well ahead of the exhibition.

"Have a look at the hotel, have a look at the ballroom and just get me the layout of the place."

The two boys had also been sent to Southampton to set up an escape route out of town by the most indirect way. Yiddel knew that once the shit hit the fan, the police would go into hyper drive and cover all the roads out of town to London and anywhere else. Yiddel had been looking at maps of the south coast and he had seen another way. He now wanted the boys to test it to see if it would work. While the show was going on in Birmingham, there was plenty of time to check out where he could place the stolen jewellery. He knew from the catalogue exactly what was there and what were the best pieces to go for once they were in the hall.

'There was three important cabinets to go for…the rest was only a lot of antique rubbish', he thought. Once he had drawn up his attack plan, everyone who was taking part would know exactly what to grab. Yiddel started to sketch out the approach on a large piece of white board. He had done this before but not in such detail. He was pleased with the layout, adding sections as they came about.

He phoned Jeremy Store, who had now also become a member of his elite band. He wanted a couple of items for the attack. Store said they would be delivered anywhere he wanted.

The two boys, now back from the coast, were given a shopping list. Yiddel expressed that the usual care must be ensured when buying any of the items; he knew he did not have to say it but always felt better when he did. He had seen the power of nail guns, delivered one day when he stopped to watch a builder putting a timbered roof on a house, and he made sure he included one of these

105

on the boys' 'to get' items. 'One of those will get into the glass cabinets without wasting any time at all,' he thought.

The show had now left Birmingham and was in London, but Yiddel by now had the whole plan in place. Roger had given him all the details about *The Grand*. The boys had also passed over the town layout, roads and car parks. Sheila had phoned to confirm she had managed to be taken on working at the *Grand,* and passed over some more useful information - all added to the 'Game Board'.

'Roll on Southampton,' thought Yiddel, 'let's get this one on the road.'

The London show was left entirely alone; Yiddel felt that he had everything he needed. The show repeated itself in every town now and there was no reason for it to change by the time it got to Southampton. The boys sat down with Yiddel to go over the plan together. All the equipment was ready including the lot from Mr Store. Several stolen cars had been secreted away near *The Grand*. Yiddel now called together the whole team, except Sheila, for a final brief as to what they had to do on the day. Sheila had sent up a hand-drawn map showing the layout of the ballroom and the entrances and exits to the service area at the rear of the hotel. She said she would jam the door from the yard into the ballroom to keep it from closing and there were empty beer kegs outside the doors. All this was added to the board.

With this final piece of information, Yiddel could now complete the Game Board and now finally see where everybody should be at 'Show Time' as he proudly called it.

"Sam, I want you close to me as we go in through the back door. As we go in throw the tear gas in four different directions so that we get maximum cover of the room. Anybody, and I mean anybody, who comes near me, you take 'em out, Sam. Harry, you

106

head straight for the main cabinet," pointing to the cabinet on the board. "You can't miss it, it's the biggest one in the room and it is always in the same place, position wise. They haven't changed it yet. After you hit it with the nail gun move away fast to this one here," again pointing it out, "you can't miss it, it's got a huge gem sitting on a stand...you remember it from Manchester?"

Harry nodded.

"If you feel that the gun has not blown a big enough hole, hit the fucker again and again if you have to. I don't want to get to the cabinet and find I can't get in. Then go for the smaller flat cabinet set off to the other side, here," pointing it out on the board. "We will follow you as you go from cabinet to cabinet clearing each one of what we want. Just three cabinets, that is all. It should take under a minute. As soon as we have what we want, we leave. Sheila should already have left before we arrive, so do not look for her. Roger by now should have set off all the devices, so there should be absolute pandemonium in the street. Once I have all the gems, watch my back and head for this door, here. Once we are through them, close them and quickly pull some beer kegs and block them...the kegs are stacked up outside by the doors. Start to remove your overalls and gas masks, put them into the spare bag which Harry will be carrying and slowly walk out of the yard towards the seafront."

Although not in the actual hotel, Roger was given the task of setting up two diversionary explosions at two different places on the roads leading out of town but near the city centre. The explosions would be in two of the stolen cars and placed at locations near to a bank or a building society, giving the impression that a bank gang was attacking them. Yiddel guessed that this would take care of a lot of the local police force. Roger would

107

trigger the devices at the same time as the main force was attacking the cabinets in the hotel.

Stopping for a drink and to gather his thoughts, Yiddel went on, "Is that all Ok to where I've got to?"

The two nodded, and now he resumed. "I need to underline the point that you must, after you have done your own job, Harry, protect us from anyone trying to stop us. I will keep moving from cabinet to cabinet collecting the gems so I will be very occupied, so watch my back. I can't believe anyone will be able to see properly, not even that big bastard, but just in case, keep 'em peeled. Right, once we are out in the yard, Sheila will have got the van and be just outside the gates by the main road. The back will be open - throw the bags in and jump in fast - she will then drive off two hundred yards towards the shops." Again, Yiddel was pointing out the features in question on the board. "When Sheila stops the van, get out and walk to the shopping area. Sammy: you are now the driver, so drive the van to the bus terminal, letting Harry and me out. Park the van and leave it, get the other car and drive back to us at the terminal…we will meet you there. We then head for Fareham. When you park the van, keep your head down until you get into the car."

Yiddel stopped for another drink and then continued still studying the board. The sweat was visible on his forehead, but this was what is was all about at this stage – handling all the things that had to be thought of and controlled; making it clear to all what their precise roles were, and that there was absolutely no margin for error on this job. "I don't want any street cameras getting a good look at you. Sheila by now should be at the station with Roger waiting or getting on a train bound for London. We are going to take a nice ride along the south coast as far as Fareham, then we head for

London, getting well clear of Southampton." Yiddel took a deep breath. "How's that, have I left anything out?"

Nobody spoke. They all knew this was the crucial moment in getting the preparation right. Get it wrong and it will be 'game over' for the rest of their lives. They sat and studied the Game Board for a few minutes, then Sammy said, "Roger is Ok with the radio controls. I went over it with him and he knows exactly what he has to do. As soon as they explode, he is to walk away or run with the crowd, whichever. I think all the bases are covered, Yiddel."

"Good, I want to leave for Southampton as early as we can, so I will be up very early tomorrow, and I expect you two villains to be up and washed and ready to go!"

The next morning, much earlier than the hour he usually got up at, Yiddel was showered and dressed before making a phone call to the boys to ensure they had not lain in. Harry answered it, sounding all pumped up and ready for what might come. He told Yiddel they would be outside their flat at 7am as promised.

As soon as Yiddel arrived, they loaded the gear and were on the road heading west to pick up the M3 motorway. The plan was to leave the first car at the halfway stage, change into the stolen car and then on to Southampton. The changeover went well, there was no one about, and soon they were on their way in the stolen *Vauxhall Vectra* towards the city centre. Sammy dropped the two off and then drove to the car park from where he picked up the stolen van and picked up the other two who were waiting at a bus stop in the dock road.

The exhibition would start at 10am. Just ten minutes to go now. While they were on their way back to the hotel, Yiddel and Harry changed in the back of the van. Sammy slowed down when he heard Harry say that he was ready; Harry slid into the driving seat behind him and took over the van. Sammy quickly changed into his overalls. Harry stopped the van at the rear of the hotel, at the spot Sheila had been told it would be parked. They took the bags with all the final gear that was needed. Harry had the nail gun, and Sammy and Yiddel two tear gas grenades each. They were now approaching the back door and at this point all three put on their gas masks, baseball caps and gloves. Now fully rigged, there was no going back. Yiddel gave the two boys a quick visual check-over, indicating 'Good'. Harry had the handles of one of the bags over his shoulder and Yiddel the other.

Opening the door that Sheila had cleverly wedged with a piece of card earlier that morning, it was now bang on 10am, and the trio, headed by Yiddel, swiftly made their way into the huge ballroom. They threw the tear gas grenades in four directions. Harry closed the door to keep the gas in the room. The heftily-built security guard lurched towards Yiddel, who thumped him with a smashing blow to his jaw; he went down and was out for the count. In just a couple of seconds, everyone else was rubbing their eyes, the air filled with screams of pain and terror, including the second security guard.

Harry, followed closely by the other two, was at the first cabinet. Another guard, unknown to them in all their planning, appeared from nowhere and tried to grab Yiddel, but Sammy expertly knocked him down and then trod on his chest like a man who had just shot a wild beast. Harry's first shot into the glass and the power of the nail gun surprised him - the cabinet glass exploded leaving the gems within completely exposed. He felt Yiddel close by and moved off as instructed beforehand to the second display cabinet. Exactly the same sound as the glass smashed into a thousand pieces. Amidst all the chaos caused by the tear gas, the sound of the gun somehow seemed deafening. Again, he felt Yiddel give him a nudge to move on and he was over at cabinet three... No looking back; he knew that Yiddel in turn was being shadowed by Sammy, both carrying out their respective parts of this audacious operation, and he knew that Sammy was guarding any brave or foolhardy attack that might come from security or the public.

As Yiddel had predicted it was all over in literally one minute. Yiddel was shouting commands that all was clear and to move out; the only obstacle, it seemed, was the sheer amount of people who were staggering wildly in all directions, in abject fear of what was suddenly and violently now happening in this magnificent ballroom. The whole place was a seething mass of people who were blinded and falling about. The trio skilfully negotiated around them and left by the same door. Yiddel noticed that the first guard was still out cold on the floor by the exit; Sammy pulled the door closed as Harry, with the help of Yiddel, pulled the beer kegs over to block the exit. They then headed for the van, taking their gas masks off as they went, but keeping everything with them. No evidence would be left for the police. The back doors were already open and they threw all the gear into the back and jumped in with it.

A woman was in the driving seat; the engine was running and she drove off sharply as soon as they were in. Yiddel looked twice at this woman - whom he did not recognise. Sheila's disguise was convincing to say the least. The gorgeous blonde-haired woman he knew was now jet-black in hair colour; she had buckteeth and glasses. For one horrible, disconcerting moment, he thought they had got into the wrong van - her appearance had changed that much. 'Well done,' he thought.

Sheila stopped the van up the road about two hundred yards away where she got out and as instructed walked away, not even a glance back to the centre of town to her current lodgings. Sammy dropped into the driving seat and drove off towards the car park. The trio were now out of their overalls and caps. They stowed the whole lot including the gas masks into one of the empty bags. Yiddel and Harry got out after a few hundred yards and left Sammy to head for the car park to leave the van and pick up the car. Sammy parked the van away from all the others against a far wall. As he got out, he primed the incendiary device with a one-minute delay. He got out and walked casually towards the car, keeping his head down – not just to avoid eye contact with anyone but because of what was about to happen. As he got into the car and drove out of the car park, the improvised device went off and the van exploded with a deafening crash behind him.

He left the scene with people who had been unfortunate enough to be nearby at the time of the detonation now screaming and running in blind panic away from the car park. He drove to the prearranged pick up point for the other two. As he arrived there, he could hear the sound of alarms going off; it seemed to be all around them as they left this area of dual terror.

Yiddel jumped in the front and Harry in the back. "All right, mate?" asked Yiddel, already smiling and seemingly relaxed.

"Yeh, fine. Did you hear the van go up from here?"

"Not much, it was that fucking loud! But have you heard the other stuff? Sounds like Southampton itself is under attack - all yer can hear is fire engines and police cars. While we was waiting for you, about four police cars rushed past in the opposite direction to the hotel, so I don't think they've got the call for that one, yet. Ok, Sam, you know where we're going so let's get on and get out!"

112

They drove along the coast road for a few miles before turning north and heading for Fareham. As they approached the town centre, Yiddel stopped the van and dropped all the clothes and equipment, except their gloves which they kept on, into a business' rubbish container which was about to be loaded onto an approaching council waste collector lorry. They parked nearby and watched the bin men pick it up using the grab on the back of the truck and tip all the contents inside the vehicle which, Yiddel said, were guaranteed to be in the county incinerator within the hour. With the satisfaction of seeing that, they drove off towards the M27 motorway and eventually onto the A3M towards London. They then cut across to the old M3, and to where they had left the car, for the final changeover of vehicles.

They removed all the bags from the stolen car and left it at the side of the car park. Still wearing their gloves, they got into Yiddel's car and headed for London. Now in high spirits, the trio recalled the events of the morning.

"Did you see Sheila?" Yiddel asked them. "I couldn't believe my eyes when we jumped into the van...frightened the bloody life out of me, but I'll tell yer, she did look good!"

"That big bastard was coming for you, Yiddel, like a raging bull...he was stumbling forward in all that smoke, about to grab you even though his eyes must have been covered with tears from the gas canisters, and I hit him right between his eyes! He went down like a sack of spuds!"

To which Harry added, "The noise was so loud from them all screaming and shouting I almost dropped the fucking gun! After I hit the first cabinet it just blew up, then I felt you pushing me on, Yiddel. I really got the buzz then and hit cabinet two with two nails. The whole front of it exploded, and then number three - I couldn't

113

wait to get to it and when I did, I was floating. I must say, Yiddel, that was the buzz of all fucking buzzes, that was. Don't know if I should ever have another one like that in my life." And then he added, prophetically – more than he could have imagined at that moment - "I don't think whatever we do in the future will ever equal that."

"Well, all being equal, we got everything we came for, gents, and maybe when we check, a little bit more," Yiddel reckoned, sitting in the front seat looking very pleased with the outcome of the job. As he spoke, yet more police cars were flying past, south towards the scene of the 'job' in Southampton.

"Bye-bye, boys, we are going home now!" shouted Yiddel, as they sped past. "You're all too late – again!"

As they drove on, Yiddel could not help thinking about the job. Those thoughts included hoping that Sheila and Roger had also got away Ok.

'Still,' thought Yiddel, 'I guess we'll find out later.'

They had an uneventful drive back, going straight to the boys' flat to have a proper look at the haul, Yiddel, as always, saying as soon as they were in the flat: "Put the kettle on, H, my throat's like the bottom of our budgie's cage. I'm gasping!"

Tipping the bag onto the carpet, Yiddel and Sammy looked at the haul in amazement...Aztec gold and American diamonds, mixed up all together in a pile of sparkling jewels.

"Harry, fuck the tea for a minute and come and look at this lot!" exclaimed Yiddel.

"Fucking hell," was Harry's response, as he walked in with three cups of tea. "Is that all for me, mister?"

"You cheeky sod!" Yiddel gave him a little slap on the face, then added, "No, now you should ask, it's all for me!"

That was the signal for letting off steam, tea or not; the two boys grabbed hold of Yiddel, Harry taking his tea away from him pulled him onto the floor alongside the haul. Sammy picked up a handful of it and let it drop onto Yiddel's head as they howled with laughter at their achievement as a team.

"You rotten lot, I meant you as well!" he gasped as they held him down on the floor with what might well turn out to be a fortune in diamonds and jewels – all in that flat in humble Hackney.

8

Celebration and Double-Cross

It was time to relax, but it wasn't that easy. The 'standard' celebration supper of fish and chips was eaten with the three sitting there on the floor surrounded by an absolute wealth of gems, but for the moment they were quite happy to ignore it all – what mattered now was to enjoy a good old working-class meal from the newspaper it was wrapped in. As they finished and started to unwind a bit more, the hoard of treasure once again drew their attention hypnotically. And now the extent of what they had just carried out began to sink in – now, they really couldn't take their eyes off the diamonds.

It was time for media coverage: the radio and TV networks were red hot with bulletins of the robbery being 'upgraded' every ten minutes. Downing Street even issued a formal statement, and Scotland Yard constant updates.

By the morning all the national papers were having a field day with a lot of speculation as to what and who was responsible for the crime. Naturally, most reports were way out of proportion, which frequently made them burst out laughing as they sat and watched the TV news.

Variations of the truth emerged like a species of animal struggling to evolve in a barren environment. Reporters, male and female, were given the unenviable task of making it sound feasible and informative as they stood there so awkwardly at the scene: 'a band of disillusioned SAS officers' were currently held as being responsible, with 'timing that could have only been executed by a trained force'.

Different channels competed it seemed, to create ever-more outlandish concoctions of the truth: 'The ballroom was invaded by a small but deadly group of IRA terrorists.'

'The woman was a Russian special agent working with her Russian Mafia colleagues'.

'At least thirty very experienced and ruthless, world-renowned jewel thieves carried it off.'

Yiddel shouted at the TV. "It was us, you silly bastards, from Hackney, not Russia!" But, as he sat on the floor staring at the treasure, he began to seriously start thinking about where he could place something so…so priceless.

"What yer going to do with it then, Yiddel?" Now, Harry was wondering the same thing.

"I think we should leave it for a couple of days and then I'll see if Sid knows anyone."

"Off the top of yer head, Yiddel, what do you reckon it's worth?" asked Sammy.

"From what the papers are saying, it could be in the region of twelve million, but that could be bullshit put up by the Americans for insurance purposes. As I say, let's leave it for a couple of days and see."

Both the boys nodded and reflected for a while, saying nothing, but possibly wondering how Yiddel could safely place all the items – very 'hot' items at present and likely to remain so for some considerable time.

The next day Yiddel checked with Roger to confirm he was all right. He phoned him from a call box and then met him in that same little park near to where he lived.

"How did it go, Roger? I take it you got clear Ok?"

"Yeh, the bombs went very well, I was a bit trash about setting them off because of all the people walking past, but when the time came, I knew I had to go, so I pushed the button. The first car didn't explode, but seemed to catch fire inside first, which gave anybody walking past a chance to clear off, then the windows blew out and the petrol tank exploded making a hell of a noise, by which time everybody was well clear and watching it go up. When I see that, I thought the other one would do the same...it caught light inside, blew out the glass and then exploded in a fantastic ball of flame. Whoever you got them from, Yiddel, knows what they are doing all right – yeh, good stuff and no one got hurt."

Roger was now gushing with excitement at his part in this audacious raid, but was aware that Yiddel needed a proper report. "The police got there pretty quick and the fire brigade too. They closed the roads, and Joe Public made it even better by panicking all over the place and beyond. I watched it all for a couple of minutes to see that it was what we wanted and did as you said - I put the radio control bit into a bin at the other end of the high street, about half a mile away wrapped up in newspaper. I went to the station, had a cuppa, and got the next train out for London. What I'm glad about, Yiddel, is that no one got hurt."

"That's right, mate, the bloke I got the stuff from knew that was how it should work. So, no one could see you with the controller, Rog?"

"No, I kept it in a paper bag all the time even when I pressed the button, so that it looked like I was getting some item or other from the bag. The noise down there was really something else and then the smoke was black and billowing all over the street. It really did the trick."

118

"Good, well thanks again, Roger me old mate. I will only call you now for the next pay day. I'll try and make it a good 'un, but as yet we don't know the worth. Still, leave it with me and I'll get the best for us all."

"Ok, Yiddel, thanks for that, keep me in mind for anything else, I enjoyed that one!"

Yiddel shook his hand and left Roger in the park. Next, he called Sheila. A quick call to her, and the pair met in the local supermarket. Yiddel waited for her in the entrance, and when she appeared they both walked into the huge store with a trolley as if they were a couple getting the weekly shopping.

"How are you, love?" he asked her, cautiously.

"Fine. And you?" Outwardly, she was playing the part well.

"Better now I've seen you as I know you. I've just left one of the other team members, and he was telling me how much he enjoyed the caper, mainly because his role went so well. You frightened the life out of me when I first see you in the van, I did a double take, I thought 'who the fuck is this?' but when I heard you speak, I was Ok."

Sheila couldn't help but laugh out loud, causing a couple of nearby lady shoppers to look round at her.

"Did you like the make-up?"

"Like it, you nearly got knocked out; I thought we were in the wrong motor!"

Sheila smiled with pride at Yiddel's words, for she knew he was in his way giving her a pat on the back for doing what she had been required to do, and that was to confuse everyone with her disguise.

"I got the glasses when I used to work on Saturdays at the opticians in the High Street. They are only plain glass, specimen ones for the frames. The teeth I got from a shop in Covent Garden, they sell all theatrical make-up. And my lovely blonde hair I got rid of by using a temporary dye, it just washes out. I must tell you, Yiddel, that big bastard - the security guard - he was trying to get his leg over the night before...kept on asking me to come up to his room. I told him I was getting over an operation on my tackle and that it would not be possible.

"He swallowed that and then left me alone. But, generally, everything went well. I kept my working gloves on all the time I was in the hotel. When I got back to the flat after I left you and the boys, I washed off the dye, got rid of those awful teeth, then I cleaned the whole room before I left. I even used my own towel to dry my hair so that I left no trace of my hair in the room...I walked through the city centre after I left the flat - it was absolute chaos. There was police and fire engines rushing all over the place." She paused and looked at him. "Was that all your doing, Yiddel?"

"'fraid so, luv. My man in town started it off as we was working the hotel over."

"I thought so!" she said with a little chuckle. "I watched for a bit then made my way to the station. I dumped my teeth and the towel on a building site fire near the station. There was no one there; I think they had all run down the road to see the action. I watched it burn and then headed for the train."

"Well done, darling, how much do I owe you for the teeth?" he cheekily enquired.

"I'll treat you to those, Yiddel!" She punched him softly on his arm.

"Ok, babe, I'll be in touch as soon as we get weighed off and I'll settle up with you then, Ok?"

Kissing on the cheek, the pair left the trolley where it was in mid-aisle and exited the store, each going in different directions.

Yiddel was very pleased with both of his new team members. Sheila and Roger had acted and done exactly what he had asked them to do on the day. They had carried out their tasks to the letter and he was doubly impressed by the added touches Sheila had organised off her own back. Roger, too, had carried it off perfectly. The paper bag cover-up was all it needed to protect him from being seen detonating the cars – these two were now definitely on the team. And the two boys? They had obeyed his commands to the letter, 'and that is why we are all back in Hackney and not banged up in a police cell in Southampton,' he concluded with great satisfaction.

The newspapers were still in full cry about the band of villains that had pulled off the hotel crime. They were all still speculating about the 'Mob that had perpetrated such a dastardly crime on the exhibition of artefacts from the United States of America'. Front-page banners were getting bigger and bolder. Yiddel was keeping a close eye on the total value figure. The Americans were still talking about an 'irreplaceable loss' but not saying how much was 'irreplaceable'.

Yiddel and the boys were scanning all the TV bulletins on UK and CNN to see if anyone was coming up with a figure. The British newspapers kept on publishing figures, but they all knew these were unreliable, and Yiddel wanted facts, not hype. He went to see Sidney.

"Is this down to you, Yiddel?" Sidney was pointing to the front page of *The Sun*.

"Yeh, it sure is." He looked at his old friend with big sheepish eyes.

"I thought you might have had a hand in it." Sidney was visibly impressed.

"In fact, Sid, it's the reason I've come round to see you, not that I need a reason to see your lovely face of course, but as you have so rightly put it down to me, I will definitely be needing your services in shifting it…so you're on a nice little earner, if you want one?"

"What's the stuff like?"

"We've only had a little look at it, but it seems good. The catalogue tells you all about it, where it all came from, but that's about it…it don't give you a value. I want to leave it for a bit and see how much it is really worth. I'm hoping the Yanks will release a figure. Who do you think will be interested in it?"

"I don't know, to be honest. You can probably get a better price all round if you break it up – see, broken up it is easily sold as just gems, not as an identifiable piece of jewellery. But let's do as you say, wait a bit for things to settle."

Going back to the market after leaving Sidney, Yiddel was startled to see a large gathering of police all down the street.

"What's going on?" he asked one of the stallholders, trying not to show his anxiety.

"Hullo, Yiddel. There's been a report about a dealer selling guns to someone in Ridley Street and they're all over the place looking for them right now."

'Fucking hell, the electrician', thought Yiddel as his blood seemed to turn to ice. 'I'd like to bet he's said something to someone and they've gone to the police. They could be looking for me!' He needed to breathe – this fear was suddenly starting to overwhelm him. 'But wait...if anything, they've been speaking to Jeremy Store in Hampstead, so why come here?'

He walked down to the market, trying not to let his worries show to the world. Despite the strong possibility that he could be a principal suspect, he casually strolled right up to the blue and white police control tape.

"*They have arrested Ansel*," announced one of the onlookers despairingly, "for having guns in his caff...they've brought out two boxes full of guns." He stopped as he noticed the familiar figure of the popular Yiddel. "Oh, hullo, Yiddel...didn't see you standing there. 'Ear about old Ansel? He's bin nicked for 'aving shooters in the caff!" The trader was clearly mesmerised by such an event happening here in Ridley Street.

Yiddel therefore had a moment in which to gather himself. "Yeh, I just heard, it just goes to show you don't know what's going on in this market, do yer?" He was trying to look as innocent as he could, but inside was feeling a huge relief that it was not him or the boys.

"You're dead right there, Yiddel!"

Yiddel then found out from another stallholder that Ansel was doing one of his Yardie mates a favour by looking after a box. He claimed he did not know what was inside, had no idea it was guns. The mate got picked up by the police for another felony in connection with his car. When the police searched it, they found he had a hand gun under the front seat. In fear of a long sentence, he told the police where all the others were stored...Ansel's café.

Ansel was locked up until the next day and then released after his solicitor explained to the police what had happened. The Yardie mate had now calmed down and told the police that the box was his and he had left it with Ansel, who did not have anything to do with it. And so, Ansel was allowed to go free – for now.

A very relieved Yiddel was also well pleased for Ansel, despite his immense euphoria that the raid by the police in the market was nothing to do with him.

Later that day, Sidney phoned Yiddel to say he had seen a news report that the police were very close to catching the Southampton gang, adding, "Can you hear any sirens, mate?" with some sarcasm.

"Fuck off!" was Yiddel's curt reply.

"And the Americans have said that the total value is twenty-two million dollars."

"Well, at least now we know how much all that Tom is worth. How much is that in pounds?"

"Hold on, I'll work it out." Yiddel could hear many clicks coming from Sidney's calculator and then heard him say, "About fourteen million pounds, give or take a dime."

"That's not bad, is it, Sid?"

The next morning the boys got the stall out early like nothing had happened on their 'day off' and were busy stacking the toys, talking to another stall holder.

"Did you hear about Ansel?" the man asked him.

"Yeh," replied Harry. "A bit rough that - do a mate a favour and finish up getting your collar felt."

"Yeh, but did you hear that Ansel had been watched by the fuzz for dealing as well, even though it was only ganja!"

"Never!" exclaimed Sammy. "What, old Ansel?"

"It worked out that the police had been watching him for quite a long time and what with the other thing had done him for the lot."

Sammy looked at Harry and the look was enough for his friend to read 'police has been watching' on his face. At the first chance they got to speak alone, Sammy said: "Did you see anyone like the police watching down here?"

"No, but we've got to be fucking careful now, just got to be," said Harry, visibly shaken by the Ansel episode.

Sammy was more optimistic about their chances. "Can't you see why Yiddel is so good? He never takes a chance, he always makes sure that no one sees - whatever he does."

Just then, Yiddel arrived at the stall; without saying a word, the boys knew that he had heard the news about Ansel…nothing was said.

Ansel eventually came up at the North London Criminal Court and as it was his first offence got away with a big fine and a caution to be good. Yiddel met him when he came back to his café.

"You all right, Ansel?"

"Yeh, though I feel very low. Man, it's really taken the wind out of my sails. Talk about 'when it rains it pours'. I suppose you've heard all about it?"

"Yeh, you're a silly old bastard, falling for that 'look after me box, man' routine without checking what was inside. And the weed, I didn't think you were into that too?"

"I know, what a prat, I got mugged from left, right and centre, Yiddel!"

Sidney phoned again to say that he had a man paying him a visit later that night and could he bring the goods over for a check-up. He said the man was one hundred percent kosher.

Yiddel with the boys and a bag of jewellery arrived at Sidney's bang on the arranged time. Sidney was there with his man. Sidney introduced him as George.

"Hello, Yiddel-Sammy-Harry, nice to see yer," he said with a broad grin, giving Sidney a wink. George was a really affable, genuinely likeable character, who had seen a hell of a lot in his seventy years, much of it rather close to the line of illegality, but his real strength on the wrong side of that line was in knowing a good diamond when he saw one, and he had made quite a nice sum of money in his time because of it. Only once had he been 'cornered' by some nasty rogues and they had left George with a permanent reminder of who not to deal with when it came to criminality. As he limped awkwardly over to the jewel box, the others were reminded of this sad fact and all felt empathy and comradeship for this good old soul.

The first thing that George took an interest in was the huge diamond, which was the centrepiece to the whole exhibition. He looked at it closely through his small magnifier and then put it to one side on the table top. He then picked up the other pieces one at a time checking each as he went. Yiddel and Sidney sat back in silence as he checked each item, both feeling quite elated that such a huge fortune was here on Sidney's desk being appraised. But it wasn't to be the verdict they were expecting.

"A lot of fucking shit!" George almost exploded with rage. "I have never seen such bad imitation gems in all my life - I could have got my two-year-old son to make better stuff from a *United Dairies* fucking milk bottle!"

Yiddel was visibly shaken and could only remain sitting in his chair. "What do you mean 'shit'? It's worth twenty-two million!"

George looked him in the eye and said, "Yiddel, I would not give you twenty-two pence for that load of crap. I'm telling you, that is one hell of a load of rubbish, absolute crap."

He got up and said to Sidney, "Call me when you've got something for me, Sid, anything but this shit. Nice to meet you, Yiddel. No offence, but you know what I mean." He nodded at the boys as he left.

The four remaining men sat speechless. Sammy was the first to break the heavy silence. "Those dirty bastards, they are still saying on the news what a tragic loss it is to the American nation and that it can never be replaced...replaced? Now we find out it's a load of shite. So, what are they on about?"

Yiddel looked at Sidney and the wily pair had it completely sussed from the second they had heard 'rubbish'.

"A scam, mate, a fucking great scam. You can bet on it that what we did was exactly what they wanted to happen to it. They must have been praying that someone would rob the collection, and we did, and no one outside the organisation knows it's a load of shit but us," Yiddel advised.

"What a load of dirty-eyed bastards," muttered Sidney. "A scam and a very good scam at that, but now *we can turn it round on them* and make more from it than you thought, Yiddel."

Sidney then called for an immediate conference. He ordered beer, food, and the war-type conference swung into motion.

"Right, let's get down to business." Sidney had taken it on himself to chair the meeting. No one had any objections to the grand old timer doing just that. To have Sidney on board at a time like this was not only superb but also very necessary. 'A wily old fox,' Yiddel called him.

"Firstly, we have got to get these bastards by the Jacobs and squeeze. We will have to make contact to let them know that we know what they are up to. Maybe they were hoping that after the crime had been committed, we were not going to do anything about it and they would then get away with their own crime of deception, if you know what I mean. Second, the main thing is that we have the evidence to their crime; we have the merchandise, the so called precious jewels, in other words the proof of the scam that they have pulled, and finally, we are not fucking paupers, we are four *very rich* men - we can get them by the bollocks and make them pay. Why do I emphasise 'very rich'? Because we can do anything we like to get them, we are not skint, so we can chase them anywhere, agreed?"

All three agreed with nods, no words, and so Sidney continued. "I propose that a phone call is made to the boss of the exhibition and the cards are laid on the table as to our knowledge of his tricks. If he wants to negotiate, fine...if he wants total disclosure of his swindle, no problem at all. We have nothing to lose, but by fuck he does. He has so much to lose. He would be very disgraced if it all came out. He has so much to lose at this time. He must be praying that the lot goes and is never seen again. That would suit him fine. He'll collect the insurance money and carry on. I don't think he reckoned on a little British team who would take him on at his own game. He could not afford that fucking show over in the States."

The other three let him talk, because all he was saying sounded correct.

"Yiddel, I want you to make the call. I want you to tell him that the game is up. Tell him we will do nothing for a while – but no more. Tell him we have the entire worthless Tom, a lot of worthless antiques and that we are willing to trade." Sidney was now in full flow and slightly out of breath in his haste to choose the right words and think at the same time of what the plan was going to be. "Tell him that we have him by the short-and-curlies and that we are prepared to meet him - but only on our terms!"

They packed up the meeting and left Sidney with his thoughts, so much was he engrossed in them that he did not even say goodnight as they left.

9

Enter Mr Moores

The next morning, Yiddel, fully prepared, took a taxi to the City. He found a phone box at the back of Liverpool Street Station from where he phoned the number in the catalogue, wanting to speak to a director of the exhibition. A man came to the phone, and the affluent voice announced, "Gerald Moores here."

Yiddel gave him the number of the phone box and asked him to phone back regarding a sensitive issue which was 'very much for your own sake'...Yiddel did this to make sure in his mind that the phone call was not being listened in on by the police. The phone rang within seconds of Yiddel ringing off. It may have been Yiddel's carefully chosen tone of voice that made the man think, especially the advice: 'for your own sake'. Whatever it was, there was no doubting that this Moores character had suddenly got a hell of a sinking feeling - this was precisely the call he had definitely never wanted to receive.

Yiddel picked the phone up. "Who am I speaking to?" He needed to make sure.

"My name is Gerald Moores...who am *I* speaking to?"

"Mr Moores, you are speaking to a man who has got your bollocks in his hand and is about to give them the biggest squeeze you have ever had in your life. Also, I have got your so-called treasure in a brown paper bag because that's, as we both know, all it's fucking worth. A load of worthless shit!"

Yiddel carried on, underlining his first salvo. "All that crap about it all being worth twenty-two million dollars is pure shit too.

In fact…my jeweller has put its worth at about one pound sterling. Are you getting all this, Mr Moores, or do I have to spell it out in another language?"

A silent Moores was desperately taking time to reflect on what he had just heard. Yiddel guessed this and waited. "Are you still there, Mr Mo-o-res?" Yiddel deliberately dragged out the man's surname. "Or shall I repeat the important bits?"

"No...no, there is no need for that. I hear what you are saying. Look, I'm a bit thrown by this call, as you can imagine. Can I call you after I have had a word with my 'colleagues'...er, don't worry, I did not mean the police."

It was Yiddel's moment in which to pause, just to turn the screw a bit more. "…I'll phone you again tomorrow about the same time." With that, he put the phone down.

He furtively left the call box and stood a reasonable distance away for ten minutes, just to see if the police turned up. No one arrived and then he knew they had their man well and truly by the proverbial *Jacobs Cream Crackers*.

Getting back to Sidney's, Yiddel told him what Moores had said.

"Ok, as you say, Yiddel, 'Game On' - let's see what he comes up with and then we can take it from there."

"Ok, mate, I'll go and phone him again tomorrow and come straight back here afterwards."

Yiddel left him and headed back to the market where the two boys were working the stall.

"Had any tea yet? I don't know, if I didn't turn up you two would die of thirst. Right, H, go and get us some tea and three cream cheese beigels." As they were having their tea break, Yiddel told them about the morning phone call to Moores. Both the boys agreed that he sounded a 'devious bleeder' and should be shown up and disgraced, even after they settled on the anticipated deal.

The next morning Yiddel, a man of such wealth but also of immense professionalism, got a bus down to the City and made his call to Moores from another phone box inside the station on the concourse. This way he had many exits to choose from should a quick exodus be necessary. Dialling the number Moores had given him the day before, his call was picked up quickly, with a noticeably anxious Moores answering.

"Gerald Moores here."

All Yiddel said to start was: "I phoned yesterday..." and waited to see what the response would be. But nothing came. So he went on: "Have you had time to talk to your colleagues?"

"Yes, I had a discussion about what you said yesterday and we are prepared to meet you...on neutral ground."

"I think I would like to hear a bit more dialogue before it comes to that. I would like to hear a figure first. And then, maybe, we can talk about neutral ground." Yiddel's tone of voice was unequivocal.

"Yes, I meant that, but we do not have a figure to give you yet," said Moores. "I will have, in a day or two - but not yet."

"Mr Moores, let me say one thing to you. Do not for one minute try to fuck me about - am I making myself clear?"

"Very clear, but at the moment my hands are tied."

"Mr Moores, listen to what I am about to say. My firm will not be messed about so I suggest that you untie your fucking hands and put them into your shitty wallets and come up with a figure, pronto, and I don't mean a woman's. I am talking money, fucking big money, Mr Moores, or we go public. And by that I mean to the American press. This could make Watergate look like a fucking tea party. Remember, all I've got to lose is a day's work at the hotel

132

and a few days planning the robbery. I can put it down to experience...you can write off your credibility in the good old US of A forever."

With that, Yiddel put the phone down, muttering 'What an arsehole.' Taking a moment to re-focus back in 'civvy street' mode, he moved away from the call box to another a few hundred yards away and called Sidney. He told him what had been said by Moores and Sidney agreed that Yiddel had said the right things and now they had been said he felt sure Moores would realise they were not messing around. "Leave it for a couple of days, Yiddel, and let the bastard sweat a bit!"

Yiddel felt he should inform Sheila and Roger as to what was happening. Not going into the major problem that the stuff they had helped to steal was a load of rubbish, he broached the issue in terms of there being a hold-up in the sale. They both were quite happy to leave it to Yiddel. He felt that almost all the people he knew were thieves or villains in one way or another; yet they were far more genuine than these pretentious bastards that were scamming the public and their country on a so-called 'exhibition of American artefacts and treasures'. All of his true friends were villains, yes, but friends who would help each other when they were in need or trouble. 'A far different breed,' thought Yiddel.

Two days passed and Yiddel again phoned Moores. "Is that you, Mr Moores? Yes? Good. You know who this is. What have you come up with?"

"I've been waiting for you to call; I thought you would call yesterday?"

"No," said Yiddel, trying to sound as cool and casual as he could. "I have been sorting out some business elsewhere. So, what have you decided?"

"My colleagues and I feel that we have no alternative but to meet you on your terms...I can only put it to you that we keep the whole thing under wraps between ourselves and that yes, we work out some sort of a deal to satisfy both sides. We feel that a compromise can be worked where we get what we want and so do you. But, I must emphasise this: 'within a sensible boundary.' Is that clear?"

Yiddel saw the red mist. "We realise that what you tried to pull off has blown up in your face. We have gone to great lengths to also pull off a job and I think we, although now sitting with a pile of shit jewellery for our troubles, did our part much better than you. My man was absolutely gob-smacked and couldn't understand that you've put such an exhibition on full display and that no one else had seen it for what it really was. How you had the nerve to put such rank shit on display - he said he could have seen it from the other side of the room."

Moores took a deep breath and said, "Look... we don't want to keep going over the same ground, we know what we have to do, we want you to play the game with us and we will look after you and your gang. We have sat through the night working out a solution and we have come up with this: get rid of the stuff; let us put in a claim for it all and then we will pay you out when we get the final cheque. Does that sound fair to you, Mr – I don't think I have your name?" A pause. "Unless you think there is another way? And to be quite frank I don't think there is. If you throw in with us, we all get something. If not, as you so rightly said, we are disgraced, and you finish up with - in your words - a pile of shit worth nothing."

It was Yiddel's turn to think and he quickly came to the decision that the man was right, that there was only one sensible answer...but only providing they played the game. He must play the game. If he don't, I can still hang him from his balls, and he will lose the money for what!

"Ok, Mr Moores, I'll go along with that, but please remember, we know who and where you are. All you've got on us is a phone call and my voice - always from a different call box - so you have nothing. I think at this moment in time, I hold all the aces."

"Yes, you do, and that's what we were hoping you would say, and for that we must thank you."

"Right," said Yiddel. "I will call tomorrow and give you a phone number so that we can stay on talking terms." That was the end of that, for now.

"Gotcha!" said Yiddel under his breath (or so he thought) as he walked away from the phone box past a middle-aged woman pushing an old pram.

"No, you ain't," she shouted back over her shoulder. "I'm a free woman!"

Yiddel was too engrossed in his thoughts to fire back a reply. He was soon on his way back to Sidney's place.

After listening to Yiddel's story of his conversation with Moores, Sidney came out with nearly the same, saying, "Got 'em. Ok, all we can do now is wait for them to make the first move."

"How long does it take for a claim to go through?" asked Yiddel.

"It could take fucking ages. It all depends on the circumstances, and in this case it could grind on for months. Don't forget, a crime 'as been committed here, which is only the beginning..." His voice tailed off as a more uncomfortable thought entered his mind. "Oh, blimey, I've just had another thought, say that it all comes on top of them and they are investigated - they go down and we get fuck all."

With that last comment of Sidney's ringing in his ears, Yiddel left and made his way to the market, where he found Sammy minding the stall. Harry, mindful of Yiddel's words about never getting a cup of tea, had just gone over to Ansel's to get some. Sammy ran over to the café and shouted to him to make it three.

"How'd it go with the man?" asked Sammy cautiously as Harry came back, swearing that the cups were burning his hands and saying, "Take a cup off me for fuck's sake, Sam!"

Ignoring Harry, Yiddel answered Sammy's question. "Yeh, Ok, the man looks like he could be on our side. But we have got to see what type of game he wants to play, a straight one or a crooked one. He can't just leave it, we will not go away, and he knows that, he has to include us no matter what. We are a major factor in his original scam and he bloody well knows it."

He started to tell them about Moores' proposal, but then shut up as a market official came up to their stall. "Hallo, Yiddel, I ain't seen you for a while."

"No, you ain't, and no reason why you should because you are never down here early enough, you lazy, fat bastard. I should let the council know about you; all I hear from everyone is that you spend all day getting your leg over the girl in the butcher's, out in the back of the shop. If her father finds out he'll cut your bollocks off on his chopping block and have them hanging on a hook in his window before you ever realised they were gone."

"ME?" exclaimed the market inspector. "I don't know what you're talking about, Yiddel," smacking Yiddel on the back but not hanging around for any more abuse, even if it was truthful. He

136

carried on ambling down the market laughing his head off, shouting back over his shoulder, "You are a one."

Yiddel shouted back: "And you won't have one if he catches you, Smiler!"

Back to the boys. "I had to go shtoom, then. Don't ever trust that bloke, he's all ears with plenty of rabbit. More than Sainsbury's got on their shelves. Right, where was I? Oh, I know. We left it that I'm phoning tomorrow to give him our phone number to continue the negotiations."

Both the boys jumped off the edge of the stall they were sitting on. "Our number? Are you fucking mad?"

"No, you silly pair of sods, I'm not mad. Sam, do me a favour and go down to that phone shop and get me one of those Pay-As-You-Go phones. I heard someone talking about it up the market."

"Yeh, you're right, it's a phone that you can buy, and no one knows who you are - you just buy a card. Right, I know the one." And he rushed off up the market.

"Is Ansel all right?" Yiddel wanted to know.

"Yeh, he seems Ok, he looks a bit shaken, not the old normal Ansel. He'll get over it - knocked him sideways, though, getting both charges at the same time." Harry said what he knew, then added, "Oh, yeh, he wants to see you."

"It's a good job I asked about him, isn't it? Otherwise you would have forgotten." Yiddel reprimanded his disciple with only faintly disguised mockery.

"Yer like an old woman, Yiddel. I would have told you, don't worry!" replied a reproachful Harry. Yiddel, however, was glad to have the opportunity to see what Ansel wanted. Harry went with him out of curiosity.

"Ansel, me old china, what's the matter with you, then?"

"Hullo, boys. Thanks for coming over." And then, in a hushed voice, he said, "I think I may have a problem, which I am told, you may be able to help with. My friend, the one that did me no favours, wants to get hold of a passport so that he can go to the USA. Any ideas?"

"Passport? He nearly put you away and now he is asking you to get him an 'ooky passport. Ansel, I thought you had learnt your lesson with this mate of yours. Anyway, that's the first time I've been asked for a dodgy passport...if I hear of anyone, I'll pass it on," but really thinking, 'Fuck his mate, let him find his own.'

"Thanks, Yiddel, want a cup of tea or a roll?"

"No thanks, mate, I've got an important call to make. See you later."

"Be lucky, Yiddel," Ansel shouted.

'Yeh, it's you who needs the luck - with friends like what you've got,' thought Yiddel.

"Did you get one?" Yiddel asked Sammy as the 'boy' returned.

"Yeh, it's the one you wanted - you just buy the phone and then buy a phone card. Untraceable it is...apparently."

"Great, that's just the ticket. This is going to save me going up to the City just to make a bloody phone call."

Sammy was busying himself installing and unpacking the new phone. "I think you shouldn't make the calls to Moores around here though...calls can be traced to a zone, so still move around," he advised, a bit concerned over Yiddel's newness to modern technology. "I've put a ten-pound voucher on the phone, so it's all primed and ready to go."

"Righto, thanks for that, take it out of the till what you spent, as you're obviously down to your last pound now," was Yiddel's parting remark, loud enough for several stallholders nearby to hear. Clutching his new toy, he left, his mind whirring with new plans, starting with Mr Moores.

"I am now going to give you a name for me," he informed his reluctant new partner-in-crime. "Call me... 'Fagin'."

There was a pause the other end. "Good morning, Mr Fagin," said Moores, slowly. "So, now I have your phone number and your name."

"How did you get that?" gasped a genuinely astonished Yiddel.

"Because it has just come up on my screen."

Totally confused as to how this could be possible, Yiddel heard himself say: "Well, Ok, you've got it now, great. Ok, what's happening regarding our arrangement?"

"At the moment, absolutely nothing, Mr Fagin. We are, as you know, still with the police in their investigation. They know nothing at all and I know everything. We can only wait until they give us the clearance and then and only then will the insurance company pay up."

"Are you going back to America?" asked Yiddel.

"No, we can't leave England while there is an investigation going on. Remember *we* are being looked at as well. Scotland Yard has informed us that a member of the FBI is coming over to cover the American side of the crime. All of this, Mr Fagin, we contemplated. So, we have to sit tight and wait. At least we know that they will not solve the crime - unless you or one of yours becomes very clumsy. I take it that you have covered all the bases, Mr Fagin?"

Yiddel kept silent.

"As far as we can gather from talking to you, you are a very careful man. We were discussing you and your team, and we unanimously agreed we could not have pulled it off better ourselves. We are only glad that you did the job, we were praying for a hit... so we compliment you. So, let us spin it out without spoiling the final furlong. Agreed, Mr Fagin?"

"Yeh, Ok, agreed...Mr Moores." Now, Yiddel was talking to him like a business partner. "Let's leave it there...if you hear, call me," and clicked off the phone, seeing he had already used one pound of his ten.

He remained deep in thought as he walked back to the stall, just to get his head around what Moores had said, and to what the future planning was going to have to be. 'There's no need to give me all that bollocks about how good we are - we know that. Now it's time for a Sidney war conference.'

Yiddel called the meeting for that night at the boys' flat, just the four main players: Sidney, Harry, Sammy and Yiddel. As usual when Yiddel was planning something, he had to lay it out on paper so that he and the others could see it in black and white. He put all the known facts down, who was who, and what was what - the Moores camp and the Yiddel camp all duly laid out like a battle formation. They spoke about the possible formulae of Moores' strategy.

"Pulling strokes and doing a runner," was Sidney's verdict.

"They could easily do that," agreed Yiddel, "once they have the insurance money, which will be a very large amount of money...they could easily fuck off to anywhere in the world, and then what about us? What would we do? The world could easily swallow them up and with that amount of money, they could hide anywhere. They could live in Brazil, leading the life of Riley, and no one would ever find them."

"Ok, let's work down on that line," suggested Sidney. "Say they did a runner and not pay us. I think what we should be doing now is preparing ourselves in case they do that. I suggest Sammy goes to the hotel where they are staying to find out what they look like without making it obvious. We must keep our eye on them and get as much on them as we can." He now looked at Sammy directly. "If you can get a picture, great, but don't overdo it in getting one. Just keep your ears open and see the state of play. If we get all that, we will be a good step in front of them. Understand? They do not know what we look like, but we will know them. Money in the bank, my boys, money in the good old J Arthur Rank!"

Yiddel nodded his approval. "Oh, another thing, Sid. I want the stuff put away somewhere safe, because at the end of the day that is our insurance as well. If nothing else, we can use that."

"I know just the place," Harry chipped in. "I'll take it down Auntie's in the morning and hide it. I think you know where?" touching the side of his nose.

A week went past and they had not heard a word from Moores. The newspaper stories dried up to just an occasional piece on the inside pages. Southampton City Council were the only ones who kept it going by seeking some sort of justice for the car bombing in their streets and about making the gang pay for frightening the good people of south Hampshire.

Sheila bumped into Yiddel in the market and politely asked, in a coded greeting, asked how the 'family' was.

"Not bad," he said. "We still haven't heard from my uncle in America, though."

That was enough for Sheila; it was equivalent to a hundred words. Roger passed the stall later in the day and asked the same question. Yiddel gave him the same answer. Again, that was all Roger wanted to hear and he disappeared back into the crowd. To anyone keeping watch on certain people in the market, such as Sheila, all they would have seen would be shoppers coming up to the stall and appearing to make an enquiry about a teddy bear as though asking, "How much is that one?" At the same time, both parties were passing on valuable information to each other. They could have phoned, but being able to see each other was more important.

Very early the next morning, Yiddel's phone made a deafening, shrieking noise that Sammy had set up, nothing like a normal ringing tone, which made Yiddel leap out of bed, thinking the worst.

The voice on the line was unmistakable. "Mr Fagin – it's Moores. I think we will be able to talk next week. The police have said that they have not had any new leads as to who committed the crime and they fear that the stolen pieces are now out of the country. I have had a word with the FBI agent and he feels the same. We are meeting the insurance agent today, who is flying in from L.A., and is coming straight to the hotel from the airport. I will phone you later today and tell you how the meeting went. Oh, and sorry to wake you so early, Mr Fagin."

Yiddel immediately phoned Sammy and told him about who was arriving and what Moores had said. "Get down to the hotel as quick as you can, and keep your eyes peeled for this man. He is arriving this afternoon, but get there early. I will take care of the stall. Tell Harry to meet me in Ridley – and quick!"

142

Yiddel then phoned Sidney and told him of the call from Moores. He told him he had sent Sammy early to the hotel, just to keep an eye on any movements. And mainly to watch for the arrival of the insurance man. Sidney agreed.

Sammy arrived at the hotel, *The Hilton* on Park Lane, with a cutting from *The Sun* newspaper. The details had been published in most of the papers of where the Americans were staying, along with a good photograph of Moores with a colleague outside the hotel. So, with his picture of Moores in his pocket, he said to himself, 'We know what you look like now, Mr Moores'. He tucked himself away in the small coffee shop across the road with a newspaper and surreptitiously kept watch on the comings and goings at this superior hotel.

At 2pm, a well-built man arrived with two cases, both with L.A. stickers on their sides, being helped in by the porter. Sammy shot out of the coffee shop and stood as close to the man as he dared at the check-in desk, looking at a car hire brochure.

"Hullo, I have a room reserved in the name of Lionel Cooper, thank you," came the heavy American drawl.

The young, good-looking receptionist checked the reservation list on her computer screen and smiled as she said, "Yes, Mr Cooper, would you please sign in for me with your passport number?"

Cooper signed in while Sammy stealthily glanced at him again, and could observe the room number being allocated to him. He kept up the pretence of looking at the brochures for just a bit longer, but his narrow window of opportunity was rapidly vanishing, and he knew it. Fortunately, Cooper now finished checking in and then asked the girl for the room number of Moores whom, he announced, he was meeting. She smiled again and went back to her screen. "Yes, sir, it's room 560 on the fifth floor."

Sammy noted that Cooper was on the fourth floor, room 442.

"Could you please give Mr Moores a call to say that I am here in room 442?" asked Cooper, politely but business-like and clearly used to staying in top-quality hotels and receiving prompt, efficient service.

The girl said she would. A young porter then carried Cooper's bags up to his room. Sammy went over to one of the lobby phone booths and discreetly called Yiddel.

"Our insurance man's arrived - his name is Cooper, Lionel Cooper, here to see Moores - who's in room 560."

"Righto." Yiddel was relieved they now had eyes on Cooper and, hopefully, soon Moores as well. "Hang around where you are, they may be staying in. Give it an hour and then come home. Well done, son!" He felt praise was due to Sammy for his efforts.

All the new information was added to the Board, and Sidney was informed. The Board was looking very impressive; it was housing all the facts about the Moores group. All the relevant cuttings from the papers including the picture of Moores and company were attached.

The Sun that morning was printing and assuming that a gang from Europe had pulled it off in Southampton, and their hacks duly went into some detail about the items that had been stolen. As Yiddel was reading the article, he saw that the paper had printed an itemised list of all the pieces that had been stolen. There were items in the list that he knew he had not touched, but were nevertheless there...

144

"The slippery bastard, he's slipped a few more bits away, the devious bastard!" He cut the piece out of the paper and added it to the chart for future reference.

Sammy got back from Park Lane and advised Yiddel that Cooper and Moores had not gone out. Yiddel went down to see Sidney, leaving Harry and Sammy on the stall. When Yiddel arrived, Sidney was sitting at the window looking down into the street.

"Yiddel, I get this nasty feeling that this is going fucking tits up and completely pear-shaped. Moores is in a good position, true, that we know, but he has had so much time now to plan exactly what he and his mates are going to do. All the time he is giving us the Mr Nice guy routine he is in reality just playing for time. We do not know what his plan is, but I think we have got to start putting our final plan together - just in case." Sidney's piercing look betrayed his strength of feeling. Then he sighed and adopted the old Jewish posture of raising his shoulders with his hands outstretched on either side. "I'll keep talking while I've got it in my head. Stop me if I get carried away. I think, Yiddel, you should start now by putting your team on this if it goes wrong. We do not want to find that Moores and his whole team are on a plane back to America before we realise what has happened. We need to confront him in London where we are, here! We need to look him in the face and frighten the fucking life out of him. We cannot let him get away. Let's prepare him for a fucking good hiding or a complete settle up!"

Sidney's passionate but reasoned logic was acknowledged by Yiddel in total agreement. "I see your point, Sid. I have been thinking along the same lines and I feel that we have been playing Moores' game, and he's in control. It's time, as you say, to stop letting him rule the deal. As you may know, I have several other members to our team, whom you have only heard about and not seen. Each one is more than capable of working my plans to the letter. I know this because they have been tested. I feel that as both of these were part of my Southampton team, they should now be included with us. That gives us a total of six. I can also call on the service of two others, and although both of these have not been tested, I know they would be Ok."

He sat down and thought further. "I agree we should do something now. How do we know that this bloke who has just arrived is an insurance agent? And what about this so-called FBI agent? Let's make a move now and put the shits up Moores, just to say, 'enough is enough' and that we're not fucking about. Ok, Sid, leave it with me, I'll give you a ring and tell you when and what."

The next stop was the stall to tell the boys of the new plan.

"Ok, Sam, start getting the usual gear together. I want overalls for all - cater for four, and vary the sizes. Four full-face masks, gloves and caps. A maid's uniform and a chauffeur's outfit. We will need a limo and a 4x4. I was thinking about weapons, but I'll leave that till later. I would like them all ready in two days' time."

Sammy left straight away for Euston, where he knew he could get most of the items. Harry departed to sort out the procuring of the two vehicles and Yiddel kept up the appearance of an average stallholder – he knew this was still vital if they were going to successfully maintain their 'cover'. In his mind, he knew the war was on. He was now mobilising his force for ever-more demanding ambitions...and this time it was Moores who was the target. He phoned Sheila and Roger and put them both in the picture as to what part they were going to play and put them both on immediate standby for two days' time.

So now he had to leave the stall with a man he knew who was out of work and was looking for a way to earn some simple money; the man was pleased to be invited to work while Yiddel and the boys 'had a little business to take care of elsewhere'.

The whole team of Yiddel, Sammy, Harry, Sidney, Sheila and Roger were on their way to Mayfair for 9am. Each one had their own instructions. They were all for it 'Big Time', they said. "The time for messing about," pronounced Yiddel, with obvious determination as they neared the West End.

Arriving at *The Hilton*, Roger was driving the limo suitably dressed as a chauffeur, and his instructions were to stay outside the front entrance and not move under any circumstances; the four-track was put on a meter nearby. The team boldly walked into the hotel and took the express lift to the fifth floor. In the stairwell, out of sight of anyone, they all changed, pulling on overalls, putting on masks and gloves. Sheila slipped into her maid's uniform, all done in seconds. Yiddel checked each one to ensure everybody was ready. He took a quick glance into the corridor to make sure it was clear, confirmed it was 'Ok' and they were off to room 560.

Sheila knocked gently on the door saying; "Maid. I have a parcel for you, Mr Moores!"

The door opened, only a little… it was Moores dressed only in a robe. Sheila deftly stepped to one side and away to allow the combined force of Yiddel, Sammy, Harry and Sidney to bulldoze their way in, and in a second they had forced Moores back into the room and onto the bed. Harry closed the door and leant against it with his arms folded. Moores' face was a picture of fear. His former confidence had evaporated now he found himself looking up at four fully masked men of whom he could see only their eyes, which served to increase his fear. No faces - just eyes. Yiddel had him by the throat, speaking quietly but unequivocally, inches away from his face.

"Good morning, Mr Moores, if you haven't guessed it, I'm Mr Fagin. We would like to take you with us. I would be obliged if you would get dressed – and quick!"

Moores nodded; he could not speak because of Yiddel's hold on his throat.

"When I let you go, do not attempt to make a sound because I really don't want to have to talk to you again."

Moores was in no doubt that he had no option but to do what he was told and absolutely nothing else. They watched him slip on a pair of trousers and a roll-neck pullover. He pulled on a pair of socks and shoes and was ready.

"Let's go," said Yiddel. "And not a sound…"

Harry was first into the hall. A quick wave over his shoulder told Yiddel it was all clear and the group left the room. At the lift, all four removed their masks with Moores' face pushed into the lift doors. The smoothness of the plush Hilton lift contrasted starkly with the tense atmosphere inside it. After what seemed an eternity, arriving at the ground floor they walked swiftly but calmly through the reception area out into the street and straight into the open door of the limo with Roger at the wheel. Yiddel noticed Sheila already behind the wheel of the Range Rover parked behind them. Sidney joined her and the two vehicles left the front of the hotel in tandem.

Moores was jammed into the corner of the vast interior of the stretched car by Sammy. Yiddel was the first to speak as they drove down Park Lane. "I just want to prove to you, Mr Moores, that we

148

will not be fucked about by you or any of your colleagues. If you have any thought at all of pulling a double cross on the deal - forget it. We have enough resources to find you, no matter where you go. I want you to take this little excursion with us as a warning. I do not want to have to threaten you any more than what we have done today. Do I make myself clear?"

Moores, still in a tight half-nelson grip courtesy of one of the boys, was in no doubt. "Very clear, Mr Fagin. I know that I am dealing with a very resourceful man and...aggh, please release me...I would not even attempt to...." He didn't need to finish to convince Yiddel.

"Good, I'm glad you have understood the reason for this exercise... Ok, stop the car at the next bus stop," calling out to Roger, "and let the 'gentleman' out." He pulled a five-pound note from his pocket and gave it to Moores. "Your cab fare, Mr Moores." The limo stopped for just a few seconds, and Moores needed no second invitation to 'escape' the ordeal. Visibly shaken, he stumbled out of the limo, which now sped off followed by Sheila driving the 4x4.

Two blocks away from where they dropped Moores, Roger pulled into a car park and they all got out taking their bag of gear with them to join Sheila in the Range Rover before heading back to the east side of London. Sammy later dumped the 4x4 on the border of the City and Shoreditch in a 'safe' car park, thoroughly clean of any fingerprints; he only took his gloves off as he left the vehicle. Meeting them all back at the flat where the discussion was going on about the encounter with Moores, he heard Yiddel saying, "I think the man got the message. He now realises that we could hit him anywhere we chose."

149

I feel he wouldn't try it on now, agreed?" speculated Harry. "The whole exercise proved that. I took a good look at him at that bus stop and he had literally just shat himself, he was so frightened. He knows what we are now even if he doesn't know who we are, that's obvious."

Yiddel then thanked Sheila and Roger for their part and said he hoped that it would speed up the payday for them both. They all left, the two boys back to the stall and Sheila and Roger to do their own things. Sidney stayed for a drink with Yiddel.

"What d'yer think, Sid?"

"Yeh, you got it right what you said to him, not too much and not too little, just right." Sidney was sure of that.

Just then, Yiddel's mobile rang. Yiddel lifted his eyebrows at Sidney, as much as to say: "That was quick," and answered it.

"Mr Fagin…Moores. We will settle on Friday. We will not be paid for a few weeks, but we will at least clear it up with you. We must have the pieces back from you, though, so that our man can destroy them. We don't want them to surface at another time. I will phone you tomorrow and tell you exactly the amount, which I hope will be quite generous."

All Yiddel said was, "Thank you," and clicked off.

Sidney was uncontrollable when Yiddel told him what Moores had said, repeating aloud: "Not too much and not too little!" adopting the old pose of hands out and shoulders up.

Yiddel was more cautious. "Now, we have got to be careful, Sid, now we are vulnerable. He will have us out in the open and I am still not sure if we can trust him." Sidney knew his friend had a good point.

"You're right, once money has got to be moved and placed in a certain area we will definitely have to look over our shoulders. And what do you think will be 'generous'?"

"It's got to be a nice round figure, say five to six million. I reckon they will get about ten to twelve…. Anyway, that's tomorrow, Sid. C'mon, I'll treat you to a nice salt-beef sandwich up the Hill."

"Oh, you really are the big spender everybody is talking about!" Sidney put his arm around Yiddel and they departed.

Yiddel decided to have an early shower and breakfast, and then get to the market sharpish in order to help the boys set up the stall. Saturday was a good market day. They seemed to do very well on sales on the last day of the week. Not that they really needed it. But it gave them that cover, to be trading 'legit', and boasting to all the other stall holders that they had had a good day or occasionally maybe a bad day, just like most of them. Yiddel got the stall set up with the boys. Leaving them in charge, he went over to see Ansel. As he was about to enter the café he noticed out of the corner of his eye a man watching him – a bit too intensely - then quickly look away as Yiddel responded by locking his glance upon him. 'That's funny,' he thought as he went in, 'who was he looking at?'

Once he was inside, he greeted Ansel and at the same time put himself in a position where he could observe things through the café window. The same man was still hanging around, nonchalantly, between the stalls, but definitely trying to watch for people in and around the café. As he uneasily became more aware that something here wasn't quite right, Yiddel tried to at least pay superficial attention to Ansel, who was going on about all the aggravation he'd had since his arrest and the drama over the guns.

Yiddel gave it a few minutes, hoping the 'observer' had disappeared, but a second check revealed no such thing: the man on the other side of the road was all too obviously tracking either Ansel or Yiddel, and was by far not doing a very good job of it. Yiddel turned to his friend and expressed his concern.

"Have you got anything else here, like drugs or guns?"

"Fuck off, Yiddel, what do think I am – bonkers? Why?"

"Because, Ansel, you are being watched. By a bloke on the other side of the road. Don't look yet…move over here a little bit, get me in the middle of the shop and look over my shoulder as though you are talking to me. You can just see him, tall bloke with dark, cropped hair."

Ansel was clearly taken aback. "Yeh, I see him, a big bastard in a black overcoat." His usual Jamaican exuberance was suddenly gone. "Yiddel, I am clean, man. I would not have anything here. I'd be down the road faster than anything. You know that."

Yiddel knew what to do. "Keep your eyes on him. I'll send one of the boys to front him up!"

Back at the stall, he briefed Sammy of the what and where, and the two of them went over to see the man, Yiddel leaving Sammy to make the move. Standing a short distance away, he could hear Sammy say, "Excuse me…can I help you?"

Yiddel moved a bit closer so that he could hear the answer.

"No, mate, everything's cool. I'm waiting for a friend."

"You seem to be doing a lot of your waiting looking at that café, there." Sammy pointed at Ansel's place. "Do you know the owner?" he added.

"No, I don't, but, like I just said, I'm waiting for a friend."

"Well, in that case, I suggest you fuck off and wait somewhere else because your card 'as been marked and you're frightening the

152

old ladies in the market. Get my drift, mate, or shall I call your desk sergeant and tell him what a bad job you're doing on observation duty?"

The man glared at Sammy and for one second it seemed as though he would react violently to being told what to do, particularly by what seemed to be some market trader. But, then he had second thoughts. "All right, whoever you are, have it your way," he said, and he walked off towards the main road and the police station, clearly angry at having been rumbled.

Yiddel stepped up to Sammy. "You're right, he has got to be Old Bill."

Inside the café. Ansel had been watching the scene.

"Who was he?" he asked, nervously.

"He didn't say, but I know you won't see him again," said Yiddel, pleased he had been able to help his old friend.

"Who do you think, then?" Ansel couldn't let it go.

"At a guess I'd say Old Bill, checking to see who visits you. You never know there might be someone in Hackney that they think might come your way and visit one of the brothers, so they look everywhere," was Yiddel's verdict.

Ansel looked a bit forlorn. "After all these years of staying on the right side of the law, I am now being watched."

Yiddel put a consoling arm around the big man and patted his big round face saying, with a grin, "Well, who's been a naughty boy, then?"

Ansel had to chuckle at Yiddel's justification for things as they now were. He knew he needed the big Yiddisher's advice and friendship more than ever now. He tried to laugh it off, but at the back of his mind he knew he did not like it at all. This was uncertainty and risk at their worst as far as Ansel was concerned.

10

Moore Trouble

At 10am, Yiddel's phone rang. It was Moores.

"Mr Fagin, we have arrived at a figure…which I hope will satisfy you. We are proposing four million pounds."

Yiddel kept quiet for a few seconds before answering. "Mr Moores, I thought I had made myself quite clear yesterday. We know what you will be getting, *fourteen* million pounds, which makes it a hell of a lot of US dollars. Our figure is six million pounds and that is the one and only figure we want to hear from you."

It was Moores' turn to go silent; Yiddel suspected he was checking with his colleagues.

"Very well, Mr Fagin. Six it is, and that's it. We will exchange money for the jewellery at a neutral location for both of us. We will leave you to arrange a place and call us. We will have the money by tomorrow at midday." The phone clicked, and he was gone, leaving Yiddel looking at the mobile phone and saying to it: "The soft bastard didn't even haggle!"

Calling the boys to meet him at Sidney's as soon as they were finished in the market, they were all quick to start working out the changeover. Yiddel opened the proceedings.

"Hold it; let's take this bit steady. I can't help it, but I still feel that Moores has a bundle of money in one hand and a fucking great machine-gun in the other. I still have my doubts… it just seems too easy. It's a fucking lot of money to say the least - not four million now, but six. I can't help it, gents, it may simply be that old

154

Yiddisher gut feeling, but that's the way I feel. If it runs out Ok, I will be the first to say I was wrong, but until we have the money in our hands I am not taking my eye off the ball."

Again, the boys could see the perspiration on his forehead as his mind ravaged itself with various nasty outcomes that Moores & Co. might be planning for them. "He wants us to arrange a place and a time for the exchange, so let's consider too that he has something up his sleeve. I want us to decide a *perfect* spot – for us - for the handover. Where?"

"It wants to be somewhere we can, if it goes pear shaped, get away fast," said Harry.

"Right. So what ideas have you got on venues and locations - complete with escape routes if we need them?" Yiddel sensed he had to nail this down otherwise one or all of them was going to get seriously injured. He went on.

"Central London: somewhere very busy, where we can use the whole team, which, in theory, gives us more players than he has. Let us assume that he uses what we know he has got - and that is four, possibly six, bodies. If that is the case, I think the two Yankee security guards will come into play, so let's go along those lines. We can only hope that it runs smoothly, we don't want after all this to lose the evidence and the money… and…and then we finish up with fuck all! And those bloody Yanks fuck off back with the lot."

Everyone listened to Yiddel's heated words. They hadn't seen the Master this troubled and nervous before. Harry recalled seeing him close to tears one day – when he had carelessly asked him about his parents and grandparents – just out of curiosity, nothing more, and how he had been shocked at his boss becoming so choked and unable to speak for a while afterwards. He had forgotten that day until now. Yiddel forced himself to breathe out slowly. Perhaps those troubling personal demons were at play again...

After a lengthy, uneasy pause, he continued: "Maybe you all feel the same as I do. We can lose it all by being sloppy and falling for any one of Moores' many dirty tricks. Now," regaining his composure, "Where would you say is the perfect spot?"

Sidney, who had also noticed the change in Yiddel, was the first to speak. "I'm just thinking out loud, but what about Victoria Station? It has three different underground services. Surface trains to all over. Outside, a maze of streets with buses and taxis right outside the main door."

They all sat back to consider this idea.

"Ok, let's give Victoria some thought for the place," said Yiddel. "Stop me if you think it don't sound feasible. I agree it's got a lot of exits and all that Sidney 'as said plus lots of people - two things we need. Yeh, I think it is just the place. Well done, Sid. Ok, shall we say Victoria then, gents?" They all nodded. And Yiddel got a large white board out to mark up the plan.

"Now, I want the whole team, as I said earlier, to be involved. Here we go: I want a black cab outside the main entrance with Roger in the seat. Sammy, get a cab from under the arches at Bethnal Green - the taxi companies park 'em there day and night waiting for drivers to hire them, so just take one. I want no disguises at all, but all to be suited and booted, City style. Sheila will play the most important role, she will take the money, which should be on a luggage trolley, run it out to the cab and leave with Roger. No matter what goes down in the station she must be got away. I will be the one who fronts up Moores in the middle of the station concourse. The Tom will be put into a left-luggage locker, so all I have to do is hand over the key, all right so far?"

156

Nods all round. "Sammy and Harry, I want you ready as 'blockers'. If it gets away from us, step in and deal with his heavies. Sid, I want you to be ready as our other way of getting the money out of there if Sheila is stopped in some way or other. Have a luggage trolley with you standing by. Get yourself a ticket for the shuttle to Gatwick and stand by for a train ride with the money. Ok, Sheila out the front door and Sid out through the back to the shuttle...we will take care of the middle area. How does that sound?"

"Not bad," said Sidney, impressed by the detail Yiddel could so often demonstrate in planning. "In such a short time we have a fine, little plan," he added, smiling.

"You've got a bloody cheek, Sid, you only came up with Victoria Station!" said Harry, trying not to laugh.

"Yeh, I know, but I have to lay claim to some of the planning."

"Oh thanks, Sid, without you we would of course be fucked," said Harry.

Yiddel phoned Sheila and Roger, briefed them on their roles, and left the rest to the boys to get all the necessary things that were needed, such as a taxi. He then phoned Moores to tell him where they would exchange.

"Mr Moores? Mr Fagin. We will meet you in the middle of London Victoria Station at 4pm tomorrow. By the middle, I mean under the clock on the main concourse, sharp at 4."

Moores was ready. "Fine, we'll be there," and rang off.

Yiddel had purposely said 4pm because he knew that at that time on a Friday afternoon, Victoria Station was a mass of people coming and going for the weekend, and that it would be an ideal cover for an escape into the crowds.

One thing that worried Yiddel was the size of the money parcel; he estimated from the Oxford Street caper a big bundle, as big as would fit onto a luggage trolley.

He sat and detailed on the board all the moves and places where the team would be, and after a while of studying, he was well pleased he had covered it all: the tickets for the train to Gatwick, the taxi outside the left luggage locker, the trolleys all in place - well before Moores and his crew arrived.

He thought now that Sidney's idea for the venue really was perfect. 'But I'll only tell him that if it works,' he reasoned.

Sammy went down to the railway arches on Friday morning and 'borrowed' a black cab and brought it back to Hackney, parking it where Roger would do the pick-up. Sheila had decided to add a bit of theatre to her role and applied the change to her looks. In just a few minutes, she became an old lady.

The rest went looking extremely smart in suits, as ordinary villains.

Roger left with Sheila in the cab to the station to get the ticket and to put the jewellery in the locker. The others left together in a taxi and were in place by 3.45.

As Yiddel had expected, the station was full of people rushing home from work or leaving for Gatwick airport. Yiddel met Roger outside the station and got the key to the locker from him. Roger duly parked his taxi in the taxi-rank area. Yiddel spotted what he thought might - just about - be a Sheila lookalike hanging around the area of the meet with an empty luggage trolley. Needing to take another look, he realised with no small surprise that it was her in another of her disguises. 'She's getting into this, big time,' he thought, as he checked, amidst all the confusion of travellers and commuters, that the two boys were also in place. He could now spot Sidney loitering with a trolley and was satisfied that the team were ready to rock and roll. 'Ok,' he thought, 'let's get it on.'

Looking up at the clock, he saw the time was now 3.58. He ambled around in roughly the same spot, in a broad circle, but always looking through the crowds of people hoping to catch sight of Moores approaching. Suddenly, there he was. Yiddel looked over to Sammy, and was relieved that Sammy had seen him, a subtle nod as the signal. And Harry too.

Moores strode up to Yiddel with an extended hand, but Yiddel was in no mood for shaking; he slapped it away.

"Have you got the money?" he asked, with distinct menace in his voice.

"Yes, it's being brought through the crowds by one of my men. I came on in front to meet you. And the jewellery?"

"Yes, that's also here. As soon as we check the money, you will get it."

Just then, one of the security guards – in fact, the same one that Yiddel had knocked out at the hotel - trundled up pushing a heavily-loaded luggage trolley, giving Yiddel a mean look. It somehow seemed like an extraordinarily large load to Yiddel…into whose mind came the two million from Oxford Street, which did not resemble even a fraction the size of this.

"We would like to confirm that it is what it is supposed to be," said Yiddel, keeping an eye on Moores and the guard. He nodded at Harry, who now stepped out of the crowd, to come over and start checking, whilst keeping Sammy in reserve, hidden by the crowds of permanently jostling people. Yiddel told Harry to check all of the bundles. Furtively producing a blade from his pocket, Harry carefully but swiftly slit open each bundle, checking they all contained fifty-pound notes, and using the bodies of Yiddel, Moores and the heavy to hide from Joe Public what was really happening under their very noses.

"All fifties," he announced.

Looking across at Sidney, Yiddel beckoned him over, and, leaving his standby trolley, he pushed through the crowd. Yiddel gave Sidney the loaded trolley, and he and Harry pushed the haul in the direction of the Gatwick train. Yiddel had chosen the back way instead of the long front route with Sheila. Sidney assumed the switch was because of the size of the loaded trolley as he proceeded to head for the train.

"Now, Mr Moores, here is the key for your stuff, it's in a left-luggage locker over there." Yiddel pointed towards the far side of the vast station. "Don't worry, it is all there. If you like, you can send your man to get it to prove that I am genuine, even if I am, in your eyes at any rate, still only a common thief."

"I trust you, Mr Fagin, I think I know you by now." Moores exuded confidence despite his surely not being used to this kind of situation... "We will go together!"

And so Yiddel Davis and Gerald Moores walked off towards the left-luggage area. Yiddel noticed that Harry had gone with Sidney to help him on the Gatwick train. 'Good,' he thought, 'that covers Sidney and gets the money away from here.' Yiddel knew that Sammy would not leave his back uncovered and a little look over his shoulder as they were on the way to the locker assured him that he was not far behind him. Moores' heavy was also close to his master's back, the four of them now easing across the heaving station.

At the locker, Moores withdrew the bag. Calmly, it seemed, he stuck his hand in it, withdrawing a handful of the pasted gems. A quick look was all he appeared to need to be satisfied that all the pieces were there.

"Very nice to meet you at long last, Mr Fagin. And good to do business with you, too, if not somewhat unexpectedly."

"Unexpectedly?" Yiddel was incredulous. "This was your plan before you left America. Your problem would have been if no one had hit you, then you would have been in trouble. You know as well as me that I have done you a big favour, Mr Moores."

Yiddel turned his back on this villain and headed for Roger's taxi at the main entrance, anxious to get well away.

"Right, Roger, head for Gatwick, we will pick the others up there."

Yiddel signalled for Sheila to go home and briefly watched her leave, keeping her wig on and walking with just a slight stoop, 'so convincingly with her old-lady make-up,' he thought, again impressed at her ability for self-transformation. Assuming that all was well, Yiddel, Sammy and Roger then drove out of the station to head for Gatwick to meet Sidney, Harry and the money.

Traffic was heavy and it was a while before they arrived at Gatwick train station. Worse, upon arrival, there was no sign of Sidney or Harry. Their unease turned to a gnawing anxiety as they searched in vain all over the station area and the terminal building – perhaps, for some reason, they were waiting there? After a fruitless search, Yiddel decided to go back to London, assuming they had decided it best, for reasons best known to themselves, to make their own way back to Hackney.

Yiddel's thoughts were sharply interrupted as his mobile rang, just as they were leaving the airport. It was an unnerved Harry. "Yiddel, we've been done over…whoever it was tied us up and bundled us into the back of a van at Victoria, at the back of the goods yard. We've only just now been released by some railway blokes, who heard me banging on the side of the van. I had to tell them that we had been left there by some of our mates who were fucking about, otherwise they would have called the Old Bill." He had to pause for breath, and Yiddel could only imagine the trauma they had been through.

"Shit, Yiddel, we fucked up. What do you want us to do?"

"Is Sidney Ok?" asked an anxious Yiddel.

"Yeh, he's Ok, but the two of us are bollocksed, we have lost the money, Yiddel! The whole fucking lot, gone!"

A stunned Yiddel with his brain racing into overdrive as to who was responsible told Harry to go back to Sidney's place and wait for them there.

The other two sat patiently for Yiddel to come off the phone to find out what the conversation was all about.

"Sidney and Harry have been done over. Someone's jumped 'em at the back of the station as they were going to get the Express, took the money and left 'em tied up in the back of a van. A railway worker has just freed them. What a bastard, I thought we were home and dry and now it has really gone tits up and fucking pear shaped all in one go!"

"Did Harry or Sid recognise anybody, Yiddel?" Sammy wanted to know.

"He didn't say. Wait till we get back to Sidney's place and then we can try and sort it out."

All the way back to London, the three sank into a depressive silence. Roger was driving, he too knowing when to say nothing. Yiddel was deep in thought, and feelings of revenge, once

162

exclaiming, "Moores, you bastard, you fucking bastard! You are dead for this!"

Yet they seemed to get back to London in record time. After dropping them off at Sidney's, Roger took the taxi back to the arches in Bethnal Green and left it close to where Sammy had borrowed it, before heading for home.

Sidney was sitting behind his desk with his head in his hands as Yiddel and Sammy walked into his office. Harry was sitting in the corner looking drained. They both looked as though they had lost blood, they were so grey-looking.

"You all right?" asked a concerned Yiddel, addressing both men. "You didn't get a spank or anything, did yer?"

Both men shook their heads and remained silent, still in a state of shock that was too deep to allow them to be able to talk about what had happened.

"Sam, do me a favour, make some tea and put a drop of scotch in all the cups," said Yiddel.

After they had all had a swig of the hot laced tea, Yiddel started the questioning.

"What happened initially after you walked away from me?"

Harry, more recovered than poor old Sid, spoke for both men.

"We were pushing the trolley, we had a job trying to get through the crowds to the train…anyway, we was doing quite well, really whizzing along once we got it moving. I thought it was you who caught us up, I got a push from the back, I turned round and it was a bloke I hadn't seen before, an' he said to keep going, to get over to the right of the departure area. I looked back again and now there was four altogether on us. One on my back, one on Sid and two others covering them. They pushed us once we was round the goods yard to go faster to the van. We was nearly running by now.

163

We got to the van; one opened the back doors, and two of them threw us in and tied us up with tape. The big bastard said that if we made a noise now it would be the last noise we would ever make. So I thought, 'fuck it, we're captured, well away from the station and we won't get a prize for being brave right now,' so we both shut up and did as told. The only thing I can say about the one on me is that he spoke with an accent, not American, more like Irish. Know what I mean?"

Yiddel nodded and turned to Sidney. "Anything you want to add to that, Sid?"

"No, it all happened so fast that I didn't even have a chance to look round at them. The only time I looked at them was when we was in the van and I only see these four big bastards with their collars pulled up to their faces and taping me hands up. Who do you reckon it was, Yiddel?"

"It's got to be Moores, it's got to be, no one else could have been set up for a hoist like that without the information as to what we was up to. Fucking hell, I thought we was being clever and now we have lost the fucking lot. That slippery bastard Moores has got everything - all the money and the Tom. Just as I had feared!" Yiddel seemed defeated, about to give up on the whole life of crime and capers. "I think I will listen to that inner voice next time," he added, despondently.

They all sat drinking the hot tea, listening to Yiddel and working on their own theories as to how the enemy had pulled it off. They all came up with the same answer as Yiddel. "It's got to be Moores!"

Yiddel started back to the beginning of the meeting at the station and put the pictures in his mind as to where all the players were at the time when the final exchange took place.

164

"Right...listen up and let me talk while I think out loud and see what we can get from it. Ok, we were there early, about five minutes before Moores and his heavy with the money trolley caught up. Sid was about four yards away to one side. Sheila was about four yards on the other side. You two," (looking at the boys) "were well placed as cover and Roger in the cab outside. I could have nodded at Sheila to take the trolley out front to Roger, but I did not. I thought that getting Sidney away to Gatwick would be the best bet and clear of any action, but they had that covered as well, because as you said, Harry, they was on you in seconds. If there had been only one little gang they would not have been able to get through the crowds so quick. That makes it two gangs, covering both sides with Moores and his minder in the middle."

Yiddel paused to collect his thoughts. "There could have been a third team, just in case. So, he had all the bases covered, didn't he? It can only be Moores. So Moores owes us six extra-large ones. His other master card was taking Sammy and me to the locker, giving them more time to take care of Sid and Harry. He wanted us to go to the locker area; he drew us away from going after Sid with the money and protecting it. Which left only you two to get the train and get mugged in the process. This man is one clever fucker, he has turned us over good and proper, and I bet he's laughing his fucking head off that he's done this on our own turf. You can bet your life that all that money will be put back into the bank. The rubbish jewellery is on the bottom of the Thames and the whole team is on a plane right now heading for America, laughing their heads off that they have fucked the Limeys. Well, gentlemen, the East End mob – us - have just been promoted out of the English league and we are about to extend our business interests into the United States of America. We are going after Mr Moores big time.

I will not be fucked by a Yankee prat like him. We frightened the life out of him once and we will do it again, but this time get him proper and get back what he owes us."

11

The United States of Revenge

The next day brought an all-out meeting of the core team and its new members. Yiddel asked Ansel and Elvis if they were interested in joining the team with a possibility of earning a lot of money. They jumped at the opportunity, along with Sheila and Roger coming in on more of a full-time basis. Sheila and Roger were also keen on going after Moores, as it was their money as well that the man had stolen from them.

Ansel was delighted to be included as money was a bit short after his recent brush with the law. He said he needed to get away from the market for a while and that he needed a break and would enjoy working for his friend. Elvis jumped at the thought of working for his long-time mate, 'as well as the Lord,' he said, with a chuckle. So there they were. Yiddel had forged a few more links to his chain of villains.

Sammy was sent back to *The Hilton* to see if the enemy had all left. Exactly as Yiddel had guessed, Sammy phoned him from the hotel to say that the reception desk had told him that Mr Moores' suite of rooms had been vacated since yesterday morning, and they had left no forwarding address, only to say that they were all travelling back to the USA.

Yiddel arranged for the whole team, including the new members, to meet at the boys' flat that night. He got Harry to stock up with beers and food, cold drinks and coffee for everyone. The meeting got underway at 8pm. Yiddel opened the meeting, explaining to Ansel and Elvis what had gone down and what had happened over the last couple of weeks. Now they all knew the score. Yiddel opened his plan as to what was going to be done to get the money back and what they were going to do to get even.

"Right, here we go. My plan basically is for us all to go to America and to get back what has been taken by Moores & Co, that is, six million pounds. I am going to put a plan together that will not only do that, but will expose Moores as the deceiving liar he is, and put paid to his scheme for continuing to cheat us out of what's ours. I know we are no better than he is, but at least we are what we are and that is open villains. This man has deceived the Americans by putting on an exhibition of artefacts that do not exist. I should think he is heavily sponsored by the government to promote the country, which he does quite well, with a load of bogus crap. How he got it set up, we have to guess. He must have friends in high places. What I would like you all to do is to put a plan together so that we can shake him. I will find out where he is based, I can do that quite easy, I have a friend who has a contact at the American Embassy, so once we get that we can plan where we start. Right, anyone got an idea to kick off with?"

Sidney, now completely recovered from his bitter experience at the station, opened. "Once Moores and his cronies are back in the States, I think they will feel pretty safe…what I suggest is that we lift him like we did before, but this time don't drop him off with a warning like 'pay up or you're dead', but this time hold him until the money turns up. We are taking a huge chance in doing it because kidnapping in the US is a big offence and we will be putting our heads on the block if it goes tits up, but we have got to fight fire with fire and this man dearly needs a lesson - from us."

"Yeh, I think we all agree on that, Sid" said Yiddel.

168

Elvis was the next to endorse Sidney's plan. "Once we have the man, we have got to make it quite clear to his deputy, whoever he is, that 'No money, no man' is the bottom line."

"So!" said Yiddel. "We will go for a straightforward snatch and detain plan on two issues: money for the man and a total exposure of the exhibition and all its rotten contents. We know or we think we know that the jewellery is at the bottom of the Thames. We have lost the evidence to prove that the stuff on exhibition was a load of crap. There was a lot of stuff in the other cabinets that we did not touch, that also could be rubbish. I wonder where that is, or did we take it all and not just the top shelf stuff? I want to say to all of you that as far as I am concerned I want no expense spared on this caper. I personally will sponsor the whole operation, and when we get what we are going there for, we split the whole lot into equal shares. That should give us all seven hundred and fifty thousand pounds each. I will get Moores to pay all the expenses on top of what he owes us. All I ask of you is to keep on your toes, think – before acting - all the time; once we start the operation if you can add some extra detail to it, do it, as long as it doesn't harm the final plan. So, are we all happy about that and going to get the bastard?"

Everyone in the room was in total agreement with the plan.

"I'm now going to phone my friend to get the address of Moores, so all get stuck in with the drink and food." Yiddel thumbed through his dog-eared contact book and dialled a number.

"Hallo, Jim…yeh, Yiddel. Look, can you do me a favour and ask your mate at the American Embassy to get me an address of a man in the States that I would like to talk to. Thank you." Yiddel returned the man's good wishes. "The man's name is Moores, Gerald Moores, he was here recently, he's an exhibition director.

Ok, Jimbo, call me back on this number, Ok mate… I'll wait for your call."

Yiddel gave him the mobile number and hung up.

"Right, let's leave him doing that. I've just realised I haven't eaten all day; let's have one of these lovely ham sandwiches," and then, with a sideways glance at Elvis, "Have you had one, Elvis?"

Thirty minutes later, the phone rang. Sammy answered it. "It's your mate," he whispered, passing the phone over to Yiddel.

"Hallo, Jim, any luck? Great. Gerald Moores?…34th Street…Statton Building, New York City. Yeh, got that…phone number 001…4258…97876. Ok, Jim, that's it. Look, send your mate a case of the best scotch and a case for you, too, and I'll come in tomorrow and settle up. Thanks, Jim. God bless, mate."

Yiddel sat back, tossing the little mobile phone back to Sammy and his face now one big smile. "Lady and gentlemen, it's not what you know it's 'who you know what knows'. Our mate in the embassy - he works there on security, Gord bless 'is cotton socks - has just given us what we want. Now we know where Moores is and where we are going: New York! Is everyone Ok with that? I want to get away as fast as we can. The longer we leave it…well, could be bad for us if he suddenly moves on and we lose him. Can you leave the café, Ansel?"

"Yeh, no prob, I'll ask my sister-in-law to look after it while I 'have a break,' Yiddel."

"Elvis?"

"Yeh, I can get away anytime, we have our four deputies at the school. I will just say I am visiting relatives in America. Oh, by the way, in New York, we will be very welcome. My other half of the group, you know, the ones we did a favour for, he lives there."

"That's handy," Yiddel noted with distinct satisfaction. "So, we have friends there too? Good stuff. 'as everyone got a passport?"

Everyone was Ok for travelling and so the plan began. Sammy got the job of booking the journey for them all, including a good hotel in Manhattan.

Harry handed the stall over to the man who, desperate for work, was now thrilled to be in work, even if it was only for a short time. Harry told him they were going to America to buy toys for the stall. Yiddel told no one anything. Sidney left his brother-in-law to run the transport side of the business and the foreman to run the repairs. Sheila and Roger were free agents and ready to go at any time.

Two days later, the whole team was at Heathrow boarding a British Airways flight to JFK, New York.

Yiddel wasted no time. He was hungry for revenge, and for the first time in his adult life had felt the agony of failure. And it had hit him hard. At night, he saw his parents laughing and joking just minutes before the crash. And then the blackness. Yiddel dreaded the blackness, but at least it signified the end of the nightmare. But, it was the same each night, and the impact was wearing him down. He just wanted to get going to America to find and punish Moores – whose face now cropped up in Yiddel's nightmares. It had become the face of the lorry driver who had taken his parents from him. The Devil.

The three days and nights of waiting for the New York flight were at last at an end. Yiddel, tired but relieved to begin the hunt for Moores, slept virtually the entire flight across the Atlantic, and, arriving at the huge American airport, started to regain his energies, confidence and affability – all essential Yiddel qualities to the core that the team admired so much. Everyone was now feeling the momentum that was unmistakably picking up as they all focused on the job in hand. It was great to be in America and soon they were all in two taxis heading for New York City centre, checking in at *The Hilton* hotel.

The first thing Yiddel did, once they were settled into their rooms, was to check out the Statton Building. Sheila decided to walk with Yiddel to see the city. And there, unmistakably, right on the front hall corporate names' board of the Statton Building was GERALD MOORES Inc. They did not stay there long in case they were spotted.

"And that," said Yiddel, "would spoil the surprise that is in store for Mr Moores..."

The next morning the whole team was given tasks to do. Elvis was despatched to his contact whom he briefed as to why they were there in New York. Ansel and Yiddel went back to the Statton Building to check the ins and outs of the place, front and rear entrances and exits, summing up quickly the general layout. The boys were given the task of checking out car hire companies that supplied eight-seater vehicles. Sheila and Roger were sent into the building - she was looking very attractive in the guise of searching for a client on the same floor as Moores' office - such that they could find out the floor layout and where exactly his office was. Sidney was sent shopping for 'special purpose equipment'.

Later in the day, everybody met back at *The Hilton* in Yiddel's room to put together their findings and results.

At the rear of the Statton Building, Yiddel and Ansel had found the service area absolutely buzzing with people, all involved in the smooth running of the place. As Yiddel said, "We could move a

172

company of marines through there and no one would take a bit of notice…the back service area is our exit point, and it's also very good for a car to wait at."

Sheila reported that the Moores business was on the ninth floor. He had one door well marked with his name on it, sharing the floor with six other companies. She said that three lifts serviced the ninth, but only one of the three went to the basement and then through to the serviced bays at the back, which Roger had looked at for parking a car. "Plenty of room," he confirmed.

The boys had found a no-nonsense car hirer in Harlem, cash on the nail, no questions asked. No need to show licences or passports. Sidney had got all the things Yiddel had listed. Elvis said that his contact would help in any way he could. He hired them a massive eight-seater with room for more.

Yiddel, now that he had all the details and gear, started to put the plan together for the morning of the next day. Sheila was told to make a phone call to Moores' office and speak to a secretary in order to check that Moores would be in the office because Sheila's boss had a personal call to make to him and it was important that he should be there. Which had more truth about it than any other subtle wording could convey. "Oh yes," the innocent secretary had said. "He will be in at his usual time of 8.30am."

"Good," said Yiddel. "Sammy, you and Roger go and get the car and bring it back here tonight, and Roger, you keep the key and park it in the hotel car park. Elvis, phone your man and ask him where we can be alone with our mate for a while, somewhere quiet. I don't want us being disturbed."

Sidney had purchased six walkie-talkie sets and clothing that were to be used by the key players.

173

"You must stay in radio contact at all times. If I ask you something, just give me a 'Yes' or a 'No,' nothing else. I want to keep the channel clear in case we need to move fast."

Turning to the two boys, he said, "Once we are on the ninth floor, put on the overalls and gloves as quick as you can. I will go straight into his office and take him out; if anyone tries to stop us, you stop them…by a word or a slap. Now, Ansel, you guard that back door. I will call you on your radio that we are coming down. The minute you see us, make sure the yard is clear and then join us to push him on, but before you do that make sure that no one is coming at us from behind and then, as I say, join us."

Yiddel continued, now in full flow and clearly in command of every aspect of the detail going through his mind. "Ok, Sheila, you stay on the front entrance in the main hall. If anything is not right, call me by saying 'Problem - Front'…if all is sweet, say nothing, and by that I know the front is Ok. After we are out with him, I will say 'GO'. You leave the building as if to go shopping; we will see you back at the hotel later. Sid, you stay with Roger, radio on and listening, again, if anything sounds bad …fuck off and get away. Sammy and Harry: I want you to play yard minders; if nothing, get in the car." He paused, as was his custom in a prep for a big job like this. "Ok, my merry men! That's it until tomorrow morning - a nice early start. Breakfast at seven. Right, let's have a drink and some dinner."

While they were at dinner, Elvis's friend phoned. Elvis quietly took the call at the table, his words drowned out by all the deliberate small talk of the others. After a brief chat, he hung up and told Yiddel that his friend owned a small warehouse in Brooklyn that they could use. He was sending over the directions on how to get there to the hotel by taxi.

174

The plan was now complete; even so, Yiddel held had a final briefing as to how they would be dealing with Moores. The failure at Victoria still hung heavily over him.

Sleep that final night was brief. Everybody woke up very early, but kept to the timings in the plan. And, now, at 8.15am, the whole team was fed, rehearsed and ready to roll. *The Hilton* was just three blocks from the Statton Building. They were there in ten minutes. Roger drove down the side of the huge building, letting everybody out to make their own way to front or back as intended. Roger then slid the motor into a bay at the back and waited. Yiddel and the two boys headed for the front hall, Sammy carrying the bag with the clothes, while the others moved on to their fixed places. Sidney decided to stay with Sheila and provide back-up in the main hall.

Once they were in the elevator, Yiddel and the boys swiftly changed into the overalls, masks and gloves. Arriving at the ninth, they went straight to the door marked 'Moores Inc'. They checked each other over, making sure they were all suitably covered - and looking even more menacing in their masks. Satisfied, Yiddel gave the thumbs up and opened the office door.

The young secretary was sitting behind her desk, casually reading some papers. Only now did she glance up – and the sight she beheld was not one she could at first comprehend - terrified beyond words, she froze as three masked men swiftly and stealthily entered the office. Yiddel bounded over to her and before she could scream had put his hand over her mouth and held her tight. The shock of it all seemed to induce her to faint. They left her seated in her chair with her head on the desktop as though, in some weird way, she was asleep, and they now headed grimly for Moores' room and revenge.

As they entered the room, he automatically looked up, that faint, semi-false executive smile on his thin lips, clearly assuming it was his attractive young secretary, but the sight of three hooded men coming towards him erased that smile very quickly. A look of disbelief – then, with horror, he realised who it was - he had been on the receiving end of targeting by Yiddel's gang before, but clearly had never thought that an amateur Limey gang could ever pursue him to New York.

Yiddel now grabbed hold of Moores by the ears, brutally and without any offer of clemency. Sammy took Moores' coat off the stand and threw it at him as Yiddel's voice rang out loud and clear. "You didn't think you would see us again, eh, Moores? Thought we were dumb-fuck Brits who wouldn't be able to follow you, you arrogant fucker! I've a good mind to pull your fucking ears off just for starters. Put your jacket on, you bastard, you're coming with us, and I will warn you now, one word or movement out of place and my friend here will cheerfully shoot you in the back of your head! Is that clear?"

Moores nodded vigorously and seemed too terrified to speak, as well he might. Looked extremely frightened and barely able to walk, he was led away past his unconscious secretary whom he glanced at, not knowing what had been done to her – as far as appearance went, she looked dead. Harry took a look at her to make sure she was breathing and not in a position where her breathing was impaired by her slumped posture. Moores did not see this check by Harry as Yiddel slipped him out of the office and in to the hall, where Sidney was holding the service lift. 'Well done,' thought Yiddel. To Moores, seeing all the gang members expertly covered up and working together in an extremely well-oiled operation, this was the last day of his life.

In the lift, Yiddel clicked his radio, asked for 'All Clear', and got a 'Yes' from the others. The lift went right down to the basement and they were out through the back doors and taking their masks off immediately prior to entering the yard. Quickly, they marched on with an unresisting Moores. This was going well; no one paid any attention to them as they walked through the throng of busy service people, all shouting and calling to fellow workers as to where received goods needed to be unloaded and stacked. The last thing Yiddel wanted was heroics from these people; he wanted it just the way it was - calm.

Roger had all the doors open on each side of the eight-seater, and they bundled in, Yiddel giving Moores a hearty push to speed him up. Sheila, after covering the front hall, had told Sidney to go and join the team, which he did, and she then left the front hall, after giving Yiddel the affirmative, and 'went shopping'.

Moores was blindfolded as he got in the vehicle, which now smoothly eased out of the service area. Having studied the route to perfection, Roger knew exactly the best way to the warehouse. Suddenly, Moores spoke. "Where are you taking me?"

"We are taking you to a place of execution," came the grim reply. Moores visibly trembled and sank into the seat. "It is the last place that you will be on this earth...unless of course you start realising that we are now very pissed off. We have been taken for fucking idiots and will not be taken so again. Who the fucking hell did you and your clever fucking colleagues think they were dealing with? But, I tell you this - you and them got it fucking wrong, my old mate, because now you are going to be well and truly dealt with."

Yiddel gave what he said to Moores a chance to sink in, making him the can carrier for the group.

"This time, Moores, if you do not settle with us...with the money, your life will finish in the Hudson River with a very heavy weight tied to you to make sure you don't float. I hope that while you are on this journey, you will take it all on board and come to a decision very quickly because, and I can assure you of this, your last moments of life before you die drowning are going to be pure fucking hell and you'll end up being glad just to get it over with."

They drove on in silence except for the audible trembling of the captive Moores. Yiddel, putting a finger to his lips asking for silence from the group, let what he had said to Moores sink in properly. After another ten minutes, they arrived at the 'small' warehouse located alongside the famous river. By their standards, this American-scale warehouse was enormous, and momentarily they all gaped at it in awe. 'Well, whatever,' thought Yiddel, 'it makes little difference.' It was, after all, situated far enough from prying eyes, and all Moores could hear was the noise of the Hudson river traffic once the vehicle's doors opened. Sensing the river, and recalling what Yiddel had said, he reasoned he was now very close to what could be the end of his life, and drowning with a heavy weight attached to his beaten and battered body was not the way he wanted it to end.

Another cloth bag was put over his head as Roger drove, very slowly now, into the huge expanse of empty, eerie space within the warehouse, deliberately going around in two circles: the first one way and the second the other, deliberately adding to the disorientation of the man inside. The boys pulled him from the car, no gentle touch for this bastard. Yiddel pointed to a pile of sacks along the back wall to throw him onto. The large doors of the cavernous warehouse were closed with a shrieking noise as they slid on a very oil-less track, incidentally adding to their victim's torment.

"Have you had time to think, Mr Moores, or shall we start the persuasion, which will start with you being plugged into the mains electricity by your toes? But don't let me rush you, think of all your clever fucking colleagues who advised you in London, just chew on it and when you are ready, when you can't endure anymore, let us know."

Yiddel pointed to Sammy to make some noise as though they were preparing some equipment. Sammy found a pile of chain and an old cable and made slight, but realistic, sounds as if some sort of lifting gear was being prepared. Slight sounds maybe, but inside the empty warehouse they generated into monstrous contortionisms in the victim's sightless imagination, and the painful echoing off the walls was magnified to a score of a hundred-fold on the rebound.

They all stood around while Sammy, now with Harry helping, indulged in more of these 'preparing' noises, Sidney giving off little whispers as though they were concocting the finale of Moores; added to the tension and pressure of being hooded and not knowing when the predicted fate would take place, he was now a broken man.

After a few minutes, Moores managed a few words. "Mr Fagin...are you there?"

Yiddel grunted, "Yes."

"You have me in a position...that you know as well as I, that there is only one solution to. You will get your money...I can see that we completely underestimated you and your gang."

Silence descended. "Yes, you are right what you said about my colleagues and...stupidly, I took their advice and now it is I and not

179

them who is left facing my death. Please - I am promising you that I will deliver the money personally to you – please!"

"Well, this is your last chance to play fair with us. I still have a mind to finish you off right now, you arrogant fucker. The next time - if you do not do what you now say - there will be no blindfolds, no car rides, no more talking because you will be dead before you hit the pavement, and that could be anywhere, anytime. If you get it wrong this time, I guarantee that you will be dead inside a week. I am a very wealthy man, I will not have your blood on my hands, I will go over the river and pay someone here in America to come over the bridge from Harlem and do it for me, I don't care how much he charges me to do it – and there are lots of them over there who will happily kill you, no questions asked. If anything happens to me or any of my team while we are still in New York, it will be on your head. I will not be fucked about any more; you did it once and made us look like fucking fools...because I trusted you - but no more. Am I coming over loud and clear?"

"Yes you are," pleaded a very disturbed Moores, now on his knees and clearly starting to break completely. "Please...let me go and I will make you this promise now: the money, all six million pounds of it...will be delivered, with no catches, I assure you...to anywhere you say...please, don't kill me!"

"I am very reluctant, Mr Moores, to let you go without giving you a fucking good hiding, knowing how you turned us over in London. I will be true to my word; you will be dead in a week if you fuck with me this time. I don't want any guards; I don't want any dramas, just you and me in a fair exchange. I gave you back that pile of shit you called jewellery so you could keep your name in the States, so play the game with us and let me never see you again after the deal is done. Oh, by the way, the final figure is now *seven* million pounds. A little learning curve for you. It's up to you now, it's literally the money or your life. And yes, your colleagues have just cost you another million."

Yiddel signalled to all the team to meet him outside the warehouse. Once they were all assembled, far enough so that Moores could not hear, he put it to them, wanting feedback to the way it seemed to be going.

"I couldn't have put it better, you have laid your cards out on the table, as you say, the money or his life," declared Sidney, confidently.

Sammy was next: "It sounded good to me, he is shitting himself, he thought he was going into the river."

Harry, in his usually more reflective way said, "You wouldn't really kill him, Yiddel?"

Ansel chipped in, "No, but I fucking will."

Yiddel smiled, slapping Ansel on the back and said: "Ok, let's get him back to the city centre. When we get there, Roger, stop at a busy subway station. Sammy - you get out with Moores, keep the blindfold and the bag on his head. Roger, drive off with us, leaving Sammy with the man. Talk to him, Sam, say something like: 'Stand still, Mr Moores,' and then quickly walk away into the subway. Leave him with the bag on his head, with you fucking off smartly."

They all went back into the warehouse, making more noise. "Ok, Mr Moores, we have decided to trust you once again. I should think you are relieved to hear that. You will not die today, anyway not by my hand. Now the money. I want it in large notes, I should think it would be very difficult for you to get that amount in pounds so dollars it will be...the equivalent of seven million UK pounds. Is that clear? Tell me it's not and I will take the gun and personally shoot you in the fucking head right now!"

"Yes, Mr Fagin, perfectly clear," gasped Moores, truly grateful – it seemed – to have had his life spared, yet he believed it could still go against him. "I will have the money for you the day after tomorrow at my office and there will be only me and my secretary there...of that, you can be assured. I don't want any more fuss. I will take care of what happened this morning in my office with my secretary. You have my phone number...please, call me tomorrow and I will tell you what time the money will be ready to pick up."

Sammy grabbed Moores by the scruff of the neck and forcibly marched him to the car, the man being now so weak from his ordeal he could barely walk unaided. They all jumped on board and Roger drove out into the main traffic heading for the city centre. The car pulled up at the first busy subway entrance Roger saw. Sammy got out, firmly taking Moores with him.

"Goodbye, Mr Moores, for now," Yiddel's tone of voice was unequivocal as he got out. Sammy spoke to Moores: "Stand still, don't even think of saying or doing anything."

And then he swiftly disappeared into the subway, leaving Moores alone. Yiddel told Roger he would wait to see the final act. Sammy walked away nonchalantly. Yiddel then told Roger to go. Roger sped away as Yiddel watched a small crowd gathering around Moores – clearly waiting for this 'street entertainer' to start doing his thing, 'a nice little degradation for such as high and mighty crook,' thought Yiddel.

Roger and Harry took the car back to the hiring company, and returned to the whole team, who now met for a well-earned lunch in the hotel grill. Several bottles were opened and consumed. Sheila had treated herself to a dress and a coat. "I could get used to this life, you know, doing my shopping in New York," she remarked

182

with obvious satisfaction. By the end of the lunch all the members of the team were, as Yiddel put it, 'happily pissed'.

They all decided to do their own thing in the afternoon. Yiddel phoned Moores at 3pm to find out exactly what time the money would be ready.

"Mr Moores, please," he said to the secretary, feeling that he should ask about her present condition, but deciding to pass on that.

"May I ask who is calling, sir?" she answered, in a shaky voice.

"Tell him it's Mr Fagin."

Within seconds, Moores answered the phone. "Mr Fagin, if you would be here at 2pm tomorrow I will have it ready to go." He was virtually breathless with the tension he felt.

Yiddel had been thinking about how the money could be transferred, and Moores' office was definitely not the best place.

"I want the money sent to an address tomorrow, which I will give you when I arrive at your office, so have all the money standing by in a car to be sent there at 2pm," he instructed. "All of my people will be operational covering every move until the money is placed in our hands. I only hope for your sake it will go very smoothly. I will see you in your office, and please don't forget my threat, if it goes tits up then you have a week to live."

Yiddel hung up and immediately was thinking of a drop-off spot. Somewhere in the open, car to car, somewhere quiet. He decided to take advice from Elvis' friend. And so, Elvis and Yiddel took a yellow taxi to go there - a very large photographic retail business on 7th Street. Yiddel was amazed to see the business being run by a rabbi or at least they looked like rabbis. Elvis introduced him to his uncle. Yiddel for the first time found out that it was not just a friend, but this lot were family. All of them looked, to Yiddel, as though they had just arrived from Israel. Business seemed good

- the shop inside was so busy that customers waiting to be served were queuing up outside it.

"You didn't tell me you had family in New York, Elvis?" said Yiddel, still shaking hands with the Uncle.

Uncle's eyes opened wide looking at Yiddel and said, "What did you call him?"

"I called him Elvis, from when we were kids at school. Benjamin used to do a fantastic impression of the great man, so the name stuck. All our mates in the East End know him as Elvis!"

Yiddel had just met Michael Katzman, head of the family that ran the largest retail and mail order business in the western world - selling anything photographic and, in the modern world, an increasing amount of new technology. It amused Yiddel to see this formally dressed religious man selling modern equipment.

The old man was highly amused that his rabbi nephew 'did a great impersonation of Elvis Presley'.

Yiddel could see that outside the shop, there were trucks from all over the USA and Canada.

"Uncle, do you send goods all over the country?" he enquired, now deep in thought, which could mean only one thing.

"Country? We send equipment to all over the world," Katzman replied, enjoying the impression it clearly was making on his new acquaintance.

Yiddel had been thinking about how they were going to get the money back to England and this, he thought, could be the answer.

"How long would it take to deliver a crate of cameras to England?" he asked.

"I can have the order on a flight in two days, delivered straight to the shop. We do it all the time, as long as the duty and taxes are paid and the appropriate custom declaration forms are on the crate

184

- it will go through with no hold-ups. Dealers in the UK buy from us because we can sell it cheaper even after duty and despatch has been paid, and they get a chance to make a few pounds on cameras, computers - in fact, anything I stock!" The old Yiddish gesture followed, up went the shoulders and out went the arms.

"If I bought some simple cameras that I can sell in the market on our stall and a couple of laptops off you, could I put some of my other...shopping in the box too?" asked Yiddel.

"As long as it isn't drugs, that's Ok. So, for a small charge, yes, of course." The Uncle was deadly serious.

"Of course," echoed Yiddel. "Right, what have you got that will be a nice little earner for the stall, Uncle, for cash?"

For an hour, Yiddel and Michael Katzman sorted out the products. Yiddel bought the whole team the latest digital camera and a laptop computer for Sammy and Harry. He had heard them talking about them on the flight over and, taking advice from Katzman, bought them one each.

"Where do you pack the boxes, Uncle?"

"Here at the back, in the shipping bay," he said.

"Good, thanks for the deal. I have enjoyed meeting you and doing business with you," announced a relieved Yiddel. "We will see you tomorrow afternoon and I'll settle up for all of it."

Elvis and Yiddel left Michael Katzman with their order to get the next part set up for the next day.

Yiddel got Sammy and Harry to go back to the car hirer again and organise a small truck and a car for the next morning. They brought them back to the hotel and parked them in the car park.

Once the whole team were together, Yiddel drew up the plan for the last part of the trip. Roger was the car driver and Sammy would drive the truck. He planned where to make the change over from Moores' car to his.

"Somewhere quiet and not far from Uncle's," requested Yiddel, looking at Elvis. "So that we don't have a long drive?" Roger was again studying his map of the city. Yiddel pointed out where Katzman's shop was.

"I've got a place about a mile from there," said Roger. "Look there!" showing Yiddel the spot he had selected. It was on the city side of the river on the edge of the financial area, with lots of small streets.

"That's it, Elvis, give Uncle a ring and ask him what's it like in that area?" said Yiddel.

Elvis phoned Katzman and spoke to him for about a minute.

"Yeh, it's a quiet area, only bars and small offices."

Yiddel checked the name and found it was called Wellington Street.

"Ok, we have a meeting spot for the exchange; I'll phone Moores in the morning and give him the name of the street at the time when the money leaves his place in the afternoon, so that they can't set up a surprise for us. No matter what we have said to him, I still do not trust that bastard, and no matter what we have threatened, I still feel that he could try another of his Victoria Station tricks. Anyway, Roger, tomorrow, you take the car, with Ansel riding shotgun. Ansel, when you get there, keep your eyes open for anything that does not seem right. Once the money turns up, park up, but stay inside the car. Sammy, you will drive the truck with Harry as your minder. I said that I would be at Moores' office at 2pm, but I am going to change that. Sheila, you go with Elvis and go straight up to the ninth floor to his office and tell him you have got to call me once the money is on the move from the Statton

186

Building. Once you have made the call to me, leave the building; if anyone stops you or nothing seems right, give me a call on the radios. If all is Ok, get away and call me to say 'Ok,' that's all, nothing else but 'Ok', and head back to the hotel. Elvis - you wait in the front hall of the Statton, act like you're looking for a business name on the board, watch for Sheila to pass you, all going well alone, and join her outside where you can watch her making the 'Ok' call to me. Once she is clear grab a taxi to Uncle's and wait there.

"Right, who's next?" he asked, looking around the group. "Sidney, you and me will go to Wellington Street and hang around for the delivery. Once the money arrives, Roger and Ansel will stay in the car and as soon as it looks Ok to do so, get out and assist Harry and Sammy on the next bit. Yeh, once the car arrives with the money, Sammy, get them to pull alongside your truck and start transferring it over. By now, Sid and me will be with you. Sid and Harry will check the money to make sure it is all kosher. Tell their driver to fuck off and make sure to watch him go. Once we are loaded, get into any seat in the motors and follow me. We are going here…" pointing to the 7th Street camera shop.

"Follow me round the back and be on guard all the time. Elvis - you should be there in front of us - tell Uncle we are on the way and we will meet you round the shipping area. We are going to put all the money into a fucking great crate with some other things I have bought. We will stay with the crate until it is nailed closed and loaded onto a lorry, then we will leave and come back to the hotel. All clear?"

He got a nod from everyone, exactly what he wanted. He could feel his brain spinning it had gone into overdrive so much. He felt that he must have a drink and sit and be quiet for a while, and not have to go over it again.

After a short pause, he decided not to allow the others to see him feeling the pressure. And so, with courage, he said to them all, "Righto, me buckos, let's go to dinner," happy to at least rest.

Harry, as witty as ever, said, "Not on the piss again, Yiddel?"

And just as witty, Yiddel retorted: "Well, with you lot I have to drink to keep my spirits up…or is it down?"

The next morning, Yiddel told Sammy to check the flight times out of JFK and to phone and check the availability for the return flight home on all their tickets. Sammy found out that half of them could get one time and the rest could catch a flight an hour later, but he was assured they all would be on the way back to England by early evening.

At 1pm, the group made its collective way to the underground car park of the *Hilton Hotel* and boarded their elected vehicles. Yiddel, Sidney, Sammy and Harry were in the truck; Elvis, Sheila and Ansel were in the car with Roger driving. They left the car park and drove along the main street through the centre of New York. They split up at a pre-determined point after two blocks, Roger heading for the Statton Building and Sammy heading for the exchange area in Wellington Street. Yiddel called Sheila on her radio to see if they were in position; she gave a "Yes, all Ok," and then Yiddel made the all-important call to Moores.

Immediately, Moores answered the phone.

"Yeh, Mr Moores, it's Mr Fagin, I hope all is going to plan and you do not have any surprises for us this time?"

"No, Mr Fagin, I have no surprises for you. I have taken on board your threat and I have no reason to double-cross you…I know

188

you will carry out your promise, and as you said to me, I do not want ever to see you again. Now..." his voice tailed off as he got his breath, "the money is in a car at the front of this building, waiting for your instructions. There are two people in the car, both of whom you have met before - my guards in England. They have been instructed to deliver the money and then drive away - those are my orders to them. Where are they meeting you? Oh, and your lady has arrived, she is with me now."

"She knows what she has to do, Mr Moores. Tell your driver to head for Wellington Street in downtown New York quite close to the Hudson, where we are waiting right now."

Yiddel hung up and waited for the call from Sheila. Sheila remained standing by Moores as he told his driver to get the money to Wellington Street - the riverside street. Moores put the phone down and attempted to make conversation with her. His lined face gave away the otherwise seemingly friendly look in his eyes. Sheila was having none of it. She gave him one of her most evil looks and deliberately said nothing. After five minutes, she called Yiddel and said "Yes."

She left Moores' office, again saying nothing, joining Ansel in the corridor outside. Elvis had a lift held ready and then the trio were in the front hall and swiftly out into the street. They got into the waiting car with Roger at the wheel.

Roger dropped Sheila off on the way and then carried on to the rendezvous with Yiddel.

Yiddel and Sidney were out of the truck tucked into a doorway of one of the huge buildings that were so vast they seemed to envelope the whole street, leaving Sammy and Harry standing outside the truck with the rear doors open. It wasn't long before Moores' big black limo came cruising into Wellington Street and pulled up alongside the truck. With just a nod of recognition, the driver got out and opened the trunk of the limo and all four began transferring the load from car to truck. Yiddel and Sidney then made their way over to the scene as Roger, with the others, arrived and parked up tight to the limo. So far, so good. No stunts yet from Moores & Co., and no one in the street seeming to take any notice of them. The tension was palpable, though, and this had gone wrong once before.

Sidney pulled out his knife and slit the wrapping paper of the bundles of bank notes. He and Yiddel checked each parcel. Ansel and Harry stood threateningly close to the two guards while the checking was going on, glaring at them and clearly this wasn't what the guards were used to having to put up with. The checking seemed to take forever, Sidney making sure that each bundle held legitimate real money and not newspaper. They were leaving no room for error or double-crossing this time. Sidney was trying to make an estimated, but reasonably accurate, count of each bundle, advising Sammy, as his back-up, of the amount he counted. Was it all there? Surely, Moores would try something? Sidney could see that all the notes were one hundred dollar bills. Harry was now with Sidney counting as fast as he could. Within a few minutes, they looked up and assured themselves and Yiddel that the correct amount was there. Yiddel, looking around more anxiously the longer this task excruciatingly went on, visibly relaxed and, breathing out fully for the first time, now stood away from the two guards and said, "Thank you, gentlemen, you can go now!"

Roger pulled his car away from its blocking position of the limo, which, with the two guards, now discreetly left. Yiddel watched them clear the street and disappear into the mainstream of traffic. Sharply, he instructed: "Ok, follow me!"

With Yiddel leading in the truck and Roger following they all headed for Michael Katzman's place.

Elvis was already there, waiting for the team. Once he saw them arrive, he went off to check with his uncle where he wanted them to be; quickly, he returned to direct Sammy to drive into the yard of the premises. In the yard at the rear of the photographic business was one of the most secure compounds Yiddel had ever seen. Katzman was there, directing Sammy where to park the truck.

"Is all this necessary, Uncle?" asked Yiddel, pointing to the high fences, the lights, cameras and razor sharp barbed wire all along the top of the perimeter fence.

Katzman pulled a face and said, "Even this is not enough; we have to keep updating our defences to stop the bastards getting in. You know New York is full of thieves, Yiddel!"

"Really!" exclaimed Yiddel. "You have surprised me!"

Katzman got one of his men to close the huge gates and another to forklift a large wooden crate over to the truck. He then drove off over to the warehouse and brought back a pallet of all the goods that Yiddel had bought - including fifty boxes of children's cameras.

"For the market stall," offered Katzman. "I'll leave you to pack the crate," he said, walking back to the main building and telling the stacker truck driver to go and get another order ready for another customer, leaving the team to pack the crate with all the money and the goods. They lined the bottom of the crate with the money, spreading it evenly, before loading all the good cameras. Laptops and children's cameras were positioned all over the top. Finally, lots of lightweight packing was added. Yiddel called Katzman, who instructed his despatch manager to nail the lid shut and then bind the whole crate with strong plastic strips. Katzman secured the customs notes to the top side of the crate at the same time as the manager was stencilling 'THIS WAY UP' on all sides of the wooden crate.

"Ok," said Katzman. "If you would like to come into my office, Yiddel, we can settle the bill."

Yiddel and Elvis followed Katzman up into his office, where, when they were inside, Yiddel asked: "Have you been burgled?"

"No, Yiddel, it's always like this, it's the way I like it, and I know where everything is. If you can find a seat, sit down."

Katzman wasn't joking. The office was so small for such a multi-million-dollar enterprise, it did not seem to fit at all. Katzman's desk was so covered in papers – invoices, delivery notes, price quotations, he obviously oversaw them all – that Yiddel could not see where it began and where it ended. After a moment, he selected a chair by moving a bundle of papers on to the floor; now, Katzman gave him a copy of all the purchased items including the shipping, packing and delivery charges. Yiddel studied the invoice, which he thought was very reasonable.

"Is everything in order, Yiddel...have I made a mistake with my sums? Too much or maybe too little?" Katzman's face gave nothing away despite his well-meant, slightly mocking tone.

"No, I thought you had not charged me enough, that's all."

Yiddel settled the invoice in cash; as Katzman was checking it, Yiddel put another bundle of cash on the table. Ten thousand dollars.

"What's that for?" asked a genuinely surprised Katzman.

"It's my East End way of treating someone who has done me a favour, Uncle."

"What the fuck have you put in the crate, diamonds?"

"Nearly, Uncle. Nearly."

They shook hands, Katzman assuring Yiddel that his crate would leave for the cargo area at JFK that evening and be in London at Yiddel's yard in two days.

Katzman came out with Yiddel to the back yard where the whole team was waiting. He shook hands with them all and gave his 'nephew' a hug. He waved goodbye, the yardman opened the gates and they drove back to *The Hilton*. Roger and Sammy took the vehicles back. Yiddel told Sammy to give the hire man an extra one hundred dollars for looking after them, and to keep him quiet. The hire man was so pleased to get a fat tip he drove them back to *The Hilton* and would not hear of them getting a taxi.

"I could enjoy living here, Sam!" said Roger, looking dreamily out of the car window as they drove back to the hotel.

"Why's that?" asked Sammy.

"I've never seen so many gay men and clubs in my life," he said, with a broad smile.

Back at the hotel, they all got stuck into coffee and sandwiches before leaving for the airport. Yiddel took the opportunity of them being all together around the table to thank them for their input into the caper.

"Without each of you doing what you have done, and doing it so well, this would not have been possible. Thank you."

A bond of steel had been forged between the band of villains. Each knew that they could in some way or another trust each member of the team to play his or her part to the full. And that no one would grass on anyone else, if it came to the worst – getting caught. But, that was not the worst of it. That was still to come.

12

Going 'Legit'...

Back in Hackney, the gang went about their own business. Ansel went back to his café; Sidney to his transport; Elvis to his beloved Stamford Hill; Sheila to looking after her father and brothers; Roger to his life of doing nothing but clubbing, and the boys back to running the toy stall. Little did anyone outside of their group know that they had been to the Big Apple and taken on someone of the standing of Mr Moores and his henchmen.

Bang on the second day, the crate from America arrived as promised by Michael Katzman, delivered straight to Yiddel's yard address. The trio were at the stall that day when Yiddel, with some relief, saw the big truck pull into the yard. He walked over to confirm that it was the delivery he was so keenly expecting. The delivery driver gave Yiddel his delivery note to check and started to prepare to lift the crate off the truck. Yiddel called out to the boys to leave the stall to a fellow stallholder for ten minutes. Yiddel signed the note, and the driver swung the crate off the back of the truck with his mobile hoist and into the entrance of the lockup shed. Yiddel, in his customary way, gave the driver a hefty tip, so much so that the driver thought it was Christmas - "Blimey, thanks Guv!" was all he could manage to blurt out as he packed up the crane and helped the boys push the crate further into the lock-up, well out of sight of any nosey passer-by of which there were always a few.

Sammy closed the doors as Yiddel started to cut the plastic binding from around the case. Harry was prising the stubborn lid open with a crowbar. To Yiddel, this seemed to take an eternity, but, once Harry had it done, they manoeuvred it up against the wall, and Yiddel, calm on the outside but with his mind racing at high speed, swiftly cleared away all the foam packaging from the top of the crate's innards, which now began to reveal the uppermost items of the children's cameras. These were piled up in the rear of the lock-up out of the way. Now, Yiddel gave each of the boys their 'surprise' present - the laptops - as well as a very up-market digital camera each. Both boys thanked him with that laddish enthusiasm that he loved so much, but of course they were naturally more interested in what was going to come out of the crate next. Pulses racing, they looked down to see...the packets of money, just the way they had loaded them back in New York.

"Thank God for that!" exclaimed Yiddel, breathing out a huge sigh. He leant on the crate for a moment.

"Amen to that," said Sammy, his voice barely audible with the tension he felt – and that inevitable dread that somehow Moores would have managed to double-cross them yet again.

They lifted the money out and stacked it up on one of the spare market stalls. As Yiddel had promised in New York to all the team, the whole lot was going to be split up into eight portions, minus the ten thousand dollars given to Katzman for his services.

With a somewhat enforced casualness, Harry went back to the stall, taking the laptops and their personal cameras with him and started to pack up for the day. Now, he was back in market-trader mode, placing cuddly toys into boxes rather than handling huge sums of money as he had done just two minutes earlier. In the meantime, Yiddel and Sammy began dividing the cash up into piles of eight hundred and seventy-five thousand dollars to each of the gang. It was easy to count: the bank in New York had obligingly wrapped each bundle into fifty-thousand-dollar bundles. They put

195

each share-out into the usual innocuous-looking, large plastic bags, which were then stowed into the back of Sammy's car ready for delivery.

A very relieved Yiddel walked on air up to Ansel's café with his share of the money on top of a market barrow, enjoying the thought of the acting he was about to perform. Knowing there was enough cash there to buy up the entire Ridley Street market a hundred times over, he nonchalantly dumped it on the floor alongside the counter and lazily remarked to Ansel: "Here's that pile of dirty books I'd said I'd lend you, mate. Don't go blind reading them, though."

Two people sitting in the café passed a remark about Ansel's need for such things and went back to their tea and *The Sun*.

Ansel – if the look of anticipation on his face was anything to go by – just about kept it together enough to nervously look into the first plastic sack and then to glance back at Yiddel, with his eyes as big as saucers. "Yiddel, you old bastard," he hissed. "These are just the ones I like!"

"See yer later, Ansel, got to go. See yer in the morning, and don't be late opening up!"

Yiddel went back to the lock-up where the boys had stowed the stall away and then the three drove around to all the team members to deliver their money. Roger was emotional. Sheila cried with thanks. Elvis simply uttered, "Oy vey." Sidney gasped his usual, when surprised, comment: "Fucking hell!"

"I think everyone is happy, don't you, lads?" Yiddel announced, feeling for all the world like Father Christmas. "I think in the end we had a result, but it was close. I don't think we will ever hear from Moores again, or maybe if we do, it will because he has been caught out as the Great American Swindler."

"What shall we do with this lot, Yiddel, let Mark Joseph put it away or what?" asked Harry, patting the sacks of money in the back of the car in an almost paternal manner.

"I've been thinking about that. I would like to be able to put it away without having to lose money on the exchange rate. Maybe Mark will do what is best and put it straight into the offshore. I'll go and see him in the morning."

The two boys would take advice from Yiddel after he had spoken to Joseph and do exactly as him.

While they had all been in *The Hilton* in New York, Yiddel had discussed the money and how he thought each member of the gang should handle it. He had made it perfectly clear that it only took one of the gang to fuck up, and they would all be in the shit, right up to their ears. They had listened to Yiddel's words intently and taken his advice and sought the services of Mark Joseph. Yiddel had emphasised the need for each member to be extremely careful.

"Remember, when we get back home, each of you will have, suddenly, a great deal of money. Think about all the jealous bastards we know...if they hear that you have got hold of this amount because of their jealousy, they'll shop you. If you are going to hold on to your money I suggest that you only exchange a few notes at a time, mainly at these exchange bureaux in the West End, 'cos they don't ask for proof of identity like a passport - they just take your money, deduct a few quid for the trouble and give you your sterling. However, remember you will have a lot of money to exchange, so if that's the way you are going to do it, be very careful. Mark Joseph is one of us, I know he charges for his services and so he should, but you will not have to worry about it, he takes care of it all. If you have another scheme in your mind, like buying

197

property in say, Jamaica, Mark will tell you who to speak to. Ok? So, it's up to you."

Yiddel had left it at that, believing his cautionary words had to be said to slow the natural rush by any of the members, like Ansel in particular, to start spending money too quickly. He still had the picture of the plain-clothes police officer who was watching Ansel that day, firmly fixed in his mind. Who was he really and why did he leave so readily, no arguments, so keen to get away from the scene, or was it really a fear of being found out? Now he thought more about it, Yiddel started to feel some unease about all that they didn't know. In New York, he had, out of all the team members, been speaking more directly to Ansel when he was mentioning buying property internationally, but now he made a mental note to stay close to Ansel, just in case.

Mark Joseph was always in his office by 9am. His first client today was Yiddel.

"Morning, Mark, got *another* new car, I see? Who paid for this one, then?"

"You did," replied Joseph, shaking Yiddel's hand warmly, pleased to see such a valued client again, which to him could only mean one thing. "Everything all right?"

"What do you mean - me? I can't afford a pair of shoelaces and you have the latest Mercedes parked outside and you say I've paid for it!"

"I'm only kidding, one of my wealthy clients bought it for me as a going away present." Joseph laughed at his joke on Yiddel.

"Why, where's he gone then?" Yiddel was nevertheless keen to know.

"Broadmoor - his money went to his head!... No, Yiddel, I'm only joking, really. You know I can't say anymore – 'client confidentiality' and all that. Anyway, what can I do for you? You know that your little investment is now making big money, don't you?"

"No, I didn't, I've been away and I haven't had a chance to read the statement yet."

"Ok, I'll take care of that today for you, and the boys too." Joseph was more than happy to always 'take care' of whatever monies came his way.

Yiddel continued. "What you can do today is make more money for both of us. I have eight hundred and seventy thousand US dollars that have got be put in the 'usual' place. The boys have each got the same amount to be put in their accounts. Oh, and I have a couple of business friends who would like to use your services - on my recommendation."

"Kind of you, Yiddel, my friend. I will look after them as I look after you. Please tell them to call me."

Yiddel had been thinking about starting a legitimate business, this time nothing to do with the market or any doubtful or dubious project, but a proper bona-fide business. He was asking Joseph how he could go about it and the advice was to "find a business first and then we'll talk about it. Won't be a problem."

Yiddel explained that he was after something that he could be kosher in, something that he didn't have to worry about who knocked at his door, all up front with everyone, no ducking and diving - even pay taxes - although that hurt him as he said it. Joseph could see him wince as if he had just had a tooth removed.

"Employ regular staff?"

"Yeh, an office girl, a tea lady."

He let Yiddel ramble on while he made the coffee and by then he had run out of ideas – and patience.

"Yiddel, just find a fucking business first, then you can hire the staff, but first things first, I've got to know: what is it that you would *like to do* exactly?"

Yiddel sat thinking, his deep brown eyes gazing into an uncertain future, but perhaps betraying a need for more security and peace of mind. Luck can turn for the worse very quickly, he knew. Joseph hadn't seen his friend like this before and was genuinely bewildered by Yiddel's sudden lack of clarity of purpose. Yiddel nursed his cup of coffee with it tilting slightly against his lower lip.

"I'll think about it some more and let you know. Give me a bit of time and I will come up with a real bit of magic to make me really legit."

Joseph sat behind his expensive desk, knowing he must be mad to even contemplate getting himself involved with yet another client's probable financial disaster - he had seen so many flop. Same old story: as soon as a client had some money behind him, he wants to chance it on some risky 'legit' business venture. 'But this client is Yiddel Davis,' he reminded himself, 'and you never know, he might well come up with some little gem and shut me up.'

By the late afternoon, Mark Joseph had taken on four new clients, all keen for his services, and all thanks to Yiddel Davis Esq. As well as Sammy, Harry, Sidney and Yiddel becoming the richest men in East London, Mr Mark Joseph was doing all right as well.

Yiddel went back to the stall and found that all the children's *Snappy* cameras had gone. Sammy told him, with a dead-straight face, that as soon as they put them on the stall they were being literally 'snapped up'.

"Too cheap, I suppose, we've gone too cheap!" mourned Yiddel.

"I don't think so," was Harry's verdict. "The reason is that they are unique, they are not in this country yet. Even Hamleys don't have 'em, so one lady said!"

"Well, now," said Yiddel, scratching his chin thoughtfully. "That's not a bad business to be in, get your new product out early and blanket the markets, in and out, quick kill stuff. Did anyone argue about the price?"

"No, they couldn't get hold of one quick enough," Harry replied. "We marked them up double the price you paid Katzman including the freight and taxes and they still sold like hot cakes!"

Yiddel ambled up to see Ansel and to have a coffee, still thinking about the cameras.

"Hi, Yiddel, you all right?" Ansel greeted him in his usually bubbly way.

"Hullo, mate. Yer, I'm fine, just thinking about an idea…"

"Count me in."

"No, not that kind of an idea, you old rogue. Buying and selling. D'yer remember those little cameras we got from New York? Well, the boys put them out on the stall this morning and they have all gone, all sold out. And they were priced up right. So, I've been giving it a bit of thought as it might be a way to start an import business."

Later in the day, after the stall had been put away, Yiddel put it to the boys if they were ready to move on to something bigger than the stall. Both agreed it would be nice to have a go at something else. And that was all Yiddel needed to start the ball rolling.

"If anything else comes along, we can do that and still have an upfront business," he assured them with great confidence.

Yiddel had a meeting with Mark Joseph about his idea. He needed advice about the legal setting up and financing of a new venture. Joseph's main concern was that Yiddel had no other supplier contacts except for Katzman in New York.

"It's not what you know, Yiddel, it's who you know. Would Katzman be good enough to tell you where he gets the cameras? If he feels that you are not treading on his toes he might cut you in. And these days, what with all the different game toys coming onto the market, you often hear that the big retailers cannot get hold of the product. I'd say, give it a spin and bell him. The cuddly toys that you sell are available for anyone to buy from warehouses all over the UK, but what you want are the special ones like the cameras because no one else can get them readily."

"Maybe not only the toys, Mark…maybe we could try lots of other things as well," suggested Yiddel, causing Joseph to smile just a little, seeing his rogue-friend getting the feel of setting up a new trading company through legal means.

"Today's acorns are tomorrow's oak trees, Mark, or something like that."

Yiddel's initial idea started to generate a whole load of avenues of thought into all sorts of trading; it began with toys and soon had developed into large-scale industrial imports. Joseph eventually had to call a halt to Yiddel's rush for the new business by warning him that only he knew about his hidden wealth and the British Government certainly did not – and could not be allowed to. Questions could be asked by the Revenue, amongst others. Such as where did all the money to buy all this come from? After all, you did not earn that sort of money running a toy stall in Ridley Road market, or at least most people didn't! So, a softly- softly approach had to be made first, just so that the whole venture would not run aground before it was floated. Yiddel took Joseph's advice; he always did when it came to matters like this, and he agreed to make it seem more 'kosher' because he was going to have to appear to start the new business in a small way, from scratch, and slowly let it grow. 'Look round for premises but do not go and buy a building the size of Selfridges just because you can afford it,' was, he knew, blindingly obvious, but it was tortuous not to get carried away with all the possibilities that would have been open to him had all his 'finance' been gotten legally.

"Get a small place first and no one will have a reason to investigate; pay your taxes and VAT and let it slowly happen. It isn't as though you're hard up, Yiddel! So - slow down a bit, please." Joseph was adamant. And clearly worried about Yiddel's ambitions. Why couldn't he stick to crime?

Yiddel agreed for Mark Joseph to set up the new company, finding a name for it and registering it with Companies House. The name proved harder than first thought. Between all of them, it turned out to be quite a struggle, and it went on for days, each of them coming up with what they thought was' the one' - only to be knocked down by all the others.

The final name came about through Sheila, who had just met Yiddel in the market. She had heard that he was going into a proper business and said to Yiddel, "There is only one name you can use, call it 'FAGIN UK'! He was a trader of sorts, Ok, I know only in purses and silk handkerchiefs, but I think the name is a name that sticks…if you know what I mean, Yiddel!"

And so, FAGIN UK Ltd was launched and accepted by all. With the help of a local estate agent, Yiddel found secure premises on the edge of a small trading estate close to Ridley Road market in Hackney. It was a factory-style unit with office space on an upper floor and a large open-plan warehouse at ground level with a large electric roll up shutter and a separate personnel door entrance. Within a few days, they had taken possession of the place and the local carpet dealer had fitted a new carpet for the office. Yiddel bought five desks with their own chairs and of course chairs for 'guests' as well.

The phone lines were installed; other furniture for the office was bought and delivered, along with many electrical gadgets for tea, coffee, toast, and a microwave oven. Everyone was invited to the 'house-warming' party from the market along with his or her friends – all were made welcome. After everyone had left, Yiddel, Sammy and Harry were left finishing off the final bottles of beer and eating the last of the food, when Yiddel posed the million-dollar question: "Right, lads, we've got the place, so what do you think we are going to put in it now?"

Yiddel had by now sold the toy stall to the man whom he used to mind it whenever they were 'away'. The man was overjoyed, becoming a lifelong friend of Yiddel. "It's what I've always wanted, Yiddel, you're a diamond geezer!" he exclaimed with barely disguised glee. He had been pestering Yiddel for a long time to let him have first offer if he ever sold it. So that was the stall out of the way. The two boys were now elevated to company directors; Yiddel would be Managing Director and Mark Joseph their business advisor/accountant.

On the first day of opening the doors of FAGIN UK Ltd, Yiddel got a phone call from Michael Katzman in New York, apologising for missing the opening, but promising Yiddel 'Mozzeltoff' any support he could give him in the future. Yiddel was grateful for this and told him he might well take him up on his kind offer...

It wasn't long before word got around, and Yiddel knew the visitors would start appearing. And, so it was one day when he was sitting at his office desk, looking for all the world like a management professional, when the door opened and who should Sammy bring in but Alfie Smith, the notorious south London gang boss. Yiddel was truly taken aback at the sight of this infamous villain, so well-known far and wide for his extreme gangster methods, yet still an acquaintance of sorts, albeit in a different league to Yiddel. He hadn't seen Smith for a long time, and now here the giant was, six feet four, smart in appearance but bloody assertive with it. Standing behind him was one of his minders - shaven headed, a hard, staring look with a nose that had clearly been broken more than once.

"This gentleman wants to see you, Yiddel!" said Sammy, urgently, standing aside as Smith moved forward regardless of Sammy.

"Hallo, Alfie...." Yiddel was now standing up to shake his hand. "Blimey, I haven't see you for years, how are you keeping these days?" He heard the words tumble out of his mouth, playing for time and probably a bit too transparent for Smith not to notice, but Yiddel knew he could not afford to offend this particular 'gentleman'. Nevertheless, he was desperately thinking to himself, 'What the fuck does he want with me?'

"Yeh, I'm Ok, Yiddel," came the gruff reply. Smith didn't do niceties. "I heard about the new business and I thought..." he paused as he looked around. "I thought I might as well come along and black my nose and see what you are up to here." Smith's eyes were everywhere, deliberately showing Yiddel who the real boss was. Smith always made sure he didn't miss a trick anywhere.

"Well, it don't take long for news to get round, Alfie...please take a seat. So...you found us all right?" Yiddel's casual enquiry was carefully worded, and everyone in the room knew it.

"Yeh, no problem, my boy here knew where this place was, he said he had screwed one of these places a few months ago."

"Oh good, remind me to put extra locks on the doors, Sam!" replied Yiddel, his cheeky grin lightening the mood for a short instant, and giving Alfie Smith a little wink. Smith said nothing.

"D'yer want a drink, Alfie?"

"Yeh, I'll have a cup of coffee, Yiddel. I've been told by my quack to leave drinking out for a while, the kidneys can't stand the pace, so I've eased up."

Sammy made him a coffee, which he prayed would be all right for Smith. Yiddel, in the meantime, went on, still puzzled by this man's sudden appearance.

"What's on your mind, there's got to be something, Alfie, you don't just pop in even if it's just to black your nose."

"Yeh, you're right. I have a business idea. I'm gonna run it past you and see if you're interested." Smith looked at Yiddel with a degree of menace, and Yiddel could feel his soul being penetrated by the look on Smith's hard face.

With Yiddel and Smith seated at Yiddel's desk, the minder stood guard by the door. Sammy knew this was a conversation that might not be for his ears, but he loyally stayed with Yiddel - feeling the mood becoming more tense - now that the two rogues were about to talk business.

"I need someone who is kosher like you, Yiddel, to come in on a deal. I've heard that you are not a prat when it comes to handling a deal – a very big one - and I wondered if you would be the man. Don't forget, I know a lot of villains, as you know, and a hell of a load of villains know me - some of them to their cost...Yeh, some have tried to turn me over or stitch me up on a deal and I've had their bollocks cut off. You know this, Yiddel...I will not be fucked about. You know what I'm like. I've not built up what I've got by being a soft fucker and I don't like to be taken on, right?"

Yiddel suddenly thought back to the lorry load of whisky that they had inadvertently stolen from Smith and wondered if he had just found out about it...and was this Smith's way of levelling the score by telling him he was about to lose his bollocks as well? 'Inadvertently' or not, Smith wouldn't make any distinctions.

"Yeh, right, Alfie," Yiddel heard himself reply, getting very uncomfortable as he felt his heart begin to race uncontrollably and still wondering 'where the fuck is this meeting going to?'

"I've got an idea that will make you a rich man," Smith continued, his menacing stare again boring into Yiddel's soul as he took a swig of coffee. "See, I had this idea, and when I found out you had a legit business, I decided you are the man for it."

Yiddel glanced nervously at Sammy, who instinctively responded with a tiny shrug of his shoulder in what was maybe meant to be an imperceptible reply, just in case this animal of a man or his equally animal minder standing behind him saw it and then decided that Sammy was taking the piss and took his revenge by removing Sammy of his priceless possessions.

The pause in the conversation wasn't lost on anyone. Perhaps Smith was enjoying the moment. Then his eyes took on a strange glint of lightness. "I'm going to going to import Jelly men!" he proudly announced, smiling through gold teeth at Yiddel.

'The man's gone stark raving fucking mad,' thought Yiddel, rooted now to his chair. 'We have one of the meanest, fiercest villains of all time, and now he's saying he wants to import Jelly men…'

"Why Jelly men, Alf?" asked Yiddel, becoming even more anxious than before – and silently praying that it didn't show. But he knew Smith was far too experienced not to know the effect he could have on people.

"I think they are going to sweep the country and I want to be in on the early killing…they're going mad for them in Japan, can't get enough, it's said, and the kids was killing each other to get 'em. What d'ya say, Yiddel?"

"Well, Alfie. It's the first time I've heard about the Jelly men, so, er, where do we start looking for them?"

"Right, well, that's why I've come to you, Yiddel. I want you to find out for me."

Yiddel took a quick look over Smith's shoulder at his minder to see if his expression gave anything away, but from the 'out at lunch' look on the man's face he guessed he had absolutely no chance with him on this one. The minder was programmed only to maim and kill. Yiddel doubted if he was even mentally in the room with them let alone giving a hint of what his equally nutty boss was talking about.

"Ok, leave it with me, Alfie, me old china, and I will get back to you as soon as I can. I'll make some phone calls this afternoon and see what I can learn about it. Ok?"

208

"All right, Yiddel, don't leave it too long though, in case someone else 'ears about it," he said, now looking more intensely into Yiddel's soul.

And, on that note, the notorious villain Alfie Smith, followed by the minder, turned and left the office. No 'cheerio' or 'thanks' was given or could be expected.

Looking at Sammy, Yiddel seemed in a daze.

"I do not believe it...that man is two sandwiches short of a fucking picnic, he is. I am fucking sure he should be measured up for a straitjacket. And the minder...I thought at one time he would come out of his trance and just for the fun of it, cut us to pieces, while his loopy governor looked on." Yiddel took a deep breath and tried to re-focus. "Sam, what the fuck are Jelly men...? And do me a favour - lock the fucking door in case they come back."

Yiddel shuddered to think how many men had fallen foul of that man and were either entombed in concrete pillars or had been chopped up and fed to pigs. He knew one thing: he had been given an order by Smith, and there was no room for failure.

"That takes the biscuit; he has gone for sure into space. Whatever we do, we must treat him with care, that is one dangerous mother fucker."

For the rest of the day, Yiddel could not shake the thought of Alfie Smith from his mind. 'What am I going to tell him? What if he blames me for not finding out where you can get these damned Jelly men? Who the fuck can I ask? Fuck it...I'll phone him and give him some cock-and-bull story about them being out of production or something. But first I'd better check if there is any such thing. What the fuck are Jelly men?'

The next morning, after a sleepless night of anxiety and demons, Yiddel phoned Sidney and told him of the visit the day before.

"What should I do, Sid, the fucking man's a psycho and he expects me to come up with a product of Jelly men. Do you know anyone I can phone to check it out?"

After recovering from the initial shock, Sidney had an idea. "The only thing I can think it might be is a *Star Wars* game or something similar. Give me five minutes and I'll phone my sister and get her to ask her kid if he knows anything about it. I'll phone you straight back." Sidney rang off, leaving Yiddel with at least a little hope.

Five minutes went past and Yiddel's phone rang again, making him jump. His usual composure had vanished, and he was edgy, thinking the worst if he couldn't deliver for Smith. Hesitantly, he reached for the receiver.

"Hello...is that you, Sid?"

"Yeh, she's asked her little 'un and he said he's never heard of it. I don't know anyone else I can phone, Yiddel. Sorry can't help on this one. Let me know how you get on, won't you?"

This was not what Yiddel wanted to hear. A friend's best wishes were of no bloody use right now. What he wanted was practical help. Nervously, he phoned Hamleys and local traders, searched through the *Yellow Pages,* but drew a complete blank on them all. Sammy checked with Harry, and Harry checked with some young people he knew, but all with no luck.

Yiddel decided to bite the bullet and phone Alfie Smith and tell him that he couldn't trace the Jelly men.

He was dreading making the call; he knew he was dealing with a real loose cannon, who might easily blame him for not trying hard enough. Yiddel was not a man to be afraid of most things that happened in his life, but he had heard many stories about Smith, none of them good. And what he had seen for himself in his office was enough to make any normal man truly fearful of the consequences of this lunatic.

He made the call. He heard the ringing tone and could only imagine Smith's phone at the other end, ringing away, maybe, with any luck, in an empty house? But would Smith be there?

"Hello...is Alfie there?" he asked the female voice that answered. "It's Yiddel Davis. Yeh, Ok, love, I'll wait." Putting his hand over the mouthpiece, Yiddel told the boys, both sitting on the edge of Yiddel's desk, that it was his wife and she had said, verbatim: 'He's having a crap and won't be long.' Suddenly, he heard Smith pick the phone up and grunt: "Hello?"

"Alfie, it's me, Yiddel. It's about that bit of business you came to see me about...Jelly men, Alfie."

To his utter astonishment, Yiddel then heard Smith say: "What the fuck are you talking about? I ain't seen you for months. What the fuck are Jelly men, Yiddel? You gone mad? And business - what fucking business? You're not trying to have a fucking laugh with me, Yiddel, are yer, because you know what I'm like if I think someone's taking the piss...I get very upset!"

"Er, no, Alfie, I wouldn't do that to you, you know me better than that. It must be a mistake by one of the boys and one of 'em mistook someone else for you, very sorry, Alfie mate. Look, I'll send you round a crate of light ales by way of apology." But as he said it, he remembered he had made another mistake... Alfie Smith had stood there in the office and told him he was on the wagon. 'Christ,' thought Yiddel despairingly, 'he said it loud and

211

clear…how could I have forgotten? The man just had a cup of coffee.'

The disbelief continued. "Yeh, Ok, Yiddel," came Smith's unmistakable voice. "I like a light ale. All right, mate, I accept your apology," and with that he put the phone down.

From a seated position when he had started the call, Yiddel now found himself standing up to finish it. Now, he dropped back into his chair, lifeless.

"I feel like I have just run the London Marathon - I am fucking drained. What did he say yesterday about drinking, Sam?"

"He said he was on the wagon because of his kidneys. Doctor's orders."

"Right, well, I made a mistake, so I thought, by offering to send him round a drink and then he goes and thanks me for it! In addition, he was *not* here yesterday; in fact, he hasn't seen me for months." Yiddel's face was now in his hands, elbows resting on the desk. The boys honestly thought he was about to start sobbing, and looked anxiously at each other. "That sadist is one hell of a very loose cannon and I don't want to be around when he goes off. What with him and the minder, there's a pair well suited to each other."

It took a few days for Yiddel to get over the experience of the Smith saga. The more people he told about the story, the more horrific ones he got back. "The one thing you must not be is an enemy of Alfie Smith," they all advised, claiming that his younger brother was even worse.

"I don't want to meet him either," declared Yiddel. "One's enough."

In the meantime, Yiddel tried to get his mind off it by keeping busy. He phoned Katzman, and the New Yorker kindly gave him the

212

contact number for the 'kiddie' camera supplier in Taiwan. He told him that when he phoned, to mention his name and the people at the other end would look after him. Katzman started to laugh while he was giving him the phone number.

"Only because you're Jewish, Yiddel, only because you are one of us is why I'm giving it to you, my friend."

Although he was born Jewish, from a Jewish mother and father, Yiddel had never taken up the faith in a serious way. In his younger years, it was customary to go to Hebrew classes, but as he got older he had left all that behind. He hated to hear 'One of us' and the 'Chosen Race'. He felt he did not need religion in his line of work; his faith was all about getting a living. Most of his true friends came from a mixed-race crowd, and seldom spoken about were religions of any kind. He had been to a school in Hackney that had some Jews but the larger percentage were Christians, and he had never been troubled by being 'Jewish'; most of his mates at school had been 'Gentiles'.

His parents, from what he could remember about them, had never forced it on him, and father had, after all, been heavily engaged in 'business' right up to the car crash with that cursed lorry that had mercilessly taken them away from him. Where was God on that day? The memories started to crowd his mind and he knew he needed a bit of space in which to absorb their agonising impact once more. He couldn't let the boys see him like this. As the world started spinning again, he hurt with the painful anguish of losing them, and he suddenly felt as vulnerable as a child. Because that was what he had been when they died. He yearned for mum's kind caresses, and for dad's jovial roguishness. And he found himself verging on praying for protection against Smith's very real psychosis. Yiddel saw his face in his visions and he knew he had to

213

get a grip. 'Only natural,' he consoled himself, concentrating on breathing deeply, wanting the world to stop, just for a moment. 'Mum and dad imparted their feelings as to what I should do and left it to me to sort it out. Yeh, that's it. We'll all find out one day what it's all about. Meanwhile, I have things to do.'

And so Yiddel Davis picked himself up, remembering the business he had built up from virtually nothing; he had people skills, life skills and he knew how to use them. As for religion, he knew he never went out of his way to make friends with people because they were Jews; he took people as he found them and nothing else came into it.

He phoned the number in Taiwan and asked for the man whom Katzman had recommended. The man came to the phone, and in very good English introduced himself as Mr Dong Lai. After a brief chat of introduction about who had given him the phone number, a deal was struck for a thousand cameras and a new line that they were marketing, at a reasonable price. Dong Lai said that he needed a banker's draft for the total amount and that as soon as he got it, the order would be despatched.

"Lovely Jubbly, we are up and running, boys! The first order has been placed with the man, a Mr Dong Lai, who sounds like a very easy going bloke. He is sending us a thousand of the cameras and a new line that they have just finished and which aren't on the market yet. He needs a banker's draft which I will see to down at the old J. Arfur. As soon as he gets it, he says he'll send it all to us."

Yiddel was pleased that he had called Mr Lai; he now felt that the new business had the solid, legal foundation it needed, and if this little deal worked out, it would be all to the good of FAGIN UK Ltd.

Over the next few days the trio had a constant stream of visitors to the new office, some of them coming to see the place just to be nosy so they could go back to the market and boast that they had been to 'Yiddel's new place'. 'All the better,' thought Yiddel, 'now everyone knows where we are.' One of the visitors was a sworn enemy of the Smith brothers: a certain Ernie Black, a somewhat smaller villain than the Smiths but just as evil in his ways of dealing with people that he did not like. Yiddel had known him for a long time; they had gone to the same school. Yiddel always felt safer with him than the likes of Alfie and Charlie Smith, but he chose not to tell Ernie about the frightening visit from Alfie, simply because he did not want to talk about him, especially to this man.

"How's it going, Yiddel? Impressive warehouse and offices...pity you haven't anything in the place, though!" Ernie remarked, smiling.

"We've only just started, Ern, give us a chance!"

"Only kidding, mate, I know you've just started, thought I'd pop round to see you meself, like!"

Ernie's eyes, like those of Alfie Smith, were constantly searching, probing all around the office, not missing a thing; such men as he were self-trained to home in on anything that they could either steal or gain something out of.

"The other thing, Yiddel, is I might have a bit of business to put your way."

Yiddel thought: 'Oh, fucking hell, here we go again...what crazy, non-existent thing am I going to be asked to get this time?'

"Anytime, Ernie, just give us a bell!"

After Black had left, Yiddel sat behind his desk and started to have serious doubts about whether he had done the right thing in opening the business; already he had visits from two of the biggest East End villains. He knew what the visits were for - each in their own way wanted to muscle in on a legit business that had barely begun as they could see the potential in using it to launder their plunder. Talking to the boys later in the office, he said, "I am beginning to have my doubts about the business. I think we should go back to what we know best, which is not sitting in an office being a target for all the lunatics on this side of London. They breeze in and you can see 'em planning what they can use us for whilst they're all the time just looking after themselves. We don't see them for yonks and then all of a sudden they appear out of the fucking woodwork."

Both of the boys agreed. "But what can we do about it?" asked Sammy, especially uncomfortable after Smith's visit.

"All right, I'll tell you what we can do. Let's leave it set up as we planned and when we do get visits from the villains, we'll just go along with them, but do fuck all. We can always make some silly excuse why we could not handle their request or whatever they want. I don't want to blank them completely, just in case they might come in handy one day."

Yiddel was right in what he was saying about the gang leaders; they could change like the wind, one minute their friend, the next - for some smallest of reason, possibly a figment of their imagination that something had been said about them - they would be at Yiddel's throat.

He lay awake again that night. 'Very funny ground, like walking on eggshells. I only hope that I can keep them at arms' length and, as I say, be 'casual friends'. I don't want to be involved in any of their jobs, but there might be a day when I need them for us. They are nuts, and that is why they are gangland bosses because they are fucking crackers. They have got where they are because they are afraid of nothing or no one. Yet someone like me has to show some sort of solidarity with them. Let's hope I never have to go back on my words.'

13

Safe Enough

Yiddel looked up from reading *The Sun* as he was drinking a cup of coffee in Ansel's cafe to see a new face – a female one - talking to Ansel. After she had left, he asked Ansel who she was.

"She works in that auction place, at the back of here, you know, they ain't been there long. They sell nothing but bankrupt stock and things - anything from razor blades to cars, most of it, she was saying, from companies that have gone skint and can't afford to pay their debts. They send in their own bailiffs, who take what they owe in property, if they can't pay, and the seized property is then sold at auction. She was babbling on... they only deal in cash and are just having a large safe being delivered this morning to put the cash in overnight until the next morning when the boss can take it to the bank."

Yiddel looked interested, but said nothing. Ansel continued: "They have one sale a week on Thursdays; it starts at 11 and finishes at 4.30 in the afternoon."

Yiddel's mind had already begun to conjure up an idea as soon as he heard the word 'cash'.

"Thursdays?" echoed Yiddel, deep in thought.

"Yeh, at 11." Ansel went back to serving customers, leaving his friend to his plan of action, which wasn't far away, now that Yiddel's mind was concentrated on the potential of what he had just been informed of.

'Maybe I'll have a look next Thursday, they might have something there that we could use...' ran his thoughts.

He was still musing on the words 'Safe' and 'Cash' when Sammy came into the café to say that someone was looking for him at the warehouse. He walked back with Sammy, telling him about what he had just heard. At the warehouse, he had a visit from the local council officer, telling him if any time he needed to take advice to please call.

On Thursday morning, Yiddel and Harry had a walk around to the auction rooms for the start of the sale at 11am. It was laid out all over the old factory floor. All the sale items were marked with a raffle ticket number. There was a vast amount of goods, covering everything that had some value to help recover the debt outstanding. But, for now, Yiddel was much more interested in the layout of the place, what protection was on the windows and doors. He had already briefed Harry to have a good but inconspicuous look around to try to see where the safe was. They had only been there a few minutes when Yiddel caught sight of the girl from the café coming down the stairs carrying a bundle of papers and placing them on the auctioneer's table, ready for the start of the sale. He watched her go back up the stairs and then whispered to Harry.

"The office is up those stairs - see if there are any alarm fittings up there."

Harry moved over to the stairs and started to go up. He got as far as the second floor before someone came out of an office and asked him what he wanted, as it was not allowed for the public to come up off the sale floor.

"I'm looking for the gents, please, mate?" he expertly lied, and was directed back to the ground floor.

The duo stayed at the sale which attracted many keen buyers, all of them bidding for each item with much desire and that bargain-hunter spirit.

"They must take a few bob here," breathed Yiddel. "Look…see how everything that comes up is sold straight away. It looks like they clear each sale of every single item."

The lots were selling fast and furious. Yiddel had decided to stay until the end of the sale to watch the whole event from start to finish. At the end of the sale, each buyer made his or her way to the cash point, which was a window hole in the wall covered with heavy gauge metal netting except for the slot at the bottom for passing money through to the cashier. They furtively hung around close to the cashier window and witnessed hundreds of pounds being paid in exchange for a stamped ticket to then give to a porter for the appropriate sale item. The buyer then took the bought and paid-for goods away. A big sign over the cashier's window advised, 'All sale items left after the sale will be disposed of'.

Yiddel had seen enough to realise this was a valid target, especially for the amount that would be in the safe. 'All just waiting for me,' he reflected, contentedly.

The next day he told Sammy to walk around to the auction house, checking all the entry points, windows and doors. Sammy returned with the news that the building was too secure to get into the normal way, but that he had also paid a visit to the adjoining building, which was a rag-trade business with virtually no security at all...

He had even been able to get up to the roof to have a look at the top part, and found it was an apex, slated.

"It's the way in, Yiddel," he said, excitedly. "Once we climb over the dividing wall, all we've got to do is take a few slates off their roof and we are in. The slates are very old and crumble as you touch them. And when we leave, come back the same way."

"Ok, that's the way we go in then," confirmed Yiddel.

Harry had said that there were no cameras on the two floors he had visited before he was caught, so the floors above must be clear too. Yiddel started to seriously plan this next job, now that he had all the information, for the next Thursday night.

"Do we need any gear?" asked Harry, ready to do his 'shop'.

"Just overalls and gloves," replied Yiddel.

"What about the safe?" Sammy wanted to know. "Have you got any ideas on that?"

"Leave that to me," said Yiddel, with a mischievous grin.

Thursday came. Harry had the necessary gear and the trio were ready to go.

They left it until 9pm to go to the building. Sammy had checked out during the week that the clothes makers' firm in the adjoining building worked all night.

"It's a real sweat shop," he told Yiddel. "They never close."

When they got there, true to what Sammy had said, the door was wide open and every light in the building was on. They walked up the stairs to the roof, but could see no one. They climbed over the small divide between the two buildings, edged their way around to the other, less conspicuous, side of the apex roof just in case anyone came up on the opposite roof and saw them removing the roofing slates. They stacked each slate as it was lifted off and in minutes they had a three-feet square hole in the old roof and could look down into the attic area. Harry climbed in using the wooden roofing timbers to support himself and then he smashed his boot into the plasterboard of the ceiling. With hardly any effort at all, he had broken the plaster to make a hole big enough for them all to get through.

Harry lowered himself slowly and then dropped the last couple of feet to land gently onto the floor below. Despite the darkness, he could see that he was in the main office. Feeling out for the nearest desk, he quickly swept its top clear of all its clutter and pulled it across so that it could be used for Yiddel to lower himself down onto, followed by Sammy.

As they did so, Harry was using his torch to locate a sturdy box, or something similar, to stand on, ready for when they were leaving and would need that extra lift up into the hole. He shone the torch on the target of their raid: the company safe. Yiddel had a good look at the size and make.

"What d'yer reckon?" whispered Harry, trying to make out he knew a bit about safes.

"I don't know too much about safes, but what I do know is that they do not like being dropped from great heights," was Yiddel's reply.

"What the fuck are you going to do, chuck it out of the window?" Harry asked, a note of disbelief in his voice, and giving Sammy a queer look.

"No, of course not. Downstairs was a large baggage trolley, remember? Go down and bring it up here…"

He waited for the boys to do so.

"Right, push the safe up on its edge, just a bit so that I can get the trolley underneath it."

The two boys shoved hard but at first the safe refused to move, not even an inch. "C'mon!" hissed Yiddel, and again the tried. Again, failure. Gasping, the boys stood back, cursing the safe and yet refusing to be beaten. A third time, and now, reluctantly and as

222

if fighting back all the time, the edge of the safe lifted just enough for Yiddel to get the leading edge of the trolley under it.

"Now pull it back to me," he instructed.

All three pulled the monster of a safe until Yiddel had it firmly on the trolley. They had never known anything so heavy.

"Christ, c'mon, lads! One more heave…good. Ok," he paused, struggling to get his breath. "Go out and break the banisters down…so there's a nice big gap - the same size as this bugger," referring to the safe's dimensions.

Both the boys kicked and snapped the wooden handrail and banisters until there was nothing there but the landing and the middle well that went all the way down to the ground floor, which, Yiddel had noticed on the initial visit, had a solid concrete base. This helped explain why he sounded so confident when he mentioned his 'Idea', followed by 'Leave it to me'.

Propping the torches so they could see their way in the otherwise overpowering darkness, they pushed the overladen trolley right up to the edge of the well in the staircase. Yiddel gently nudged the trolley slowly forward and the safe very slowly tipped over and fell into the dark expanse of the well. To them, standing there as if after a battle, it seemed an age before it hit the concrete floor below. They had expected one hell of a noise when it eventually hit the floor, but the sound of the impact was shattering - the whole building seemed to shake, and the trio were temporarily deafened by it. Then they looked down the well between the broken rails and were relieved to see that the safe had split in two and the huge door was hanging open...

They knew they would not have much time and rushed down, as fast as the limited torchlight provided, to the ground floor to observe the contents spilled out all over the floor. Large bundles of five, ten, twenty and fifty pound notes were everywhere. As Harry was scooping up the paper money into a plastic sack, he also picked up a small wallet and without thinking threw that into the bag with the banknotes.

Yiddel was reading the words on the front of the safe and said, "Listen to this! 'Tested to withstand Dynamite'. But, I'll tell yer what we could add to that: '…but they do NOT like being dropped four floors onto a concrete surface!'"

This was Yiddel at his professional best – calm, witty and yet focused on the task in hand. It was time to go. They knew they would have to leave all the coins behind and headed back up towards the roof to exit through the entrance they had created. Once all three were on the roof, they eased around the apex, jumped over the divide onto the other roof and then swiftly down the stairs to the street. As they exited, although careful, they came virtually face to face with an old man who was standing in the street, looking up at the Auction House building.

"Did yer hear that?" he said over his shoulder as they quickly passed. "I think the floors 'ave collapsed in there, or there's been an explosion."

The trio said nothing and slid away into the night, leaving the old man looking at the building and muttering to himself.

Back at the boys' flat, they eagerly tipped the contents of the bags onto the table. Sammy began counting the money, helped by Harry. Yiddel noticed the wallet and opened up the flaps to find that it contained a key - and a ticket with a Bond Street jeweller's name on it. This was more intriguing, and he sat back in an armchair, superficially observing the boys counting the money, but already deep in thoughts that led in many different directions. If they had looked up at him at this point, they would have recognised the expression on his face – it said, quite simply: "Idea…"

"Eleven thousand, nine hundred and forty pounds exactly," announced Sammy, sitting back in his chair and looking at Yiddel.

"Not a bad night's work," reflected Harry, flicking through a bundle of fifty-pound notes.

"What was in the wallet, Yiddel?" asked Sammy.

"A key…and a jeweller's ticket in Bond Street, nothing else."

"Let's have a look?" Sammy was curious now. Yiddel threw it over to him. Looking at it closely, he read the key: 'Number 125 Waterloo'. And the ticket: 'Hammonds, Jewellers. Bond Street'. "It could be a pawn ticket…and the key could be a left-luggage key for Waterloo Station!" he exclaimed, getting very interested now.

"Oh-oh, Yiddel," came Harry's sarcastic response. "We've got Sherlock Holmes with us! We should be honoured with such a detective in our humble flat," trying not to laugh.

"Piss off. I only read what's written on 'em," said Sammy, uncharacteristically angry at Harry's comment.

Yiddel stepped in quickly to bring the debate to an end. "Ok, lads. Put the money away in the hidey hole, we'll sort out the other thing tomorrow, yer never know - it might be the Crown Jewels…"

But Sammy was still annoyed. "Oh, you're both starting now, aren't yer - what's this, then - funny night in Hackney?"

"You're a miserable fucker sometimes, Sam. Ain't you had your end away lately?" Yiddel's tone indicated that was enough. "Oh, come on, let's get some sleep and we'll sort it all out tomorrow… night-night, lads, see you in the morning."

As he left their flat, he could hear police sirens in the distance, coming from the direction of the Auction House area. His drive back home took him past the building and he stopped the car to join the throng of people gathered there.

"What's happened, mate?" he casually asked a man in the crowd.

"There's been an explosion in that building, they think it's gas," the man reckoned.

"What, in that big building - the one with 'Auction House' sign on it?"

"Yeh. That old boy over there heard it and called the fire brigade…they're being very careful in case it goes up again." Yiddel's new companion was clearly enjoying the excitement of it all.

Yiddel asked no more, keeping his thoughts to himself as he nonchalantly strolled back to his car, of course knowing exactly what had gone 'bang' in the building - and it definitely had not been gas. And he did not want that 'old boy' identifying him.

The next morning in the Ridley Road market, everyone Yiddel met was talking about the robbery at the Auction House: how the gang had got in and opened the safe by dropping it four floors, making it sound like an explosion. Yiddel listened, shaking his head and nodding in all the right places during the telling of the drama, making no personal comments at all; he just silently listened, encouraging them all to theorise.

The local police were all over the area with cordons and barricades, carrying out door to door enquiries of who saw what, and when. Predictably, they had no information at the end of the day - because no one had seen anything.

Yiddel heard from talkers in the street that the amount stolen was in the high tens of thousands, which made him raise his eyebrows. Also, that the Auction House was putting up a reward for any information and recovery of other items that were in the safe.

'That's the interesting bit,' thought Yiddel. 'Must find out what that is all about.'

The local paper, the *Hackney Gazette*, did its thing, its front page covered with the story and pictures over each of the next few days, detailing the extent of the robbery and what had been taken, augmented by comments from the managing director of the Auction House, who said he was very keen to retrieve the other items that were in the safe, with he himself putting up a substantial reward - in fact, one that was far above the twelve thousand pounds that had been in the safe. All of this made Yiddel more curious as to what these 'items' might be...

14

The Box

Yiddel knew he had to leave it a couple of days to let things cool down, and then he sent Sammy to Bond Street to check out the jeweller's shop whilst he went to Waterloo Station, where he found there were two blocks of lockers, in various sizes. He made no move to go close to them, but simply checked that no one was tasked with keeping a watch on them all, and, above all else, no cameras. He bought a newspaper and found a seat nearby to just sit and pretend to read, all the time furtively checking around the entire area. In the aftermath of that raid, was anyone doing the same? He gave it an hour in which time he noticed nothing…no one out of the ordinary hanging around. This was it, then. Now to approach the lockers, get there quickly in just a few purposeful strides, walk past them slowly now, checking out the numbering system.

Hell, where was number 125? He had trouble locating it, and knew with each second that he was becoming more and more conspicuous. Herat racing – now, at last, there it was; he noted its position exactly. But it was still too risky to try it now, so he did a one-pass, 'casually' returning and at this point making the decision that it was as safe as he could ever achieve: 'Try the key, now, Yiddel,' he told himself. He slid it into the lock, which he covered with his handkerchief, and, as he held his breath, it opened.

Despite all his years of criminal experience, he was aware his body was tingling with the vulnerability that now was the time, if any, to feel that fatal hand drop on his shoulder and for him to be arrested. But no hand did drop. Just as well because there was no going back now. Inside the locker was a leather briefcase which was removed in a split second; leaving the door of the locker open, Yiddel did a swift about-turn and walked smartly with the flow of people in the station and down into the underground, catching the first train going east.

Exiting at Liverpool Street, he headed for the shops on the street level, and bought a cheap holdall at a travel shop to conceal the leather briefcase, before hailing a taxi to take him back to the 'office'. Once inside the taxi, he felt so tempted to have a peek in the briefcase, but, fortunately perhaps, the driver started to talk about 'last night's game' and a load of other trivia, which kept Yiddel in polite conversation with him until he got back.

Sammy was already there with the news that the shop was not just a jeweller's but also a pawn shop, and what they had was a pawn ticket for something that had been deposited at the shop.

For his part, Yiddel proudly produced the briefcase - the two boys hovered close by, such was the air of mystery about this item, and, with the aid of a screwdriver, Yiddel now snapped the little lock open. Looking inside, he could see several small parcels wrapped in newspaper. He opened the first one – it seemed to be a printing plate for twenty-pound notes. The other ones, it turned out, were for five, ten and fifty-pound notes.

"Fucking hell, look at this lot!" gasped Yiddel as he passed over the twenty-pound plate.

"Plates for making money, big time!" exclaimed Sammy, excitedly. But then he thought about it; this would be new territory. "Who do we know who could help us with these?"

Yiddel was too busy looking at the detail of the engraved plates to answer for a few minutes, and then he said, "Make your own money…maybe!"

"You must be joking, Yiddel, one thing's for sure: we're thieves, not forgers," Sammy retorted, wondering if he had heard Yiddel right.

"I'm only kidding. What I meant was - sell 'em and earn a load of money and let someone else print the actual money." Yiddel looked at Sammy. "What's the price on the pawn ticket?"

"There's nothing on it, it just says 'Redeemed Pledge', with a number."

"Well, phone up and give them some cock-and-bull story about your aunt who has just died and you found the ticket in her purse, and so on...y'know: 'could you tell me if it's worth coming all the way from,' say...'Glasgow, to redeem it,' and see what they say."

Sammy dialled the number and spoke to a woman in the shop, giving her exactly the line Yiddel had suggested, at the same time giving her the number on the ticket. "She's checking now," he whispered, his hand over the mouthpiece. "Hello...yes...Ok, thanks."

He turned to the others downheartedly. "She says it's *not* a pawned item - it's been locked in the vaults for safekeeping, all paid for. But she could not say what it was," he said.

Yiddel sat back in his chair, thoughtfully looking at the ceiling. "Now, if our mate at the Auction House knew about it, why is it in the pawn shop at Bond Street? Are we going to walk into a trap if we go and get it? The only chance we've got is if he did not make a note of the ticket's number, an' if that's the case...we're Ok."

"She sounded all right, not edgy at all, just normal. If she was on guard, I could have told." Sammy was able to reassure them that much.

"There is a way, now I'm thinking about it, that we can get hold of it without finishing up in the nick. That is - get someone to collect it for us…I have an idea! Look, for the moment, leave it for a bit and see what more comes to me. In the meantime, let's see if I can find a home for those plates."

Yiddel spent the next hour on the phone to a chosen few of his many contacts; he played his cards very close to his chest, giving nothing away and just saying that he had been asked by an 'acquaintance' to help place them for him. After he got off the phone, he turned to Sammy: "This is a very specialised business - forgery - everyone I talk to makes out they don't know anything about it, and all the time I'm talking to 'em I can hear the printing presses in the background! They must all have good plates already. Some of 'em said they'll come back to me later if they 'know of anyone'. Well, at least I've put the feelers out."

Later on in the day, Yiddel called the two boys into the office from down in the warehouse regarding the pawn ticket.

"I've got it - what I said about getting someone to collect it for us. We get a courier to collect the parcel. We can be outside when he comes out of the shop, where we can watch if he's being followed. If he is clear, we will take it off him in the street…what d'yer reckon?"

"It's worth a try," answered Harry. "How will we get a courier to work for us without it coming back here, though?"

"I'll phone a company. No, on second thoughts, that won't work because they'll want an address…Ok, what about a mini-cab firm? Yeh, send him to the place, let him go in and get the parcel and we'll wait for him outside. Then we'll follow him back to the address we've given him and then take it off him, paying him what he asks for, with a drink on top…well?" Yiddel looked at the boys for encouragement for his idea.

"Maybe that'll be Ok," reflected Sammy with a slight frown. "You mean...use any address, do yer?"

"Yeh, we can wait outside the Mickey Mouse address and take the parcel off him. As long as he gets his dough, he couldn't give a fuck about the parcel. Does that sound better, Sam?"

"Yeh, we can't lose out, let's give it a go!" pronounced an ecstatic Sammy.

Next morning, the trio set off for the West End. They parked Yiddel's car in Harley Street, quite close to a very imposing building - 'Harley Clinic'. Just around the corner, they had spotted a mini-cab firm, and noted the number as they passed it. Within a couple of minutes, they had phoned the cab company and asked for a taxi to go to Harley Street, giving the street number of the clinic with orders to meet a Mr Fry there to then go to Bond Street for a collection, and afterwards back again to the clinic.

"No problem at all, sir," said the very efficient telephonist, only too glad to get an order for Harley Street. "Our car will be with you in ten minutes."

Telling the boys to wait just inside the clinic doorway and to give the mini-cab driver the ticket when he arrived, Yiddel waited a little way up from the clinic, ready to hail a taxi to follow the mini-cab to Bond Street.

Exactly on time the cab pulled up outside Harley Clinic; the driver got out, went into the premises and was instantly met by Harry with the ticket. Harry told the driver his exact onward destination and what to do once he had the parcel. The driver, smiling, obligingly took the ticket, saying, "won't be long, sir," and got back into his car to make for Bond Street followed by Yiddel in his own taxi, subtly acknowledging the boys as he went past.

The mini-cab was at the jeweller's in no more than five minutes; Yiddel in his taxi was right behind him. The driver got out and went into the shop with Yiddel now on the pavement looking at the display as if simply 'window-shopping'. With that classic furtiveness born of many years of criminality, he watched the driver pass the ticket to a woman at the counter, who then went through a door to the rear of the shop, disappearing into its unknown depths. Yiddel waited anxiously out in the street, knowing that he couldn't stay here much longer without arousing suspicion. After a very long couple of minutes, she came back and passed over a box to the driver. Yiddel moved swiftly now to another black cab as the driver left the shop and placed the mysterious box on the passenger seat of his car. Yiddel, knowing where the next destination would be, had directed his driver to the Harley Clinic, his driver disbelieving, initially, the instruction to 'follow that car'.

Yiddel, however, was also anxious that no one was following him, and he kept looking back to make sure of this. In the heavy central London traffic, this wasn't always easy to tell, but it did seem there was nothing to worry about in that respect. 'Good', thought Yiddel, 'now all should be well as long as that driver doesn't get too curious about what's in that box he's just been handed.'

As both vehicles approached the clinic, he could see Harry standing on the top step outside the main front door. Yiddel saw him greet the driver, pay the fare and then gave the driver an extra tip for playing his part, completely unknowingly, in a nice bit of criminality. Yiddel's brief to Harry was, once they had the parcel, to go into the clinic for no longer than one minute, to unwrap the parcel and give the contents – whatever they were - to Sammy, who must then leave the clinic by another door at the rear. Harry was

233

then to dispose of the parcel wrapping in a bin within the premises and follow Sammy out the same way.

Yiddel was now back in his own car waiting to pick the boys up at the back exit and swiftly away from Harley Street.

"Sweet as a nut, boys, sweet as a nut… no hitches at all in the clinic?" he said, once they were safely on their way.

"Only a receptionist wanting to know where I was going as I walked through. I told her I was from the council about the blocked drains and my mate was going to be following me shortly. All she did was nod and go back to speaking to a lady," said a very proud Sammy.

"Well done, lads, right…let me stop and we will have a look and see what we have got for our troubles."

Yiddel stopped the car in a discreet parking bay where Sammy passed him the box, the mystery of which now had them all virtually holding their breath.

"There wasn't much wrapping, just a bit which I took off and got rid of, like what you said, Yiddel," said Sammy.

The box itself seemed to be a very decorative, red, leather-bound jewellery case with two small catch locks on the front. Yiddel sat with it on his lap as he undid the two catches and lifted the lid to expose, set into the recess of blue velvet, a diamond and ruby necklace with matching earrings and a pendant of the same stones…at that precise moment, the sunlight hit the stones which spontaneously burst into a wild spectrum of colours as though the whole treasure were on fire.

"Fucking hell, what beauties!" gasped Yiddel, who was virtually speechless with this heaven-sent magnificence. "What an absolute beauty!"

The two boys took it in turns to hold the box and gaze at the gems, each marvelling at the wondrous sparkle of the stones.

"They look very old," said Sammy after a lengthy pause in which no one spoke, all three men staring as though hypnotised by the box's contents. "But what a box of gems we have here!"

"Let's go to Sidney's place and then he can give his mate George a ring and see if he can have a look at them for us and give us some sort of a estimation," was all Yiddel could say for the moment because although he had that 'feeling' that they really had something here, he also knew they were way outside their normal comfort zone of stolen acquisitions.

Arriving at Sidney's, they found him in the yard with one of his mechanics trying to fix a lorry engine.

Yiddel knew how to have a friendly dig at Sidney. "What are you up to then?" he asked plaintively, "making out you know all about engines…are you the technical advisor to the engineer here?"

"I am keeping my hand in, Yiddel, as it happens," responded Sidney, refusing to take the bait. "When I was on the road I used to keep my old lorry going with bits of string and wire…now I've got these new lorries, I can't even work out where the engine is, let alone fix it!"

They all laughed and Yiddel gently advised him to leave it to the man who knew what he was doing.

"Anyway, Sid, I want to see you about a bit of business," he said, more quietly.

Yiddel passed him the jewel box once they were all seated in Sidney's office to show the man what the 'business' was about.

"Fucking hell!" gasped Sidney, his eyes suddenly like saucers.

"That's what I said when I see 'em, Sid…smashing ain't they?"

235

"Smashing is not the word – 'amazing' is better, I reckon, Yiddel."

"What I want, Sid, is for your mate George to pop round and have a look for us and see what he says."

Sidney immediately picked up the phone and dialled George's number, asking him if he was free and could he come around right away as he had something to show him. Yiddel and the boys noted Sidney didn't give anything away in what he actually said, but the tone of his voice certainly did just that.

"He's on his way," said Sidney, taking another look at the gems. "They really are nice, Yiddel. May I ask where they come from?"

"We did a little job a while back and it was part of the parcel with some bank-note plates. I've tried to place the plates, but no one's come back yet. Still, they can wait, I'm in no rush. They're not eating anything."

Ten minutes later and George arrived.

"Hello, Yiddel-Sammy-Harry, nice to see yer again," he said with a broad grin, giving Sidney a wink. George's affability never failed to impress them all; here was a gentleman-rogue of the old sort who could be counted on for anything, but, summoned by Sidney for today's evaluation of Yiddel's acquired treasure, it was his extraordinary knowledge of diamonds that would be indispensable now. George limped painfully to a chair offered by Yiddel, who saw the pain in George, and marvelled at how he could look so cheerful whilst enduring so much.

Sidney passed over the box to George and said: "Have a look at these then, my friend, and tell us all what you think of them."

George opened the box as he sat down, not really expecting anything out of this world, but the expression on his weathered face said he had now seen just that. It wasn't often George was stunned into complete silence, but not one word did he say as he gazed, transfixed, at the box's contents. His expression was noted by Yiddel and Sidney, who both gave him time to collect his thoughts. Initially, all he could utter was that he was more than impressed with what he was looking at.

Out came his jeweller's eyepiece from his expensive waistcoat pocket as he picked up the necklace, going immediately to the biggest diamond, which was on the drop of the necklace.

"At least, without putting a gauge on it, this is a twelve-carat diamond. They all range down to about a four-carat and the emeralds and rubies are magnificent, all beautiful stones. All set in twenty-four-carat gold." He continued going through the contents with his glass. "The earrings, well, they are the same...at least eight-carat diamonds...And this pendant...again at least a ten-carat diamond surrounded with emeralds and rubies." George paused to breathe out fully. "Truly remarkable pieces of jewellery, Yiddel. I take it that these are yours?"

"Acquired on a job. We was wondering what sort of money would they fetch, George?"

George ran the necklace through his fingers, picked up the earrings and then the pendant and had another look with his glass and said, "These are the finest I have ever seen in my life and I have been in the trade for over forty years. I should think, straight...eight million pounds, maybe more. However, there's something you should know..." As his voice tailed off, Yiddel suddenly became uneasy. How could there possibly be a problem with diamonds worth eight million pounds? Surely the money couldn't elude them now?

The tension in the room grew. Just a few moments ago, all had been anticipation – a building up of excitement as they had all held their breath, awaiting the expert's verdict. Now it had changed. George resumed his analysis. "Yes, worth a huge amount, but as they are...y'see, you would not be able to sell them because these are a one-off. The minute a collection like this came up for sale, you would be nicked. The only chance you've got is to sell them as single stones. But even then, the big stones are so identifiable they would definitely ring an alarm bell to someone and that could be dangerous for you."

"What do you suggest then?" asked Yiddel, uncomfortably.

George was unequivocal. "Personally, I hate to see something as good as this get cut up - it's like cutting the middle out of a priceless painting...you get part of the painting, but you have destroyed its beauty by doing that to it. Because of which, the painting will now never be the same again. It's finished being a work of art. D'yer see what I mean, Yiddel?"

"Yes, I do, George." Yiddel wasn't going to let go though, not having come this far. "So, as I say, what do you suggest?"

"Well, to get yer money, there's only one thing you can do and that is to cut this work of art up and sell the stones separately." George looked quite sad as he said this, and he avoided eye contact with anyone. "It's the only way to avoid being caught with the things as they are."

"Thanks for your help, George." Yiddel wanted to give him some crumb of comfort. "But as we was talking, I had an idea about who might be interested in them as they stand. If not, you can have them to cut up and make us all a few bob. I know your feelings on the subject – you've been totally honest about that, and I respect your views, but would you be prepared to do that for us, if it comes to it?"

Perhaps George wasn't. There was another awkward silence as he considered Yiddel's request. His blue eyes had lost their sparkle of earlier on as he gazed with despairing protectiveness at the treasure trove in front of him. Finally, he got to his feet and, without looking directly at anyone, thanked Yiddel for showing him the jewels and for giving him a chance to earn some big money; without committing himself to an answer, he bade everyone goodbye and left. No one in the room spoke for quite a while.

Deep in thought, Yiddel and the boys drove back to the office. As soon as they had got back, Yiddel phoned Igor at the *Ukraine Club* in Kensington.

"Listen, Igor, I've got a bit of business that your 'friend' might be interested in. See if you can make a meet for me - he could come over to me if he wants... Yeh, I've got an office in Hackney. I'll wait for your call."

Harry had made them a cup of tea and was bringing it over to Yiddel's desk as the phone rang. A voice with a thick Russian accent spoke: "Mr Davis, I spoke to Igor and he gave me your number. He says you have something good that I would be interested in...so tell me...how do you define 'good'?"

Yiddel explained what he had: plates for printing English bank notes and the jewellery. The Russian was interested. He would be at Yiddel's business premises for the next morning at 9.30.

"We might get both the lots away at the same time here," Yiddel said with quiet confidence as he put the phone down. "He seemed interested; anyway, we'll soon see..."

Bang on 9.30, a big black Mercedes pulled effortlessly into the front of the warehouse yard. The stocky Russian, preceded by one minder and followed by two others, approached.

"Good morning, Mr Davis," he said, shaking Yiddel's hand firmly. Without wasting time on pleasantries, Yiddel took the Russians up the stairs into his office. Sammy poured them all a coffee while Yiddel unwrapped the plates first and laid them out in front of his guests. One of the 'minders' came over, produced a jeweller's glass from his pocket and scrutinised each plate separately. Then, looking at his boss, he said in English, "They are very good."

'That went well,' thought Yiddel. 'Now let's see how the jewels go down.' And so he opened the box and placed it in front of the Russians. The boss's eyes opened to almost the size of dinner plates when the sparkling of the stones caught his attention. Again, the Russian with the glass was beckoned over to check them. In complete silence, Yiddel saw his eyes nearly fall out when the man beheld the display in the box. Not saying a word until he had checked every stone, which took quite a time, the appraiser stood up straight and again turned to his boss. He didn't need to say anything. Yet again, the jewels had entranced he who had ventured to look at them. "Again, also very good, boss", he said with more of a hoarse whisper than a normal tone of voice. Returning to his seat, he was still shaking his head in disbelief with what he had just checked out.

The Russian boss drew a deep breath and looked directly at Yiddel with that air of gangster confidence that was designed to send a very clear signal. "And so, what is the price for the plates, Mr Davis?"

"Two hundred and fifty thousand pounds," replied Yiddel, thinking that it sounded right.

"And the jewels?"

"I am asking four million pounds for them all. They have been valued at ten." Yiddel was now in full flow.

The Russian glanced meaningfully at his appraiser. Yiddel noticed a subtle nod.

"I will give you four million pounds for the lot, Mr Davis!" he pronounced.

Playing the same game, Yiddel looked at Sammy as though he was asking for advice, all a big act for the Russian, and then at Harry. He deliberately waited a minute, then stood up and offered his hand to the big Russian.

"It's a deal," he said.

The Russian evidenced no emotion outwardly, but simply said that his appraiser would be back later with the money to clinch the matter.

Thanking Yiddel for his hospitality and for offering the deal, he swept out of the office followed by his team.

When they had gone, Yiddel sat down and looked triumphantly at the boys. "Not a bad morning's work, lads. We have just earnt one million and three hundred thousand each, without even breaking into a sweat. I will give George and Sidney a drink for their bit and later I'll go over to Kensington and square up Igor for his help. Oh, and George will be pleased he won't have to cut the jewels up!"

Three hours later, as all three were having their customary 'working lunch' of beigels, the Russian appraiser returned with the minders to pick up the plates and jewels. The four million pounds was in a large case, all in fifty-pound notes. The two boys and

Yiddel, with the minders looking on, checked the cash. Establishing it was all there, Yiddel produced the plates and jewels once again, and the Russians checked they were the same as their boss had seen earlier that morning. They then simply put them into a bag and with barely a word spoken, left the premises.

"I know you checked the money, lads, but out of all the people that I have ever dealt with, I am sure the Russians are the ones that would never turn us over. They are too fucking serious in what they do; I don't think anything like that comes into their heads - ever."

It was at about this time when Yiddel heard that the people in the Auction House had upped the reward and were very keen, to put it mildly, to get any information about the burglary of their premises. Harry had a stroll around to their building and watched the nightlights and CCTV cameras being installed on all sides, 'a little bit late for that, now,' he thought to himself, with more than a little amusement. The roof was now being divided by a large central metal screen fence, topped out with razor wire.

"You should see what they are doing with that place, Yiddel - it looks like a combination of the Berlin Wall and that fence in the Falls Road, Belfast. There's workmen everywhere working their nuts off and there's me watching them and I couldn't help wondering: 'All this is a bit pointless, lads, hasn't the horse already bolted?'

The next morning, Yiddel took the underground train to Kensington to see Igor at the *Ukraine Club*. The man was always pleased to see Yiddel and his face lit up as his friend came through the door.

"I've come over to give you a bollocking, Igor."

The club owner's face turned abruptly from a smile to a frown. "What have I done, Yiddel? Did those Russians fuck you about…why do I get a bollocking?" Igor really was worried; he resembled a persecuted fugitive whom the world had decided to vent its anger upon.

Yiddel let it go on for a few more seconds, keeping a straight face and then he had to let it all out with a huge roar of laughter. "I'm only kidding, Igor! Cockney humour, me old mate! We did a deal and it's all done and dusted. I've come over to have a drink with you." Lowering his voice, he added: "And to give you your little bonus for letting them know what I had."

He deftly pulled a bundle of fifty-pound notes out of his pocket, placing them on the bar top just inches in front of Igor. "That's for being good. Now come on, let's have some of that special Russian 'Wodka'."

With another quick glance around to note if anyone could possibly see it, Igor flicked the bundle of notes excitedly and could immediately see that he had earned himself a few thousand pounds for a one-minute phone call to the Russians.

"Any time, Yiddel, any time. Right, the drinks are on me!" he said exultantly.

Hearing this pronouncement, a couple of the regulars ambled over to the bar and were treated to a healthy slug of the finest vodka. Within an hour of Yiddel's arrival, word had gone around that there was a party going on at Igor's club and that the drinks were on the house. An hour later and the place was bouncing. A couple of Ukrainian musicians who were drinkers there revelled in reproducing their nation's cultural music on traditional instruments and from that moment the party really got under way. Ukrainian songs, Ukrainian dances and to top it all, some of the regulars were members of a Ukrainian choral group and started into the famous cultural ballads. Laughter, tears (about the old country) homesick Ukrainians - the whole lot was let loose in the club. The party spiralled into one to remember, and dancing girls shrieked as they whirled around the floor.

Hours later, Yiddel was unable to leave unassisted; his legs would not function enough to stand up. A taxi was called for and a huge Ukrainian who carried him like a baby placed Yiddel on the back seat. A bottle of 'Wodka' was put into his jacket pocket 'for later', he just about heard Igor say as the cab door closed and Yiddel passed out. The taxi arrived at the office where the boys were waiting, tipped off by Igor that he was on the way back. As Sammy and Harry attempted to help the big man out of the taxi, he said to them, "What a party, what a fucking party," and promptly passed out again.

It was a very fragile Yiddel who was up and about the next morning. It took several cups of black coffee to start to bring him back into this world albeit a bit shaky. He was sitting at his desk with his eyes closed when his phone rang. It was Sheila, who wanted to meet him to talk about a 'bit of business' that she had heard of. Sammy organised transport for Yiddel on the basis of 'take it easy today, please', and soon Yiddel and Sheila were meeting at their usual place on the forecourt of the local supermarket at Dalston.

Taking a trolley, they walked into the huge store together, making the customary small talk as they pretended to peruse the products.

But, Sheila was keen to update Yiddel with precisely what the 'bit of business' was. "My girlfriend phoned me yesterday to have a chat; she told me that her partner had got a job in a casino in Southall as a croupier. He reckons the place is far from kosher; it's an illegal set-up, catering mainly for wealthy Asian businessmen. The partner said they're taking a hell of a lot of money every night, but the big night is on Saturdays when they get packed to the rafters." She paused as other shoppers passed by, then continued: "It seems a large Indian syndicate backs the place and the partner says that no expense was spared for the décor in the place. They would like to get a licence for the gambling, but that is out of the question from the local council, which is a bit old school, so the place is being run underground as a drinking club with a licence and the gaming bit operates well out of sight. She said her bloke reckons the place is huge. Apparently, it used to be an aircraft maker's building, being that close to Heathrow." Sheila stopped and looked at Yiddel. "So, what d'yer think?"

Yiddel's mind was working overtime – despite the hangover. "Ask your mate exactly where it is. Get the address off her and see if she can get her partner to get us an invite or tell us what night we can go and have a look at it." He gazed at Sheila affectionately. "Anyway, it's about time we had a night out together. You remember I promised you that months ago? We'll go there for a drink and see how it shapes up. Now, are you sure you're up for that?"

Poor Yiddel was still trying to focus his eyes beyond his nose, and Sheila thought it quite endearing. "I thought you'd never ask! Ok, leave it to me. I'll give her a ring tonight."

And so they left each other with Sheila giving Yiddel a little kiss on his cheek. 'Well, that's a nice surprise,' he thought.

Later that night Sheila phoned Yiddel. "We can go any time, you don't have to be a member to drink in the place, you just sign the book when you arrive and that gives you a temporary membership and makes it legal for that night for the local council. She gave me the address - it's not far, just a couple of miles from Heathrow," she reported with clear excitement in her voice.

Sensibly making it for the following night, Yiddel felt a bit elated that for first time in such a very long time (he could not remember when) he was now actually taking a woman – and a very attractive one at that - out for a social night out, albeit to research a job, but it was a night out nevertheless and he felt so good about that he realised he had feelings for Sheila.

The night out called for a new suit, something else he had not done for a quite a while, which of course opened the floodgates from the boys as to, "Where are you off to then?" plus all the usual comments of, "Going for a job interview, Yiddel?"

He had to smile at their well-meant jibes, knowing how close they all were to each other, and he was in great form when he picked Sheila up at her home - she was waiting at the door and as she came down the steps, Yiddel could not help giving a low whistle, she looked so good. Her blonde hair and blue eyes reminded him of something truly angelic, and he couldn't help noting her long legs and wonderfully natural femininity.

"Hallo, love, you look nice!"

"Thank you very much, it's such a long time since I've been out for a drink, except when we were in New York, but that was when we was working." She paused and realised for the first time that he was attracted to her. She smiled shyly as she said, "And this is the dress that I bought in New York...d'yer like it, Yiddel?"

"You look great, you really do," he replied with spontaneous admiration, feeling as though she was the only woman in the entire world – and he the only man. As they made their way to the evening's destination, he couldn't help thinking to himself 'And why not? She is quite a girl. Beautiful…and a trusted member of our business. She's been so good – how could I have left it so long to just take her out?'

And then, 'Wish I'd done this before.'

15

More Than a Gamble at the Casino

They found the club with no problem, Sheila from reading the map located it tucked away off the main road in Southall. Yiddel parked the car and they walked the short distance to the club. Their tip-off was right: it was a very big place all right, looking more like a public house than a club. A multitude of exterior lights covered its one entrance doorway, which was staffed by heavily-built doormen.

"Have you been here before, sir?" one of them asked Yiddel as he and Sheila approached. Although dressed immaculately in a well-tailored dinner suit, the doorman was clearly not in the mood for anyone giving any wrong answers.

"No, it's our first time, we heard about you from a friend," replied Yiddel, effortlessly putting on his charm.

"Ok, sir. All you have to do is sign the visitors' book as you go in and that will take care of your membership for today for you and your good lady."

Thanking the man for his help, Yiddel and Sheila duly signed in as 'Mr & Mrs Heath'. "Why not?" Yiddel quipped later. "It's as good as any and we are quite close to Heathrow airport." As they made their way through from the reception and signing-in area into the main room, the place suddenly changed dramatically. They were now in an enormous, fabulously well-decorated expanse adorned with beautiful wall-mirrors and from an astonishing ceiling hung chandeliers on a scale and expense that Yiddel and Sheila had never seen before. Below these aristocratic adornments, attractive girls were handing out drinks and selling cigarettes. Yiddel looked across to the bar, where there were even more girls, clearly 'dressed to impress', serving more drinks behind a bar that was all of two hundred feet long. It was still reasonably early, but the place was already three-quarters full.

"Blimey!" gasped Sheila, when she had recovered from the surprise of the opulence lavished on this area. "She wasn't joking when she said her partner reckoned it was all posh and decorated, was she?"

Getting their preferred drinks, they chose a table in the middle of the room. While they sat and gave the impression they were just talking generally about life, they both keenly observed everything around them, especially the way the place seemed to be run. At the end of this main area, Yiddel noticed the employed heavies escorting a few people out through a small door to somewhere he could at this stage only guess at. From where he was sitting, it looked to Yiddel like a service door at the end of the bar.

Keeping his voice low, he asked Sheila, "Did you see that, love?"

"Yeh." Sheila was curious where that door led to. "Must be the invite-only casino."

They both sat and watched as more couples were taken through the door. Yiddel ordered some more drinks and asked the girl who brought them back if there was a restaurant.

"No, sir," she said with some surprise, "there's no restaurant, but food will be served a bit later for all - a running buffet."

Seeing an opening for a question, Yiddel casually remarked to her: "Oh, I thought that was where all the people were going down there," pointing to the door at the end of the bar.

249

"No, sir, that's a special invitation area for VIPs only." She would not be drawn on the subject, Yiddel and Sheila noted. "No restaurant, sorry," and with that, she promptly left.

The pair decided to make a night of it and stay, having more drinks and food when the buffet was served. While Sheila was being served by a waiter with her and Yiddel's selection from the buffet table, a man in a dinner suit asked her if she had been before. Sheila put on her 'little girl who never comes out' voice and told him: "It's my first time and why I am here is because my friend had told me all about how lovely it is and that we could have a good night out gambling, so me and my husband," pointing to where Yiddel was sitting, "have come all the way from Surrey to have a night out here." She deliberately paused to change the tone of her voice for specific, emotional effect. "And now I find that it's only for invited guests and I am very disappointed…" She let her remark tail off into an awkward silence and her mournful gaze fell upon the floor as though she was going to cry.

The man appeared to take the bait. "What line of business are you and your husband in, madam?"

Sheila confidently picked up on the searching question, which was really what she had predicted, and more like, 'Are you sure you can you afford it?' and she replied, "We are in the building business, we have two companies, roofing and foundations. Why do you ask?" Her sparkling blue eyes fixed on the man's face.

"The reason, madam, is that the side of the business that *I* run is more exclusive…for specially invited VIPs who can afford to use it."

'More likely to *lose* it,' thought Sheila.

"If you would like to use the, er, facility, you and your husband are quite welcome to do so," he said smoothly, smiling.

Sheila thanked him and went back to Yiddel, who had noted - with a little concern - the man's attentions upon Sheila. He could only guess at what questions he was asking her.

"We have been invited into the back room," she informed him excitedly. "I think we should eat something first and then I'll get him to take us in. I think he is one of the guvnors. He acts as if he owns the place the way he talks. Oh, by the way, you're a builder with two businesses and we live in Surrey." She had to smile as she saw how impressed Yiddel was with what she had found out so quickly.

"I *don't* believe you," said Yiddel, gazing with unconcealed admiration at her. And then he laughed. "You was only over there for two minutes and suddenly we are in - and a friend of the guvnor as well!"

"Not quite a friend yet," she cautioned. "Give me time."

Yiddel looked at her and felt more attracted to her than he had ever done before; he loved her modest yet professional style. He did not have to ask her to do things, she just did it off her own back. Like Southampton and New York, he knew he could leave her to do something and she did it better than he could plan it - unlike any woman he had ever met before. This was something new in his life. Where he had always had to explain everything to most people, in her case, he found she did it herself.

They finished their food and drink and then walked down to the small door and the man in the dinner suit.

"Mr and Mrs Heath," Sheila said to the man, who now identified himself as Mr Khan.

"That's fine. Shall we go through?" he gestured toward the room behind the doorway that was so intriguing them.

Mr Khan escorted them through the small door, which had a sign on it saying 'STORES' and then through a corridor, which now opened up to an even greater sight and scale than the expanse they had just left. This room had to be nearly the size of a football pitch, Yiddel reckoned. Everywhere was a gaming table of some sort. They were both given a glass of champagne and the blessing of Mr Khan to 'do well and have a good time', as he left them.

They had both noticed as they came through the corridor that a small camera screened each person's face as they passed it. The enormity before them was equally beautifully lit, giving a deliberate mood of calm and assurance.

'All to help the gamblers to gamble and lose more money,' thought Yiddel.

Recovering from the initial shock of the closely guarded secret that they now found themselves in, Yiddel asked Sheila, "What d'yer reckon, love?"

Keeping her voice down and making sure her expression gave nothing away to anyone that might be observing them, she replied, "Very impressive and...quite moody."

"Check the exits and security, love. I'll walk round the other way to you and meet you at the other end. Don't rush, look like you're making your mind up about where you're going to lose *my* money," he said with a faint smile.

Sheila raised her eyebrows. "I'll take you up on that", and strolled off.

They both drifted apart in different directions to eventually meet at the top of the room. They found a table to sit at and sipped their already charged champagne glasses to compare notes, going over their observations quietly together so that they both had a good picture of the layout of the room.

"Shall we have a go at the roulette table, then?" asked Yiddel.

A butler-type character was standing by on all the main tables to change up money into chips for each punter. Yiddel gave him four hundred pounds which was exchanged into round plastic chips from behind a glass-fronted window set in the wall on one side of the room.

Giving Sheila four hundred pounds' worth of chips, Yiddel remarked, "And don't lose it!"

Sheila smacked his hand, giggling, and retorted: "And you be lucky, darling!"

They emerged from the casino in good spirits in the early hours of the morning for, despite both of them having lost their money, they now were leaving with a wealth of information about the place, and also with the blessing of Mr Khan to return again. They had become official members of the casino.

"I'm sure that we were being watched and by losing the money he decided we were a good bet to be made members…but who knows, maybe one day I'll get my money back!" He turned to Sheila and his deep brown eyes gazed at her adoringly. "Would you fancy it again next week, love?" he asked her, searching for not just a 'yes' but more of how she said it.

"I'd love to," came the immediate, enthusiastic reply. And then, with a light-heartedness that he found so endearing in her, she simply stated, "And it made a nice change from sitting indoors looking at the telly!"

Yiddel thought to himself, 'Where have I heard that before?'

Getting back to the plan, he proposed a course of action. "In the meantime, I want to put all the information together that we have got now and by the time we go back it should add up to a lot more.

We must find out where the money room is for sure, which I think has got to be the window room. Can we get at it from the back? We will check that out too. Anyway, let's leave it till later and I can draw it all up. I've enjoyed our night out and you never know - it might turn out to be a little gem."

On the way home, Yiddel asked Sheila if she would like to go back to his flat for coffee before he took her home.

"I would like that, yes."

And so, Sheila stayed the night at Yiddel's flat. The next morning, Yiddel served her breakfast in bed and although they had known each other for years they both felt it was long overdue that they should now be together.

"I was hoping that you would ask me in New York," she said with an air of innocent confession. "I was feeling rather amorous there, what with the glamour of the hotel, the city and the job. It turned me on in a small way and I began to see you in another light. And when you were giving us our roles, I just felt right with you then."

"I also see you in another way," Yiddel replied, "not just as a friend I've known for a while, but more so as an intelligent woman that I knew I could trust. Southampton was the first time when I saw how you handled your role through that clever use of make-up, and again in New York. And when I saw you coming out of your house...I had never looked at you in that way before. You looked great and that was it. I think I fancied you then. I'm glad we went out last night and I'm glad we spent last night together." He paused to allow his words to sink in, still a little concerned that Sheila might get nervous and withdraw from him – and his life of crime. "If it's all right with you...I'd like to see you more often."

Yiddel had never felt or spoken like this in the whole of his adult life. From the time that he was thieving alongside his father until the time he was left to fend for himself, he'd always had to be on his guard. That was how he had seen the world – then. Always on guard, always watching out that he never made a mistake and never able to trust another person fully, not even with the boys. He felt he was still teaching them anyway, so he could not let go. However, with Sheila he felt, like last night in the casino that he could back up a little bit and trust her to the limit.

Sheila knew Yiddel was reflecting on things and gave him time to collect his thoughts. Then she put her coffee down on the bedside table and rolled over to be nearer to him and kissed him on the cheek with her customary giggle.

"I would like to be with you too, you lovely man, the whole team thinks you are a great man, they all love you in their own way. The boys treat you as their father. Sidney treats you like a son. And I love my new boyfriend…I think the world of you."

Yiddel, for the first time in his life, felt a bit overcome with what Sheila had said. He had never given much thought about how others saw him; he had always seen himself as the leader of the gang and had never really considered how even they saw him. He was, therefore, quite affected by what she said.

It was mid-morning by the time he dropped Sheila off at her home en route to the warehouse office. The boys had been in for a couple of hours and were waiting for him with great anticipation.

"How'd it go, Yiddel?" asked Sammy.

"It went very well. It really is an unbelievable place, on the scale of a huge supermarket, full up with gaming tables and slot machines like what you would see in a Las Vegas casino, just like you see in the films. The frontage is a pub-like place, deliberately so in order to camouflage what's really going on in the back. We were very lucky, we had only been there less than an hour when this big geezer asked Sheila if we would like to be members - and then we was in!" He paused to convert his new-found knowledge into a working plan.

"We're going back next Saturday night to have another recce and see if it stays the same. I want one of you to go during the day as I think it's best in the morning because it will be all closed up, which means you can check out the back of the building. I'll show you what I mean, I'll draw you a diagram. There is a large field out the back so take a dog with you as though you are out walking it and if anyone sees you, there won't be any questions for why you are around the back of the place." Yiddel looked at both the boys intently. "Check the whole of the back out, even the fields. See where they go and what backs onto the other side of the field as well, and then get out. Get me a complete check of the area. Ok?"

Sammy volunteered for the trip and was pleased they were back in action again; he had long felt he needed something to do to keep busy. Harry was given another task by Yiddel: to go to Southall and discreetly check out the business side of the area.

"Make out you're thinking of opening a business there and see what feedback you get from the locals, but don't overdo it!"

Two days later, Sammy and Harry had obtained all the relevant information that Yiddel wanted and the chief started to put his Game Board together again, centring on a large piece of white card with a detailed plan of the casino building, drawn as accurately as possible based on all the surrounding information gathered by the boys. Yiddel sketched out the inside, from bar to casino, with every door and window added. And the interior of the casino itself with as many of the table positions marked on the board as they could remember. He had the exterior shape of the building and the doors to the money room. But there were some important, unanswered questions. How many men were on duty in both areas? Where were the cameras? What roads were at the back across the field? How many local business traders used the place? And so on until he had all the facts he could possibly get about the 'Target Casino' on the Board.

Yiddel had estimated that on the Saturday night he and Sheila had been there, there must have been nearly two thousand people in the casino.

What Harry had found out backed up what Sheila's friend had said about the place. It was being run completely non-kosher. The general feeling out on the street was that it would not be long before the local council found out and closed it down.

"Not before we do!" pronounced the enterprising Yiddel, really switched on with the planning, and everyone knew that there was now no going back – this was it, the casino was going to be hit Yiddel-style, good and proper. The plan steadily began to take shape with lots of the right information from the team.

Yiddel was in his office taking a phone call when Harry came up to say that a crate was being delivered from Taiwan.

"Got to go, darling, see you later," as he bade farewell to Sheila. As much as he loved any time spent being or talking with her, Yiddel was particularly excited to see what was in this consignment. Quickly descending the stairs to the warehouse floor, he watched as the truck off-loaded to just inside the warehouse, the driver using his hydraulic crane to push the crate inside.

257

As soon as the driver had gone, Harry was instantly cutting the binding tape from around the box as Yiddel was taking the document pouch off the crate, and keenly opened it. He said nothing while Sammy, with some effort, started to prise the lid off the crate with a crowbar.

Before it was even half off, the trio had cleared the protective packaging away and could see, initially, the boxes of cameras along with the new product Mr Dong had sent. Sammy opened one of the many boxes…of little, quite ingenious, mechanical plastic dogs. Once the batteries had been fitted, the *Little Fido* did all kinds of tricky moves, from sitting up and begs, to barking. It twisted each way, and when Harry placed it on the lid, it would only go to the edge, turn around, and not fall off. However, its clever bit was in responding to the human voice. When it was told to sit, it did, and so on, performing many tricks, which they all found very entertaining.

"It's like a robot," exclaimed Sammy. "What a great little toy, I do like that!"

It came in a very attractive box, looking very presentable in any high street shop. Taking a couple of the cameras and dogs up to the office, Sammy and Harry were given the job of seeing how they would be received in the trade, and to work out costings so that the business would have a realistic price for both items. This had to factor in Mr Dong Lai's price, the shipping and then the final FAGIN UK Ltd figure.

Sammy phoned Hamleys, the major toy buyer in Regent Street, to make an appointment to demonstrate the two toys. Yiddel was quite surprised to hear that the buyer had said they had not seen either of them, but would be happy to do so as soon as possible. So, the boys put on their best suits and with an impressive-looking briefcase to carry the merchandise, took themselves off to the store.

As they were leaving, Yiddel, with the caution born of years of experience, told them: "Tell them nothing but the price. You don't have to – and mustn't - reveal where they come from. Ok, good luck, boys!"

Yiddel had worked out the price of the cameras that Katzman was selling in New York and then calculated what he could get for them in England, and so he went for the same extent of mark-up for the dog, and this appeared to give them a very nice profit for both items.

He had some business cards and letterheads printed by a small trader in the market so when the boys arrived at Hamleys they were well presented. Within the impressive surroundings of the large business premises of this famous store, they were shown into the chief buyer's office where a Ms Janet Floyd, a small, portly woman in her mid-forties, met them with what seemed to them a superficial politeness rather than genuine enthusiasm.

To the boys, who were used to taking people at face value and talking directly, this went down awkwardly, but they tried not to let this show. They duly demonstrated the dog on her office desktop and showed her the clever little camera.

"Will we be the sole buyers or are you taking them to the other stores?" she eventually asked after some initial hesitation.

Sammy recalled what Yiddel had said: give nothing away. "I'm afraid we can't promise you that…not at the moment, anyway. We all know that these sorts of products have one killing in the markets before they're superseded by the next, so if you really need a guarantee today, we would have to say 'no', I'm afraid."

Ms Floyd had already realised that the multi-nationals would love to get some of the action on these: they were both perfect for the present day and her hungry commercial instincts were telling her they would sell like hot cakes. After the usual bluff and counter-bluff prevalent in taking a product to market the world over, the meeting finally ended with the chief buyer of no less a store than Hamleys promising (verbally only) to make a firm order within the next two days.

Once out into the street, the boys paused to collect their thoughts. Sammy stopped Harry by holding his arm. "Harry, me old china, correct me if I'm wrong, but I think we have a market-killer here – what d'you think?"

Harry agreed. "In that case, while we're up in the jolly old West End, let's go and see the right people at Harrods and Selfridges and see if they would like to make us a 'firm order' as well!"

With rising self-confidence in this new game of marketing innovative products on a scale still beyond their true comprehension, they called in at both stores, completely cold as a business call, and found themselves again shown into each buyer's office and achieving the same response from both. All three meetings were identical, they reflected later, in terms of the conversation, the questions asked, the surface hesitation and then the poker-game of testing the other side out.

When Yiddel was informed of their actions, he immediately suggested that all the supermarket buyers should be invited to have a look as well. Again, the response was staggering: every buyer who saw the products was falling over themselves to get hold of the goods, and not one of them seriously contested the price (which included Yiddel's confident mark-up of one hundred per cent, after expenses).

Yiddel held back on the order to Mr Dong Lai in Taiwan until he knew exactly how many this really could be for.

Two days later, he knew. Twenty thousand of each item, split between the stores, and that was just their first order.

"See how the sales go," they all said, "and then, all being well, we will give you another, bigger order."

Yiddel phoned Mr Lai and placed the order with express wishes that the order be dispatched as quickly as possible.

"Mr Lai did not sound at all surprised by the size of our order. He just said 'Thank you, Mr Yiddel, just pay the same way as your first order on banker's draft'," Yiddel informed the boys, congratulating them on their very successful business outing. "He then gave me a grand total, which, once I worked it out, is cheaper without Katzman's bit that he put on."

After a long discussion amongst them all, Yiddel decided not to release any of the stock they had down in the warehouse to any of the stores until the main order was delivered from Taiwan so that all the London orders could be delivered to simultaneously, giving them all a chance to start trading – and competing - together. Sidney's haulage company was given the task of delivering each order to the depots of the stores.

After all this feverish activity, there was then a 'calm' in which there was nothing else to do but to wait until the shipment arrived. All the invoices had been made out, ready to go with each respective order.

Yiddel sat back in his 'chief exec's' chair, as the boys called it. "So, gents, seems like we really do have a legit business. And by the way it's started, a successful one - all trading from our new premises." He lifted his mug of tea and pronounced a toast: "To FAGIN UK!"

"FAGIN UK!" echoed the boys.

Yiddel and Sheila had become a very close item. They had decided on the timing of their second trip to Southall for a closer reconnaissance of the casino situation. When they arrived - again Sheila looking stunning in a beautifully cut dress that seemed to wrap naturally around her elegant figure - Mr Khan was at the main door welcoming guests for the evening.

"Mr and Mrs Heath, how nice to see you again! I hope you both have a lucky night," he wished them, with his well-practised, wide trademark smile.

Yiddel was duly impressed, even a bit shaken by the man's extraordinary memory for people's names. He had begun to think that he was easily able to judge what made Khan 'tick', and therefore what motivated him, and how to anticipate his way of doing things; after all, Yiddel had - all his adult life always been so perceptive, so shrewd in his almost uncannily accurate estimation of others – but he was now starting to doubt himself, especially as they had only met once before…and the sheer volume of guests arriving was surely too great for individual recognition. But now Mr Khan was himself escorting them to a table, beckoning a waiter over to get them both a drink.

"On the house," he instructed the waiter, who clearly knew who his boss was. Turning back to Sheila and Yiddel, his voice flowed: "Call me or one of my men to escort you through when you are ready, please."

They both sat and enjoyed their first drink, at the same time making notes on how many 'heavies' seemed to be on duty compared to the last time they came. After a couple of drinks, they were ready to go through and Yiddel called one of Khan's men over to show them through to the casino room.

"What do you make of it so far, love?" he whispered.

"I'm seeing about the same amount of minders and staff in the bar area as before," was Sheila's analysis.

Once they were in the casino, a member of staff got them their gaming chips. And exactly like before. they went their own way, meeting at the far end of the room, where they got a table with another free drink and compared notes as to how much, and precisely what, if anything, was different to last week.

"Still the same," said Sheila after a long pause. "It don't seem to change one week from the next."

"That's good, just the way I like it. Well, darling, I'm sure we are being watched," Yiddel said as he glanced at the bulbous- type camera pods fitted into the ceiling. "So, let's go and bet!"

All the time they were gambling, they both checked out the inside of the fire exit doors to see how they were secured and took a good, long, but surreptitious, look at the strong room which Yiddel noticed had three staff inside, changing and stacking the money. He managed to get a better analysis when he went to change up some money himself, and as he stood scrutinising the room, he could see over the tellers' shoulders to what the inside of the room really looked like close up.

"Mr Heath, there's no need for you to change up money yourself, that's what I have staff here for!" Khan was suddenly alongside an immediately rather unnerved Yiddel, who had possibly become a little too engrossed in checking out the strong room.

"Oh, I'm sorry, Mr Khan. I forgot, in my haste. I'm enjoying the game so much that I'm just rushing to get some more chips and get back to the tables."

Hoping Khan had swallowed this lie, he was glad to get away from him and get back to the tables, but not to gamble. He joined Sheila, who was standing by a blackjack table.

"Did you see that? He was on me as soon as I got to the window."

"Yeh, I saw him move pretty rapidly once he saw you standing there." Momentarily, she had gone rather pale at the thought of Khan being onto them and she had to force a smile upon catching a glimpse of one of the minders looking in their direction. Under her breath she told Yiddel to do the same and to point to the table as though they were purely concentrating on the table itself.

"They are very sharp, Yiddel. They really don't miss a thing. Greeting us by our names when we arrived. Then seeing you at the window. We have got to be good, darling, or they might come and hold our money for us." She forced another smile, just as she lost another fifty pounds' worth of chips.

They knew they had, now, to stay the full course, and tried to enjoy the free buffet and drinks, and when the last of the chips had gone, it was with huge relief that they made for the exit. Again, Khan, who seemed to be everywhere, now appeared at the main door shaking hands with the guests as they left. It came to their turn, and they both knew they had to act this bit very well indeed.

"Good-night, Mr Heath, and of course the lovely Mrs Heath. Thank you for coming," was all Khan said, but the look on his face said something else…or did it? In spite of all his experience of reading people, Yiddel was struggling with this one.

They were both glad to leave. Halfway up the drive to their car, Yiddel couldn't help looking back over his shoulder to the door. "Smooth bastard!"

"Oh, I don't know, he's quite charming," Sheila said softly, taking Yiddel's arm and raising her eyebrows at him.

Yiddel grabbed her tightly around her waist and whispered in her ear, "I think *you* are very charming, you beauty, and don't try to make me jealous!"

"Meeee? I don't have to do that, I love you too much." She kissed him on the lips.

They now had every bit of information they needed for the caper. The next day, the Game Board was amended and Yiddel decided it was time to bring together all the players who would be needed for the hit.

He had decided that Elvis and Sidney were not required this time and instructions were given to say nothing about the job to them. He needed Roger as main driver and Ansel for added muscle, making a formidable team of five. Ansel agreed immediately to be part of the group.

"Without a doubt, man, count me in, don't even think of going without me!" was his ecstatic Jamaican response.

Roger was also invited and he readily agreed. Sheila was sidelined because once Yiddel had laid out the plan it was clear there was no job for her to do.

"Anyway," said Yiddel. "She's done her bit already."

Yiddel's plan was to use the same sort of tactics that they had used at Southampton. A large diversion of noise and commotion, all mixed up with tear gas and explosions.

"Right, listen up, gents. This is the game plan. I want three motors. One of 'em a four-wheel drive. A change motor for number two and another for a detonation outside or near the club. The detonation car primed with the same stuff that we had at Southampton. The four-track will get us there and then get us away across the field at the back of the target to the main road where number three car will be parked. Get a large powerful motor for the third, H. Ok?" He paused and they all nodded agreement.

"Right, I want incendiary in the four-by-four when we leave it. The detonation car has to be parked, Roger, as near to the entrance of the club as you can without drawing too much attention to yourself. So ideally, be suited and booted as if you are going into the place. Once you've parked it, walk back to us and take over the driving of the four-by-four, then drive us all round to the back of the casino, here!" Yiddel pointed to a small service road which ran around the back of some houses nearby and then on towards the casino back door itself.

"Stay with the four-by-four. As you see us go in the back door, detonate car number two. You'll have the same gear as at Southampton, so you know how well it works, Ok, Rog?"

Getting thumbs up from Roger, he went on.

"Wait for us to come out to you, have all the doors open slightly - not closed - for a quick entry. Sammy, I want you to help Roger to have the two cars prepared for detonation before we leave for Southall. I don't want you doing anything once we get there, all right?" Sensing the particular importance of this element of the plan, they confirmed they understood what to do.

"This is the main road here, Roger," pointing again to the plan board. "When we leave you, cut across here where the third car will be parked from the day before. Sammy - you detonate the four-by-four as we leave it. Then we drive up the main road towards the

266

North Circular here, and away. Get a fairly big motor for number three just in case we have a large parcel of money to handle."

This got whoops of joy from the team.

"Right, back to the casino. I will blow the back door with one of the explosive packs. As you follow me in to the main gaming room, throw the tear gas in all directions, using as much as you like, and make sure there is plenty of gas in the room. I will head for the strong room and blow the door with another of the packs. Each of you will enter the strong room carrying a large GPO sack. Again, throw the tear gas into each side of the room. As soon as you can, start loading the money into the GPO sacks. By now, the second car should be well and truly alight causing mayhem outside. Ansel, take up a rear-guard position at the door and take out anyone who wants a fight. There are three men in the strong room, but they look like bankers, no obvious muscle, but just in case deal with it. Keep your eyes on each other's backs as you are working." Yiddel paused to drink some water.

"As soon as you have your bag filled, check that we are all ready, and leave together, straight out the door we came in through. Roger will be in the four-track. You know the rest. Ok, Rog?" Again, a firm nod. "Harry, here's the shopping list: gas masks, balaclavas, overalls, gloves, four GPO bags and three motors. I will get the explosives and gas from our man.. Any questions?"

Getting a positive reaction from the team, Yiddel concluded. "This coming Saturday night, gents, be ready to rock and roll at 11pm."

The whole team, including Yiddel, were naturally now buzzing and it was hard to wait for the 'off'. The minute the plans were put on the table and the brief was given out, the adrenalin began to flow. The gang were on a high once more, Harry reckoned. "There is nothing like this in the whole world for such an all-time feeling. I don't know, but I should imagine that the troops must have got a rush like this when they were coming out of the trenches, to meet an unknown situation, either with a bullet or with success. We're like them, we just don't know what we have in store for us, do we? And *they* don't know we are coming, do they?"

Harry was in one of his of his philosophical moods, and his words hit the spot all right. Everyone in the gang agreed with what he was saying.

Sheila had sat through the briefing, listening with admiration to the new man in her life, who seemed to her to be the whole world itself. She thought a lot, but for now said nothing. She watched the faces of the team, and could see exactly what she had seen before, and this she told Yiddel. They were Yiddel's men through and through. They take in every word that he tells them. Why should there be 'any questions' at the end? His plan was laid and that was that. They all trusted Yiddel to the core.

Although she had been left out of the final action, she felt she should do something to help, so she suggested to Yiddel later that night that she would bring another mini-bus to pick them up from the third vehicle. Then there was no need to bring it back, they could leave it anywhere en route. Yiddel could see her logic and agreed.

"A good idea, babe. I'll get Harry to get another motor. And for that I'm taking you out for a slap-up dinner. Pie and mash, and it's on me!"

"What a gentleman you are, Mr Davis!"

Yiddel now left the toy business in the hands of Sammy and Harry, as he had said he would once it was established. It had a good future ahead of it and, once the big order had arrived from Taiwan, the boys could take care of the orders and despatch using Sidney's transport company.

"As soon as the first order goes in, leave it a couple of days and phone 'em again. Follow it up with a personal visit and that should help keep them on the boil," Yiddel told them.

He made another phone call to Mr Lai to say that the order had arrived Ok, and how pleased he was with the merchandise. The main reason for his call was to somehow get assurance that Lai would let FAGIN UK be the sole importers for the whole of the UK, and he found himself being pleasantly assured by Lai of exactly that. This had been his plan all along, he said. Yiddel told the boys later: "I like to have one company in each country; it makes doing my book work a lot easier!"

The week passed uneventfully, with all the necessary items for the casino job being obtained through theft where this was better, and by Friday night, everything was in place including vehicle number three. The other stolen vehicles were locked away in Auntie's just for the night, where the explosives were fitted and primed with their detonators. The tear gas canisters were put into the four-by-four with the gas masks and clothing.

Saturday morning had a bright cold start about it, not bad for a November day; the team all in their own way were doing their usual thing. Ansel opened the café at his usual market day time of 6am in order to cater for the stallholders, who were busy setting up and getting the merchandise out on display before the first shoppers appeared at 7.30am. Yiddel was up and about, walking through the market at 7am to have an early cup of tea at Ansel's. The two boys were at the office by 8am; not being able to sleep beyond 5am due to their minds becoming so focused on Target Casino, they had to get up and get on with things – at this stage, anything - just to stay cool and focused and not let the nerves get in the way. Roger never got up early on a Saturday, but today he couldn't sleep either and also was up and moving around. The whole team were, in their own way, preparing sportsman-like for the night's action.

Yiddel loved the market; he was fascinated by the characters in it. From the man who sold brown paper bags, and the stallholders for their sales, to the man who sold crockery in vast quantities, and doing a showman's performance in his selling technique of how 'unbreakable' his product was, and to the one who boasted (only to his friends) about the large villa he owned in Marbella but who, to everyone else, was always 'doing bad' and never earning enough money to pay the rent, Yiddel loved it all. A typical Yiddish ploy, it was, to say that out loud so that everyone hears how bad you're doing (it could, after all, be the taxman standing nearby).

Walking through the market everyone liked to have a chat with him; they all found a natural affinity for the man – it just was how they saw him: a large amiable man who would not do his own down, and always ready to help out, even if it is just to right a tilted stall or to help pick up fallen stock.

Ansel cooked Yiddel his usual bacon sandwich with a large mug of tea. Not a word was spoken about the forthcoming job. Only friendly banter, sometimes 'taking the piss' about something they knew about one of the stallholders in the café having his breakfast before the day's trading got started. Jokes were often rife: the dirtier the better; current affairs, politics, boxing, the Arsenal, Tottenham Hotspur and all the rest about an East End market way of life. There was a joke for everything.

Yiddel and Sheila were now living together. Sheila would occasionally go home to make sure that her brothers were looking after their father and to supervise all the washing that needed to be taken care of. She was feeling that she had given so much over so many years of being their 'housewife' that she needed her own life now with Yiddel, and the family applauded that.

16

Target Casino: Game On

By early evening all the team had assembled at Yiddel's flat. Sheila was effectively the hostess and she made sure they all had something to eat and drink, even though most were nervous and finding it difficult to even think of food.

Harry had acquired a Space-wagon mini-bus for the trip out to Auntie's to pick up the other two vehicles. The conversation was that of those getting ready for the big event. Everyone tried to hide their nerves by talking about light-hearted topics of the day or maybe just some gossip from the market.

Yiddel looked calm on the outside and had been searching the true state of the team as he watched them talk. But now he called the gang to order, to go over each of the roles for the final time. It was the last chance anyone would get to avoid misunderstanding what he was to do once the job started. At the end of this, Yiddel could relax a little, and reassure himself that everyone was indeed fully aware of their responsibilities. As was his custom, he now sat back and let them all continue the pre-hit banter that each knew was necessary to manage the anxiety they all naturally felt, and to be able to 'gel' before show-time.

They drove over to Auntie's, collected the other cars, and then they were on their way, each in their allotted vehicles. Sammy and Harry had already parked the third car in a side road at the back of the field on Friday. The drive over to Southall took slightly longer than expected as the roads were quite busy with Saturday night traffic, and the boys wondered at how unsuspecting so many people were of villains like themselves who had other, very different, motives for this particular Saturday night's activities.

Sammy and Harry checked that the third car was still there after which they went to the club to rendezvous with Roger, who was driving the second car which would be detonated, and with Harry, who was driving the four-by-four. Roger parked up as close to the casino as he could without arousing suspicion and then walked back to where they were waiting in the Range Rover, of which he now became the driver to take them to the back of the casino.

Once they were all dressed and ready, Yiddel gave the 'Go!' Now it began. They leapt out of the car and followed Yiddel to the back door. Yiddel raised his hand to Roger for the signal to hit the button at the same time as Yiddel blew the back door off. The noise was ear-splitting as the car went up and the back door disintegrated under the force of the explosives. Kicking the splintered remains of the door to one side, the gang moved forward to the strong room door. The others were already scattering the gas grenades in every direction as Yiddel detonated the second door - the strong room. They burst into the room, again spreading gas grenades. In this split second, Yiddel glanced up at the clock on the wall - ten past one - and at the same time caught a glimpse of no less a figure than Mr Khan through the window in the gaming room. The tear gas was billowing all around the money room and now it was spreading with such unstoppable energy, it seemed, through the window into the gaming room. As Yiddel knew, it was rapidly becoming very dense and choking, and he could hear the screams of the stricken from the gaming room.

The team knew what to do and how to so it: pouring bundles of money that were all nicely piled up on the racks into the mailbags. Foolishly, one of the tellers made an effort to prevent Ansel from loading his bag. Not good. Ansel felled him with a solitary punch to the head, and Yiddel saw that both the others were too busy hiding their eyes from the gas to offer any resistance. Within just a few minutes, the four had cleaned out all the racks and lockers of any remaining bank notes. And in all this mayhem, Yiddel could hear the panic the raid was generating - even through the walls and despite the noise that immediately surrounded him - and he knew that, as planned, the diversionary bomb was doing what he wanted it to do and was causing chaos and panic out front.

He looked around and, checking that everyone was clear, shouted: "OUT! GO!!"

They pushed through the dense gas and into the open air, heading for Roger.

'Good old Rog!' thought Yiddel in that raw moment as he saw the doors flung open and Roger there, waiting for their getaway.

But, just as they were pulling away, two of the club minders caught up with them and threw themselves at the four-track. Roger slowed as Sammy, Yiddel and Ansel jumped out and hammered the two to the floor, leaving them both battered and very bruised for a long time for their troubles.

Roger waited for the trio to get back on board and then carried on with the set plan and headed at speed across the field to car three. As the off-roader lurched from side to side with Roger careering over the field like a mad thing, Yiddel threw a glance that clearly required reassurance back towards the casino from where he could see fierce, orange-tongued flames thrusting themselves out of car number one, and – more importantly - no else in pursuit.

Feverishly, but with the professionalism gained from their collective experience, they rapidly transferred all the moneybags into car three and drove off. Harry was holding the detonator and, right on cue as soon as they were a hundred yards away, hit the button. But nothing happened. The Range Rover appeared not to want to explode. For the first time in this operation, Yiddel felt very uneasy. Everything else had gone so well. His mouth had gone dry and for a moment he didn't know what to say or do. This wasn't what he, the Master, was used to. He could see, out of the corner of his eye, that the boys couldn't believe the four-by-four was still intact. What had gone wrong? This moment of anxious concern seemed to last a lifetime, and Yiddel's mind was tortured with what to do. He was about to make a command to Roger (they would never know what it was) when suddenly the Range Rover took off in a giant fireball of exploding glass and metal, destroying the vehicle completely.

"Oh, thank God for that," exclaimed Harry. "I really thought the button had failed."

Now back on auto-pilot, they all removed their overalls, balaclavas and masks, which Sammy put into a big sack. After driving at a cautious pace for a couple of minutes, Yiddel looked across and could see Sheila driving alongside them smiling. He signalled for her to drive behind and told Roger to pull into the first lay-by so that they could transfer over to Sheila's Space-wagon. Roger's instructions were to pull in to a car park once they were well clear of the scene, and then to get in with them. This would take them into west London, a good few miles away. Roger drove into a large public car parking area near Chiswick. Checking all around them, they watched Roger leave the vehicle at the far end against a wall and, as he walked back and got into the big Space wagon with the others, Sammy detonated Roger's previous car - only by this method could they be assured that no clues had been left in the three vehicles. The detonation kit in this one was similar to the one used at Southampton: no big bang, just internal combustion, setting light to the inside. They watched it start, and, seeing the resulting flame, made good their departure.

Looking back over his shoulder at their faces - each one grinning mischievously back at him – Yiddel felt the need to congratulate them all.

"Well done, boys, fucking marvellous, just like clockwork! And fucking magic, bang on cue, just what yer muvver ordered and all the other things I'd like to say, but for the life of me I am still ten thousand feet up and I am fucking flying!"

Harry was sitting on top of the bags of money; Sammy was pinching his cheek saying, "Who's a clever boy then?"

Ansel decided it was time to break into a rap number and Roger for his part just sat and smiled.

They were now driving along the North Circular Road from the Chiswick roundabout, when Sheila - although really glad all the boys were safe and sound – checked behind them again as she had already done a couple of times out of an anxiety that was niggling away at her. Yes, sure enough, there was a big black car that seemed to be following them very closely.

"Yiddel," she gulped. "There's been a big Merc following us for a while now…d'yer see him? He's had several chances to overtake us, but he's staying where he is…" Her voice tailed off, but everyone could detect the note of near-panic within it.

Yiddel heard loud and clear and took a look through the back window. "Ok, let's take no chances, might be something, could be nothing. Slow down as though you're going to turn left and see what he does!"

Sheila slowed and the Mercedes slowed as well.

"We'll try him again, slow right down." And, so did the Mercedes. The tension in the car was palpable. No one looked back as that would give the game away, but it was almost unbearable to feel like sitting ducks and be powerless to do anything about it.

"Ok, we know now that we've got a tail on us. Roger, slide in the back of Sheila and take over the driving. Sheila, get right in the back, down low and keep your eyes on him. Everybody else get ready for a ruck!"

The transition was made safely, with the vehicle's speed only slowing a slight amount. But would their hunter guess he had been rumbled?

"Ok, Rog, start to take the speed up to about seventy and let's see what he's going to do."

The big engine of the Space-wagon roared as it opened up and devoured the road…and so did the Mercedes.

Yiddel had made his mind up. "Roger - it's all yours now, take it to the fastest it will go and then brake hard for an emergency stop. Traffic's almost non-existent this time of night." He turned to the others to issue the next command, this time raising his voice above the engine being pushed to its capacity: "Get ready for a crash, gang, he will either hit us or go round us…if he goes round - Rog, go with him and take him off the road. Just sideswipe him as he goes past. Right, ready? Ok, mate, do it!"

The Space-wagon with its three-litre engine was very capable of doing the speed that they were now travelling at; looking over at the speedometer, Yiddel could see that it was now at one hundred and twenty miles per hour which, as Yiddel and all of them well knew, was suicidal on this road, and now he shouted, "Brace yourselves! Right, Rog! Hit the brakes!"

The big Space-wagon had the brakes to match its engine capacity - superb. The vehicle nearly stood on its front sending up a huge plume of tyre smoke, with the determined Mercedes driver still travelling at one hundred and twenty. Thinking he had Yiddel's team on the run, he had fallen into the trap of becoming too obsessed with closing in on his prey, and it was too late when he realised Yiddel's tactics: with the Space-wagon suddenly halted in mid-flight, the pursuer had no option but to hit his brakes to instinctively try to miss slamming into the back of the Space-wagon.

He could never have stopped in time. Swerving to the near side of Roger, it was in that same raw moment that Yiddel gave Roger the command: "Nearside, Rog!" as the Mercedes careered past, still at almost full speed.

Amidst the screeching of tyres and the forces of gravity throwing them all around, Yiddel somehow got the look down into the Mercedes to see what he needed to know…Who the hell were these people? It was no surprise. In that split second, he saw the agonised face of Khan staring up at him like a mad thing from the back seat of the car. But it no longer had the look of the hunter. Now it was a look that Yiddel would never be able to forget. Not just fear written all over his face. Khan was in the 'death tunnel' – when someone knows his time is up and there is nothing he can do to avoid it. All the precious things he holds dear flash before him, and his mind goes into that death-trance.

Now Roger violently swung his steering to the left and hit the Mercedes right between its front and rear doors. The big car hit the kerbstone and became airborne. With such momentum of speed behind it, and with all control lost, it flew in the air for about

278

seventy feet and crashed through a furniture showroom window, bursting into flames as it did.

Yiddel couldn't care about Khan and his cronies. Instead, he calmly asked Roger how the Space-wagon was after that impact, concerned about its ability to get them to safety.

"It's fine." Roger confirmed. "I think all we lost was a hubcap. His speed took him out. I only had to clip him and he was gone." Curiously, Roger seemed far less stressed than anyone else amongst them, and they had to admire him as he resumed a normal speed.

"Well done, Roger! Just in case there was an eyewitness, let's get off this road. Take the next right and we can cut through Hampstead to Holloway Road."

They all settled down to a quiet, uneventful journey back to Hackney. No one followed them now, and the 'incident' back on the North Circular was left behind with no obvious witnesses - hopefully. Sammy took the vehicle out of the borough and parked it in the grounds of a block of apartments that he knew well, wiping all the surfaces down as he was driving it, and by the time he arrived at the drop-off the inside was ninety per cent clean. A final rub and check and it was time to leave. Harry, who was following, drove them back to the office, where they could recuperate and get their thoughts together and relax a little.

"It's a shame that it had to finish like that, but it was their own fucking fault. They took us on and they fucking well lost. What a prat - the bloke driving the Merc. Christ knows where his brains were, up his fucking arse I should think." Yiddel Davis was clearly distressed at the outcome of the crash. He did not like to see anyone get hurt in such a way that they cannot get up and fight another round. It was against his age-old principles of 'rogues' fair play'. The boys stayed quiet – they knew their chief needed to articulate what he felt and this was the best way.

"Yeh, get your man…but you don't have to kill him," he went on, pacing up and down. Catching his eye, Sheila beckoned to him to sit down and she put a consoling arm around his shoulders.

He took a deep breath. He did appreciate her kindness - and love. "All right, lads?" he asked the boys.

Both of them, sensing his mood, just gave him a thumbs-up and poured themselves a drink. They had been speaking about the Mercedes crash on the way back and both of them marvelled at how well Roger had handled that situation that had so suddenly developed on the North Circular Road.

"He's a funny fucker, old Roger." Harry reckoned. "One minute he's all done up in beautiful clothes to do the gay clubs… and the next he'll take on the heavies and beat 'em hands down. And he don't even turn an 'air!"

Sammy saw it differently, however. "What you forget, H, is that Roger, dear old Roger, don't know any different. His entire family are villains. Things like tonight come naturally to him - he don't even have to think about it, it just comes. Yiddel didn't have to tell him where the Merc was. He knew. And he knew exactly what he had to do to take him out before Yiddel even said a word. Gay or not, our Roger is a great chauffeur."

All through the night, Yiddel saw Khan's face in the back of the car demonically staring up at him. He just could not get that picture out of his mind. It proved a long, tortured, sleepless night. Sheila knew this and kept a comforting arm around her man all the time.

The next morning, they were both up early. After showering and coffee – neither had an appetite for any breakfast - they were off to the office and the legitimate business. Sheila left Yiddel at the premises and went to see her family. The two boys had both said they could not sleep, and Yiddel Ok'd it for them to go to the gym for an early but well-deserved workout and sauna.

Yiddel had asked all the gang members to be at the office as close as they could to 8.30. Everyone was there on time.

"Anyone heard any news yet?" asked Yiddel anxiously, clearly expecting someone to have heard something, but they all shook their heads.

Yiddel sighed and sat down heavily. "The coffee's on - help yourselves. Go and lock the door downstairs, Harry, and make sure the grill in the door is covered…you know what a lot of nosey bastards they are round here. And, then, gentlemen, we'll start the count."

They tipped all the mailbags out onto the floor.

"Pile it up in thousands, and put an elastic band round each bundle. Keep the notes in each value - it will save a lot of messing about later."

They all got to work with the task of counting, many of the notes being still in their counted bundles, but they did what Yiddel had asked and counted each and every one. It took a couple of hours of them all working, and they needed to stop for yet more caffeine at about midway. Eventually, they arrived at a total of nine hundred and fifty thousand pounds - with a lot of rupees, Irish punts and American dollars not counted.

For the first time since the heist, Yiddel smiled. "Well, I guess that is not a bad night's work, lads, well done!"

They divided it up into shares of one hundred and thirty-three thousand pounds, with the rest - once it had been sorted out and exchanged - to follow.

Harry took the big bag of clothes and masks down to an incinerator at the local hospital, where he knew he could burn the whole lot by giving the man in charge there a few twenty-pound notes for his troubles. Physically, they could all leave now, well satisfied with the share-out, but in reality all of them were trying to fight off that vision of the crash that stubbornly lingered at the back of their minds.

"It's a shame that it had to happen," said Ansel, as they were leaving. "But, y'know, if that driver had had his way it could have been us."

Roger agreed. "He was coming for us and that's for sure, he was under instructions from his boss to keep with us. He tried to miss us, and maybe get in front. Yeh, I've been thinking about that all night."

"Well, that makes two of us," said Yiddel. "But I'm still glad you did the right thing under the circumstances...we had to get away or we would all be busted now."

"Or smashed to pieces," murmured Sammy, deep in thought.

"Yeh, we are all Ok." Yiddel tried to put on a calm and confident air as he got up to go, but his voice betrayed his state of distress.

At that moment, Harry arrived back with the early editions of the *Evening Standard*. Over coffee and cheese beigels and doughnuts, they scanned the paper with some anticipation.

"Anything in there?" Yiddel wanted to know, and the sooner the better.

"There's nothing on the front page." Going through the rest of it as fast as he could read the headlines within them, Sammy continued, "And nothing on two or three." Skimming through the paper, he began to realise that he was going to have to disappoint Yiddel. "No, nothing at all." He avoided Yiddel's agitated, searching frown and waited for the moment to pass. Harry had also been watching the chief, and wanted to reassure him. "I'll go down lunchtime and get the midday edition," he offered. "Bound to be something in it then."

Sammy turned on the television as the morning news began.

'Last night, in the early hours, violent explosions rocked west London and shook local residents out of their beds when two vehicles blew up in Southall. Police are not ruling out another incident on the North Circular Road where two men were killed, and two others badly injured, in a horrific crash.'

That was enough to galvanise them. All in the room were drawn hypnotically into the pictures that were being screened of the front of the club and of the furniture store with the remains of the Mercedes car. The news report continued: 'There is a possibility that both incidents are related to a racist attack on the club recently. The owner of the club had reported a similar racial attack two weeks before.'

Yiddel was not impressed by that claim. "A cover up...a fucking cover up! So now they're calling it a racial attack to hide any truth coming out about Khan's illegal gambling casino."

"How the fuck can they do that when the back of that place was blown up as well?" Sammy wanted to know.

"They must have closed the back up and told the police that all that happened was the car that blew up on the front drive. If they lock the small door at the end of the bar and stick another exit door

283

on quickly, no one - detective or otherwise - need go down there," Yiddel surmised, his mind racing once more with what was being claimed and how far it was from the truth. "I reckon they could put it down to a service area or a kitchen or whatever. And the chase down the North Circular was down to chasing after the racialists, leaving Khan's place squeaky clean, and then two of them getting killed 'heroically' in the action trying to do it." Yiddel's expression changed dramatically as another thought occurred to him. "That Khan's going to be buried as a hero – a brave, bloody hero!" He paused to try to think ahead – what were the authorities really up to? What was going to be their next move?

He looked straight at Sammy with clear anxiety in his face. "Sam, where did you leave the Space- wagon last night?"

"Tottenham, in a public car park next to a pub."

"Take Harry with you and torch the fucker, just in case there *is* something in it that could come down on us. Especially now that we know that two of them died. The Old Bill will be keen for it now, so when you get there, well and truly check it out before you do anything…any sign of anyone watching, leave it and come back. Ok?" Yiddel was rapidly wishing he had instructed this last night.

In just a short time after the boys had left, his phone rang. It was Sammy.

"Yiddel…we're here and the Space-wagon ain't. So, we went into the pub for a drink and sat at the bar 'cos everyone's talking about the police having nicked three boys who apparently had stolen it from here and who was stopped going towards the M25 in it. The lads had a lot of gear inside to do a job, so people are saying. Tools and safe blowing equipment. Seems the unlucky fuckers had to steal that motor and then got stopped. But don't worry, Yiddel, I went over that motor last night and wiped all the inside down, there

284

was nothing of ours in it. We cleaned it inside and out, all the doors, handles, seats - believe me, it's clean! And then the Old Bill came back here and told the landlord the story after checking him out too. They kept on asking him if he knew whose motor it was…told him it had been stolen from Aldershot last week. Now, I got it from a car park in Islington, so it looks like we had it second, and someone else had it before us."

He paused to check around him and wait for Yiddel's questions. But none came, so he continued: "It looks like those poor sods that were captured are going to cop it unless they can clear it with the police, don't it?"

As Yiddel finished listening to Sammy, Sheila arrived at the office to tell him what she had heard on the TV.

He listened attentively even though it told him nothing new. Remaining seated behind his desk, he looked distant and troubled. "Yeh, two dead and two badly injured." He went on to tell her about the phone call from Sammy.

"That's unreal," she gasped. "That motor had been stolen and used three times for something or other? Well there's nothing you can do now, it's in someone else's court, not ours."

The television news was putting out another news flash. 'Three men have been arrested in connection with the club attack and the incident on the North Circular Road in the early hours of today. The vehicle that they were driving, when stopped, was identified by an off duty police officer on his way home from a party. The two men that were injured in the crash are in a serious but stable condition in Hampstead Hospital. The Metropolitan Police are asking for any eyewitnesses to the explosions in Southall to come forward as a matter of urgency.'

A long pause ensued, then Yiddel finally spoke. "What d'yer reckon, love?"

"I think the best thing to do right now is to get the team together, pay them all off with the divvy-up and forget it. Let us back off. What happened on the road was their fault for chasing us…it was either them or us, and they were the ones who lost."

Sheila was adamant. What she said made sense to Yiddel, who tried to focus on: 'unlucky for them. Those in the Mercedes and those who stole the Space wagon'.

"Right, let's get the gang together, Babe, as soon as the boys are back."

Sheila phoned Ansel and Roger to meet up at the office – 'effective as soon as possible'.

Within one hour, the whole team was assembled. Yiddel went through the latest news with them and they all agreed 'it was them or us,' and to leave the subject well alone from now on.

Yiddel was starting to return to normal, which the team was glad to see. "Ok, my lovies. The share out. The total, as you all know, was eight hundred thousand. We had fifty thousand expenses for explosives and extras, which leaves us with seven hundred and fifty thousand. Split into six gives everyone on the caper one hundred and twenty-five thousand each. I've put your money into bags." And then his eyes twinkled as he looked at each member of the team. "Be careful as you leave, though, boys. Don't get mugged!" He paused, hoping to see a smile or two. But there were none.

"Right, who wants a coffee? Ok, coffees for all please, darling," looking at Sheila who raised her eyes to the heavens in mock indignation. "And a sugary doughnut each!"

Away from the news, the conversation took on a rather different turn; they discussed football, local gossip, the weather - all those things that made up the minutiae of life. But, suddenly, the TV put out another news report about the Southall job. It immediately sentenced the room to silence as they listened.

'One of the survivors of the fatal crash on the North Circular Road was the co-director of the club: Mr Amit Khan. His condition is critical but stable. The other survivor is a cousin of Mr Khan who works for him, who is also in a critical condition.'

Yiddel's eyebrows raised and once more he could see Khan's agonised face in his thoughts as he looked up seconds before the crash. After Ansel and Roger had left, and leaving the boys down in the warehouse, and Sheila generally tidying up, Yiddel was thinking deeply and eventually he said "Yer know he see me, don't you, just before he crashed?"

"I knew there was something else on your mind," Sheila was relieved he had at last told her. "You didn't sleep, did you? Was that the reason?"

"Yeh, I kept seeing his face, he had a look of rank fear - and I can't forget it. But what I'm thinking is that he saw me without a mask on, so he knows who did his place over. One of his punters, Mr Heath...I know we covered our tracks, but he still knows it's me, doesn't he?"

"Did you not hear what they said on the news? The man is in a critical condition, and hardly in a position to worry about you right now, is he? The man is fighting for his life. He may make it or he may not," Sheila replied matter-of-factly. "Leave it at that and if - and it's a bloody great if - he makes it, your dear little face will be well and truly forgotten by then. And if not, we will just have to do

287

something about it. Now, come on, you old fart! Let's go and get drunk somewhere local and then we can roll home stoned."

Getting some comfort from her words, Yiddel and his 'luvverly' Sheila finished the night having a riotous time in the *Ridley Arms* and were eventually asked to leave by the landlord as he wanted to close and go to bed. Already jaded by lack of sleep the night before, Yiddel was more than ready to comply and he and Sheila did indeed roll home together and not another word was said about Mr Amit Khan.

The newspapers were going big on the 'racial attack' in west London. Over the next few days, exaggerated as always, everything was blamed: from the National Front to the Klu Klux Klan. But, strangely, not a word about the actual robbery. There were a couple of column inches about exploding vehicles. There were a few lines about the three young robbers who were detained with the Space-wagon and formally charged with other crimes – none of them related to Southall, and that was it; on the face of things, nothing like enough to put it in the big league.

The days ticked by and the big order from Taiwan was delivered. The boys threw themselves into the business of looking after all the clients who were waiting for their orders. They arranged for Sidney's small fleet of vans to make the deliveries, all arranged by phone to be at the various stores simultaneously so that no one could claim that a competitor had received the products first. By late afternoon, Hamleys, Selfridges, Harrods and all the other multi-nationals that had placed their first orders were on the phone to FAGIN UK re-ordering and anxiously wanting to know what the earliest date was that they could have the next delivery. On the strength of such demand, Yiddel immediately phoned Mr Lai to place an even bigger order and likewise requesting a definite time by which they could expect it.

But Mr Lai was again ahead of him. "Mr Davis, I hope you do not think me presumptuous, but I knew you would be on the phone making this kind of demand of me, so, five days ago I sent you the same two items, doubling the order size from the first delivery! Am I making myself clear in English, Mr Davis?"

Yiddel had suddenly learnt a lesson in big 'legit' commerce. "Mr Lai, you are making yourself very clear and I thank you for your awareness. I will send you a money draft first thing tomorrow morning, covering the cost. I shall of course double up the amount of the last invoice for all the items and the delivery costs. Thank you, Mr Lai."

He hung up the phone and turned to Sammy.

"That man is one hundred percent, you know. Not only has he sent your next order before waiting to hear from us, but he has doubled it!"

"He must be getting orders coming in from all the other buyers. He's gauging the world demand on the toys; he's one clever old bastard. He'll clean up before it dries up and then go on to another little gem," reckoned Sammy.

"He can't be daft to know when to do all that," said Yiddel. "So, we will have them in a couple of days, wont we?"

Harry and Sammy spent the rest of the day phoning around like good business people looking after their customers, assuring each one that they would have their order within the next few days.

At the end of the day, Sammy sat back in his chair and looked over to his business partner Harry. "Well, what a good day, I must say," he remarked with obvious mirth.

289

"What about me, then?" asked Yiddel.

"Oh, and you as well, Yiddel, how can we leave you out?" The mood now lightened considerably – all due to their first-ever venture into legitimate business. Soon, they were all falling about laughing at the extent of success this innocent foray at being legit was having – like it was trying to compete with their irresistible urge to be crooks and villains. "It's insane – it's like a bloody gold rush!"

Later that night at Yiddel's flat, Sheila had prepared a candlelit dinner for them both, with some beautiful wines. After they had dinner, Sheila put everything away and they sat back with another bottle of wine to watch the film on TV.

"I'm glad we are together," said Yiddel, relaxing with her on the sofa. "It's so good to have someone here to share my life with, more so – a million times more so – because that someone is you, Sheila, and I know I can trust you…I'm not afraid if I slip up and say something which I shouldn't. I know the boys are Ok, they are set up now. They are very rich young men. And my girlfriend, whom I love to bits, is also a very rich lady and is well able to look after herself." He looked at her with that big Yiddel smile and took her hand.

"I think that is one of the reasons we are so happy," she said. "I trust you too, Yiddel, you are the nicest man I have known, and I don't want anybody else."

There was a pause as they looked deeply into each other's eyes. Nothing and no one else in the entire world seemed to matter for those precious moments; it was such a magical feeling for them both, and, eventually, it was Yiddel who broke the silence. "Sheila, I've been thinking about…well, us, and I wanted you to know something about…" As his voice tailed off, he seemed to change his mind about something, and then he said, "Sheila, would you marry me?"

Sheila, who hadn't looked away from his deep brown eyes - such fathomless pools of love and affection – was more than a little startled, and immediately began to assume her man was perhaps embarking on his usual 'wind up'. But then she realised that Mr Yiddel Davis - the big, affable man whom *everyone* liked - was for once not joking. And by the look on his face he meant every word of what he had just said.

Time stood still.

"Oh, darling, you're not joking, are you?" she heard herself say.

"No, I am not," her man replied, his voice deep and sincere.

"Well, in that case, Mr Davis…I accept your proposal and yes, a million times yes! I would love to be your wife!"

17

The Art Caper

Early the next morning, Yiddel left the flat before Sheila awoke and set off for the warehouse to make some business calls. When he arrived at the entrance he noticed a large Mercedes parked in the driveway to the units. It drew his attention because of its clean, black bodywork, by far not the usual type of car to be parked around the streets of Hackney.

'I wonder who that belongs too...' he thought, as he opened the main door to the premises.

Deep in that same thought, he hadn't realised that he was not alone. A voice behind him said, "Mr Davis?"

Startled, Yiddel turned to see a tall, smartly dressed man.

"He's not in yet," he said, mindful of possible repercussions emerging from the Southall job. "He usually gets in about ten o'clock. Who shall I say called?"

"He does not know me. A mutual friend has recommended me. My name is Joe Morris...from Texas, USA."

Yiddel then realised that the chances were that the man wasn't there to blow a hole through him - he *seemed* too genuine a person to be carrying a twelve-bore - and also, the fact that he was alone, reassured Yiddel slightly.

"Who's his mutual friend then, Mr Morris?" he enquired.

The American was no fool, however. "You have come very highly rated, Mr Davis, very highly...from a man who tried to, how do you say it over here? Ah, yes, 'do you over' and failed, and who has since then held you in great esteem." He let the clue sink in. "A

Gerald Moores from New York City. Do you remember him, Mr Davis?"

Yiddel certainly did. But, after Khan and the events of the Southall job, even Moores seemed a lightweight adversary. So, he invited Mr 'Morris' into the warehouse and then upstairs to the office, away from the street and any listeners.

"Do I remember him, Mr Morris?" he asked, rhetorically, when he had made them both coffee and they had sat down. "I would have gone to the other side of the world to get even with him for what he did to me here in London and - luckily for him - I was somehow in a good mood when I finally caught up with him in New York and only took off him what was rightfully due to me."

Yiddel wondered, however, why Morris wanted to know, and if Morris was trying to gauge his reaction to whatever it was that he was going to tell him.

"Naturally, I do hope he is all right and hasn't been arrested?"

"I'm sorry to bring it all back to you, but no, he has not been arrested, in fact he owes it all to you that he is not in the county jail. You know why? He is a business associate of mine…Now, no more will I say about it than that. As I said, you come very highly recommended by him."

Yiddel met the gaze of his new acquaintance full on and somehow felt assured that this man Morris was kosher – ironically, by, of all things, his knowledge of Moores.

"And how did you find me, Mr Morris?"

"I simply looked up your company name - FAGIN UK - and hoped I had found you. I knew it was you when I saw you at the door. Gerald gave me a very good description of you and it fitted like a glove."

293

Just then, the two boys arrived. Yiddel introduced Morris as a friend of Gerald Moores from New York. Both boys immediately tensed up, not knowing in what capacity this stranger was in their office.

"It's all right; he has sent Mr Morris to see us, not to harm us."

Sammy gave Harry a look and shrugged his shoulders.

"Ok, Mr Morris, what do you want?" asked Yiddel.

"The reason I am here in London is that I have a job for you to do. A job that I could not in a million years handle myself. I have a partner with me here in London whom you may have seen at Gerald Moores' hotel when he was here. A Mr Lionel Cooper - he's in the insurance business in the USA."

"Yeh, I know him," said Sammy. "I watched him when he arrived at the hotel to meet Moores. Yeh, I know what he looks like!"

"Good. Well, Lionel and I are, as you say, 'in business' together." He paused as if to let his words sink in. And then he looked deep and hard at Yiddel directly. "We would like to use your services for a job here in England. A job for which money is no problem. If that is Ok with you, of course?"

Yiddel was already more than a little interested but, as was his normal practice in such situations, tried not to show it. Instead, he looked at the boys for their reaction, and they both shrugged their shoulders to indicate they had no major objections, so Yiddel, not wanting to commit his team to something he didn't have the full facts about, simply said for now: "Sounds very intriguing, Mr Morris…why not tell us some more?"

Now it was down to business, and they all knew it. Another caper; another risk that something would this time go wrong, yet once more too irresistible to decline.

Morris, secretly delighted that Yiddel had accepted his offer, opened up with what this particular job was really about.

"We have a client in the USA who is a secret collector of art - the masters, in fact. His collection contains works of art that have been regarded as lost to the art nation, due mainly to the Second World War in Europe. He was in a position after the war to purchase some of the finest paintings produced by the great art masters of the world - from those that had *stolen them – the Nazis*. Do I make myself clear, gentlemen? My client wishes to expand his collection by getting hold of a particular painting, which is here in England. My client is a very wealthy man in Texas; his financial standing is beyond any figure. Money is a rude word to him, all he wants he gets, by one way or another. He employs me to get what he wants. He has made me a multi-millionaire just for working for him, so I say again: money is no problem."

The trio listened to Morris's story without interruption.

"The painting that he is after is in a collection which belongs to a certain man in Oxfordshire, who was a Nazi officer during the war. My client found out from a reliable source exactly where it is and this man, like my client, keeps all of his stolen masters locked away in specially prepared viewing rooms. If I told you that my client has a house in Texas which has another house built below it, completely separate from the top section, which holds only his works of art, this, I hope, will give you an insight as to what a keen collector he is."

It was time for Yiddel to say something, having listened to Morris's story so far. "And you want us to get the painting for your client, right?"

"Perfectly right, Mr Davis. He will pay the price without dispute as long as he gets it intact. He stipulates that he wants no contact with you and you will get none from him. I am all you will get. Should this go wrong, Lionel Cooper must be no part of it - just me, that's the risk I take on his behalf. I have the details of where the house is and I have a photograph of the painting taken in Poland during the war. The only guide for you *is the photograph*. It is such a 'busy' painting that it would be hard to describe, anyway."

Yiddel was now fully on board with what was required and was already visualising how they might do the job. But, instead, he again said nothing and looked directly at the boys for their response, deliberately so in front of Morris whom he wanted to draw more information out of – particularly before they started discussing Yiddel's 'fee'. He valued the boys' opinions – they had already been through a lot together and were fast becoming good strategists at evaluating the feasibility of a 'caper'.

Sammy read his thoughts and spoke carefully, although not without some obvious enthusiasm in his voice. "Well, we like a challenge, Yiddel." And, turning to Morris, said: "If we do it, we'll certainly give it our best shot, Mr Morris."

"How much is the painting worth?" Harry wanted to know, thinking only about the financial side of the job and how much they were going to make out of pulling the caper off.

"The painting itself, gentlemen, is priceless, one cannot put a price tag on it. If it came up for auction, the price would be astounding. It is a Van Gogh and we know for a fact that his *Sunflowers* fetched twenty-seven million pounds at auction in London in the early 80s, so I guess…well, much more than that!" Now Morris wanted some answers. "Anyway, I ask again and must have a definite answer, please: will you do the job?"

Yiddel sat silently looking at Morris, shifting his look from Morris to the boys. The stillness hung heavily in the air and everyone felt the tension that was suddenly upon them. But Yiddel wasn't one to let the awkwardness of the moment influence his decision. It was no bad thing to let anyone asking for their expertise to sweat just a little.

At last, he had made up his mind to give Morris his answer. He had in fact made the yes/no decision a while ago, but Yiddel Davis was an experienced operator when it came to negotiation.

"Yes, Mr Morris. We will do the job and get your client his painting. Our fee for doing this will be ten million pounds. I am making no demands on your client, but I would like the money deposited in my accountant's hands before we even get the car out of the garage."

Morris stood up, looking relieved. Relieved that Yiddel had not turned him down and had taken the burden off his back after his previously unsuccessful search to find anyone suitable and capable of doing the job.

"I am pleased that we are doing business, Mr Davis. I will give you all the details by this time tomorrow. I will be back here with my colleague in the morning." And then, smiling for the first time since he had arrived at the premises that morning, he said to all three: "And thank you, gentlemen!"

They all shook hands and Harry took Morris to his car.

As he watched Morris leave, Yiddel reflected on the meeting to Sammy. "Talk about 'money comes to money'. And what d'yer think about that shit-head Moores? He only recommended us! How does that work? I had him down as a right wanker…"

Harry came back from seeing Morris off and repeated exactly what Yiddel had said. "What a prize prick Moores is. What d'yer think, Yiddel? It's a nice little earner, thanks to you."

"If we get the right info from Morris, we can make it a smooth operation. Let's see what the details are in the morning."

As promised, Morris was back at the warehouse with the insurance man bang on time. Both men were dressed immaculately in expensive suits, which impressed Yiddel.

"Good morning, Mr Davis," said Morris. "Allow me to introduce Lionel Cooper. I believe that you did not quite meet up formally the last time he was in England."

"Good morning, gents. No, we have not met before, but I was informed of his every move while he was here with Moores. And talking about Moores," said Yiddel staring into Cooper's face, "I take it you were his insurance man for the exhibition?"

The bespectacled, slightly overweight Cooper answered him directly. "Yes, I was. I had the whole trip covered in case of any, er…accidents as well." He tried to put on a brave face, and his grey-blue eyes spoke of a highly educated man who knew how to use such 'education' to good effect in his trade - the interests of wealthy, ruthless businessmen.

"I bet you did!" Yiddel was still glaring at the man.

"Can we get down to business now that the introductions are over please, gentlemen?" suggested a suddenly unnerved Morris, clearly having underestimated the hostility arising out of the dealings between Moores and Yiddel. He was starting to seriously worry at what could be a dangerous hindrance to his client's wishes. Anxious to get the deal underway, he tried to defuse the tension with a few pacifying comments, but Yiddel did not like Cooper and he could not help voicing it.

Uneasily, they all gathered in Yiddel's office to hear Morris begin outlining the specifics of the forthcoming job.

"We have a detailed layout of the premises where the painting is hanging; we believe it is up to date. It was acquired recently but we cannot validate it." He paused momentarily to check Yiddel's reaction, but there was none.

"The house is in Oxfordshire, in a village called Waterperry. I believe it is not that far from London. The house is called Klein Manor - the name of the family that own it is Klein. They are Germans. They arrived from Germany after the war and have long been involved in trading on the London Stock Exchange. The son, Albert Klein, is the head of the family although his father is still alive and living at the house. Albert's grandmother died two years ago. Albert has a young wife with two sons. The father, who is Heinrich Klein, was an officer in the Gestapo and a firm Nazi party member, who somehow survived the Nuremberg trials after the war because of an accepted plea of non-collusion, rather than non-involvement, with the annihilation of the Jews. It seems he got away with it because he was in charge of only minor operations of supply movements, which happened to include his own illegal appropriation of works of art for his personal collection."

Again, Morris paused – this time because something was telling him that what he was about to say about the Jewish element of Klein's past might affect Yiddel's thinking. The name 'Yiddel', Morris realised belatedly, spoke of a Jewish ancestry, and Morris for the first time wondered if he had made the right decision in requesting Yiddel Davis' help.

But it was too late to go back now, although this dawning of truth, combined with the hostility between Yiddel and Cooper, made Morris wish he could rethink his plan. He knew the others were waiting for the next element of information and Yiddel was already watching him, wondering what he was thinking.

Uneasily, he continued. "This was not known at the time; he had been very clever in covering his tracks and had all of his ill-gotten gains hidden away from the reach of the authorities' searches. Technically, he was squeaky clean and he only got a minimal sentence for being a member of the Nazi party. However, Klein engineered that so-called 'verdict' with some of his stolen Jewish money, which kept him off the gallows. Therefore, at the end of his sentence, he brought his wife and family to England, complete with all his 'possessions', and started a new life here. He became a very wealthy man by occasionally selling some of the vast fortune that he had gathered up from the Jews - people who were no longer in a position to care about their belongings. He had been party to whole families being wiped out, leaving bastards like Klein free ownership of their treasures, be it art, jewellery, property and land." Morris had chosen, after all, to play the Semitic card.

Yiddel listened intently to the words of Morris. He, like many Jews, was affected by the Holocaust, wiping out distant family members. He recalled his father telling him that he had lost all of his family who had remained in Europe in the death camps. Suddenly, Yiddel felt he was now involved. He was being asked to go to a man's house, a man who had stolen property from people who could not prevent it happening, and take it off him. It gave Yiddel another slant to stealing from this man Klein. Morris' plan had worked.

Yiddel gathered himself and took a deep breath. "I am going to steal something that this man has claimed as his for more than forty years and I am going to have great pleasure in taking it from him. It will be the first time in my life that I will have come close to a Nazi bastard, and yes, Mr Morris, I am going to have great pleasure in doing it to him. I will inflict some more pain to the man by taking more than just the painting for your client; we will hurt his pride where he thought he was safe."

"I'm a simple east London man, who was far removed from the sufferings and near-annihilation of the whole Jewish race, and it seems to me that a vast majority of the guilty got clean away with it after the war. They got away with the mass murder of people…people who were only interested in getting on with their lives and they got away with stealing everything that countless families had worked for."

Yiddel's emotions came out fully, and the boys wondered if their boss was going to lose it completely. They could only watch as he opened up.

"I remember reading that they not only killed everyone from certain Jewish villages - they then torched the village until it was totally destroyed and to this day that village is not on the map. Not only the Jews, Mr Morris, but also anyone who they did not like. And when Hitler got fed up with killing ordinary people he started killing his army commanders when things did not go to his liking. A most disgusting man and best dead along with his cronies – all of them. Sorry, Mr Morris, I have this thing about Nazis, not because I am Jewish, but for all the people in England who suffered the air-raids, and then no one escaped. Everyone in England lost someone they knew in one raid or another."

Morris had underestimated Yiddel's strength of feeling, yet it had worked; Yiddel Davis would not only do the job, but would give it one hundred and ten per cent.

"I fully understand your anger and the plight of everyone in Europe at the time of the war, Mr Davis, so maybe it will make this particular job a lot easier than most to handle. And as you rightly said, we will be stealing something back from a man who killed to steal by organising the deportation of people away from their homes so that he could ransack them and take what he wanted."

Morris went on, feeling that he had also vented some anger about this man Klein. At last, he came back to the task in hand.

"Here are the details. All laid out in document file. We have as much as we can without the Kleins being aware. I cannot give you any more; it is now up to you, Mr Davis. We are staying in London until the job is done, that is my order from the client. We will leave, hopefully, when we know you have succeeded in your task. Anything that you want to ask me, you can contact us on this number." He handed Yiddel a business card. "It is a non-traceable mobile phone. It will be switched on day and night. I only want to hear one thing from you, Mr Davis, and that is 'come and get it'." Morris got up and his mood lightened considerably as he had not only outlined the task, but also had found the man whose its responsibility it was to be.

"I wish you and your team the best of luck, but I have to say that what I heard from Mr Moores in New York is that you are good, so we will undoubtedly speak soon, and the money will be deposited with your accountant as soon as we see the painting."

They all shook hands and Morris and Cooper left, more than satisfied at having Yiddel and the boys so enthusiastically committed to the theft of the painting, although in Cooper's case it was as much relief to be away from Yiddel as it was anything to do with the painting.

Yiddel laid the documents out across his desk ahead of starting the 'Game Plan' once more.

"I'm getting that feeling again," said Harry, smiling and showing them his trembling hand.

"I think we all are, mate," replied Yiddel, quietly.

They spent the rest of the morning shut away in the office poring over the papers. By lunchtime, Yiddel could see the course of action.

"Tomorrow morning, I am going to the village to case the place and have a little listen and see what I can pick up. You come with me, Harry. You stay here, Sam, and look after the shop; we will give you a ring when we get there."

Next morning the pair were on the road heading for the M40 and the tucked away village of Waterperry. They arrived just before noon and parked at the only pub the village possessed, right in the middle. A sleepy place by London standards, Yiddel noticed there were a couple of shops catering for the villagers' immediate needs: a family butcher, a baker and a hardware and newsagents all within a hundred yards of each other. At the end of the village, sited in one of the immaculately-kept terraced cottages was an estate agency with a huge sign over its front displaying the name 'Browns'. Leaving Harry in the car, Yiddel took a seemingly casual stroll there.

"Good morning, sir," a girl said as he entered the shop.

"Morning" said Yiddel.

"Can I help you?" she asked in her well-educated voice.

Yiddel went through one of his yarns about always loving the village from a child and now that he had returned from the Far East a wealthy man, he was thinking about buying a place there. Yiddel watched the faces of all three staff when he mentioned the well-chosen word 'wealthy', and true to form, everyone smiled and coffee was immediately offered. The girl then handed him over to her 'senior property advisor' - a clearly affluent man in late middle-age named Jim Clarke. Yiddel introduced himself as Charles King, right off the cuff as he had just glanced at the headlines on the front page of *The Daily Telegraph* - something about Prince Charles. Yiddel was thinking of a line about Jim Clarke, but thought he would say nothing, just yet.

"What price range are you looking at, Mr King?" Mr Clarke affected that rather false, sickly smile all too readily betraying the commercial interest in a potential client of such wealth.

Yiddel detailed a rough amount of land and size of property and thought he would not go too high. "About two million."

"I'm afraid you won't get very much for that sort of money around here, Mr King. In fact, most of the larger properties are fetching in the region of three million pounds and upwards."

"What would a large manor house fetch, just to give me an example?" asked Yiddel.

"Well, sir, if you remember the area as you say, you must know the big house on the other side of the river, it's now called Klein Manor, after the present owner. That would set you back a cool fifteen million just because of the sheer size of it, the amount of land it has and of course, the river rights."

"Yes, I see what you mean, Mr Clarke, so my two million won't go too far here, would it?"

Realising he was losing a potential buyer with a nevertheless substantial sum of money to spend, Clarke was quick to say, "We have some very nice houses that would easily fit your price range.

Maybe not so big, but quite spacious nevertheless. Some would need a little work doing to them to bring them up to today's standards, but we've got one or two in some really excellent locations, and, in the end, each would turn into a very nice investment."

Yiddel thanked him for his help, with a promise to return for a deal, and left with a good local Ordnance Survey map of the area to help him look around.

Walking back to the car, he was thinking 'how the fuck did a Nazi bastard find this place - in such a beautiful part of England? Why come here, to this particular area?'

Still trying to figure this out, he was relieved to be able to at least talk to Harry in a normal voice.

"Ok, H. I've sorted that bit for us, let's go and have a drink, and keep your ears open!"

The duo sat at a small table near the bar after ordering their beers and sandwiches. The landlord of the *Duke of Wessex* was a large, jovial man, more like a family butcher than a publican.

"First time to our village then, gents?"

But Yiddel was thinking something different: 'Here we go, the third degree from a nosy fucking landlord!'

"Yeh," said Yiddel, purposefully stuffing a large ham sandwich into his mouth.

"I thought I hadn't seen you before," ventured Nosey.

"No. We're just passing through and stopped for a quick beer and a sandwich." 'Now you can fuck off,' thought Yiddel. But, no, Nosey was staying the course.

"What brings you through here, then?"

"We had to see someone," said Yiddel, now feeling pissed off and wondering how much of this his patience could stand before he got up and did something. Suddenly, however, the door opened and Yiddel was saved by the arrival of a couple of locals.

And Nosey was instinctively on at them at once. "Hello, Tom, Ruby. I heard the bad news with your sister, Tom, what a shame and so young, too!"

The young man appeared grateful for the expression of sympathy. "Thanks, Bill. Yes, we were knocked sideways by it. One minute as right as rain, and the next - dead on the floor."

'All trivial rubbish,' thought Yiddel, 'which I don't really want to hear.' But then it all changed in an instant.

"The Kleins found her on the Great Hall floor. She had just finished cleaning the stairs. The doc reckoned she was dead before she hit the floor. 'Instant,' he said."

The Kleins…Yiddel's ears were now like an Indian elephant's. 'What about the Kleins and the sister?'

Fortunately, the landlord also wanted to know more, but the young man wasn't able to say much that Yiddel was directly interested in.

"This is the first time we've been out since she died. Still trying to get over it, aren't we, Ruby? She was only twenty-two. The funeral was very good; the vicar said so many nice things about her."

'Tell me more…'Yiddel thought.

In the silence that followed, Yiddel and Harry kept their heads down while they drank their beer. Even Nosey kept his mouth shut for a couple of minutes, but was soon in action again.

"What are you going to do about her little flat?" he asked.

"It's in the hands of Browns the estate agent. We're clearing out all of her things and they are going to let it out for us. Her job is advertised in the local paper, but we've heard that no one wants

306

the job because they pay so badly," declared Tom, gazing mournfully into his pint.

Yiddel's mind was racing. An empty flat and a cleaning job at the exact place they want to get into...

He told Harry to eat up and the pair left with Nosey telling them to 'come back soon'.

The pair got in the car and Yiddel phoned Sheila.

"Hello, love. I've got a favour to ask of you. It's to do with the American who came in the other day and offered us a job… well, it's on. It has all dropped into our laps. Stay by the phone, I'm going to get a local paper and give you a phone number."

Harry was already out of the car and on his way to the newsagents, from which he brought back two of the local papers. Yiddel drove out of the village centre and pulled in just before a farmyard and stopped the car. They each took a paper and scoured the jobs columns.

"Here it is!" Harry had found it. "CLEANER REQUIRED, phone KLEIN MANOR, and the number."

Yiddel phoned Sheila, explaining to her all about what they had heard and what he wanted her to do. "Apply for the job!" he said and gave her the phone number.

There was no time to lose and Sheila was making the call within seconds of speaking with Yiddel.

"Good afternoon, Klein residence," a man in a distinctively 'cultured' voice said.

"Oh, hallo, I'm phoning up about the cleaning job advertised in *The Chronicle*," said Sheila, putting on her little 'Miss Innocent' voice.

There was a pause. "Yes…we currently have a vacancy for a cleaner, who will be required to work four days a week, which are

Monday to Friday but not on a Wednesday. The pay is seven pounds and fifty pence per hour, and the appointed candidate will be required four hours each day." The man said all this without drawing breath - as though it was all too much effort to have to speak to a lowly, would-be cleaner.

Sheila wasn't going to allow this to put her off; there was simply too much at stake. To have someone on the inside would be an absolute gift for the team. She responded, again in a tone of voice that came far from naturally. "That sounds very reasonable to me. Would it be possible for me to come and see you in the morning?" she enquired politely. If this went well, she would be well and truly in control of the operation in its infancy.

The man paused again, as if for effect of some kind. "Yes, very well, tomorrow will be fine at ten o'clock. Would you please ask for Mr Cane. I am Mr Klein's secretary. I will expect to see you then. Goodbye."

It was an excited – and relieved - Sheila who quickly phoned Yiddel to confirm that she had succeeded in gaining an interview at Klein Manor at ten the next morning.

Yiddel was impressed. "That's great, darling. I'll also take you to the estate agent to get you a flat. I know he has one, so you'll have an address near here. We're on our way back now. See you soon."

While they were on their way back to London, Harry was searching the accommodation columns and found a flat to let, just come on to the market at Browns.

"That's got to be the sister's place, Yiddel," reckoned Harry, drawing a circle around the advert.

"Who's a lucky boy, then?" was Yiddel's response. "You know what the word is…it's 'Mozzeltoff' and I have fucking shit loads of it when I need it." Yiddel's face broke into that big Yiddisher grin as he looked skyward. "Thank you, Lord."

He drove for a few miles deep in thought and then said to Harry: "Phone Sheila, give her the phone number of Browns, read the advert to her and tell her to make an appointment to see the flat for about nine am tomorrow - just in case someone else wants it."

Harry made the call and passed on the instructions. Five minutes later, Yiddel's phone rang and again Sheila had good news: the viewing was all fixed up for the morning.

Yiddel's mind was firmly in gear for this forthcoming caper and he had a hundred thoughts racing through his head right now. "While you're on the phone, darling, go out this afternoon and get some changing equipment. You know: hair, eyes, teeth, like at Southampton....and clothes, some cleaners' clothes...Ok, babe, I'll leave it to you."

They drove back home discussing the way the day had panned out and how it was going to be played the next day. By the time they were back in east London, Yiddel had the formation of the Game Plan in his mental filing cabinet. And this one was special.

After they had returned to the premises later that day, they all huddled around the desk in Yiddel's office, with the map of the village spread out. They were checking where the village was in relation to Klein Manor. Sammy was given the task of going out and acquiring a stolen car and fitting it with false number plates.

The next couple of hours were taken up in going over Yiddel's plan in ever-increasing detail together, and, after just a few hours' light sleep that night, the foursome were on the road early the next morning to Oxfordshire in two cars for the first meeting at Browns.

Sheila was continually assured and complimented by Yiddel on how 'fantastic' she looked in her disguise.

"Even your own mother wouldn't recognise you," remarked a very impressed Yiddel.

Sheila paused. "I bet she wouldn't, she left me and my dad when I was a baby."

Yiddel bit his lip and went on. "The man who you will see is a bloke called Jim Clarke. Don't make any remarks about him being fast with a car or anything, will you?"

"Jim who?" asked a truly bewildered Sheila.

"Oh, never mind. Just let him show you the flat and you make up your own story about wanting to live out here."

They neared the village and changed cars, Sheila now with her own. Yiddel let her drive off alone through the village to Browns and parked a safe distance away to watch her get out of the car and enter the estate agency.

It was just a few minutes before they saw Sheila and Clarke come out and get into Sheila's car. They watched the car drive off to the other end of the village and stop. Yiddel decided they would stay where they were and wait for them to return. Fifteen minutes later, Sheila and Clarke came out of the flat, drove the short distance back, and parked outside Browns. Another twenty minutes went by and Yiddel's patience was beginning to be tested, but then to his relief he saw Sheila leave Browns and drive towards him. As she drove past she made a signal to follow her. As they exited the small village, what few dwellings there were rapidly gave way to woodland and then open fields full of crops, with just one or two agricultural workers toiling in the morning sunshine. Two miles out of the village, she pulled up off the road into a farm drive, got out and joined them in Yiddel's car.

"All right, babe?" he asked her, confident but nevertheless needing to know all was going well.

"Yeh, fine, it's a nice little flat. One bedroom, lounge and a little kitchen, all furnished, and I've paid for a month plus deposit – cash - and I've got the key."

"Ok, let's get over to Klein's place and get you your job. You still Ok for it, darling?"

"Course I am, silly sod, why shouldn't I be?" she mocked in that special Sheila way.

"No, I don't mean anything by that. It's when only one member of the team is doing all the work, I sense it can be a bit unfair…you know, when it's all on you."

"Don't be daft, I'm enjoying every minute of it. Come on, let's get the next bit done, then we can go for brunch or lunch."

"What, dressed like that?" he said, looking her up and down in false astonishment. He prepared himself for a slap, but all he got was one of Sheila's looks.

Again they followed Sheila to as near as they dared go to Klein Manor. She slowly drove up the substantial driveway, bordered by well-tended, extensive garden lawns, and after two minutes she then could see the manor house itself.

'Fucking hell, what a house,' she said to herself. And it was. It seemed like a step back in time – nineteenth or perhaps even eighteenth century. For a moment it made her feel very, very humble – maybe this had been the desired effect on visitors over the years. 'It certainly would keep 'working' people in their place,' she thought, reflecting on the task ahead of her now. She stopped the car at the main entrance where a man was working on the garden.

"Excuse me, I've come about the cleaning job," she ventured in a talked-up accent.

The gardener couldn't have cared less. "Well, don't park your car there, then! Go round the back. Only the Klein family are allowed to park there," he said, turning his back on her.

Sheila forced herself to say nothing in response. Closing the window of the car, she muttered under her breath, "And fuck you too."

At the rear of the massive house was a sign: 'Deliveries and Staff'. 'Ok,' she thought. 'Tradesmen's entrance. Must be me.'

As she walked towards the doorway – which had clearly seen many years of horse-drawn and then motor vehicle deliveries made to it - she was met by a tall, elderly man dressed in a morning suit.

"Have you come about the vacancy as a cleaner?" he asked.

"Yes, I phoned yesterday afternoon," she replied.

"That's right, you spoke to me. I am Mr Cane. Right, well, I haven't much time, so if you will follow me I will show you what your tasks will be."

Sheila followed him around the huge manor house, pretending to be excited at the prospect of working for the Kleins as a cleaner, but inwardly taking in all the interior layout of the house and learning which doors led where. It was quite labyrinthine: passages that servants of times past had bustled back and forth along, serving their masters obediently, never disagreeing with their superiors and working all hours of the day and night. Sheila felt she was about to encounter a scene from *Downton Abbey* at any moment, but she quickly reminded herself of why she was here, and that one word out of place now could wreck her prospects of getting this job. Mr Cane went on showing her what her duties would be in his rather aloof, slightly condescending, manner.

312

"You don't have to worry about the beds, they are made up by another member of the staff, all you have to do is clean the rooms after she has finished making the beds and then look after all the other rooms in the house. If a room is being used you will leave it until it is free, is that clear?"

Sheila nodded.

"Good, all the cleaning material you will need for doing your work is kept in the servants' quarters, where you will have your breaks, for fifteen minutes – only - each day." He looked at her again in that way of his that Sheila had already taken a serious disliking to. After a long pause that she found uncomfortable, he then asked her the question she had been waiting to hear: "When can you start?"

She forced herself to appear grateful and one again avoided her east London voice, though with some impatience. She didn't like it here – it reminded her of all the things that her own ancestors must have suffered and struggled against. Looking straight at Mr Cane, she answered, "I can start in the morning if you want me to."

"Yes, we need a cleaner to start quickly so that will be fine. It has been left for a few days because the lady whom you are replacing had an accident." He looked rather distant for a moment and then took a deep breath, striking a speck of self-imagined dust off his jacket as if to underline his authority or perhaps some equally imagined aristocratic sense of values.

Sheila waited patiently for the next move, but was thinking 'Yeh, she died doing this demeaning work for a bunch of snobs for a fucking pittance.'

Mr Cane had resumed. "Be here at 9am sharp, please, we do *not* tolerate unpunctual people. Oh, and what is your name?"

"Mrs Brown," Sheila quickly answered, off the top of her head.

"Well then, Mrs Brown. The Kleins pay cash, so there is no tax to pay and there is no need to have a National Insurance card."

'Perfect,' thought Sheila, although a little astounded. 'Suits me. You are playing it right, just how we want it, exactly what I wanted to hear.'

Driving away from the house to meet the others, Sheila thought, 'Why do people stand for this crap, especially from men like that arsehole? I wished I could have punched him.'

They all met up and drove a decent distance away from the village before pulling into a pub car park for lunch, where Sheila told her story of how she had got the job and what she had seen.

They found a quiet corner table where Yiddel showed her the picture of the painting. Unfortunately, it hadn't been part of Sheila's travels within the house that morning. "This is what we are after, find out where it is in the house. Check the alarm system…anything else I'll leave to you. While you were in the manor, I've decided to stay here with you. The boys can go back home and make sure everything is cushtey there. Will I be able to get in and out of your flat Ok?"

"Oh, yeh. It's got its own entrance, no communal door. You will be able to get in and out without anyone seeing you; it's got a side entrance, babe," said Sheila, thankful that she was not going to be left out here on her own, and having her man with her comforted her immensely.

Before the boys returned to Hackney, they all went into the nearest town to shop for the immediate things they would need at the village flat.

The next morning, Sheila reported for duty well before the required time, to be met by another girl who told her she was the bed maid.

314

The girl showed Sheila where all the cleaning material was kept and then left her at her first cleaning area: the main entrance and hall.

The girl said she would come for her when the first bedroom bed had been made up. For a moment, Sheila was in awe of the lavish house, with its splendidly wide staircase sweeping upwards like a huge fan to the first floor. Beautiful marble floors and magnificent carpets. Each room contained furniture that she had only seen in films of the period. Obediently, she got on and swept and dusted, cleaning the inevitable dirt off the floor in the entrance hall and scuffs off the door.

The hallway displayed life-size paintings in bronzed frames, ornately decorated and embellished with Latin and other inscriptions; these went all the way up the stairs, and each wall could boast stunning paintings and portraits its entire length and height. Keeping her professional eye out for the target, Sheila checked the large lounge off to one side of the hall and also the grand drawing room, which was so vast that it seemed to stretch into the distance on the opposite side of the hallway; eventually, she was able to confirm that unfortunately they were both clean of the particular painting she was looking for. As she was finishing the hall, the young maid came down the stairs. She tip- toed over to Sheila in a manner so nervous that Sheila wondered for a moment if the girl was all right; she whispered that it was now in order for her to do the bedrooms, and told her 'not to worry as they are all out'. And one real morsel: that the alarm system only went on at night, so she could open any doors during daytime.

'Wow,' thought Sheila, 'free range to look, and look I shall.'

The maid took her up and showed her the rooms that had to be cleaned: three bedrooms which were in constant use, an office and the hallway. The maid then left her to go and do her own work, going back downstairs. It was now that Sheila felt she could at last take full advantage of there being no one to disturb her searching. She swiftly checked each room…but no luck. There was, however, one room at the far end of the hall corridor that she thought led to the wing of the house. Trying the door, she knew she taking a risk: this room was not on her official list, so what excuse could she offer if found out?

It was locked. Sheila wanted – indeed, needed – to know why. She noticed that outside this room was an art pot containing a floral decoration; automatically, she slid her hand down into it and at the back along the bottom edge, she found what she had desperately hoped for: a key. But was it for this door or somewhere else? And why keep the key in a pot right next to the door if what was behind the door needed to be kept out of sight? She quickly ran back to the top of the stairs to check if the maid or anyone else was about. Seeing it was deserted, she ran back to the locked door and slid the key into the lock.

The huge door swung open to reveal a multitude of art treasure: all along the walls of the room were many different sizes and styles of paintings: landscapes, portraits and groups of people, and in the centre of the room was a large display cabinet with an assortment of jewellery, ranging from pendants to rings to tiaras. Sheila knew she didn't have much time. That girl would soon be back, possibly any second. She was about to give up searching for the Van Gogh – there were just so many paintings - and the eyes of the characters in the portraits seemed to stare back at her with hostility, following her as she looked with increasing desperation for the target. She heard a sudden noise downstairs which startled her; this was getting too much - her nerves were on edge and she knew she had to leave.

Yet, turning back towards the door to get out fast, something caught her eye; it was as if one of the paintings spoke to her, reaching out in some strange, mystical way.

She forced herself to look back: it was the Van Gogh. No mistake. Sheila breathed out for the first time and could have shouted for joy, but there was definitely someone coming now and she had to move fast – there would be no excuses, no second chances if the girl even suspected that she was up to something improper – and improper it definitely was. Satisfied that she had now identified the painting required by Morris' client, she quickly but silently locked the door and returned the key to its place inside the pot. Rushing back to her designated work in the bedrooms, the girl was already there.

"Everything all right, Mrs Brown?" she asked.

"Yes, thanks, it's a bit dusty, isn't it?" Sheila was seriously wondering how the girl could be so simple as to not suspect anything – or was she?

"Yes, sorry about that, it hasn't been touched for weeks." The girl was looking straight at her – almost into her, Sheila felt.

"The last cleaner the Kleins used had an accident, see."

"Oh, yes, I heard about that." Sheila kept her voice level but friendly. "So…what happened, then?"

"She was cleaning down the stairs when she slipped and fell down to the hall. A bit of a surprise to us, because she was such a fit girl…to just fall off the stairs like that."

Just then, the door of the bedroom opened and the secretary came in. "Come on, then, no talking, let's get the work done and you can talk later," he said, looking angrily at the maid, as if this was not the first time. Sheila kept her head down and carried on with the work and the young maid scurried off to do another of her

317

jobs. Sheila was relieved that the secretary did not linger to question or rebuke her in any way and he instead went his office near the main bedroom of the house.

She patiently saw the rest of her shift out, moving from room to room and as she was leaving to go home the secretary called her over and told her how pleased he was with the way she had done her work. He had evidently been checking her work for all, or most, of the morning. 'Hopefully,' Sheila thought, 'he doesn't suspect me…'

Getting back to the flat, she was understandably anxious to tell Yiddel about locating the painting and in which room it was, and where the key was to be found. She went on to inform him of all the other paintings and the cabinet with the jewellery. She gave him a rough description of the paintings that she had seen and then told him that, according to the maid, the alarm system was only triggered at night.

"There are some lovely things in the cabinet. Beautiful jewels, they look like," she said, more than a few times, Yiddel noted.

"Good, that's ours then. Them could be our little perks!"

He telephoned the boys to advise that he and Sheila were both Ok, and then the Yank to see if he could get some information about the other paintings.

"Yes, Mr Morris, it's all going fine…we've found your item and also a lot more…Yeh, quite a lot more. Look, if I describe a few to you, can you see if you can put an artist's name to them…yeh, just a couple… Ok, here we go." Yiddel went on to describe the paintings which Sheila had seen in the room.

He listened for a few minutes as Morris informed him about what they were that Sheila had seen.

318

"Fucking hell! Oh, I'm sorry, Mr Morris, I didn't mean to swear like that on the phone, but is that right what you just said? That they are paintings by some of the greatest artists that ever lived? And to think that this arsehole Klein has got them or, should I say, has stolen them, and they have been hanging on his walls all this time…?"

Yiddel phoned the boys back and updated Sammy because now things were changing and very, very soon, they would be happening.

"First thing in the morning go down to Ansel's café and put Ansel on the case. Tell him his services will be required and I will let him know when. We will need a large furniture removal lorry, some very decent tools like power screwdrivers and drills. All the usual gear - masks and clothes for just the four of us. Get some sort of rope as we'll be needing to tie a few people up, I reckon. And anything else that I have forgot, Sam! You know what to do. I'll phone you in the morning."

Morning came, and Sheila went in to work on day two, an equally important day in Yiddel's Game Plan. She was armed with a pull-out tape measure and a small video camera. Yiddel's instructions to her were to try to do a rough measure up of the large paintings and shoot a bit of video so that he could then see what else was in the target.

She tucked both items away out of sight and carried out her duties. Keeping to the act of being a conscientious, diligent new employee, she was working away on the stairs waiting for the young maid to call her when a hand touched her on the shoulder.

A tall, grey-haired man with an unmistakable Germanic, seemingly aristocratic, bearing stood smiling down on her. Sheila froze.

"You must be the new member of our staff. May I welcome you, Miss. My name is Heinrich Klein."

Sheila acknowledged him by saying, very humbly, "Good morning, Mr Klein."

There was a silence that for Sheila seemed to stretch out into eternity and she could see the old man's eyes looking down at her bust and then to her hips with a half-lecherous smile on his face.

"I hope you enjoy your employment with us; if there is anything I can do for you, please don't be afraid to ask."

And he carried on down the stairs. Sheila shuddered at the way he had spoken to her and looked her over. She had felt that hideous power he exuded and knew she had been given the once over by an ex-Nazi officer, a man who had ordered the deaths of countless civilians, Jews and non-Jews alike. She watched him leave through the main entrance and into a waiting car to be chauffeured away, and the next second she was rushing up the stairs to the locked room. With her heart pounding so hard it was almost audible, she checked the bedrooms were clear, and then, knowing she had seen the maid go down the stairs during her encounter with Klein, Sheila headed for the locked door and its supposedly hidden key. Once in the room, she quickly ran the tape measure along the bottom edges of the paintings she had been told about, mentally logging each one's height and depth.

Next was the video camera which she slowly panned around the room, pausing on each painting and then spending a few precious seconds on the jewellery cabinet. Job done, she put the tape and camera back into her cleaner's uniform, locked the room up and breathlessly returned to the stairs within just a couple of minutes. Now it was high time to quickly but properly clean all the rooms she was responsible for before going back to the stairs and main hallway. It had seemed to go well, but there was an icy silence that hung heavily throughout the house, and Sheila's nerves were being severely tested. Anxiously, she scribbled down the measurements she had taken and concealed the small piece of paper about her person. At 12.30 prompt, she was called by the young maid to come down for her lunch break to join the other staff members in the lower part of the house. She noticed the young maid was sitting alone, looking very sorry for herself. Sheila had to ask. "What's up, love?"

"Oh, it's nothing," the girl replied, but the look on her face gave the lie away. She was more than sad, more than withdrawn; something serious was troubling this girl – to the point of her spirit being broken - by someone or something against whom she felt she could do nothing.

Sheila felt a pang of sympathy for this poor creature. "Come on, you don't look like that over nothing."

The maid looked around to see if any of the other staff could hear her and quietly said, "It's that dirty old bastard again. He got me on the bed, pulled my clothes up and…was dirty…with me," and she choked back a sob.

Sheila had suspected as much. 'I knew it,' she thought, 'I sensed that this morning, what he's up to.'

"It's not the first time," the girl went on, fighting her tears away, but struggling as they tried to come back. "But please don't say anything, will you, to the secretary? I depend on this job and if they knew I had told anybody…I'll be dismissed," she said, with a tear rolling down her cheek.

"Has he done this many times before to you?"

"Yes, he held me down and put it right in last week and told me to say nothing. Said he would get me some more money. I don't want to lose the job, I have to look after my mum. Please don't say anything will you, please…"

"No, I won't say anything, darling." Sheila tried to calm her down and put a comforting arm around her little shoulders. She could feel the girl's body shake with the trauma of her experiences, and Sheila knew she had to tell Yiddel.

"What did you say happened to the other cleaner?" asked Yiddel, once Sheila had got back to the flat and began relating the story of the girl – and of her encounter with Klein.

"She apparently 'fell off the stairs'," she said.

"When you get in tomorrow, ask the maid what else she knows about the dead cleaner, but be careful." Yiddel was realising there was more going on at Klein Manor than he had ever imagined. He was grateful to Sheila for all her hard work, and gave her a little kiss on her nose.

"Right, Baby, what else have you got for us today, then?"

Sheila wrote down all the measurements and together they looked at the video footage.

"Good…very good, luv. That's all I think we need. One or two days and we will do the job. I'll check with the boys and tell Ansel to get himself ready."

Yiddel phoned Sammy and told him the same; Sammy was to get the lorry and all the gear and stand by.

The next morning Sheila was in early and started her work before 9am. The young maid arrived, still looking distressed.

"Are you Ok, love?" Sheila asked her.

"Not really, I'm not looking forward to today," she said. "In case he wants me again. He has started on me ever since the other cleaner died."

"Do you know if he was playing about with her?"

"Yes, she was, I was told, to say nothing or else, but she got pregnant!"

Just then, another staff member arrived so the pair shut up and went off to their work.

'That's it,' thought Sheila. 'He pushed that poor girl off the stairs, the bastard.'

She spent the rest of her day fuming about what the maid had told her, but keeping her wits about her. Would she be his next intended victim? At lunchtime, she overheard the secretary telling the cook that the family was going away on Friday morning for a trip to Germany and would be back on Monday.

"You will all do a normal day on Friday," he said. "And, Mrs Smith - I would like just you to come in and ensure the place is clean for their return."

'*I* sure will,' thought Sheila, 'me and my boys.'

The day passed with no sight of the Kleins. After work, she hurried back to the flat to tell Yiddel the news about Friday and the story of the cleaner.

"I had a quiet word with the maid and she said that the cleaner was pregnant by Klein. And I reckon, to cover up, he pushed her off the stairs. By all accounts, the maid was the only one that knew anything about it."

"What d'yer think, darling?"

"The bastard, he deserves a lesson for sure!" she said, fuming. Yiddel had never seen her like this before. "So they buried a pregnant girl, then? And I bet her family don't know about it…"

"But they soon will." Sheila was adamant.

"Too fucking right they will!" agreed Yiddel. "Leave it to me."

Yiddel phoned the team that night. Ansel and the boys were ready. The lorry had been acquired along with all the gear needed. Sammy told Yiddel that he had got the lorry from a yard in south London that handled bankrupt companies, so the furniture lorry would not be missed at all. It was still in its full company logo and markings and looked authentic and credible for the caper. Sheila and Yiddel spent the last part of the evening cleaning the flat of any evidence that they had ever been there.

The lorry, complete with Sammy, Harry and Ansel, was on the M40 heading for the village of Waterperry before 8am. They arrived at 8.45, parked up and waited for Yiddel's signal. At 9am sharp, Sammy's mobile rang.

Yiddel gave him his instructions. "Drive through the village and I will meet you at the far end - slow down just before the junction and I will jump in."

Sammy drove the big lorry to where Yiddel had said, and could see him coming out of the flat. Yiddel threw a bag into the cab of the lorry and joined the team.

"Morning," he said, exuding his normal Yiddel-like confidence. "Everyone ready?"

They all passed their usual remarks about getting up early and that it was all right for some.

"Oh good, so you're all Ok, then," said Yiddel with a smile.

At the junction, Yiddel directed Sammy to turn left and then to pull over about one hundred yards up the road so that they all could get changed.

"It's only about a mile from here," he said.

The team changed into their working clothes complete with masks and then they were off to Klein Manor. Sammy drove the huge lorry up the drive to the house and was directed in the final stages by Sheila to the back of the house.

Yiddel jumped out, followed by Ansel and Harry. Sheila pointed to the door in the lower area of the house, the servant's quarters. It was a clandestine operation; never had getting into the target building been easier or gone smoother, but once they were inside all members of the staff that were there had to be overcome swiftly without anyone being able to raise the alarm. The boys went about this professionally and in a matter of a couple of minutes, the staff were each tied up with tape and a new piece of kit that Harry had found for sale: plastic ties, used for gathering electric flex together, for their wrists and ankles. Once it was applied, the tie had to be cut off.

The gardener, cook and the young maid had all been together in the kitchen, having a cup of tea before starting work. The secretary had been telephoned by Sheila and asked to come downstairs to sign for a parcel. He arrived, unsuspecting, to be firmly accosted by Yiddel while Ansel secured his arms and legs. They were then all put into a large pantry room and the door firmly locked.

"Ok," said Yiddel. "Let's go to work!"

Keeping their masks on, they followed Sheila up the stairs. She opened the door to reveal the paintings – and they were all stopped in their tracks at the sight of so many true masters -it was absolutely staggering. After this unscheduled pause, they all began working on unscrewing the brackets that held them onto the walls. Once it was free, each one was taken down the stairs and carefully loaded onto the lorry. The glass cabinet, incredibly, was not locked; all the contents were lifted out carefully and loaded into a bag. The room was totally cleared in less than an hour. Not one painting remained, but it had been, and still was, high tension, and anything could go wrong at any time. Leaving only the carpet on the floor and an empty glass cabinet, they all left the room.

As they were loading the lorry with virtually the last painting, it happened - the unexpected visitor. Who should call at this delicate stage but the postman with the Kleins' mail. Luckily, Sheila was covering what Yiddel had termed the 'public side' of the lorry – facing outwards from the house so that the 'business side' was facing inwards with the loaders out of view – unless anyone particularly nosey intruded that far around. Sheila could see the postman coming up the long drive and had thought of how to handle the situation long before the elderly man arrived at the house.

"Thank you, Mr Postman," she said with a smile, hoping he would just go away. But he was too inquisitive for that.

"Are they moving out, then?"

"No, these men are just picking up some old things," she lied, rather elegantly. "Nothing more than that."

"Oh, I wouldn't have thought the Kleins would have parted with anything…" And he began to edge closer round the lorry.

Sheila quickly intercepted him, but for an elderly, country postman he had moved even quicker.

"Oh, looks like quite a lot going out. Still, none of my business, I suppose…"

With that, he waved goodbye and started to walk back up the drive. 'Too right it's none of your business,' Sheila thought, glad he was going. But it was his frequent glances back that troubled her.

Before she could advise Yiddel of the unwelcome visitor, the boys announced that the lorry was now loaded. Yiddel was glad they had the extra strength of Ansel with them; some of the paintings were very heavy and awkward to handle due to the huge frames that some of them were in. Getting them off the wall, down the stairs and into the lorry through the narrow areas was a feat on its own. By the time they had taken the last one off the wall the four felt that they had been working for hours; all four were breathing heavily and sweating profusely.

With the lorry's rear doors closed and all the paintings secure inside, Yiddel and Sheila went back inside Klein Manor to check on the staff in the larder. Seeing that they were all sitting as comfortably as they could, Yiddel signalled for them to leave. Sheila went over to the maid and whispered in her ear so that only the young girl could hear.

"We are going to get that bastard, good and proper, love," she promised, and gave her a little kiss on her cheek before leaving with Yiddel and closing the door to the pantry behind them.

"Ok, my lads, I want to get away from here as far as possible before the shit hits the fan. The staff are all Ok, they are safe where they are. I'll make a phone call when we are well away and tip the Old Bill off."

Sheila departed in her car and the others left in the lorry, encountering no one as they trundled slowly up the drive and away from Klein Manor. As they were driving along the M40 motorway, Yiddel said: "And there are another couple of phone calls I'm going to make as well!"

Arriving back in Hackney, Sammy reversed the lorry into the warehouse and they all set to and got it unloaded. Sammy then took the vehicle back to the lorry park in south London and Sheila's old car was disposed of after Yiddel had removed the false number plates. It was now early afternoon, so Yiddel phoned Morris for him to come over to the warehouse and see the merchandise. He then went out in his car well away from Hackney to phone the Oxfordshire constabulary.

"There are some people locked in a larder at Klein Manor, Waterperry, needing attention," was all he said. He drove back and arrived at the same time as Morris and Cooper. The big black Mercedes elegantly pulled into the yard, blocking the entrance to the unit, within which, standing up against the wall and looking ridiculously out of place was the Van Gogh - just propped up in a warehouse, not up on the wall of a gallery or a beautiful home. All around the unit were fabulous works of art in similar positions. Morris and Cooper stood and gazed at them for quite a long time, unable to say anything until they had taken in the splendour of the masters' works.

Finally, Morris spoke. "I take it…it went well, Mr Davis?"

"Yes, Mr Morris, it went very well all due to this lady," pointing at Sheila. "No damage to anything and no damage to anybody, maybe a few dented prides somewhere deep in the Oxfordshire countryside – so, all good."

There was no need to tell Morris and Cooper about how luckily the whole caper had come about, and, in any case, that was another matter that Yiddel was going to take care of later.

"What are your plans…now that we have got the merchandise, Mr Morris?"

"I think, because we are in front with the acquisition, that we should spend our time setting up the despatch. I will have a talk to my client to see if he is interested in any of the other works that you have."

Cooper was already walking around the warehouse taking stock of what there was there, making notes on each one. Again and again, though, Morris would return to the Van Gogh and stand there gazing at it.

"You don't realise, Mr Davis, what a fantastic painting this is, do you? If you understood art as you love football, shall we say, then, that this is the FA Cup, the European Cup and the World Cup all rolled into one? Along with the best players in the world. Moreover, the rest that you have taken from that Nazi is equal to anything you would like to compare it too. I am going to leave it all in your safe care and we will be back tomorrow with some sort of plan as to when we are going to ship it back to the States."

They all shook hands and the American duo left. Looking at Sheila and the others, Yiddel remarked, "I'm glad you didn't say anything about the tomfoolery because that is going to be our little earner on the side. Now...I have a very important phone call to make. Come with me, Babe."

They went up to the office and Yiddel phoned *The Chronicle* newspaper in Oxfordshire, using his mobile phone.

"Good afternoon, can I speak to the editor please? Oh, he don't know me....Yes, a news story, love. Just say a friend..." He winked at Sheila, then broke into the famous Yiddel grin. "Hallo, is this the editor? Great. I've got a very good tip-off for a story for you..." and went on to detail all about the cleaner and her sudden death in connection with the ex-Nazi living at Waterperry, Oxfordshire.

After *The Chronicle* call, he phoned the police in Oxford and told the officer in charge what he had heard about the death of the cleaner not being as clear-cut as it first seemed. "The death of the girl should be investigated," Yiddel stated flatly, "regarding a relationship she had with her boss - a Mr Heinrich Klein of Klein Manor, Waterperry. It has emerged that the murdered girl was carrying Heinrich Klein's baby. Ask the young bed maid at the Klein manor house - she is also being abused by him."

"Who is this speaking?" asked the officer after having listened to this extraordinary revelation.

"A friend, a caring friend!" and Yiddel promptly hung up.

"Well done, my darling," Sheila congratulated him. "In more than one way, that is going to spoil the Kleins' weekend."

They all set about covering up the paintings and left, locking up the unit, leaving - unbeknown to the vast outside world on their very doorstep - a vast fortune of the world's greatest masters in some anonymous, unremarkable warehouse. Sheila and Yiddel went back to his flat. Sheila needed to wash the black dye out from her blonde hair and to relax for the first time in what seemed a long while; she put other aspects of her disguise, such as the teeth and glasses, back into her 'props drawer', as she called it, while Yiddel looked with wonderment at the Klein jewellery.

The next morning, Joe Morris excitedly phoned Yiddel and, without a breath drawn, told him that he had spoken to his client - there were indeed a couple of the other paintings that he would like as well. He had detailed the ones, and agreed a figure with Yiddel of another two million pounds.

"The paintings are going to be shipped out with a lot of absolute rubbish that has been bought by a Texan art dealer as a cover for the good ones. In the shipping itinerary, they will be substituted. The rubbish paintings will be destroyed and the Van Gogh and the Renoir will travel in their place. A world-famous shipping agency will come to your warehouse and prepare them for their journey to Texas. The other paintings... he is not interested in, so you can sell them yourself as a side deal, Mr Davis. All the money owed to you is being drafted to your account through your Mr Joseph right now."

Morris rang off and promised to arrive at the warehouse at the same time as the shippers.

At that moment, the boys arrived back from a meeting with a supermarket chain with the news that the buyer wanted to place an order for the same toy products that the multi-nationals were selling.

"How's it going? asked Sammy, referring to the paintings.

"Very well. I've had a good morning. We've just added another two-mil to our total with Joe Morris, and his client wants one of the other ones, a Renoir. I've never heard of him, have you?"

Harry said he had; Sammy looked as blank about it as Yiddel.

"Never mind, when Morris gets here he can sort out which one it is. So, you did all right with the supermarket man?"

"He wants to order a thousand to start off with, just to see how they go. I told him that I can't get hold of them very fast, but he said he will try a small order first. What a schmendrick!"

Yiddel consequently phoned Mr Lai and put in another order to be included with the new one that the boys had had today. Lai again promised shipment within two days.

"What a business this is turning into. We can't get them here quick enough!" exclaimed Yiddel. "Crazy really, 'cos we don't really need it, do we?"

18

The Marriage

The international carriers arrived to pack up the two valuable paintings for transportation to Texas. Yiddel couldn't help being nosey to see what they were leaving the United Kingdom as, so he glanced at the despatch docket which read: 'Two paintings by Alfred Griggs,' (then the sizes) 'value £300.' The despatch fee was in fact greater than the value of the Griggs paintings. Morris and Cooper had come along to supervise the shippers and to make sure, as Yiddel said later, that he had not done a runner and given the shippers the wrong ones.

"Would I?" mocked a very amused Yiddel.

Once the paintings had gone, the two Americans stayed while Yiddel checked that the money was in the bank, that is, with Mark Joseph, who assured them that it was. The two thanked Yiddel and the boys, and left.

"What are we going to do with the others?" Harry wanted to know.

Two days later, Yiddel was reading *The Sun* and gave a low whistle. "Listen to this, 'Heinrich Klein of Waterperry, Oxfordshire, has been charged with the murder of twenty-one- year-old Valerie Gough after an anonymous tip-off to the police that Mr Klein was a Nazi officer during World War Two, and had made Miss Gough pregnant during one of his many sexual assaults on her. During an argument with her, she had fallen to her death from the top of the stairs to the hall inside the manor house. Further investigations by the Oxfordshire police have revealed that another staff member of the family house was also being sexually abused by the same man. Heinrich Klein has admitted all the charges.'

Yiddel looked up from the newspaper. "And no mention of the paintings being stolen…Well, I suppose, how can they? Officially, there are no paintings - he can't claim for something that he should never have had. That would bring more disgrace on the family. You can bet your life that the staff was told to say nothing, and I should imagine that they had had to pass off the pantry bit with something like 'it was just a staff member larking about'."

"The son, Albert, must be in total disgrace, what with his business being in the City," said Sheila. "So, really, there are no paintings are there? What we have in the unit and what is on its way to Texas don't exist, do they?"

"I bet the Kleins must be right in the shit now. The old man charged with murder and a rape charge to follow and all of his 'hoard' cleared out by us," reckoned Sammy.

"It makes me feel a whole lot better. I don't like grassing someone up, but those two phone calls that I made got that old Nazi bastard dealt with. He's put his hands up to the charges because they've got him bang to rights!" Yiddel was ecstatic, rubbing his hands with glee.

Later that night, Yiddel and Sheila were at home finishing off a second bottle of red wine and both feeling a bit light-headed.

"You know, darling, we got another twelve million pounds today," he giggled, child-like. "I remember, not so long ago when I was lucky to say after a hard day that I had earnt twenty pounds and I was so pleased, so pleased that I had got a little money for the next day….Do you know, my little flower, that I am worth a bloody

333

lot of money? I haven't got twenty pounds these days…I've got bloody millions, far more than I could ever have imagined." Yiddel was lying back, his head on Sheila's lap, contented, relaxed and slurring his words.

"I think that it's about time we…that's us…got on and got married, darling, don't you?"

The next day Sheila returned to her family to tell them the news that she and Yiddel were going to fix a date to get married. Yiddel told everyone he met as he strolled through the market chatting to all the traders and anyone else who even looked at him. Ansel was given the job as caterer. The florist outside Ansel's café got the job of supplying the flowers.

"Yiddel….Yiddel!" It was Ansel calling out from the café. "Come 'ere!" Yiddel went back inside the café.

"Why don't you have proper caterers do all the catering, and give all the other things to people who do this for a living? We're just market traders. Just invite us to your wedding."

Yiddel looked at the market florist and he was nodding in agreement. "Yiddel," Ansel continued, his voice lowered now. "You are a fucking multi-millionaire and you are still doing it cheap - for fuck's sake, man, do it right and do it fucking big. It's your first – and only - time. And Sheila's. Don't fucking spoil it. You're a very rich man, remember?" Despite his excitement, and to Yiddel's relief, Ansel had kept his voice down so that the well-meaning, but possibly rather nosey, florist did not hear the 'millionaire' bit.

"Yeh, you're right, Ansel. I'm a prat even thinking like that. I am so used to watching the spending that I was automatically just wanting to give you all a bit of work to earn yourselves a few bob."

"Yiddel, remember that I'm also a very rich man now, thanks to you. Let me come to your wedding and we will make it one of the best weddings the East End of London 'as ever seen."

Yiddel had to agree with this friend, who was beaming from ear to ear. He gave the big man a huge hug, promising to see him later and strolled back to the office still telling people about his wedding plans.

"You're going to a vedding, a lovely Jewish vedding, and the vedding you are going to is mine," he sang as he came into the office. Both Sammy and Harry jumped up from their desks and swung him around.

"At last, you old sod. Now, let's see, who are you going to marry?" Harry winked at Yiddel.

"Oy, Oy, Oy, Oy Mozzeltoff...Oy, Oy, Oy, Oy Mozzeltoff, we're going to a vedding," sang all three of them at the top of their voices while they danced around the office crashing into the desks and chairs until it was all interrupted by the telephone ringing. Putting his finger to his lips for quiet, Yiddel answered it: "Good morning! FAGIN UK! Oh, hello, Mr Morris. Yeh, all's well, and you? It all got there safely...good. Great news. Oh, another thing. I'll send you an invite - I'm marrying Sheila. Yeh, the one with the teeth and black hair!"

Sheila busied herself over the next few weeks, putting the wedding plans together. The day, the place and where the reception would be held. Yiddel wanted to invite everyone he had ever met. Yiddel had decided not to have a Jewish wedding in a synagogue. He was quite happy with a registry office 'do' in the local Hackney Town Hall.

335

"I don't go to church all the year round, so why should I want to get married in one?" was his comment when asked about it by Sheila.

Sheila hired a very large hall at the community sports centre. It was a vast room used by the members for basketball and other court games. She did this because of the guest list that Yiddel had compiled - by the amount of people that she was going to invite, she knew that a conventional hall was not going to be suitable.

After all the arrangements were in place, the wedding was planned for the first Monday in June – three weeks' time. It had to be a Monday because most of the guests were market people and most markets always closed on a Monday giving them their other rest day, and what could be a better day for a wedding?

Yiddel had given Sheila a completely free hand for the overall wedding plan: "I'll leave it all to you, Darling!"

Sheila booked a firm of caterers to serve all the guests a lunch and an evening buffet, laying on all the delights of an East End wedding. The florist told her that they would take care of all the flowers for her from the guests and the tables in the hall. Yiddel and the boys were having their suits made by a bespoke tailor, all in the same material and colour, in Bethnal Green. Sheila's dress was being created by a local dressmaker, well known locally for their style and creations. The entertainment was going to be a mixture of 'Old-Style' dance band and disc jockey, combining new music with the oldies. The photographer had been instructed that all the photographs he took throughout the day's event were to be given to each guest and to give Yiddel the final invoice. It had taken Sheila and her friend a week to write out the invitations. The wedding had grown into a marathon event, surpassing any other that had been held over past years.

336

Sammy and Harry invited all their families. Elvis, Roger, Ansel and Sidney were also told to bring whomever they like. The wedding was turning into a vast potpourri of peoples from all walks of life, all living and working in the East End. Mark Joseph, Jeremy Store, Igor and even the Smith brothers - all got an invitation.

In the meantime, the FAGIN UK company was trading non-stop on all the toy imports - as fast as one order came in, another went out, and immediately they had to phone Mr Lai and repeat the order. One day, the enigmatic Taiwanese told him that he had a new item which was being produced and that he would send a sample of it with the next delivery, just so they could test it out with their clients. He told Yiddel that it had not yet gone out to any of his customers, so FAGIN UK could be the first in England to have it. Yiddel thanked him and at the same time invited his Taiwanese business associate to the wedding, who apparently thought it highly amusing that he, for the first time in his life, would leave his native country to go to a wedding in England. He thanked Yiddel for his kind thought and said he would try to be there.

Naturally, Yiddel wanted to move the former-Klein jewellery on; he was getting uneasy by it simply being in a bag in his attic. He still had no idea of its worth and secondly, this just wasn't good practice to have such items at his own address – he might easily get a visit from the police...and what explanation could he possibly give?

He phoned Sidney to see if he could arrange for George, his expert appraiser, to come over to the office and give him a rough estimate. Sidney phoned back inside a minute to tell Yiddel to bring it all over to his office instead the next morning. Early the next morning, after a restless night, Yiddel got the bag down from the attic, dusted it off and drove over to Sidney's place. George was already there, his eyes sparkling with the anticipation of something big – this was what George lived for – but he obviously thought he would pull Yiddel's leg first.

"I hope it's not like that other bag of crap you got me over for, Yiddel!"

"So do I!" retorted Yiddel, tipping it out onto Sidney's desk.

Keenly, George produced his eyepiece and began inspecting the first piece very closely, taking care to look all around it. Again, the silence hung heavily as he took enough time to carry out his examination thoroughly. Yiddel and Sidney waited patiently. George eventually sat back after checking each item and looked straight into Yiddel's face.

"Where the fucking hell did you get this lot?" George wasn't accustomed to swearing – Sidney in particular knew instantly that this was going to be something big.

But Yiddel, who did not know George so well, was straight away thinking: 'Oh no, not another pile of shit!'

"Why, George, is it no good?"

"No good, this fucking stuff is the dog's bollocks. It is marvellous, the gems are unbelievable, it's the best set of mixed gems I have ever seen in one piece of jewellery, absolutely incredible!"

He took another look at one of the larger pendants, gently giving a low whistle at every turn of the item.

"Yiddel, this is the crown jewels, mate. In fact…some of these stones are better than the Crown jewels!"

Also on Sidney's desk in front of George was a collection of the necklaces, rings, brooches, pendants and a tiara.

George regarded them cautiously. "This out of my league, gentlemen. I have never seen the likes of this. Each one of these large stones," pointing at one in the tiara, "is so magnificent that they must have their own name in the international jewellery world, just like the *Kohinoor* diamond of India, they are that good. I really don't know what to advise you to do with them. As they are, complete, they would be identified, like a car number plate. The only chance you've got is to split them up and sell each stone as a separate item. I am not kidding, Yiddel, at some stage in the past, these were worn by European royalty."

'No wonder Heinrich Klein had them tucked away behind a locked door,' thought Yiddel.

After Yiddel and Sidney had thanked him for his expert opinion and promised him 'a little drink' for his trouble, George the jeweller left Sidney's office, still shaking his head and muttering "I've seen some stuff in my life of handling crooked gear, but this takes the biscuit!"

"What are you going to do with it?" Sidney needed to know.

"Put it back up in the fucking loft, I should think!"

"You can't do that now you know it's worth something, Yiddel..."

"Why not? We had a multi-million pounds' worth of gold and platinum under my aunt's sand pile in her yard in Bermondsey, so why can't I put it back up in the sodding loft?"

"I'm just saying, it should be put somewhere safe or something!" advised Sidney, disbelievingly.

"In a fucking safe, round here? That's the last place I would put it. It's far safer up in my loft, Sid."

Sidney left him to his own choice of safekeeping. Yiddel departed, but holding the bag a lot closer to his body than when he arrived. Later, all Yiddel said to Sammy was: "I'll leave it up there till some stage in the future."

A few days' later, reading *The Sun* in the office while eating his first beigel of the day, Yiddel noticed something with great interest. "Listen to this, lads: 'Heinrich Klein has been formally charged with the murder of twenty-one-year-old Valerie Gough at Oxford County Court today'." There were other charges too. Yiddel read some more about these before concluding: "Fucking good riddance, his past 'as caught up with him at last. And still not a word about the paintings!"

Yiddel phoned Mark Joseph to check that the twelve million had cleared. Mark assured Yiddel that it had. Yiddel then decided to give all the team their share of the money. He instructed Mark to make a transfer to each of the accounts, naming each and how much they should get. He divided up twelve million pounds into five different accounts. Ansel became a millionaire overnight with one million pounds deposited into the account set up for him by Mark. The two boys got two million apiece. Sheila, not because of her closeness to Yiddel, but because of the crucial part she had played in the caper, got three million and the rest went into Yiddel's account.

Later that day, he bumped into Ansel in the market.

"I was just on my way to see you," the big Jamaican declared. "Mark just phoned me and told me what you instructed him to do. Yiddel, you are too fucking much, man. I am now a millionaire with a two-bob café in Ridley Road. With this sort of money, I could go back to Jamaica and buy the whole island! All I did was to take some paintings off the wall and put them into the back of a lorry...so, are you sure?"

"Course I'm sure! Compliments of a Texan billionaire. Look, I wouldn't be able to do it if I wasn't sure. You did what I wanted you there for, and now you've been paid. All I ask is that you are careful and don't talk about it. Carry on running your 'two-bob' café and when the day comes when you want to fuck off, give the café to your sister in law. Anyway, I'm not finished with your services yet, I've got another job for you…Best man at my wedding!"

The big black man's eyes grew to the size of saucers and he instinctively grabbed hold of Yiddel to give him a hug. Yiddel looked over his shoulder to see if anyone was witnessing this seemingly over-intimate scene and said, "Steady on, Ansel, people might take this the wrong way!"

"Fuck 'em, I don't care. What a fucking day I've had and it ain't over yet!" Ansel was beaming the largest smile Yiddel had ever seen on a man's face.

The morning of the wedding came; everything was in place and ready for the main event of the day. The hall had been decorated in garlands and flowers. Ansel had added his little contribution to the occasion by hiring a steel band, who were busy rehearsing their routine in one corner of the hall. The florist was putting the final touches to the floral arrangements after decorating the hall with flowers in every shade and variety. The army of staff organised by the caterers was laying all the tablecloths, including serviettes of pink.

Yiddel had left his flat for the town hall with the two boys in a gleaming white stretched limousine. Sheila was taken by her brothers and father in another. The main street, Mare Street in

Hackney, gave an impression of gala night for the Oscar Award ceremony in America. There were limousines in all colours with a vast assortment of up-market cars arriving at the wedding venue.

The local police were called to assist and control the flow of extra traffic along with the hordes of people who had heard about the wedding and had come to see the spectacle - as well as the bride and groom.

The Hackney Gazette, along with *The Evening Standard*, was also there, eager to get an edition picture of such an event. The traffic was brought to a standstill as the bride arrived. Hundreds of lips made their 'Oooo' sounds as they saw the bride step out of the car. Needless to say, Sheila looked fabulous in her dress and her flowers as she walked up the steps, stopping at the top step for her brother as he had to push himself through the gathered crowd to whom she couldn't resist turning and waving – acknowledging all the cheering.

She thought to herself, 'This is my day and I am going to enjoy every last minute of it.'

Her brother caught up with her and whisked her through the big doors and into the waiting room, where she joined Yiddel and Ansel.

"What d'yer think, Babe?" Sheila asked, giving him a twirl of her bridal gown.

"You look smashing, Darling. I love you, Sheila, and always will," he said.

They were ushered into the registry office, where they stood alongside each other while the registrar performed the wedding. Vows were spoken, rings were exchanged, and the sealing kiss was done.

After the ceremony, everybody wanted to congratulate them. It took ages for them to push through all the guests to get outside into the open air. The crowds were now ten deep all eager to see the couple. The newspaper photographers were snapping everything that the couple did: laughing, kissing and then Sheila throwing her bouquet into the crowd. They posed on the steps for everyone to get a picture as they greeted and kissed their friends. The crowds of spectators by now had grown into many hundreds, cheering and clapping as the happy couple made their way down the steps into the waiting limousine to take them to the reception. The two boys followed on in limousines with their families. When they got back to the sports hall, there were as many people again gathered to see them arrive. The street outside the sports centre was bumper to bumper with limousines, Rolls Royces, Bentleys, Mercedes and Jaguars, along with all sorts of expensive cars.

Someone in the crowd was heard to say, 'I thought these market people didn't do well. It don't show by their cars.'

As Sheila and Yiddel entered the hall, a fanfare of music welcomed them with *Congratulations* played by the combined steel and dance bands. The hall was full of friends all keen to get hold of the couple to touch, embrace and kiss. Looking around the hall, Yiddel could see some old mates whom he had been to school with: market trader mates, Spitalfields Market salesmen, it seemed to Yiddel as he looked around that everyone he knew was in front of him. He was shaking hands with Sheila's father when he got a tap on his shoulder; he turned to see Elvis.

"I'll do my impersonation later, Yiddel," he said.

"Nice to see yer mate, you all right?"

Getting a slap on his back from the big man was enough for Yiddel as he passed on to the next person and so on. Sammy slid in close to him and put a glass of champagne in one hand and a cigar in the other. He went from group to group, while Sheila had been swept away in the opposite direction doing what Yiddel was doing and meeting the invited guests until they both met in the middle of the hall. The overall noise was unbelievable, everyone was hell-bent on having a whale of a time. It was still only midday. The band struck up and everyone started to sing along as Yiddel and Sheila joined hands and danced together. The crowds gradually moved back to the tables and other couples joined the bride and groom on the middle dance floor. The dance finished and the pair stood alone in the middle of the hall to shouts of "Speech!"

Yiddel acknowledged them and waited for relative quiet. Then he began. "Well, there's not a lot I can say right now. We are so pleased to see you all here with us. Although we know each and every one of you, we don't often get a chance to have a drink together. So all I am going to say now is: IT'S PARTY TIME – so eat and drink, it's all here for you to enjoy!"

The room burst into cheering and applause again as the band started into its routine of music. The caterers were now working flat out, they could not open bottles and cans fast enough. The catering manager brought the whole gathering, eventually, to quiet by shouting through a bull horn, which had surfaced from somewhere, for everyone to take their seats so that the food could be served. At last everybody was seated. The waitresses were like ants serving hot food to sixty tables, with twelve people to each table. The band started up again with music at a quieter volume while the guests met and introduced themselves at their tables and settled down to their meal and drinks.

It went on until the early hour; some people were carried out and taken home to their beds. Yiddel and Sheila finally got back to their flat, and fell straight into a deep, contented sleep.

Sheila slept in until late the next morning; Yiddel, on the other hand, slept until his dreams started to feature his parents, and yet again that car crash and that lorry – how he wished they could have been there on his special day; how proud they would have been, and how it could never be. Eventually, the torture grew too much and he got up, still exhausted and slightly traumatised by those hideous images again of Mum and Dad as he had last seen them.

He looked across to where Sheila was lying so peacefully, with such serenity; and it was enough for him to know that all was well with the present moment.

19

Showdown Time

Yiddel, because of the late night and his hangover, did not feel energetic or motivated on his first day of married life, and he knew that today he had to slow it down; uncharacteristically, therefore, he ambled into the office at about lunchtime. Long before that, however, there had been a knock on his street door – it was Sammy, feverishly clutching the first edition of *The Evening Standard*. He opened the paper on the first inside page to show Yiddel a half page picture of Sheila and Yiddel on the steps of Hackney Town Hall surrounded by masses of people.

'Hackney Wedding Stops the Traffic,' was the heading.

For the first time since the wedding, Yiddel realised the implications of that half page picture in *The Evening Standard*, it being a regional newspaper and therefore covering a much bigger readership than the local *Hackney Gazette*. His blood ran cold.

"Do you know what this could mean, Sam?"

Sammy had been thinking the same as Yiddel. That was why he was showing Yiddel the paper. "Yes, I do! - your face!"

"Exactly. That picture could tell certain people who are looking for a face without a name, exactly where I am. Everyone who has seen my face but did not know my name. From petty villains to Khan and the people of Waterperry. I might be very lucky, Sam, to get away with this, but on the other hand I could be a target here in Hackney for a lot of fucking people."

By now, Yiddel was stone-cold sober, his head was as clear as a bell. "I think my biggest worry is the Khans. The others I can deal with. But in the case of Khan, I have two men who died chasing us that night, and Khan, if he is alive – which I reckon he is - saw my face just before he crashed. The only one in Waterperry was the estate agent bloke. Besides, I gave him no connection with the Klein place, did I? I just asked him about buying property."

Yiddel knew he had let himself down by lowering his usually self-enforced guard. All his years of watching his back and making sure his tracks were covered, all gone. In an instant, he had committed the cardinal sin, in his book, of exposing his identity.

"I got carried away with the joy of marrying Sheila. I never gave it a thought about the newspapers making a splash of it," he said, smacking his hand holding the paper.

"What a prat…still, too late now. I can only hope that they only run it in the first edition and not all day."

Sheila had been in the bathroom when Sammy arrived, but had heard the conversation between them.

"I agree with you, darling. Leave it and see what happens. It could be nothing will come of it, so come on, let's have some breakfast."

Yiddel asked Sammy to go back to Southall to see what he could find out about Khan, if he lived or had died. Sammy left and headed back to the office to brief Harry as to what Yiddel wanted him to do and also be prepared for some action.

"They may come looking for us if Khan has survived and he sees the picture. You can bet your life he will put his soldiers on it…if he does, we have got to be ready to watch Yiddel's back. If it happens, I will get some back up so that we are well covered. You go over to Southall, be careful, and see what you can find out. Meet you back at the office."

Sammy was running the team now. He knew that Yiddel was vulnerable and he was going to do all he could to protect all their backs from an attack by any cut-throat bunch of villains. Sammy had phoned Alfie Smith just before Yiddel arrived in the office. He did not tell Yiddel he had hired the Smiths to provide protection; there was no need to - yet.

Harry returned to the office to tell them the news about Khan – the bastard had survived the crash, but was still in a bad way.

"All the shopkeepers are talking about it, so it's not that difficult to find out anything about it. It seems that Khan got blown out of the car with one of his guards, who has since died, as the car hit the shopfront. He was on the danger list for the first few hours, but because he is such a fitness freak, seems he was strong enough to pull through. The other two in the car died instantly. Khan is still in hospital with back injuries and a broken arm, but is able, unfortunately, to speak to any visitors who have been in to see him."

"Thanks, H, no one said anything to you, did they?" Yiddel needed to know.

"I never spoke to anyone, all I did was listen to them all talking, it was the only topic of conversation there."

"Ok, let's assume that Khan has seen the picture, because the man's got fuck all to do all day but read the papers. So, if he happened to see my face with Sheila…he knows us both from the casino visits, and he'll want to get even, won't he?" Yiddel's voice tailed off as he began to imagine some of the very real, very nasty, possibilities emerging. He turned to Sammy with fire in his eyes: "Sammy, I want Sheila guarded day and night, without her knowing it, just until we know for definite we are Ok. Right?"

"It's already been taken care of, "said Sammy. "I have put Alfie Smith on the case and he has put two of his more 'intelligent' minders on it. I told him to invoice me and he told me to fuck off. They should be covering it right now." Sammy looked at his watch. "Alfie said they would be there in ten."

"You're a diamond, Sam, thanks for that. Have you set anything else up for us or shall I do it?"

"Alfie thought we should have a bit of protection and he would have it ready the minute you phone him."

"I'm glad you phoned the Smiths - this is what he's good at. He has done this all his life because of the sort of business he is in. He has to guard the two of 'em. He told me once that he went to a race meeting at Sandown Park and told his minders to have the day off. That afternoon at the track, as he and Charlie were getting out of their car, they were attacked and nearly butchered on the spot. But for two coppers who were riding past, they would have been cut to ribbons. Since that day he never goes anywhere without his minders. He believes it was Ernie Black who put them on it, but could not prove it.

"That's why there is a feud between them and it was all over a bit of business that went wrong…they have been sworn enemies ever since. I heard it was over nothing, but you know what they are like. Anyway, it's just as well they're not our enemies!"

That afternoon Yiddel phoned Alfie to thank him for his help and was assured that it would be in place for as long as he needed it. After Yiddel put the phone down, he thought that whatever else was said about this man, this was the first time he had asked him for help, and he had responded without a second's thought. In his lethal trade, this evil man was supposed to be above reproach. Yiddel

349

would make sure one way or another to make it up to him; he knew that Sheila was now being looked after, although she didn't know it.

The next day started as a normal day. Everyone keeping their ears and eyes open to anything that was not normal. The boys had a load of toys delivered and spent a good part of the day putting the orders together. Sidney's transport was organised for the next day. Harry had all the delivery notes and invoices typed up and placed with each order.

What they had expected came in an unusual and very unexpected way. Yiddel answered the phone to a very quiet, well-spoken man with a slight foreign, possibly Asian, accent.

"Mr Davis, my name is Khan. The brother of the man who nearly died on the North Circular Road...my brother sends you his regards and would like you to come and see him. He is in Thomas Ward at the Hampstead Hospital. He has instructed me to tell you that there will be no surprises for you at the hospital. Will you go and see him?"

Yiddel was thrown by the man's attitude, so matter of fact, as though he was arranging a cricket match on the village green.

"Give me a minute, Mr Khan." He sat, thinking for a moment and said, "Yes, I will go and see your brother."

"That's good, Mr Davis. I will tell him that you will be along to see him in the next few days. Goodbye."

Yiddel called the boys up from the warehouse and told them who had phoned.

"I wonder what he's up to?" said Sammy "There's got to be something in it for him or he would have just sent his heavies for a fight."

350

"I've said Yes," Yiddel advised them both. "But I haven't got a clue why he wants to talk and not fight. I think we should treat this with care. The man could be setting me up on his own territory. Whatever, I want you two with me, watching my back."

Sammy suggested that as well as himself and Harry, they should bring along one of Alfie's trusted heavies. "Just in case."

Yiddel agreed and planned to go the next day in the afternoon. Sammy arranged two cars and got the Ok from Alfie to take his man with them. Not knowing which way to play it, Yiddel for once was a bit lost.

"All we can do is turn up and just see what he wants to talk about."

They all set off in the two cars, Sheila telling the boys to keep their eyes on her man all the time. "And watch each other," she said, tearfully, as they left hoping that one day this way of life would be a thing of the past.

The minder who was travelling with them was, in Yiddel's words, 'Built like a brick shithouse', and that to shift him, 'You would have to use a chainsaw on his legs'.

Arriving at Hampstead Hospital, the boys and the minder split up and checked out all the access and exit points to the ward. Sammy stayed with Yiddel right up to the ward door and then took up a position outside of Thomas Ward.

Yiddel walked into the ward, slowly looking at all the people in the beds on each side, desperately trying to see Khan before he saw him. He still couldn't see him, and he was nearly at the end of the ward – was this part of the set-up? He could hear his heart pounding as he felt that deathly threat hanging over him. Where the bloody hell was this devil? And then, right at the end of the twenty beds, there he was…just sitting up and reading a newspaper.

351

Khan looked up just as Yiddel got to the bed.

"Mr Heath – oh, forgive me, Mr Davis! Thank you for coming."

The man's smooth, self-assured manner was seriously throwing the burly East Ender. He had expected to be confronted with an angry, aggressive man, someone spitting pure venom. But, here he was, looking at a man who had a smile on his face and was beckoning him to take a seat at his bedside.

Now keeping his voice down in a manner that Yiddel for one was much more accustomed to, Khan began to outline why he had asked for the meeting. "Like you, I am a villain - all my life, I have taken chances and in many cases I have won. What you did to me shattered my pride in being the best at what I do, and I have literally been taken to the cleaners and left out to dry. The casino, as you know, was working under cover of the drinking club and it was giving us - me and my brother whom you spoke to on the phone - a very nice living. This you also know by how much you took from me that night. We are a very wealthy family and much of what we do is what you would say as 'kosher'.

Khan paused, looking at Yiddel for a reaction, but the big Yiddisher had recovered now, and he had a feeling he knew what was coming.

"Mr Davis, as you will have gathered, we have our fingers in many pies, and we are prepared to offer you and your team a job to do for us. I regret the deaths of the men who were working for me on that night but luckily for me I am still around. Their families will never go short of anything, we have made sure of that. They died in my service and they will be looked after. The driver as far as I am concerned made a mistake and it cost us. Your man did exactly what I would have done, if I had been driving and taken your car out. As a matter of fact, although we are the losers, in more

352

ways than one, we admire your tactics on the day of the attack on our casino. It was well planned and well researched and carried out in the minimum of time. That's why I am extending my hand on behalf of my brother and am asking you to consider something that we want done."

Yiddel said nothing; instead, he turned and signalled to Sammy to come and join them.

"Even now you have cover, Mr Davis?" queried Khan, looking at Sammy approaching.

"Mr Khan, just so you know, there are two more outside. Just waiting, just in case…"

Yiddel took Sammy to one side out of earshot, away from the still unknown quantity that was Khan. He told him what Khan had proposed, and let the news of the offer sink in.

"What d'yer reckon? Yes or no?"

"See what the caper is…then we'll have another chat," was Sammy's view as he glanced over Yiddel's shoulder at Khan.

Returning to Khan's bedside, Yiddel sat on a small stool alongside the bed so that he was close to the man.

"Who else is in on the caper?" he asked.

"Just me and my family. No one outside the family knows anything about what I am about to tell you - you have my word on that." Khan's inscrutable expression was impossible to read. Was this a trap, or did he really want to do a deal – fairly?

"Mr Khan, do I also have your word that the casino job, as far as you are concerned, is done and dusted and is not going to rumble on?"

"Yes, you have my word on that as well, as bad as it makes me feel. But, as I said to you just a minute ago, I admire your ability…the way you carried out the job – even though it cost me dearly."

"The reason I am asking this is because I have a huge amount of resources and I don't want you making a U-turn at some later date." Yiddel knew he could afford to be unequivocal. Again, he searched Khan's eyes for any sign of emotion. And then he breathed: "You do understand me…? I don't want to have to do something I will regret."

Khan looked at Yiddel, then to Sammy, who remained a short distance away. He identified the same expression on both men's faces, and knew their loyalty to each other was unbreakable.

"As I said, what's done is done. The casino is over." He held out his hand; Yiddel couldn't help pausing – then he shook hands with his customary firm grip, which he held for a moment whilst giving his newly-found business associate a bit of advice: "Mr Khan: my hand shake is a bond, so please never be a fool and break it."

As he got up to leave, a man who had been sitting by a nearby bed also rose to his feet, giving Sammy and Yiddel a searching look before walking over to Khan's bedside.

'So, Khan had a minder there as well,' thought Yiddel.

As they began to walk away, Khan advised Yiddel he would be called by his brother for a more in-depth talk about the next steps. Back at the cars, Yiddel told Harry what had gone down in the ward with Khan.

"Well, that's a turn-up for the books, Yiddel…I had expected to hear gunfire."

Yiddel gave him a light slap on the cheek. "And what would you have done if there had been gunfire?"

"Called the police, Yiddel, what else?" came the cheeky reply.

Just before Alfie's minder left with Harry in his car, Yiddel pulled him to one side and put £500 in his hand.

"A little something for the trip."

Without any expression, the minder looked at what Yiddel had given him. "Any time, Yiddel!"

Sheila was thrilled that the boys and especially her man had arrived back safely. She had been dreading the phone call bringing bad news. Yiddel explained every detail about what had been said.

"Strange, very strange, that this man who we turned over big time for one hell of a lot of money now wants you to do a job for him...Maybe now is the time to be really careful. You know this could be a set up to get even."

Yiddel took on board exactly what she was saying. "Yeh, you could be right. Anyway, let's wait until the Khans make contact, then we can decide how careful we have got to be."

Sheila was so pleased that her gang of men had returned safely she booked a table at a West End restaurant, simply saying, "My treat!"

Early the next morning, Yiddel was in the office when he received his first phone call of the day.

"Good morning, Mr Davis, it's Joe Morris. I have a client who is very interested in the rest of the artwork you have. I take it you still have it?"

Yiddel's mind had been on other things so much, he took a moment to recover. "Oh yes, Mr Morris. We still have it tucked up nice and warm out of harm's way," he responded.

"Good. I will be coming back to London next week to arrange with you what they are offering, and all going well the transportation. I would like to have an arrangement with you before I arrive. Can I say that I am on twenty percent of the gross figure, Mr Davis?"

"Yes, you can. I think, under the circumstances, as it's your client and that you are handling the deal, that's Ok with me. When you arrive, give me a call. By the way, I may have something else that I would like to show you. Give me a bell when you get to your hotel. I'll come over, and we can have lunch. I will bring this little lot of merchandise with me."

"Great." Morris rang off.

For three long days, Yiddel heard nothing from the Khans - then the call came through. It was the brother, Raja Khan.

"Mr Davis. My brother, Amit, will be leaving hospital next week and has asked me to arrange with you a meeting at *The Savoy* for next Tuesday, where we will outline all the details of what he has discussed with you. Are you Ok with that?"

"I see no problem with that, Mr Khan. If it's for lunch, which we prefer, I will bring my wife with me too."

"That will be perfectly acceptable. So, we will see you and your wife next Tuesday in the main dining room. A table will be reserved in my name. Goodbye."

Yiddel phoned Sheila and told her. She still felt a bit uneasy about it. "My instinct is that we have got to play it carefully. Let's have the boys with us - somewhere near, just in case."

Sammy duly reserved a table for two at *The Savoy* on the same day.

Joe Morris phoned later in the day to tell Yiddel that he would be in London on Wednesday and that he was staying at *The Hilton* on Park Lane and confirmed he would phone him once he checked in.

"It's all on the boil now," said Yiddel to the boys. "Next week is already shaping up to be a very busy – and important – one. Tuesday: the Khans. Wednesday: Morris." The boys could tell their boss's mind was racing away once again – this was always when Yiddel was at his best. There was a pause as they allowed him time to formulate the details of how to make it a successful, and safe, week for them all. Eventually, it was Harry who broke the silence.

"And this afternoon we have got a delivery coming in from Mr Lai. The shipping agency phoned to ask if it was all right to deliver. I said yes – it's on its way now."

Half an hour later, the lorry pulled up outside the unit to unload the latest novelty from Taiwan.

All three of them were down in the warehouse to help the driver reverse his lorry into the unloading bay, and watched him swing the two wooden cases off the back of the motor and onto the floor. Yiddel signed the delivery note and waited for the driver to clear the doors and leave. Harry was already anxiously prising the wooden crate open with a crowbar. Sammy checked the first layer of boxes of the ordered toys in the first crate, then the second, where he found a box of a new shape and size.

"This must be the new one," he said, eagerly undoing it. "The box label says it's 'Digital Reality'. It looks like a small laptop with a mask and a glove…let's have a go at it!"

Harry unpacked all the contents, fitted them together and after studying the instructions, put it on.

"Fucking hell, this is unbelievable. You're actually inside the computer," he said, not wanting to give it up. Sammy had to wait his turn.

"Bloody hell, this is good," he said at last. Harry stood laughing at Sammy's movements as he fought with the aliens in the programme.

"Addictive, ain't it?" reckoned Harry, itching to have another go. It was not very long at all before they had both keenly agreed that it was a very decent bit of kit, and should do well on the British market.

Sammy went up to the office and began phoning all the buyers, ticking each one off as he made an appointment to bring the new product to each of them., also advising that their present standing order would be with them in a few days. As part of this wonderfully successful 'legitimate' business enterprise, Yiddel phoned Mr Lai, thanking him for the delivery and checking with him the cost of the new toys. It was a great cover for their real dealings, and afforded a bit of relaxation before the forthcoming week, which would be very different.

Tuesday came - the meeting with the Khans at *The Savoy* was upon them. All four headed for the hotel in a taxi. At the entrance, Sammy told the driver to stop while he and Harry got out leaving Yiddel and Sheila to arrive in style right up to the main entrance. The two boys waited five minutes after Yiddel and Sheila had disappeared, then made their own way in. The two boys were shown to a table, just a few metres away from Khan's reserved table.

"A perfect spot," Sammy said, quietly. "I can see them quite good and the Khans have got their backs to us."

Sammy did the watching while Harry sat with his back to the Khans. But, was there anyone taking just a little too much interest in them? And in Yiddel and Sheila, who were already in conversation with the Khans? Raja was obviously the elder of the two; Amit, still with his right arm in a sling, extended his left hand to greet them both.

"It's nice to see you both again," he said.

Yiddel thought it all a bit strange. Here they were shaking hands with a man whom they had nearly killed a few weeks ago, and now were about to sit down and eat with in *The Savoy*.

"I hope you are feeling better, Mr Khan?"

"Yes, slowly but surely. My leg is still a bit stiff and my arm is taking its time because it was a difficult break, so the doctors tell me. My back is fine, once I am up and about. But for that, I'm Ok."

The waiter arrived with the menus and they ordered their first course.

"It's nice to see you as well, Mrs Davis." Amit was as outwardly relaxed as the first time they had met him. "The last time I saw you, if I remember, I remarked on your beauty. And even after getting married you are still a lovely lady," he added, looking at Yiddel and giving him a wink.

The food came and went and the informal conversation finally gave way to the reason for the meeting. Raja began explaining the proposed caper.

"The job that we would like you to do for us is one that we cannot be seen to have any involvement with. It is a family matter that has snowballed over the years. I will go into the finer details about it in a moment, but if I say that our father was the loser, then perhaps it will make sense. The job entails two sides - both will be taken care of when you execute the first. Number one is a vast collection of coins...quite a mixture. A precious collection of ancient gold and silver coins and a large amount of Roman coins.

"Number two is a complete collection of world stamps - all in mint condition. A great number of the stamps are those that most collectors can only dream about. They have never been seen nor have they been up for sale. They were originally collected at the time of printing. These stamps make serious collectors envious. We would like you to retrieve this collection of stamps and coins so that we can restore them to their rightful owner: our family. The family that now has them stole it from our father when they were friends. That was a long time ago in India. The value of it today is 'galactic', as my young son would say.

"This whole thing is not about the value, Mr Davis, it is about the principle. If you get it back for us, complete, then I can assure you that whatever we agree to will be paid in whatever form you would like it. We are a very rich Indian family and we still have large business interests in India and here in the UK. So, I say again, Mr Davis, what we hope to retrieve is rightfully ours. The family that has the collection lives in Holland, that's why it has been so difficult even contemplating getting it back ourselves. We have tried through negotiating, but we have been told, in no uncertain terms, to go away."

Khan let the silence descend as his words sank in. After a prolonged pause, and with no visible reaction from Yiddel or Sheila, he felt compelled to ask the one important question.

"Will you take the job?"

Yiddel had sat back in his chair and took his time. He had been thinking of little else for what had seemed like an eternity. Now, instead of giving a direct reply, he looked at Sheila, noticing a tell-tale sign of an eyebrow raised slightly, which he took for 'It's all yours!' That was enough – it was sounding like the sort of caper Yiddel and the boys excelled in, but now was also not the time to give the game away.

"I will say to you both right now - let me see the details of where it is, then, once we have looked it over, I will give you a positive answer within a day. All we need is as much as you can supply us with, and we will do the rest, Mr Khan."

"Thank you, Mr Davis. That was the answer that we expected from you. We will have all the information delivered by hand to your door by tomorrow. And one more thing, we know that you have two of your men here with you today as, shall I say, insurance? Well, naturally, we too have our men at the table next to your two, also as insurance."

Yiddel laughed and looked across at Sammy and Harry and to their right Khan's men.

Khan smiled. "The place is full of our people, it's a good job we had lunch here today – otherwise, this fine establishment would have been empty!"

The next morning Morris phoned bang on cue and said he was at *The Hilton*. He invited Yiddel and Sheila to join him for dinner. He had booked a table for 7.30 and he was looking forward to what Yiddel had to show him.

They arrived at 7.15. The desk clerk called Morris' room to advise that Mr and Mrs Davis were in reception. Mr Morris would be glad to see them in his room, room 645. They were escorted to the lift and then taken up to the sixth floor. Morris was waiting by the lift for them.

"I'm always pleased to see you, Mr Davis, and your lovely wife too. Please come in."

361

Yiddel immediately felt at ease with this man and undid the bag of jewellery. As Yiddel gently poured the contents onto the table top, even Sheila gasped at the splendour, the lights of the room catching the stones and sending sparkles of colour onto the ceiling.

"This really is some collection of stones," exclaimed Morris.

"They are fantastic, aren't they? I thought you would like them."

"Truly amazing." Morris was picking up the pendant. "Each piece is undeniably a work of art. Do you know anything about them at all?"

"All I know is that this lot is our perks for the Klein caper. So I can only assume that they come from Europe. Our man who looks after the jewellery side said possibly the royalty of an eastern European country, stolen by the Nazis." Yiddel was holding the tiara up to the light.

"Russian royalty, most probably," said Morris, still spellbound by the sheer quality of so many items, gently placing them back on the table with total admiration.

"I am blown away with their magnificence, Mr Davis. I am not a sentimental man - especially over jewellery, but this is something else. Come on, let's go and eat and then we can have a talk."

Yiddel put the collection back into its bag and they all went downstairs to dinner.

Keen to know Morris' real view – or rather his negotiating position regarding the jewellery's value, Yiddel opened the conversation as they sat down. "I have had our man look at them as I said and he too was genuinely blown away by them'. He said it would be a shame to have them cut up, but as they are, if they were to surface on the market, they would be instantly recognised... I should imagine like one of the paintings, Mr Morris?"

362

"Yes, you're right, if they were to appear on the auction or sale market they *would* be identified – far too risky. I should think they must already be listed in some very well-read catalogues of the world's finest jewellery, just like the paintings, as you say. So, the safest way would inevitably be to break each piece up and dispose of them individually. Do you want me to see what interest might be generated in the States?"

"Yeh, why not? I've got no rush to do anything with them yet. I'll wait to hear from you."

Nothing more was said about the jewellery. Next on the agenda was the remainder of the paintings.

"I've had a word with a few secret collectors that I have contact with, Mr Davis, and I have come up with two who are interested in taking what will amount to the entire collection off your hands. All I have to do is separate the whole lot into two deals. I will come over to your place and itemise what you have, then I can fax them the items and how much it will cost them, that is…after we have settled our price together."

Yiddel and Morris agreed this relatively quickly. They settled down to dinner and discussed future job possibilities. Morris seemed at ease.

"I find that to have a man like yourself available, should I have one of those sensitive jobs come up, is a real asset for me - where I know I can delegate a job and I don't have to concern myself until the job is done. It's very satisfying, Mr Davis!"

"Likewise, Mr Morris. I feel that I can always rely on you if I have something…how shall I say - a bit tasty - perhaps, that I want to get rid of."

And that was that - for the time being. All that was left to do in the short-term would be undertaken the next day at the warehouse.

363

The next morning, Joe Morris was at the unit just after 9am, carrying several books about famous painters and paintings. One was titled 'LOST ART', detailing the works of the great masters that had been lost through all manner of reasons - from malicious damage, fire, war, to the inexplicable - including those stolen and never retrieved, never to be seen publicly again.

Most of the paintings Yiddel had in his warehouse were in the last category - stolen during World War Two - and never seen since. They had never realised, until Joe Morris checked with his reference books, what a king's ransom of art they had, and it was getting increasingly concerning to have them all stacked up in their modest, unassuming commercial unit in the heart of a relatively impoverished Hackney.

Each find in the manual brought a 'Fucking hell!' from Yiddel, and a shout to the boys to "Come down and have a look at this one then...it's only another Rubens!"

Listing each one as they identified it with the catalogue, Morris finished up with a complete, detailed list of all the remaining paintings. Once he had his list, Yiddel left him alone to work out which ones he was going to tell his clients he had. This took him the rest of the morning and eventually he had two lists ready to fax to each one.

The fax letter to his clients was in a sort of industry code, but a code that Morris knew his people would understand.

"Now it's up to them," he announced. "All I can do is wait for them to come back with the all-important question of 'how much' from both of them...what price are we looking for, Mr Davis?"

"You asking me?" Yiddel was now adopting his classically Yiddish pose. "I ain't got a clue. It's all down to you regarding how much they are worth to your clients. I guess they'll negotiate, try to beat us down, but it's entirely your area, Mr Morris."

About half an hour later, the first fax came back from his number one client, saying simply: 'I will have the lot'.

The second client sent 'BUY THEM FOR ME' in capital letters.

"Well, now we know they are keen, I will fax the amount for each. Knowing these people like I do, I know I am wasting my time by telling them how much. Money is no object; in fact, to these two it is obscene to talk money, but I will anyway, and then they can't say they weren't told how much they're in for."

He sat at Sammy's desk for ten minutes doing his calculations for each painting. Yiddel sidled over and looked over his shoulder and whistled quietly. Morris looked up and said, "Let's see what they say, we can always come down," and faxed the amounts.

Ten minutes later, both faxes were returned with 'BUY' emblazoned on each.

Morris turned to Yiddel and shook his hand. "We have a deal then, Mr Davis?"

"Too fucking right we have a deal, Mr Morris!"

The deal was for one hundred million pounds split between the two buyers. It was left up to Morris to arrange the shipping of the works of art, which he did through the same channels as before. He had seen it work last time with the Texan, so why change anything? And so it was that the paintings left the shores of England bound for the States in a container with the documentation marked up: 'Paintings of a London Artist'.

Yiddel was paid out, and Joe Morris got his twenty percent plus a bonus from Yiddel that was in itself enough for him to buy an ocean-going yacht.

"A little pressy," said Yiddel when he gave it to Morris. "For working so well for us."

All the team who had been involved in the Klein caper also got a little 'pressy' from Yiddel in the form of fifteen million pounds each.

Yiddel put his money, along with Sheila's and the boys, into the offshore accounts set up by Mark Joseph, all expertly hidden away. There was nothing that the four wanted or desired that they could not afford, but for the moment, the biggest mistake they could make would be to show it.

Yiddel would, with great irony, sometimes say: "We live very comfortably, a fish and chip supper sometimes and an occasional take-away and, if we are really stretched, a night out in the local restaurant. What more could you want?"

Raja Khan phoned Yiddel as he had promised to tell him that all the details had been drawn up and they should meet to go over them. Yiddel set the meeting up at a friend's snooker hall in Islington, in a small room used for card schools.

The Khans turned out in force with three minders and another family member who was introduced as their cousin, and who happened to be a solicitor.

Yiddel's team consisted of himself and Sheila with the two boys on show, and sitting in his car outside was Alfie Smith's minder, borrowed once again.

Raja Khan opened the discussion by laying out on the table a map and details of where the place was in Holland.

"The house is in the Amsterdam area, not far from the city centre. It is easily reached by road. It is part of an old Dutch community village. The houses all belong to the family who have

366

the name of Bibi - that is their surname. They trade in anything that makes money, including drug importing and illegal firearms dealing. Most of their wealth comes from exploitation back in the old country. Today, the younger members of the family are buying and selling some very exclusive property all over Europe. They use the money that their grandfather stole to make more money. We don't care what they do with themselves these days, as you know - all we care about is restoring the coins and stamps to their rightful owners - that is, our family."

Khan paused to distribute some items. "This is a photograph of the house where we know the items are kept. Please take a look at this aerial photograph of the house – you will need to know both this and the surrounding property. This map shows exactly where in proximity the house is to Amsterdam. I will include on my behalf a member of my staff, who speaks fluent Dutch and Hindi to travel with you as part of your team. You will find him very handy to have around. I am not sending him as you might think…to watch you on our behalf, but for you to deploy as you will need his talents of language. He will obey your every word and command to the letter, Mr Davis, that I can promise you. Once you have the collection, will you be able to get it out of Holland and back here?"

"No problem at all. It all depends on how much there is. We have used a reliable way to move some other merchandise recently," said Yiddel, thinking about Sidney's false floor in his lorry.

"That takes me on to what you asked about how much there is. The complete collection consists of twenty stamp albums about the size of a popular newspaper. The coins are in wooden trays and secured in recesses - each coin has its own identity tag. Each tray would again be the size of a popular newspaper and there are twenty of those. It is quite a sizeable load. I would prefer that you did not tip the trays of coins in a bag because they are so precious that the slightest mark to the surface or edge of the coin will devalue the whole collection, so please keep them in their trays at all times. The stamps are Ok left in their albums, again, though, even touching them is not allowed. By all means leave the cabinets that they are in, they are too cumbersome to move.

"I have saved this until last. They have a modern alarm system and at night the grounds are patrolled by guard dogs. During the day, the dogs are shut away because they have young children playing in the grounds. On most days the house is left in the hands of the security staff, with the grandfather, daughters and the children. All the men are usually in Amsterdam or travelling in Europe. That's it. I have, I believe, covered it all. Have you any questions?"

Yiddel had been studying the map and the photographs while Khan was talking.

"I don't think I will get what I need from the photos, Mr Khan. I will have to go there and see for myself - the layout of the village, for example. Once I see how we can approach the house, I will be able to put it all together. I need to do this before I can say how the job is going to be carried out. I thank you for your man - as you say, he will be very useful to us if we run into any language problems. I will include him in my team. I think for now we will have to leave it at that. I will phone you when I get back from Holland."

Yiddel gathered up all the information that Raja Khan had prepared and the meeting came to an end.

20

The Dutchmen

"Fancy a trip to Amsterdam, Darling?" Yiddel asked Sheila. "We can combine it with a little honeymoon, which we ain't had yet, and a little look-see at this place. You know the type of thing - up and down the canals and twice round the sex shops will do us a treat. And at the same time help us set up this particular caper."

Sheila knew her man well and thought it was a lovely idea, but added, whimsically: "You go to the sex shops while I go round the clothes shops, Darling."

Back in their office, Yiddel phoned their agent, who booked them on a flight out of City airport in Docklands to Amsterdam Schipol for the next day.

Sammy drove them to the airport and waited there until he could see their aircraft jet off to Holland, before heading back to the office. Upon arrival, a delighted Harry informed him: "I've had tons of calls from the buyers for the new toy that we promised. They all have their latest orders and are well pleased, but they want to see the new one. I told them we could go and show some of them today and the rest tomorrow - that all right with you?"

"Sounds good to me. Now that Yiddel is away for a couple of days, let's do it!"

They both went back to the flat to get suited as appropriate for their important buyers, and left for the West End with a sample. By late afternoon, the boys had been to most of the top buyers who, once they had seen the demonstration, were eager to get their orders in. It took just the next day for them to visit the rest of the main buyers and once again they were inundated with orders – no reluctance or hesitation - the only word coming at them was 'When?' Back at the office, Sammy phoned Mr Lai and asked him: "How long will it be before they are in full production, Mr Lai?"

The Taiwanese was euphoric – he knew he had a good instinct for what would sell at any given time – but the sheer scale of commercial orders had taken even him but surprise. "They are in full production now…my factory is working around the clock; we do not stop. 24-7. How many would you like to order?"

Sammy, without hesitation, said: "As many as you can send the better, and you'd better send another load of the others as well, we are almost out of stock."

Meanwhile, Yiddel and Sheila had checked into the *Metropolis Hotel*, known as the best, in the city centre. By now it was late afternoon so they decided to have a look at the city and eat out and relax for a few hours – Yiddel and Sheila both knew this was no holiday, this was going to be all about getting the right understanding of how to effect what would be a very daring raid – and all for their one-time arch-enemy Khan.

The next morning, they hired a car with an English-speaking driver to take them around. Yiddel told him they were from England and were here to look at some property and would need him to take them to the village of Lisse, which, it turned out, the driver knew of.

"Ok, that is not far, about twenty minutes."

As soon as they arrived in the village, Sheila got into the role of the innocent tourist armed with a seemingly modest camera, walking about with her husband. But Sheila of course was only interested in one thing - the gates and buildings within the Bibi estate.

The driver, however, noticed and asked: "Why are you only interested in this house?"

"No reason," said Sheila, reassuringly. "I just like the look of the house and the way the garden is laid out."

"This house belongs to the richest family in Holland...do you know them?"

"No, I don't, but I know a lot about them – it's public knowledge that they are not nice people to know, either."

"What do you mean by 'not nice'. Do you mean evil?" The driver was now becoming a little too interested in things that were none of his business.

"Yes, you could say evil...yes, that sums them up perfectly," replied Sheila. Then she had an idea. "Come on, walk us round the village and tell me all you know about this place. I rather like it, don't you, Darling?" and she looked over her shoulder at Yiddel, meaningfully, followed swiftly by a subtle wink.

"Yes, it all looks good to me." Yiddel played the role.

They strolled around while the driver recalled other snippets of information about the village and the family. Occasionally, a local would say 'Hallo' as they strolled with exaggerated nonchalance around the Bibi estate without drawing any attention from anyone within – as far as they could see. No dogs, by the look of it, and no children, either, from inside the gated estate. Sheila casually snapped her camera whenever she felt there might be a shot for reference. Yiddel walked closely behind her and the driver, taking everything in. He knew that he could only do this sort of recce once. After that he would begin to stand out. 'So whatever has to be done has to be done now, otherwise people, especially this over-inquisitive driver, will start to remember faces.'

Yiddel had also noticed that the bell on the main gate had a CCTV system with it – no surprise – something very valuable to protect what lay inside.

Directly opposite the house was a bar-restaurant. Yiddel suggested they all have a break now, and get something to eat and drink before heading back to the city. The driver readily agreed, thinking of his fare for such likeable English tourists, completely oblivious to the real reason why they would really want to sit in a provincial restaurant for an hour and a half.

While they had lunch, chatting and marvelling at how relaxing it was in this unspoilt country, Yiddel made sure he was able to observe any comings and goings to and from the house on the other side of the road.

The driver, by now, had forgotten how unusual it was for anyone to be taking such an interest in one luxurious property in a sleepy Dutch hamlet.

'Why should I care?' he thought. 'The clock is running and here I am being paid just to eat and drink – suits me!'

The next day, Yiddel and Sheila again took a taxi – a different one - back to the restaurant in Lisse, and this time had dinner there, the purpose being to watch how and when the various members of the family who owned the house came back at the end of the day. This time, they sat alone in the restaurant and compared notes of what they had seen. By the time they left and were headed back to their hotel in Amsterdam, there was nothing else that Yiddel needed to know in order to be able to make up his plan of attack: he had it all.

A couple of days remained before returning home, and they spent the rest of the trip sightseeing around the canals, flower stalls and flea markets of this amazing city.

Then it was time to go back - back to the team, and to set up the job. Yiddel was confident that between them they had collected enough data to brief the meeting. Yiddel paid the driver handsomely for his services and was assured that if ever they came back to Amsterdam, all they had to do was to call him.

'No, the next time we come,' thought Yiddel, "we will be more than able to look after ourselves.'

21

The Dutch Khan Caper

Sammy met them at the City airport, pleased to see the Master and his wife again.

"Got lots to tell you," he said. "First, the new toy, the *Reality* one, 'as taken off like a rocket. We took it to all the buyers and all of them admitted there's no other toy like it in England. They were all very eager to have it before anyone else got hold of it. I told them as soon as we got it, they would all have it at the same time...they were a bit narked at that, but what can we do?

"And, second, Mr Morris phoned and said that he's got a buyer for the jewellery. A man who would take it all. He's phoning you later to talk about money."

"Well, that's a good start to come back to!" Yiddel wasn't surprised at either piece of news, but this, added to the successful recce in Holland seemed like the icing on the cake. "Everything else all right, Sam?"

"Yeh, but for the toy thing, it's been pretty quiet...glad to have you back."

Sheila looked at Yiddel with her 'You're their father' look, and merely smiled - she had said it all before.

Yiddel had been thinking about the present-day situation regarding the two boys. How he had restricted them from spending money, always to be safe than sorry and so on. Now that they had a kosher business up and running, there was no reason why they could not show that they were Ok on their own. There was nothing to hide, they were trading well, and the business had a very healthy bank balance and, unbelievably, the whole thing was above board with the accounts – them paying their tax and stamp, and FAGIN UK paying its dues to the Revenue as a legal set-up.

Sheila, naturally, figured highly in all his thoughts. So, now was the time for him to call them all together in his office along with their accountant.

He could see they were all curious as to the reason for the unexpected meeting, so he opened proceedings directly. "As you are all well aware, the business is doing very nicely - trading well and all legit - so I feel that after all this time of being careful, we can now spend a few bob. We mustn't go mad, but we can spend."

The accountant who had been recommended to Yiddel as a good 'un was not aware that the people sitting with him in Yiddel's modest office were multi-millionaires. All he knew, and all he had to know, was that they ran an importing business that was very successful, and under his professional commercial guidance, could do even better.

Yiddel continued: "So, I think we can afford to have a new car each, on the slate of course, and also you may want to have a look around for a new flat and," looking at Sheila, "a new house. Is that all right, Mr Jacobs?"

"Perfectly Ok, Mr Davis. Keep the cars at a reasonable price, also the flat and the house. You will have to go on market prices, and I will take care of the mortgages."

Big smiles all round from the boys, with Sheila giving Yiddel a kiss.

"When can I start house hunting, Mr Jacobs?"

"Whenever you like, Mrs Davis, just call me when you have the details."

Later that night when the two of them were having dinner, Yiddel said: "About the house, I don't really want to move too far away from round here, you know what I'm like - I love living in Hackney. I have never lived anywhere else, so when you start looking, remember: not too far please, darling. I know we can afford the best house in England...we know that, and one day we will have it, but for now let's find a nice house, where we can have a dog and maybe something else!"

"Something else?" wondered Sheila. "What 'something else'?"

"Well...you know," said Yiddel evasively, "maybe a little..." looking into Sheila's eyes, which were getting bigger with the workings of her mind.

"Maybe..." he couldn't help but grin, "a little kitten to go with the dog."

Yiddel caught a table napkin right in his face as Sheila launched herself at him, landing on his lap.

"I thought you were going to say a baby, you sod!"

Yiddel rolled up with laughter as the two cuddled, with Yiddel saying quietly in her ear: "Get the house first!"

In the meantime, Sammy and Harry had been to the BMW showroom and both had ordered the 318 series in different colours. Yiddel ordered a Volvo and Sheila a VW Golf, all due to be delivered about the same time. The boys had decided to look at the new apartments in Docklands, and Sheila went looking for houses in Chigwell, to the east of London. She had said to Yiddel, with an imploring expression: "About twenty minutes' drive from Hackney and the warehouse – Ok, Darling?"

Morris phoned Yiddel to endorse his conversation with Sammy about the jewellery. "I've got a client who would like it all, what did your man say it was worth?"

"He said it was priceless, a king's ransom and all those kind of things. Why, what do you think?"

"The stones alone must be worth a couple of million," was Morris' verdict.

"Ok, see what you can get and put in your commission as well. If he wants the lot, let him have a deal. I'll leave it to you. I won't be around for a while. We have a job on the continent, so go ahead and set it up; we will be back in about a week."

And Yiddel left it at that – his mind was now firmly on who to select for the Dutch caper. He decided to call everyone in for a conference and to lay the plan out and see what they had to say about who went and who stayed.

The whole team arrived at the warehouse.

Yiddel stood by the wall that now had small-scale maps and photographs on display. "I love it when I get the team together. Ok, everyone, I have a job that's been put to us, to do in Holland, in fact it's just outside Amsterdam. It seems straightforward enough to me but for one problem. Although I have a plan in my mind, I am stuck on how many players I will need. I'm looking at it as easy, but then again it could turn tits up and all go wrong."

He turned to Sidney. "I will need you because of the transport. Ansel, Sammy and Harry – I need you for muscle. Roger - you will be the driver. Sheila, I have a job for you too, so the only one I can't fit in is Elvis. Sorry mate, you will be on the next one. We have a translator travelling with us; he is their man – the Khans, that is - who speaks fluent Dutch and Hindi. As well as that, he is a big man, so we will have plenty of brawn if we need it, plus we have drivers and transport.

"Ok, this is it. The house is in a village just outside Amsterdam." (Sheila passed the photos around). "You can see that it is a fair size place surrounded by a high wall and that the only entrance is through that gate. What we are after is a collection of rare gold and silver coins and a very rare and valuable stamp collection that was stolen from the people we are working for and on whose behalf we are getting it back. Some sort of feud between the two families that goes back years. By the way, just so you know..." Yiddel paused and looked at them closely to gauge the reaction to what he was about to tell them.

"The family is the same ones who we robbed in Southall, the casino job. I know, it sounds a bit much but there you go, they thought we were good at doing 'em there and have given us the job. And, gang, we are getting paid by them and they don't want the casino money back!" At this last piece of news, everyone dissolved into giggles – especially the burly Ansel and the boys.

Yiddel was relieved it had gone down so well. And, certainly no objections, as far as anyone was letting on, and he knew his team – all loyal to him beyond all others.

"Ok, have you all seen the pictures, so you know what the target looks like? Good. Now, during the day, all the male members of the family leave the house and go off to work, either in Amsterdam or further afield, we have noted, so the job is best done then. Why? Because at night, as well as all the men being there, they let the dogs loose out in the grounds and they are not friendly to intruders. The main gate is controlled from the house by sound and vision. We spent an afternoon sitting in a café opposite where we watched the movements of those coming and going. They had several trucks

378

taking deliveries in. It looked like food and booze, so that, I reckon, is our way in. I want one of those trucks hijacked before it gets to the village, and us in it when it arrives at the gates of the house. The translator can be the one who speaks at the gate and he can pretend to be the driver too. The truck will be used to carry us in and carry out what we are there for. If it is full of food when we stop it, tip it all out somewhere discreet so that we can all get in. Roger will be the driver of the truck. Roger: if for some reason after the Khan man 'as spoken to them, they refuse to open the gates, ram the fuckers down. Once we're at the house we have got to move fast to secure everybody who is in there. Harry, you will carry wire cutters to cut all the telephone lines and whatever else that could be an alarm system. The women and children are to be rounded up and put into one room by Sheila, right out of our way. Check that they are not carrying mobile phones so take the translator with you, Sheila.

"If there are any men there, take some of those plastic cable binders with us, Harry, and tie 'em up. Ansel - guard the door and the ground floor and watch Sheila's back. Sammy and me will start the house search. As soon as the women and kids are secure, Sheila will join us on the search. As soon as we find it, shout out so everyone knows it's been located. There is a strong possibility that the old grandpa is in the house. Be careful, don't harm him, if he is in bed leave him there. Once we have the gear, everybody start helping get it back to the truck, I don't know how much there will be. I have been told it is in cabinets. Remember: handle it with care, don't take the coins out of the trays, take the trays complete with the coins and the stamp albums as they are.

"Harry - take care of the clothes for the whole team. Overalls, gloves, masks and four walkie-talkies. We will meet you, Sid, about two miles down the road, here (pointing to the rendezvous on the map). It's an old goods depot with a large shed. Pull your lorry round the back so that when we come back we will be all out of sight from the main road. We will leave the grocery truck there. We will all leave in a van, which we will get once we're there. Once you are loaded, Sid, get on your way home to England.

"Sammy, you get that van for us in Amsterdam to get us to the village. Take it with us when we go to the house once we have hijacked the truck. When we leave the house, use what transport you like to get away, and don't get left behind, because we won't come back for you. Sid - when we go, can you arrange to pick up a load of carpets to cover your journey?"

Sidney said nothing, but made the thumbs up sign.

"Once you've got the load on board, get as far away from Amsterdam as you can, and then start heading for the port. All clothes afterwards in one bag for burning; set that alight at the goods depot. The driver of the grocery truck can be left at the house tied up with the women. Anything else I've forgot? Oh, yeh, all split up and head for the airport and travel back the same way as you went out. Only take a small case each so it looks to the customs officers that you have some luggage. If you see any danger go away from your points of departure, head for Amsterdam and book into a hotel and stay there for a while, then try it again and if it's clear head back by train or ferry. Don't travel together. Right, is there anything you think I missed?"

A buzz of excited talk broke out, but there were no questions.

"Ok, Sidney, it's all down to you, as soon as you get a load, we go!"

All they could do now was to wait for Sidney to tell them when he had a load of carpets to pick up in Holland.

Roger, in the meantime, had been busy finding himself a house or apartment. He met Yiddel in the market and said that he was thinking of moving out of his father's because he thought it would be better for him to have his own place now.

"Where are you thinking of going, Rog?" Yiddel asked him.

"I've been looking in the Hampstead area...then I started to think it's too far from here and I changed my mind. There's some new buildings going up in Docklands that look all right. I'm on the way there now. How 'bout you?"

"Sheila's been looking at houses in Chigwell. She's gone back this morning to have another look with her friend. I suppose I'll hear all about it tonight, if she still likes it, that is. Anyway, see you later, Roger, wish you luck in looking."

Yiddel ambled off down the market, stopping to talk with some of his trader friends, during which he could see Ansel looking down the street towards him waving.

"You all right, Ansel? I see you waving."

"Yeh, I'm Ok. When I saw you here, I thought we had the word for the off!"

"No, nothing yet, mate. We've got to wait for Sid to get a load, then it's all above board, as far as anyone else knows."

They shook hands and Yiddel carried on strolling down the market, and noticed the man who had taken over his old stall pitch that he had run with the boys before FAGIN UK was launched fully. Poor old Stan was just standing there doing nothing.

"It looks like you're quiet, Stan," Yiddel observed.

"Yeh, Yiddel, it's one of those days - they obviously don't want to spend money today."

"Come up the warehouse when you can, the boys have got some new lines in and they may have a few for you to sell on the stall. It might liven up your trade a bit."

"Ok, thanks for that, Yiddel, I'll do that." This had given Stan some much-needed hope – it wasn't just today that potential customers weren't spending their money, as he had suggested it was.

Sheila came back from Chigwell to say that she had put an offer on a house she really liked, and that Yiddel should go and have a look with her.

"It is really lovely," she had gushed with such enthusiasm.

They drove out to Chigwell to see the house that afternoon and Yiddel had to agree with her – it would suit them both, and possibly more besides - and he could see it was not too far to travel to the warehouse from, so it was the work of just a few minutes for him to endorse the deal, saying: "If you like it, darling, so do I!"

The next morning, Yiddel took a phone call from the Khans, who were starting to wonder if all was well and when Yiddel and team were going. All Yiddel could tell him at this stage was: "The minute I know, I will phone you so that your man can travel with us on the same day."

"Thank you, Mr Davis, he will be ready for you, no problem."

The phone call reminded Yiddel of the Khans' seriousness to get back what they claimed was theirs, and that they were not minded to wait forever. He reflected for a moment that he had no control over when Sidney could give the go-ahead and that to get on the wrong side of the Khans could still spell a lot of trouble.

As his mind drifted onto the ugly possibilities that a war with the Khans could bring, he suddenly remembered his parents and how they had perished. That was it – the car crash reminded him of how Khan himself had nearly died – that look of Khan's, seconds before his car had impacted, was bringing back the one cataclysmic event in Yiddel's own life that had changed everything. Would he really be living a life of crime and deception if that bloody lorry driver hadn't been drunk at the wheel?

Yiddel buried his face in his hands and sobbed, thankful only that neither the boys nor Sheila were here to witness his pain. He told himself to dig deep and get stronger – that was supposed to be his automatic response to the torture – he would see Mum and Dad again one day, and he must make them proud of his achievements. Besides, scum like Khan deserved to die. Yet he hadn't died – and Yiddel thought for the first time how impossible that surely was: he himself had seen the car go up in flames; no one could have survived that, but Khan not only had done so, but the man had no burns or suchlike injuries on him whatsoever.

Very rarely did Yiddel doubt himself. But this was hurting badly – not only was Khan alive and recovering remarkably well, but here was Yiddel doing a job for that bastard and taking orders from him, after which Khan could pick him off at will with a well-chosen hit squad. Perhaps Yiddel had given too much away? What would Dad have done? No answer – he had died too early for Yiddel to form a really developed relationship with – 'so you're on your own,' Yiddel thought to himself.

He could feel his heart thumping and knew this stress could bring him down if he wasn't careful; he needed to talk to someone about all this, but there wasn't anyone whom he felt he could trust with all the detail. He forced himself to sit up and look straight ahead and just stared at the wall for a while, allowing his inner turmoil to settle, and then his response kicked in: Do or die – if

383

Khan wants war, so be it - but he, Yiddel, could take him on, especially with assistance from the likes of Alfie Smith. It was in any case too late to pull out of the Amsterdam job. Yiddel had committed himself too quickly and too easily.

He breathed in fully and stood up. 'Lesson learnt,' he thought, straightening up, now defying the pain. 'Can't keep doing all these jobs – my luck will run out eventually.' And then, speaking out aloud as if to a benevolent listener: "First, Holland; next, if needs be, Khan; then, anyone else that gets on the wrong side of me…and, finally, retirement with Sheila".

Those few minutes had transformed the easy-going Yiddel into a man with a burning ambition – one that seemed to have been sent to him by Providence itself. 'You can't escape your fate,' he mused, 'so, in the meantime, let's have some fun.'

As he moved towards the door, any further feelings were interrupted by the phone ringing. It was Morris calling from Texas with good news: his man was more than interested in the price Morris had set and so Yiddel could leave it to him to arrange the meeting and the transaction. Momentum had been restored.

All was quiet for three days. Then Yiddel got the call from Sidney - he had a load to drop off in Rotterdam first and then a pick up from the Amsterdam docks. All carpets as usual. The lorry would then come over to them at the village and then back to England all on legitimate delivery notes and invoices, making the whole trip 'as kosher as you can get it' in Sidney's words.

"Good man, when is the lorry off to Holland with the delivery?" Yiddel needed to know.

"My driver is on his way to Bradford right now to pick up the load. When he comes back to the yard, I will then give him the documents and then he will be on his way. Due to be at the port on Sunday evening, then the night crossing and in Rotterdam by Monday afternoon. Back to Amsterdam by Tuesday afternoon. He will have an overnighter there with his load and be on the road to us by Wednesday morning. We can be in place by midday Wednesday at the old goods yard."

Yiddel immediately notified all the team members: they must be ready to leave on Tuesday morning. He wanted them all in Holland a day before the hit. Harry took all the working gear over to Sidney's yard so that it could be loaded onto the lorry, and his next task was to purchase various tickets for the different routes into Holland making sure that they did not arrive in a large body of people but in ones and twos.

They were all booked into the same hotel in Amsterdam, in their own names. Sidney was Ok - he was going on the whole journey with his driver - he had chosen one of his most trusted men to do this trip, knowing that for another ninety pounds in his pocket he was guaranteed to say absolutely nothing to anyone. Yiddel and Sheila would travel together; Sammy, Harry and Roger alone; Ansel with the translator - all making their own way to the hotel in central Amsterdam.

Yiddel was relieved he could now phone Khan to tell him that his man must be at the warehouse in Hackney by 9am on Tuesday, and that Harry would arrange his ticket. Yiddel sat back in his chair with his eyes closed and tried to think if he had left anything out of the preparations for the operation. "No, it's all done, everything's ready," he thought aloud. "For Mum, for Dad. Let's get it on."

7.30am Tuesday: Yiddel and Sheila were already at the warehouse going over the plan. Sidney had taken the working clothes with him on his trip to Rotterdam. The tickets for all the party were on Yiddel's desk and ready to be given out. All cases were packed for the overnight in Amsterdam.

Just then, Sammy and Harry came in with the first man to arrive.

"Yiddel, this is our translator, Mr David Hamal. David, this is Yiddel Davis."

Yiddel shook hands with him and welcomed him to the team and quickly ran through the plan with him. Ansel then arrived, followed by Roger. Harry gave everyone a ticket and some Dutch guilders. After a brief run-through, they started to leave, all heading for their departure points.

"See you in the *Metropolis Hotel*, Amsterdam," said Yiddel, as the first left the building.

Yiddel and Sheila were the last to leave, making sure everyone was away and locking up the warehouse as their taxi pulled up to take them to City airport.

By late afternoon, everyone had arrived at the hotel. Using the internal phone system, Yiddel summoned everyone to his room.

"Any problems, gang?"

He got a chorus of 'No' and carried on. "Just to be on the safe side, I suggest we stay split up for tonight and just do your own thing, go out to eat or eat in. In the morning, all go down for breakfast, then back to the rooms, pack up, pay your bill and then walk down to the square by the canal – as you know, about two hundred yards from here as you turn left out of the main door. Sammy will have the van parked there, ready to take us to the village. Get that tonight, Sam, and park it in the hotel car park…right…all at the square at 8.30 sharp!"

They stayed together for a while, talking and comparing notes on the journey over, and sharing those two contradictory emotions - excitement and anxiety – as the adrenalin surged through their veins in anticipation of the next day's caper.

They all left Yiddel's room together, Yiddel and Sheila deciding to go for a walk and find a restaurant nearby to eat at. The others did the same, but all going off in different directions as instructed.

Bang on 8.30am, the team assembled at the square as Sammy pulled up with the van allowing them all to climb in. As directed by Yiddel, he drove straight to the goods depot where they found Sidney already parked. They all spent a few moments greeting each other, with Yiddel introducing David Hamal to Sidney, the latter handing out the specially chosen work clothes. They all got changed and were on their way back to the spot outside the village, where they were going to stop and then hi-jack the grocery truck.

"When I say so, pull the van across the road, Sam, and block his path. Everyone stay in the van until he stops except Harry and me. Once he stops, Harry, follow me to his door and get it open. I will pull him out of his seat, you gag him and tie him up and put him in the back of the van. Roger, jump up and drive off behind us until I signal you to stop. Ok, let's get it on!"

Sammy drove the van to the quietest spot on the road and stopped. They waited for the inevitable.

Bang on time, the grocery lorry came down the road towards the village.

"That's the one!" Yiddel shouted. "Right, Sam, do your thing, NOW!"

The driver of the truck came to a skidding halt trying desperately to avoid the small van, and rather innocently looking relieved that he had avoided an accident. That feeling soon disappeared as he could now see two masked men running towards him. Harry had got to the cab door in a matter of seconds and had yanked it open before the unfortunate driver had any time in which to react. Yiddel yanked him out of the cab and onto the road. Thinking that he was in for a bashing, the man naturally coiled up defensively and tried to protect his head. However, the next thing he knew was his uniform being removed and a gag and blindfold being firmly placed over his eyes and mouth. His arms were pulled back and his hands tied behind him as he was bundled into the rear of the van Sammy had been driving. Frightened and cowered by such power that verged on sheer violence, he felt people pushing past him and others pushing him into the van. Then a Dutch word spoken as if by a fellow countryman was telling him to 'be quiet or else'.

Roger was now in the driving seat of the lorry whilst Hamad put the driver's uniform on. A short distance up the road towards the house, Yiddel signalled Roger to stop to let them exit the van, and Yiddel joined Roger, telling Sammy to follow them closely to the gates and to stay behind them.

At the gates, Hamad took the lead role, looking to all intents and purposes like the regular deliveryman. He looked up at the name on the side of the truck and pushed the bell button. A female voice answered: "Who is it?"

"Schmitz Grocery. It's your food delivery, madam." Hamad's Dutch was perfect.

"Who are you? Where is the usual man?" she asked, being able to see Hamad on the video screen.

"He was taken ill suddenly this morning, and I am the replacement driver, madam," was his calm response.

There was a pause for longer than Yiddel was comfortable with. Had they been discovered? Then, the big iron gates gave off a click as the locking device was released and they began to swing open. Roger drove forward with calm deliberation, David Hamad in the passenger seat. As Roger began to manoeuvre around to the back of the house, they all heard the big gates being closed shut with a bang. The van was right behind the truck as Roger stopped.

Then it was all let loose. Leaping out of the vehicles, they began to swarm like angry wasps into the entrance of the house.

In their way were a man and a woman.

Sammy held the woman and Yiddel the man while Hamad ordered them to be quiet. This time there was more protest, though, as the woman in particular tried to scream and struggle against the onslaught of the gang. Harry gagged her and secured her hands with the plastic ties. They now had to ascertain who else was in the house – and fast. Where were they? If they happened to be near a phone... Bursting into an adjoining room, they found two more women, with three children. The women surrendered passively, obeying the instruction to co-operate. All were brought out to the entrance hall and the adults were bound and gagged like the other two before being shut away in a large broom cupboard that Sheila had found. Ansel brought the driver through and he joined the rest there.

As Ansel stood guard in the entrance hall from where he could cover any attempt at escape, everyone else began searching the house for the merchandise that they were there for.

Yiddel, Sammy and Hamad charged upstairs while Sheila and Roger searched the ground floor. Harry went back outside to find the phone and alarm wires. Whilst he was cutting these, Sammy found the room housing what they wanted. It was a magnificently large room, ostentatious in its sheer opulence, and amongst the valuable furniture were two large cabinets standing proudly in the middle of the room. These housed the stamp collection.

Looking quickly in the open drawers of the first cabinet as directed by Sammy, Yiddel could see that each drawer contained the collection of coins set into its own recesses.

"Ok, this is it! Start taking these down!" he ordered.

Sammy carefully carried the first drawer down to the lorry – emptied now by Roger, who had piled all the food alongside it - causing much of it to spill over the gravel path. Sammy passed the first drawer up to Roger, who carefully laid it on the floor. The other drawers were soon carried down by all the team and swiftly but expertly loaded with care, one on top of another.

But Yiddel had noticed something in one of the drawers – Sammy could see him pulling out what looked like some black, diary-sized books which Yiddel was taking a keen interest in, 'a reference to the collection,' he thought.

Next was more precarious, potentially. They needed to transfer the entire contents of the larger of the two cabinets – the stamps. 'Get this wrong', thought Yiddel, 'and we've wasted our time. And then to have to explain it to Khan…' This time, each tray was loaded with sheets of mint stamps all protected by a sheet of thin tissue paper. It took another ten minutes to empty the unit along with a pile of beautifully leather-bounded stamp albums they discovered were also in the drawers, all considerably well-protected and clearly treasured by their now-former owners.

All was going well. 'Soon be out of here,' Yiddel reckoned.

But it was not to be. From upstairs, David Hamad was calling him. "Problem!"

Yiddel went with him, leaving the others to carry the stamps out to the lorry.

Hamad had gone a deathly pale and couldn't seem to speak. Yiddel's mind started spinning with possibilities, none of them easy. As they both raced up the stairs to the second floor, they could hear one of the children starting to cry from down below, and then Sheila's voice trying to calm the women. A female voice in Dutch was screaming and cursing out loud, somehow, despite having been gagged; maybe a child was suffocating? There seemed to be an increasing uproar, and Yiddel reminded himself to trust Sheila's judgement in how to handle their captors, but what was upstairs that had caused Hamad to sound the alarm? In a flash, all had changed.

Yiddel knew he couldn't afford to think of that right now. He followed Hamad down the hallway, glancing in all the rooms to see if there was anything else that needed attending to. At the end of a long corridor that boasted a decorous grandeur from days gone by, they came to a very large bedroom. An old man was sitting up, his eyes wild with fear and anger. Seeing them at his door, those eyes spoke of malicious revenge, if he could inflict it upon Yiddel and Hamad, for the outrage of breaking into his house.

"Who are you and what are you doing in my house?" he thundered.

David Hamad cautiously moved closer to the bed and said, in the man's language, "We have come to take back that which is rightly ours, that which you stole from our father and which belongs to our families."

The old man was staring into David's face. Despite the trauma, and despite his advanced years, he recognised Hamad.

"I know you, you are one of the family of that mangy dog... Khan. Well, I can tell you now, it will never be yours. Can never be! It is ours by right, and we will rightly lay claim to it and have it returned to us." He stopped abruptly and was clearly struggling for breath. His right hand went to his chest and he forced himself to inhale deeply, and then the wild eyes bore into Hamads's face once more. "I never stole it from him, it always belonged to my family!"

Yiddel guessed this must be Khan's adversary, the head of this family – this was Bibi himself – defiant, but very weak from the realisation that his so-called 'right' would now be violated – the collection was no longer his. The injustice of this outrage and the impact of being powerless, physically, to prevent it, were clearly causing him chest pains, and he could for a moment only get his breath with extreme difficulty. "Bastards," he wheezed.

"You can't stop us, Bibi," was Hamad's exultant assertion. And then his air suddenly changed to one of concern. He had just realised how frail this old man really was, and neither he nor Yiddel wanted manslaughter on their hands. "Can I get you some medication?" he asked. "Are you Ok?"

Yiddel had been taken aback by the tirade from the old man, and he too realised they couldn't afford a corpse on their hands.

"What the fuck do you care? You rob me of things that are mine!" Bibi's head shot back in acute pain, and then he clutched his stomach and seemed to coil up. His old face, wrinkled by ill-health, contorted momentarily as his torture threatened to overcome him. Then his eyes opened again, but this time they avoided looking at Hamad. The old man fought back his pain. "I will make sure...one day, that you will feel the same, you son of a whore!"

David Hamad half turned away from the old man. "Fuck you, Bibi, and all your kin. I offered you my help if you needed it and

392

now, old man, you get fucking nothing but my curse on you. I hope you suffer for a long time and die in a lot of pain!"

With a look of disgust that he had been forced to say what he had, Hamad retreated. Yiddel hadn't doubted the hatred between the two families, but had been shocked at the exchange, and was keen to get away from this place, especially if the raid should spell the death of the old man. He beckoned with his head that they should leave.

"The fucking bastard, he should have died years ago!" Hamad said with everlasting, immeasurable contempt.

Down in the lower hallway, Yiddel and David rejoined the team. Yiddel was re-focusing; Hamad would take a while to calm down.

"Is everything loaded?" he got a nod from Roger. "Are all the women and kids Ok?" Another nod, from Sheila. "Right, let's get out of here."

Sheila checked the women and children for a last time; despite the screaming of earlier, she had successfully calmed things down. There was always a kindness to Sheila's firmness; the panic-stricken woman had seen that.

The van followed the lorry as they headed up to the already open gates – the boys had jammed the mechanism to 'open' for just long enough for them to get through – and, in ten minutes, they were at the goods yard depot, where Sidney was waiting to transfer the load.

He and the driver had pulled the carpets back to make room for it. Roger reversed the truck up close to the back of Sidney's lorry, both vehicles with their back doors wide open, while the whole team carried the stamps and coin trays through into the lorry. They were then covered over, firstly with some fine cotton sheets and then completely by the carpets, twenty deep. The grocery truck was taken around the back of the yard and put into a large empty warehouse and the doors closed. Sidney was satisfied with the loading – and that was good enough for Yiddel – and he wished them all luck. He and his driver now headed for the ferry boat at The Hague.

All the working clothes were put in one bag. Roger had checked that every member of the team had kept their gloves on all the time they were in and out of the back of the grocery truck, so it was completely clean of any finger prints – anything, even the slightest flaw in this element could spell disaster. Sammy poured petrol over the bag of clothes and set it alight. As the rest of the team climbed into the van, he observed with grim satisfaction the lorry going up in tongues of hungry flame.

A clear run of twenty minutes' drive took them back to the centre of Amsterdam. Sammy dropped then team off in stages until there was only himself left to park the van, which he did so in a multi-storey car park, picking up his overnight bag and walking away, heading for the station. Yiddel and Sheila, both carrying shopping bags, took a taxi for the airport for their return flight to the Docklands City airport.

Roger and Ansel had tickets for the train ferry route. Sammy flew back to Heathrow followed by Harry on another flight. David Hamad left Holland and headed for France to catch a ferry back to Dover. And Sidney and his driver plus his load of carpets were on the ferry boat, halfway across the sea – all on their way before the alarm was raised at the house.

The first person to discover the robbery was one of the older children, returning from school and unable to get into the estate through the gates. He had eventually managed to climb over the wall and found his mother, aunts and siblings, as well as the guard, tied up and locked away in the broom cupboard along with a man, whom he had never seen before, in his underpants.

As they were untied, the driver immediately went to phone his workplace to tell them of his ordeal only to find there was no connection. Frantically, the women rushed upstairs to check on Bibi - they found him in a coma, the shock and impact of the raid had taken all the strength out of him. Unable to call their doctor, one of them went outside to try to summon help from the bar-restaurant, the same one used by Yiddel to stake the place out just a couple of weeks before. At the top of the drive, however, she was met by Houn Bibi, the youngest of the sons, returning home and completely unaware of all that had gone on. He straight away called for an ambulance for Bibi.

The women were still in a very distressed state by the time all the men had arrived back.

"Who did this to us?" Houn asked, looking at the guard and then the women.

"We don't know, they were all masked. Your father was talking to them in his bedroom, we heard him shouting at them. All I caught was 'son of a whore' and then I heard a door slam and they all came down. A man looked in our room and then they all left...I heard two engines start up and that is all."

Outside on the drive all that was visible was a pile of food, in packets and loose form. The room where the collection had once been was stripped bare except for the empty cabinet and the wooden unit.

The eldest son, after listening to the story of the morning's events, rushed up the stairs to the collection room. When he saw that the room had been cleared of everything, he let out an ear-splitting shriek.

"They have taken all the ledgers of all our transactions that we have done over the last three years - they were in the bottom drawer!" he gasped, hysterically.

By now, all three sons were back in the house, all together in one room and all now realising the implications of the ledgers falling into the wrong hands. They then had to decide how they were going to handle the robbery and what was going to be said to the police – what they could disclose, as well as what they couldn't. Only then did they call the police.

At this stage, Yiddel and team had six hours' start on them. Yiddel's and Sheila's plane was landing at Docklands, and during this time he had wondered what the 'reference books' were, exactly – it would not, however, be until much later that he would find out that they were much more than what he had even tried to guess at.

Gradually, throughout the late afternoon, the team started to drift back to the warehouse. All of them very pleased to see each other and all with a tale to tell about their travelling.

Roger phoned in to say that he was Ok and back home. Yiddel was well pleased with how the caper had gone – the only thing that worried him was the old man. When David Hamad arrived, Yiddel arranged for him to stay nearby so that when Sidney got back to his yard the next day they all could go together and sort out the load.

Meanwhile, back in Holland, the stolen grocery truck had been found by the police as well as the pile of burnt out clothing. The driver was so confused that he was unable to tell the police anything except how he was forced to stop and that two men took charge of his truck. He was asked if he saw any of them with their masks off and he told them honestly: "For only a brief few seconds as two men approached my truck. When one pulled me out, I was holding my head, thinking that I was going to get beaten up and when I looked again they both had full face masks on. From then on, I was blindfolded and marched off to be put in another vehicle."

The police now knew that there was another vehicle. All that the family members could tell them was that there had been about six in the gang. Only one could speak Dutch, all the others were speaking English, which was confirmed by the truck driver.

The Dutch police had their forensic department go all over the house, checking for any possible traces of evidence - including fingerprints. At the end of the day, all they had was what they had when they first arrived at the crime scene. Nothing.

The police now had all the departure points covered, but had nothing to identify anyone leaving Holland. The bag of burnt out clothing revealed nothing but ash. A van had been found in Amsterdam that had been stolen, which also revealed nothing for the forensic team. The Bibi family reported that what they had stolen was a stamp album and some coins, which they said had been in their family for many years and was very valuable.

Yiddel and Sheila were in the office before 8am. Sheila was making them a coffee when Yiddel's telephone rang. Sidney was back at the yard.

"Everything go all right, mate?" was Yiddel's automatic question.

"Like a dream, cock, and we had time to get a bit of duty free, got you some extra fags," he said, cheekily.

"Thanks very much, they're always handy... What time shall we come over, Sid?"

397

"As soon as you like. I'm staying here with the lorry. My driver's gone home to get some kip. See you when you can."

Sammy and Harry arrived to find David Hamad just getting out of a taxi outside the office.

"Morning, David, sleep well?" asked Sammy.

"Yes, thank you. All that fresh air and activity yesterday quite tired me out."

They all went up to the office and had a coffee.

"Right," said Yiddel. "Sidney is back in his yard, let's drink our coffee, then we can head over to his place."

Just then, Ansel popped his head around the office door.

"Morning all, just to let you know I'm back," he said, rushing off to open the market café.

David used Yiddel's phone and gave the Khans a call to tell them that they were all back and Ok, and that they were going to pick up the coins and stamps at the transport yard. Sheila passed him a note with Sidney's address on it, which he passed over to them. He suggested they have a large van with them at the yard to take it all away.

"Before we go any further, David, what was your arrangement with the money?" asked Yiddel.

"Amit and Raja are bringing it with them, they will settle up with you today."

Behind Hamad's back, Yiddel signalled for Sammy to come away for a quick chat.

"Watch them all the time when they get there. I still do not trust them, tell Harry the same!"

An hour later, they were all at Sidney's yard, where Sidney was opening the back of the lorry and gently pulling the carpets back to expose the stack of albums and coin trays, all protected from dust by the white cotton sheets. The boys jumped up and helped him carefully move the trays nearer the back doors. Yiddel picked up one of the ledgers, just out of curiosity, to see how the stamps and coins were detailed. He glanced over the pages, expecting to see detailed notes about itemised stamps and coins. What hit him in the face was something very different - shipment details about drugs and contraband arriving into Amsterdam through their family business – so this was the true nature of these people.

'That's handy,' he thought. He realised that this was indeed something else, and put the black-bound ledgers under the stack of carpets and out of sight.

Just then, David Hamad appeared with the two Khans.

"I understand that it all went well?" said Raja.

"Yeh, thanks in part to all the planning, it went like a well-oiled clockwork toy," said Yiddel.

The stamps were now off-loaded and were on display for the Khans to see.

"Oh yes, they look superb," said Amit, peering closely at the coins. "Oh, and we have your money, Mr Davis, and we would like to thank you and your team for the most excellent way that you went about the job." He shook Yiddel's hand with much-evident gratitude. Raja passed him the money, which Yiddel passed to Sammy, who placed all the contents onto the tailboard of Sidney's lorry and, with Harry, began to count it.

Yiddel thought this was a good moment to announce his acquisition to the Khans. "While they are doing that, gentlemen, I think I may well have further business with you. Something else has come into my possession. Three ledgers detailing the illegal shipment of drugs and other illegal items into Holland for disposal throughout Europe by the Bibi family. They will be of great value to you when your friends, the Bibis, start to have a go at you for taking this lot away from them. I've only had a quick glance, but as far as I can tell, I think you should have them…at a 'fair' price of course!"

"Can we see them?" asked Raja, keenly. Yiddel lifted the carpet and retrieved the ledgers. As he passed them to the Khans, he noticed David Hamad's shoulders go up in reply to a question from Amit in their language. They studied them for a few minutes and then Raja said: "You are perfectly right, Mr Davis, these ledgers will do very nicely. What is your price?"

"Make it a nice round figure of one hundred 'K' and they are all yours!"

Amit looked at Raja and said: "Pay the man, Raja, it is as good as any insurance policy to us."

The deal was struck and a cheque was made out and signed by the Khans. Yiddel looked at the boys and got a nod from them both regarding the money count.

They all shook hands, loaded the Khans' van and the Khans were gone, back to Southall.

Yiddel was ecstatic. "Without a doubt, that has got to be the quickest one hundred 'K' I have - or will ever - earn in my fucking life!

"And every penny is in the cash parcel as well," confirmed Sammy.

"You know something, this business of stealing for thieves and people with so much money that they want other people's possessions is much better than working for a living," reckoned Yiddel. "Put the cheque through the business account for the toys and I'll divvy up the cash into six bundles. Minus the expenses, of course!"

"But of course," mocked Sammy, lifting his shoulders.

"Are you taking the piss, young man?" Yiddel reproached him in the same tone.

"Who…me? As if I would!"

'Expenses' naturally included Sidney getting an extra bonus added to his share for the use of the lorry, and another bonus for the driver.

Sheila's mind was all about their new home together, and she simply had to find out about the house. The agent assured her that the transaction – in her name - was being processed and that it would be completed in just a few days. And so, a truly delighted woman arrived at the warehouse with a treat of freshly baked beigels with cream cheese and smoked salmon for the boys.

While she was making the tea, the Volvo dealer phoned and told Yiddel that his new car was in and would be ready to pick up the next day after it had been checked over.

"Have you heard from any of the toy buyers?" asked Yiddel of Sammy.

"Not since they had their last delivery. Do you think I should have a ring round to see if all is well?"

"I think you should, just to keep the toy business on the boil, especially with all this spending that's going on," looking at Sheila and grinning.

"You are one tight old bastard…we are doing so well, and you still worry about spending! You have," lowering her voice, "so much money you could buy the whole of Chigwell, not just one house, Yiddel Davis…"

"I'm only kidding, sweetheart. Only getting you at it!"

"You wait until I start spending on the furniture, then we will see who is getting who at it, Darling," retorted Sheila, returning the dry humour of Yiddel.

"Oy Vey," he sung. "If I was a rich man..." singing the first line of *Fiddler on the Roof.*

A very happy Sheila left the office to go to the market, still shaking her finger at him.

Amit Khan phoned Yiddel to again thank him for the way he had carried out the job - the whole story had been reported to him by David Hamad - from start to finish. He said that he had already received the expected phone call from the Bibi family offering some sort of negotiation for the return of the ledgers in exchange for the collection. Khan said he would think about it and come back to them.

"I will let them stew for a while. The son also said that his father suffered a stroke as a direct result of the trauma of the robbery and is in hospital recovering. He said that David was there during the raid, and he said his father wishes everybody to hell, so he is still putting up a fight even though he's in a bad way." Khan rang off, saying he would phone again later. Yiddel related the story Khan had told him to the others, but all he got from them was a simple shrug. They were no longer interested – things moved on in capers in their world of crime – and it was now a case of seeing what came up next. They were entirely comfortable executing the plans that Yiddel dictated, and entirely confident in his judgement each and every time, even though, as they well knew, that could be a time when it all went wrong and one or more of them might get seriously hurt.

Two days later, Roger walked into the office, having recently got back from Holland, looking very tired.

"I decided to stay over and not rush back," he said.

"It looks like you had a good time then, Rog?" was Yiddel's piss-taking question style.

"I am absolutely fucked and I mean in more ways than one," said Roger, flopping down into a chair. "I have never partied that good before, non-stop since I left you."

"You dirty old bastard, Roger. One day it will drop off and then where will you be?"

"Fucking happier - I'll have an operation and then I'll party again!"

"Putting all that to one side, Rog, I'm glad you're here," said Yiddel, glad to change the subject. He pulled a large bag out from under his desk and threw it across to him.

"What I promised you! And a nice little bonus on top from a side deal I pulled off - we had a little windfall from those black books that we found in one of the drawers. It seems that our nice little Bibi family are running a 'naughties' business in Holland, and those books are their record of all the dealings and imports. They have phoned the Khans and have offered them a deal: books for stamps and coins. So, in the end, it has worked out well for them, lucky bastards."

Roger, whether listening or not, was flicking through his bundle of cash and had stopped counting when he got to one hundred 'K'. "Thanks for that, Yiddel, that will go towards my Docklands apartment," he said.

"We all got the same, minus the expenses for the trip and Sidney."

Whilst Yiddel had been speaking to Roger, he had heard the business line ringing. Sammy had taken the call. It was Joe Morris.

"I have the man who is interested in the products coming to London with me next week. I will phone you when we get there. It's certain that he wants the lot, so that should seal it nicely. He's certainly an expert in diamonds – I'll be interested to hear what he says about these ones."

Sammy went down to the warehouse, keen to intercept them with the news. He found Yiddel, Roger and Harry looking at one of the new toys that had just arrived from Taiwan.

"Mr Morris phoned, Yiddel. He's coming to London next week and bringing the buyer with him." He paused, suddenly worried as to the whereabouts of the diamonds. "By the way, where is the Tom? I haven't seen it for a while."

Yiddel pointed to a dustbin in the far corner of the warehouse.

"In there, naturally," he replied, grinning.

"You mean to say that all that fantastic jewellery is in a dustbin?"

"Of course - what would be safer round here? Definitely not a safe! The best place is where it is, it's quite Ok. Oh, do me a favour, Harry - check if it is still in there…"

Harry walked over to the bin, lifted the lid off, got hold of a black plastic bag and peered inside. "Yep, it's still here, Yiddel!"

"There you are, what did I say? Safe as houses!" proclaimed a triumphant Yiddel.

The office phone rang and, it being his turn to get it, Harry rushed up the stairs to answer it; within one minute he had returned, all smiles: "Our cars are in the showroom, Sam. They want us to go and check 'em over."

Excitedly, the boys moved towards the warehouse door, but Yiddel, quick as a flash, said, "Before you go, boys, give us a hand to sweep the warehouse!"

"You must be kidding, Yiddel, our cars are in…".

"Oh, well…all right, go on, then, I'm only kidding. Go on, fuck off and get your new toys, see you later."

"You bastard," said Harry, pulling Sammy through the warehouse doors, eager to go and see the cars.

Roger left with them, laughing at the repartee that went on between them all.

Yiddel was left on his own in the warehouse. He detested being on his own. No boys, no Sheila – just himself, Yiddel Davis, and he hated it. It was all too quiet for the man who thrived on the hustle and bustle of life. He went back up to the office, made himself a coffee and sat reading *The Sun*, soaking up all the drivel written about the glitzy lifestyle of showbiz and sports stars.

'I could lead that sort of life,' he thought. 'In fact, I would thrive on that sort of life…Wait a minute, I'm not far off that sort of life now, what with all the capers over all those years. Maybe stop soon? Got to let go eventually – been lucky for a long time – that can't last, can it? Ah well, maybe it's not too bad.'

Those initial thoughts on retiring from the frontline of crime – perhaps from crime altogether – were rudely interrupted as he heard the outside doorbell. Someone was paying him a visit.

"Morning, son, how's yer luck?" It was Elvis.

"Very well, thank you, Elv. Good to see you – been a while!"

"Yeh, too long, mate. Anyway, listen: while you were away, I popped over to Belgium for a few, and I met my future wife there - all arranged by the families years ago by my father when we were kids, and she is a stunner, a froomer, but what a woman. She's from Holland. You wait 'til you see her, Yiddel, blinding!" Elvis was clearly intoxicated by his new woman. His eyes blazed with the happiness of anticipating a future with her.

"Anyway, I've just heard a bit of news from my new family that might be of interest to you. They are in the diamond business, always have been, even before the war. The old man, that's the grandfather, and his family, were lucky to have got away from Poland with anything, let alone their lives and because he came here with money he made more, and then after the war went to Belgium to be in the middle of the diamond trade. The family are wealthy - stinking rich. All down to the old boy, of course… now, he let go of the business and his son and grandson now run the show. They asked me when I was there if I would be keen in putting a bit of money into a 'syndicate'. All to do with diamonds, again of course.

"They reckon I'd be a millionaire in twelve months. Well, I had to laugh - what they don't know is that I already am, thanks to you. So, I don't know whether to invest in it or not. They phoned this morning and asked me again. Maybe it seemed to them like I was stalling, but this time it went a bit further and they told me they were buying a bulk load from an American who has got a large amount of precious stones and diamonds, which once belonged to a European royal family…"

Elvis stopped talking, seeing the sudden change of expression on Yiddel's face, with his eyebrows raised and his head to one side.

"I don't believe what I am hearing here," said Yiddel. "Your man didn't happen to accidentally drop the name of the American, did he? Because, Elvis, *I* am the man who is selling the fuckers to the American. He is on his way from the States with a so-called buyer to take them off me, who, by the sounds of things, will then take them to Belgium and sell them to your new in-laws with the fucking money that I have made from stealing them in the first place! And they all come from that dirty Nazi fucker Klein, who stole them from us Jews. This is unbelievable. Elvis...if it's the same people, I want some of the action!"

Elvis had had the wind taken out of his sails, well and truly. He had rarely seen his old friend Yiddel so incandescent with rage. 'Crime is indeed a small world,' he thought to himself.

Yiddel continued. "Elvis, when we did this caper I did not have any use for you...in fact, I only took Ansel for a bit of back- up muscle, plus Shelia and the boys. What we went for, we got, and this load of Tom came about as a little deal on the side. The man that we went for didn't know anything about them, so while we were there, I took 'em. When I had Sid's man look them over, they blew him away - he said he had never seen diamonds like 'em and that they must have belonged to royalty. Now, doesn't that sound familiar to you?"

Elvis simply nodded. He knew what was coming next.

"Do me a favour and phone your man. Use that phone there, and ask him what the American's name is. Give him some cock and bull story about reading in the paper here that some Yank has been nicked for handling diamonds and you thought it might be the same bloke."

Elvis dived into the inside pocket of his black coat and came out with his address book. He found the number and dialled it. In a second, he was speaking in pure Yiddish to the man in Belgium.

He did exactly what Yiddel had told him to do. After the formalities, he slid in the tale about the wayward American diamond man.

"What's his name?" he asked, at the appropriate moment. After listening for a few seconds, he reached across Yiddel's desk and picked up a pen and wrote a name on a piece of scrap paper: 'Morris', and looked at Yiddel. Elvis repeated the name to his contact, just to be sure: "Morris. Yes, from Texas... no, it's not the same man," he said, convincingly, reverting to Yiddish. Thanking the man for his trouble, he put the phone down.

"Well?" said Yiddel. "So, it is the same fucker, Elv, me old mate... now what the fuck is he playing at? He told me he was bringing the buyer from Texas and now we find out he will leave England to sell them to your man in Belgium. This is very interesting. I think we have to work something out for our colonial cousin..."

He thanked Elvis for coming over, and Elvis left, leaving Yiddel in deep thought.

22

The Diamonds

The noise of powerful vehicle engines jolted Yiddel out of his reflections and planning. The boys had got back, both sporting their brand-new cars, and eager to show the Master what they had chosen. Yiddel acknowledged their understandable joy and after lots of 'Oohs' and Aahs', told them the story of the diamonds.

"So, what is he up to, exactly, Yiddel?" Sammy couldn't work it out.

"I don't know. Why is he telling the story about bringing the buyer with him from Texas? Why don't he say that he has got a buyer from Europe instead of all the bollocks about a Texan?"

Silence hung over them all, the elation of the new cars totally forgotten now.

"I'm puzzled," said Yiddel. "I've been trying to fathom out the financial gain and there is none. Whatever else, he's got to give us our price...Fucking hell - I think I've got it! He's trying to pull a stroke; bringing the Texan as a buyer so that in reality he can fix the price. The Texan, whoever he really is, acts like a diamond whiz kid – he 'advises' us the market price is so and so. We believe him and pay what he says, then he and Morris go off to Belgium to double or treble the money they've got from simple bloody fools like us! Right, if that's the case, I'll have George here on our behalf, without letting on anything, for when they arrive."

Yiddel immediately phoned Sidney to ask George to give him a call sharpish – he needed at the very least a rough idea of the total value of the lot.

George returned Yiddel's call.

"Hello, George. Could you pop over? Yer know that bit of Tom I've got? Well, I've got a bloke coming from the States that I suspect is trying to pull a flanker. I want you to give me a rough estimate of what it is worth and then I want you here when he comes for the deal, is that Ok? Great, thanks, George."

Yiddel sat back in his chair, his hands behind his head, his manner more self-assured now, indeed it was the Yiddel they knew: aware of what was what, who was who, and especially who was trying to do what to who. He stared at the ceiling a while, a curious ghost of a smile on his lips. Then they heard him say, "Right, let's see if that's the game or not. No one gets past me."

Sheila now returned from the market and was shown the cars and told the story of the diamonds and the American. Within the hour, George had arrived at the warehouse with Sidney: "I thought I'd do it now rather than leave it till they are here," said George.

"All right, mate. Harry, do me a favour and get all that Tom out of the safe will you!" said Yiddel, crisply with an authority and urgency they hadn't seen for a while, but then, they knew if there was one thing the Master couldn't bear, it was being double-crossed. Harry duly obliged, and went not to the safe but instead retrieved the bag of jewellery from the dustbin. Bringing the plastic sack back to Yiddel, he quipped: "It's a good job I remembered the combination, Yiddel!"

Yiddel placed all the pieces on his desktop, all neatly laid out. George, complete with his jeweller's glass, checked each piece in turn, making notes of each item. Yiddel and Sidney said nothing to him, they merely sat patiently while he went through his appraisal of the jewels, knowing George needed his time to get this right.

Sheila dutifully asked if anyone would like a drink.

"That's a good idea, love," said Yiddel. "Beers all round."

Giving everyone an ice-cold beer, Sheila joined the lookers and waited for George to give his valuation.

"Right," said George, taking a deep breath characteristic of someone about to announce something that would require a lot of careful thought and analysis. "Just going on the stone value - and *not* on the complete item value - which I believe is beyond a value...I reckon that this one," (picking up the tiara) "because it has flawless four and six-carat diamonds backed up by a bevy of smaller stones, must be worth four hundred thousand pounds. This one," (picking up the necklace) "again because of the amount of large diamonds, emeralds and rubies must be worth six hundred k. The brooches - each, I should think, about two hundred k. The pendant...well, one stone alone must be worth one hundred k. The rings, each one, eighty to one hundred k... and the cherry on the cake...well, I think again on stone value, a million pounds."

George paused, letting his words sink in. "I said to you last time I see these, Yiddel, that they are to any jeweller mind- blowing, and I say again, mate, just look at them...staggering! I still believe that the tragedy will be breaking 'em up. But, as I said, if you don't then they are a giveaway. So, let's have a roll call...just under three million, and that is a rough estimate. I haven't valued the small stones, only the large carat ones, so think on the lines of three million plus." He sat back and took a long pull on his beer.

"Thanks for that, George." Yiddel had never doubted him, but was relieved to hear him reaffirm his judgement. "All I want you to do when they get here is just to sit in on the meeting, and leave it to us to sort out what he's up to. Harry - do me a favour and put this lot back in our 'actual' safe."

Harry ceremoniously placed the jewels back in the dustbin.

Sidney and George now left, with Yiddel telling them he would phone as soon as he heard from Morris that he was in London with the buyer. Harry confirmed to Yiddel that all the gems were back in the safe proper.

"I know, the reason for all that is because the less anyone knows about where they are, the better, and 'in the safe' does now sound better than 'in a bag in a dustbin in the corner of a warehouse', do you not agree?"

Harry agreed that it did sound better.

The next day, Sheila spent the morning at the new house with the builder, going over the alterations and new decorations to the house.

"I've asked him to put a nice big patio on the back with lights so that we can have parties outside in the summer. He's fitting all the new kitchen units and decorating every room," she said happily to Yiddel. "Come over with me later and I'll show you what I mean."

Yiddel had more than patios on his mind right then and only mumbled his tacit agreement to her.

"Don't get too excited!" she scolded.

"Sorry, Darling, I was thinking about something else."

"Don't go over the top, Yiddel Davis, you might break out into a sweat."

By the next morning, Yiddel had discussed the arrival of Morris with Sammy and Harry and had decided to let Morris make the running to see what he was going to offer through his so-called 'buyer'.

He knew now what sort of price the whole bundle was worth, give or take a few hundred thousand pounds. In Yiddel's mind, thanks to George, was a figure close to three million pounds, cut up, or whatever, as they were. Sidney came over from his yard, just to pay a visit, and to see if the Yank had phoned.

"Yer know that George. He really is a master diamond-cutter - he has cut, when he was in the trade proper, some beautiful stones. He knows what he's talking about, Yiddel; he's no fucking fool when it comes to diamonds...I take it you haven't heard anything yet?"

"Not a dickie bird, Sid. I thought he said he would be here this week. I'm beginning to hate all this waiting; still, it's early yet."

Just then, the phone rang. It was Morris at last.

"Hi there, Mr Davis. We are here in London, just arrived."

Yiddel put his thumb up to Sidney and mouthed 'Morris'.

"Oh hello, Mr Morris, yes, we were indeed just talking about you. I was saying I thought you would be here this week. Yeh...tomorrow is fine. Ok, about half past nine..."

Yiddel looked at Sidney with a puzzled face.

"Are you a fucking witch? You arrive here, ask where he is, and lo and behold, the bloke phones. Anyway, you probably heard what I said...9.30am. Right, let's phone George."

The whole team was in Yiddel's office at 9am sharp, all of them going over 'who says what and who says nothing, just listens'. Bang on 9.30am, the Americans arrived. Sammy went down to let them in.

"Good morning, everyone," beamed Joe Morris, looking as unruffled and self-assured as ever. "This is my business associate, James Black, also from Texas."

413

Mr Black was a short, slightly overweight man in, as far as Yiddel could make out, his early fifties. He somehow lacked the affluent look that Morris portrayed so easily, and shuffled in with some awkwardness – perhaps a limp or a bad back – and seemed anxious to dispense with the small-talk, and commence his task. Everyone in the room shook hands and Sheila served coffee and the meeting got underway around two desks that Harry had pushed together - the jewels took centre stage.

Yiddel reached into the bag and slowly took out one piece at a time, displaying each on the desk in full view of the two Texans. James Black produced a jeweller's eyepiece and began scrutinizing each piece; he too was being scrutinised, especially by George, although he could never have known it. Everyone kept to the script and remained totally silent while Mr Black carried out his inspection. It had immediately struck George that he didn't seem used to using the eyepiece – or perhaps he was imagining that?

"Very nice, Mr Davis…In fact, extremely nice, there are some beautiful stones there, but I am sorry to say that most of them have flaws in them and the colours are not what I'm looking for. I collect blue diamonds and the bulk of these are yellow stones. I cannot deny that the actual objects are good…It's the quality of the stones that are not unfortunately up to the standard that I'm looking for – such a shame."

During this man's summary of what was quality and what was not, Yiddel took a sly glance at George, who was sitting with Sheila on the opposite side of the office. He was very subtly shaking his head, and gave Yiddel a slow wink, meaning 'Let him go on'.

Black had resumed. "They are not European royalty either; they are in fact, pretty modern. I would say about 1946. I would hazard a guess at them being copies of the Russian originals. In saying that,

414

don't think for one minute that there is no value here, but you must appreciate that if they were the tops, then the price would be much better. Yes, a great shame indeed; I don't think these are worth a great deal to anyone. Do you understand what I mean, Mr Davis?"

Sammy could read the Master's mind exactly at this moment in time: 'Yiddel Davis can take as much criticism as most people about most things, but the one thing he hates is being told that he doesn't understand something when it's in his face. What he does understand, now that it is out in the open, is this pair trying to take him and the professional advice of George for a couple of prats?' He could see Yiddel taking a deep breath, looking around the room at his most trusted friends, and then it began.

"Mr Morris, I have listened to your business associate, Mr Black, attempting to tell us that what we have on this desk is not only not any good, but is in fact nothing less than a pile of shite."

Yiddel was trying to keep his voice level, and his anger under control. Morris' face had gone a deathly pale; he knew he had annoyed a London gangster.

"I was very interested in your little act – let's face it, that's all it was. Sitting behind you in the room with us is one of England's greatest diamond experts, Mr George Somerfield. He is also an adviser to the Tower of London Crown Jewel section. He has seen this collection catalogued, which was identified as a collection stolen in 1940 from a Jewish diamond dealer in Poland, acquired legitimately before being stolen by the Nazis - and subsequently all claim to it was terminated by the slaughter of the owner and his family in the death camps. I chose not to introduce him to you in his full capacity until we had heard your judgement. Every professional who has looked at them has said that it is the finest and purest set of gems that they have ever seen - and as for the settings

415

- none finer in the modern world today." He took a sip of his coffee. The air in the room was so thick with tension it could be cut with a knife.

"Now, Mr Morris, we were a bit lucky. One of our team was in Belgium last week...Oh, I see how your eyes light up at Belgium! Yes, he was approached by a certain dealer there about a load of fantastic diamonds that were coming from England this week. The word he had been told was 'Fantastic' in terms of their quality. Yet here, funnily enough, we are now looking at what has been described as a pile of shite by your expert here.

"Mr Morris, I am many things, but one thing I am not is a fucking idiot and I do not like being treated like one...We know the approximate value, cut up, and have got a rough idea of them all as a complete set. So, now, would you like to start again, or shall I tell you both to fuck off out of my place?"

Morris remained silent, absolutely terrified of the retribution that might follow. In an excruciating mental agony, he waited for what Yiddel decided, praying that he would calm down and just let them go – unscathed. Yiddel went on. "And your man, Mr Morris, should go back to the USA and study 'kidology' on how to try to put something over on a man like me because he is clearly no fucking good to you as he is. I would not for one minute have a prat like him on my team, who had come into a situation like this and led with his chin. He should have checked out who was in the room and who he was dealing with before making statements like he did. This is not a nursery for silly kids, Mr Morris, and I am disgusted with you trying to get away with such a fucking trick! Do you understand me now, Mr Black? Christ, you bastards make me fucking angry. All my people will tell you how it takes a lot to make me like this..."

416

He paused – he had caught sight of Sheila's face, which was so despairing she looked on the verge of tears – she hadn't seen Yiddel like this before. At her expression, Yiddel thought he ought to now wrap this tirade up and get rid of these upstarts. "You who have worked with me and earned a nice few quid in the process. What really makes you try to pull a fast one on me and my team?"

Morris said nothing; he had fixed his solemn gaze on the floor such was the shame he felt. Now, he looked at Black, who clearly couldn't cope with much more from Yiddel, and of Sammy and Harry he wasn't at all sure. Both realised they had been caught out in what they had so audaciously been attempting to do – and it hurt.

"You're perfectly right, Mr Davis," came Morris' attempt at salvation. "I have to put my hands up and say 'yes, I was trying to', as you say, 'pull a fast one over on you'. I sit here now disgraced that I have even tried it on you. You are right, of course, James Black has not got a clue about diamonds, in fact he works in a shoe shop in Houston and again you are right, I should have checked out who would be in the room with us before allowing him to make a complete ass of us both - under my instructions, of course. But he only played it as I told him to, and I got it all wrong. I can only apologise profusely to you and the team - whom I have complimented over the Klein job - for even thinking that I could get away with the deception. It all boils down to greed, Mr Davis, and I have, as you say, 'fucked up big time'." Morris sank back in his chair.

Yiddel looked sternly at the two men in front of him. Finally, he spoke.

"What hurts me most of all is the fact that we have worked together. We got your paintings for your clients and more. I gave you a bloody good bonus and you have still tried to fuck me. When someone tries to turn me over, when I have played it straight with you, as far as I am concerned you are finished as a business or social friend. I feel that you and your shoe salesman should leave us and as far as I am concerned don't ever call me again, and I speak for my team as well. Now fuck off!"

The two Texans got up and without another word were shown out of the building by Harry.

After they had gone, George came over to Yiddel and said: "What was all that bollocks about me being England's finest diamond expert and advisor to the Tower of London Crown Jewel section? And my name is not Somerfield, Yiddel."

"Well, I guessed that prick - the shoe man – immediately, once he started talking all that twaddle. It was clear he knew nothing about diamonds. It was all coming out of his mouth too 'off pat', as if he had been rehearsed on what to say, so I thought, 'fuck it, I'll play the same game and play you as a trump card and blag the pair of them'. The one thing I learnt about Americans since we have been working with them is that they are very gullible and believe every fucking thing you tell 'em. Not like us lot, who doubt everything anyone tells you until it is rammed up your nose. Besides, now we have another iron in the diamond fire with a deal that's going down in Belgium with the help of Elvis. I called you 'Somerfield' because it was the first name that came to me and as I was dressing you up to such a level, I called you after the supermarket people... and they are big people, George."

As he was talking, he was dialling Elvis's number.

"Hello. Rabbi, is that you already? It's none other than me, your old friend Fagin already. I have cleared that little problem...so when you can, make a call to your in-laws and tell them we are going to do the deal and not the Yanks…Yeh, I threw them out of the office…"

"Put the diamonds back in the safe, Harry, and make sure you lock it!"

The new game that had arrived from Taiwan was proving itself as a world beater in technology and in price. Sammy had placed an order with Dong Lai for as many as he could let them have.

Every buyer who had seen the demonstration and had placed an order were checking with the office on a daily basis as to when they could expect to get their delivery.

They were not only ordering the new item but as many of the previous toy orders as well. Yiddel had not failed the toy dealer in Ridley Road market either - he had kept his word and a selection of the new deliveries were slid out to him at the stall. In a way, that poor old market trader was having to compete with the giants of Selfridges and Harrods, but he too was eagerly demanding when he would get his next delivery.

During a meeting about stock, Yiddel instructed Sammy to phone Dong Lai, and, regardless of orders from the big buyers, to obtain as many as possible of the three lines. Even now, months after the original order, these were selling faster than ever.

"At this rate, we can afford to have a warehouse full of stock and just draw the orders from here," said Yiddel. "That way, we can react better to all the urgent stuff and hopefully control things more directly – like price and profit! Sammy, get as many as he will let you have of all the lines."

23

Calm before the Storm

Amidst all this business, Sheila somehow at last got Yiddel to go with her in her new car to see their future home in Chigwell. Arriving at the house, Yiddel immediately saw the changes that had been done to the exterior and was impressed. The builder had undertaken all the additions and modifications that Sheila had wanted throughout, including the kitchen, patio and gardens. They wandered around the property, making sure that there were no more alterations needed before he finished. They were more than satisfied with what they saw and left the builder to finish off. As they were leaving, he walked out with them down the driveway. Right opposite them, a demolition team were halfway through pulling down a very desirable looking house.

"Why are they doing that?" asked Yiddel, genuinely bewildered. "That place looks in very good condition to me."

"That is a way of laundering money, Mr Davis; you buy the house with dirty money, pay to have the place pulled down, then you pay a builder to build you a super-duper one with all the mod cons and then sell it after a short while and make a nice, fat profit. And the dirty money is now clean and legit money, which can be put back into circulation…after you pay a little tax."

Thanking him for his knowledge of a subject of which he knew nothing, Yiddel filed it away into his memory bank of a brain – 'for future reference, maybe,' he told himself.

The toy business, in the meantime, was making money faster than anything. As the deliveries arrived from Dong Lai, they were immediately dispatched. Yiddel had tried hard to get the boys to hold on to enough stock to enable them to build up a UK outlet, but as fast as it came in, it went straight out.

Things were settling down nicely. A few weeks passed by with nothing non-legit happening, or of it being requested. Sheila, particularly, found this time quite wonderful – she had such dreams of the family to come once she and her man moved into their brand-new home. Just her and Yiddel. No problems or danger anymore – she could relax at last, and she could sense the same desire in Yiddel – he had even said as much several times, particularly recently. Then, on a Monday morning, Sammy took a call that changed everything. It came in the form of a woman, who wanted to speak to Mr Davis.

Sammy's telephone manner was as polite as ever. "He is not in the office at the moment. Can I get him to call you back? He should be in shortly."

She seemed to agree to that, but not without some reluctance to have the call terminated so unsatisfactorily from her point of view. She gave Sammy her name and number, and told him she was going out at lunchtime, but would wait for his call. As Sammy put the phone down, Yiddel and Sheila walked through the door, both smiling and clearly so happy together.

"Morning, lads, any calls?"

"Yeh, an American lady phoned and wanted to talk to you, Yiddel – to you only!" Sammy passed over the piece of paper with the woman's name and number on it.

"Mary Buchan…I don't know her," Yiddel remarked casually. "Did she say anything else?"

"No, she just said that she wanted to talk to you."

Yiddel looked at the number, trying to place where in London it was, but he thought no more of that and made the call.

"Good morning, can I speak to Mary Buchan please...Yeh, it's Davis, Yiddel Davis."

Yiddel would now sit and listen to her explanation of why she had phoned. Sammy dutifully left the office to allow his boss some privacy, but if he had been able to foresee what would come, he would have acted very, very differently...

COMING NEXT…

What happens in book two is truly cataclysmic… Both Sammy and Sheila had a bad feeling about this next venture; that this was just too much now, that it seemed somehow out of control. Yiddel's lust for the caper knew no moderation despite all the warning signs that were coming up. In her heart of hearts, Sheila prayed for it to end favourably, all the time knowing that it might not prove to be so.

Yiddel will take on the job proposed by Mary Buchan despite his own initial, serious misgivings – and against the wishes of his wife. The conversation between him and Mary Buchan will outline what is going to be required – but not what will then unfold.

…"Mr Davis, I have been given your number by a friend, who tells me that we might have something in common. Will it be possible to meet with you so that we can have a talk in private and, er, not on the phone, if you understand me?"

Yiddel played it slowly. "Before I agree to that, would you mind telling me who this friend is?"

"His name is Gerald Moores from New York."

"Oh, yes, I know your man. I have done business with him before." A pause. "Where would you like to meet?"

"Is the tea room at *The Ritz* Ok with you, Mr Davis…this afternoon at 3.30? I will book the table in my name. Buchan."

"That's fine with me. See you at 3.30."

Replacing the receiver, he looked across to Sammy. "Yer know, I don't understand this bloke Moores. It's the second time he's referred someone to us after we turned him over – and now he acts like our agent in New York. This bird, Mary Buchan, wants to meet me at *The Ritz* for tea this afternoon to talk about 'something we have in common', whatever that means. What are you two doing this afternoon?"

"Not a lot, 'cept taking orders for toys," Sammy replied.

"Good, you are coming with me to *The Ritz*. Slip home and put on a suit. Harry - you stay with Sheila and guard the place until we get back."

They took a taxi to *The Ritz* and were shown to a table by the maitre d'hotel, where they met the lady in question. Yiddel gave her his quick once over and guessed she was about forty-five, very attractive, extremely well dressed and looked like she knew 'what side her bread was buttered'.

"Hallo again, my name is Yiddel Davis, and this is my colleague Sammy."

"It's nice to see you, Mr Davis, and Sammy, please sit down. I have ordered tea, sandwiches and a selection of cakes for us." Mary Buchan spoke in a well-heeled, educated, but at the same time no-nonsense voice, which Yiddel could not fail to make a mental note of – he was trying to establish what sort of 'job' such a woman could possibly have.

"Are you staying here?" Yiddel was curious.

"No, I'm at another hotel. I just thought this would be a good place to meet."

The afternoon tea was served by two waiters, who fussed over everything on the table until the tea was poured, and the plates were in their correct places, something Yiddel and Sammy were not used to. Mary Buchan noticed this immediately and smiled while this was going on.

"That's what you pay for in this place and boy, do you get it. Please have your tea and sandwiches, gentlemen, and I will start to tell you the reason why I have come to you, which, as you know, is

424

based on pure recommendation from Gerald. The job I have to offer is quite complicated and could be very dangerous if handled wrongly."

She made sure no nearby patrons could overhear – she had chosen this particular table wisely – it was located away from most of the others – and that voice communicated itself so well, so it seemed. Yiddel, of course, was well aware they were being observed by this woman's minders.

"I belong to a group of business people who deal in all manner of commerce around the world. One of our group, we believe, is doing personal deals on the side - above and beyond our stipulated formula of working. We are nothing less than a multi-billion-dollar company, in fact, more than billions. We are in the outer orbit league as far as money is concerned; cash, or money, to our group is a rude word. Yet we have been brought down to earth by the amount of money that is disappearing from our business. It only became known through a new firm of accountants that we now employ. We have whittled it down to one man, very discreetly of course. All the facts point to him as the one who is pulling out more than his fair share.

"Because we deal in all manner of things, it would be difficult to actually make it a crime and give it to the police to handle, you understand, because of the nature of what we trade in.

"We want him stopped without involving the authorities, in other words, we want someone like you to do that for us. We cannot afford it becoming public; if that happens, then we will all finish up in jail. I know I can speak openly with you, Mr Davis, when I say that, to the authorities, we would be seen as a group of crooks. So, now one of our own is being equally crooked to us. We control a very large amount of, shall we say, devious business in the world, and as I said, money itself is a rude word.

"Your fee will be a drop in the ocean once we have stopped our man from helping himself. I have only outlined the situation so far. Once you agree to work for us, I will give you all the information and help that you will need. We were getting desperate about how we were going to deal with him, but last week, I was at a dinner party given by Gerald Moores in New York, whom I have known for many years, and in complete confidence I was telling him of our dilemma. Then, he said he knew 'just the man'. You."

Mary Buchan paused, letting the meaning register – and trying to read Yiddel's face. "So that's how I was told about your work, Mr Davis. You see, I also know that Gerald Moores is not all that he seems to be. I think you know what I am saying there?"

"I certainly do," said Yiddel.

Book Two of FAGIN UK by Mike Pattison will be available in the summer of 2018. Please register your interest for this via the Not Just Another Book website, and we will contact you nearer the date of publication: www.notjustanotherbook.co.uk